THE NAKED WORLD

THE NAKED WORLD

BOOK TWO OF THE JUBILEE CYCLE

ELI K. P. WILLIAM

TALOS PRESS

Talos Press books may be purchased in bulk at special discounts for sales promotion, corporate gifts, fund-raising, or educational purposes. Special editions can also be created to specifications. For details, contact the Special Sales Department, Talos Press, 307 West 36th Street, 11th Floor, New York, NY 10018 or info@skyhorsepublishing.com.

Talos Press is an imprint of Skyhorse Publishing, Inc.®, a Delaware corporation.

Visit our website at www.talospress.com.

10 9 8 7 6 5 4 3 2 1

Library of Congress Cataloging-in-Publication Data is available on file.

Cover illustration and design by Markus Lovadina

Print ISBN: 978-1-940456-52-2
Ebook ISBN 978-1-940456-53-9

Printed in the United States of America

A corner of the universe suddenly peeled back to reveal what seethed out there just beyond tidiness. What lay just north of order.
—*Infinite Jest*, David Foster Wallace

Opportunity
Came to my door
When I was down on my luck
In the shape
Of an old friend
With a plan, guaranteed
—"Opportunity," Bobby McFerrin, *Spontaneous Inventions*

PART 4
NAKED JOURNEYS

1
AN ALLEY?

From the depths of oblivion, a pair of eyelids moved. Whether they went up or down, opened or closed, was not yet clear, nor could it be said whose eyelids they were. But their movement had been perceived. Of this there was certainty.

Perhaps triggered by this perception, something immediately began to buzz into existence beneath the eyelids. A sort of tactile cloud, a pinprick tingling that spread through an area of space as though dead TV static were coalescing into a definitive shape: a body? A human body? A man's body?

All along his right side, the man could feel hardness, and against his right arm from the wrist down, warm grit. It was a familiar sensation. Yes, he could remember it, the touch of the metropolis's skin—concrete. He could smell exhaust, a dusty sourness, and the musk of dirty water. He could taste the phlegmy acid of morning breath stagnant in the back of his throat.

The pair of eyelids moved again. They were the man's eyelids. Attached to the face on his newly awoken body. But whether they were going up or down, opening or closing, he still wasn't sure, for whichever way they went all he found was darkness.

Denied light to fully rouse him, the man could feel the pull of sleep, an undertow that threatened to drag his still-mending awareness back down into the abyss of fractured slumber from which it had just arisen. Somehow, this first brief gasp of waking life felt precious to him, and without yet knowing why, he wanted to remain there. At the same time, he sensed with helpless anxiety that the buoyancy of his mind was tenuous and could do little more in his frail state than continue to blink.

Yet this very act seemed to have significance for the man, for on about the sixth or seventh blink two words came to him suddenly—Amon, Kenzaki—and immediately they began to link to various thoughts, like a hub firing lasers to all the nodes in a vast network inside his head. . . . Amon Kenzaki >>> jubilee >>> Monju >>> forest >>> Mayuko >>> forest >>> GATA >>> Mayuko >>> Rick >>> jubilee >>> Birla >>> ??? >>> Sekido >>> virus >>> bankdeath >>> . . . Then a multitude of memories burst forth all at once, everything he remembered jumbling and blurring together like millions of Venn Diagrams flitting across a blackboard, like countless droplets of water smashing each other in mid-air.

Amidst this mnemonic tempest, the man hung on to those two words—Amon, Kenzaki—and knew this was his name, his raft, nailing his sensation of blinking and warm gritty hardness to it, clinging to it with desperation until he remembered where he was, or where he *last* was. Running out of cash before he could get to the Sanzu River, he had sat down in an alley to commit identity suicide. Yes, that's what this feeling of concrete was, that's why he could smell the water. Now he had to get there. Had to cross over into the District of Dreams. The largest bankdeath camp on Earth. There was nowhere else to go.

Focusing on the little muscles beneath his brow, muscles over which he had mastered subtle control during his blink reduction training, Amon told his eyelids to drop and then lift. As expected, this brought the distinctive sensation of thin epidermal curtains sliding down his eyes and then up again, the direction of motion now as obvious as ever. But contrary to expectation, this did nothing to dispel the black void before him. He fluttered his eyelids, stretched them wide; he blinked and blinked and blinked and blinked and blinked. But however many times he tried, there was no blinking away this darkness.

To say "darkness" actually wasn't quite right, for darkness implies the absence of light. Yet this wasn't the absence of anything visible in particular, but the absence of sight itself. Eyes open or closed, Amon was blind.

And just when he realized this, another revelation came to him. Unless the metropolis had fallen into a state of torpor—a deep, quiet urban coma in which even its pulse of cars and images and people had settled into utter silence—he was deaf too.

Layered on the exhaust fumes and stench of the river, he could smell the dusty sourness of concrete beneath him, as it shook now and then, perhaps with the passing of cars or trains. In the thick humidity that seemed to settle on the ground, his skin felt sticky all over, and licking his lips, he tasted the salt of accreted sweat in the right corner. The right side of his body ached from lying on the hard ground for . . . How long? Just a moment earlier, it seemed, he'd been sitting in an alley. Then he'd committed identity suicide, cash crashing himself and demolishing his perceptions, experience itself collapsing like a house of cards. He'd been expecting to lose the overlay. The ImmaNet was obviously going to disappear when his BodyBank went offline. But what had happened to everything else? Why could he not hear or see anything? What the hell was going on?!

Amon felt the clenching of his diaphragm, the vibrations in his chest, the tearing pain in his throat, the stretching wide of his mouth, but no scream came out. Though his lungs ejected air as hard as they could, his ears picked up nothing, only increasing his terror. He began to writhe about, his arms and legs flailing, the wetness of his own spittle and tears spattering his face. When suddenly there was a sharp crack on the back of his head as Amon accidentally smashed himself into something solid and wall-like.

The impact seemed to knock sense into him, for he realized the stupidity of what he was doing and stopped moving, letting his limbs flop down limp. People had been after him. He had lost them many stations back in his invisible dash through Wakuwaku City and his train ride on the Oneiro Express. But drawing attention to himself was foolish, however small the chances were they might find him.

After his spastic fit, Amon found that the hardness was beneath his back now. With the weight off his right side, the compression no longer numbed his ribs and they began to throb with sharp tiddlywinks of pain. Still panicked, his breaths quivered in and out rapidly, and Amon started his blink reduction, instinctively seeking calm in this habitual exercise. As always, it would transport him back to his apartment in Jinbocho, to that sanctuary of frugality where he had practiced every day. As always, it would reassure him that he was saving money and advancing towards his dream. As always, it would make him feel like he was doing something significant with his life. But right now it was accomplishing none of these things and whenever he lifted his lids during each blink cycle, the feeling of having his eyes open and yet not being able to see only magnified his unease, so that he gave up within seconds and clamped them shut.

It was then that Amon noticed his throat was parched, his skin oozing with moisture in the heat. While one perspired constantly just staying still in the stifling, sultry air of Tokyo summer, he had been hurrying like mad through the metropolis before cash crashing, frantically struggling to save Mayuko, weeping. Now he'd been thrashing about without taking in any fluids after lying there in the alley for who knows how many hours, assuming he was still in the alley. That was a disturbing thought. How did he know he hadn't been moved? Or hadn't sleepwalked? He'd never been somnambulant before, but he'd never been bankdead before either, not to mention deaf or blind. From the smells, the rumble of the ground, the sickeningly warm feel of the concrete, and the dull throb in his head from when he'd smacked against some wall-like surface, it certainly seemed like he was in the alley. But how could he be sure?

As though powered by wills of their own, his hands began to feel their way around his vicinity: the hard, rough, dustiness beneath; a lumpy but smooth plasticky material rising vertically to his left, and groping upwards only empty air. Reaching to his right, his fingers brushed over more concrete and, recalling that the alley ought to have a wall just a meter or so in that direction, he got to his knees and warily began to crawl towards it. *What if you're touching premium real estate?* the voice of his nerves whispered. *What if you're headed for the road?* He knew it was irrelevant who owned the surfaces and what they cost now that his BodyBank was turned off. But that didn't lessen his feeling of guilt for possibly wasting money, and his concern about the road wasn't totally without basis. Nonetheless, he forced himself apprehensively onwards, only a few knee-paces to go, his awareness concentrated into his right hand outstretched ahead of him as it felt along the ground for signs of danger like a curb or a train track or passing shoes. His fingertips hit something, and he recoiled in fright. Then, gingerly extending them again until they touched whatever it was, he traced upwards while edging closer until he could flatten his palm against it and felt a wash of relief when he found a flat plasticky surface like the other.

Being ensconced between what could only be two walls, he felt certain for a moment that he was in an alley (the faint, muggy breeze telling him he was outside and therefore not in a room or hallway). But even if it was an alley, he realized, he couldn't be sure that it was *the* alley. He'd only been in it for a few seconds before blacking out, and in that brief interval his mind had been swirling with stress and fear and remorse and thoughts of Mayuko and countless other distracting things, so his recollection of his surround was highly suspect. He did a series of subtle twitch-gestures with his fingers to open up the seg of the moment before he cash crashed, but obviously that didn't work. And the realization that he was hopelessly lost, unable even to access his LifeStream and check how he got here, came slamming down on him like a bag of sand so that he flopped down flat on the ground. There he curled up close to the wall he'd just discovered as he shook in the darkness that was not dark enveloping him, trying to force the question of where he might be from his mind.

But this only awakened a second question and without thinking, he glanced into the bottom left corner of his eye, where, of course, he found no clock overlaid, only the same void abiding everywhere else he looked. Not only did he not know *where* he was, he didn't know *when* he was. He wanted to think he'd only been lying here for a few hours. Yet perhaps it had been longer. Was it morning? afternoon? evening? If he thought about it, the warmth of the metropolis felt subdued, suggesting night. But if so, was it the night after he sat down here, or the following night, or maybe the night after that . . . ?

As his trembling began anew, Amon reverted to blink reduction, but the experience of not seeing with his eyes open only brought terror quivering outwards from his chest again and his eyelids spasmed uncontrollably. Accepting the counterproductive futility of the exercise, he automatically switched to the next stage of his frugality routine—breath reduction— focusing on the muscles around his diaphragm to extend his breath.

With his nerves frazzled, he found himself *panting* uncontrollably, and decided to overcompensate with *deep breathing*. Since this action was more expensive than regular old *breathing*, he began to feel guilty for wasting money, and his stress intensified, until he realized that the cost probably didn't matter. No, it *definitely* didn't matter. Keeping his eyes closed was no longer more expensive than *opening* them or *blinking* or *squinting* or *winking*, just as *deep breathing* was no longer more expensive than *wheezing* or *hyperventilating* or anything else. In fact, none of his actions were any more or less expensive than any other. Now that he was severed completely from the ImmaNet and GATA's vigilant tallying, his actions had no price at all, nor did blink or breath reduction bear any relation to his savings. If he thought about it more carefully, he didn't even have any savings, couldn't have any savings. This meant that trying to save money would not help him get to the forest. Therefore, there was no connection whatsoever between conserving his actions and the realization of his dream. But this truth undercut everything that made these practices meaningful. They were pointless!

All the same, he found the deep breathing calming. And although a certain part of him—the self-monitoring, ambitious part—told him that this calmness merely distracted him from his aspirations, making him anxious for not taking shallower, more affordable breaths, he continued to breathe deeply and gave himself fully to the feeling. *Amon, this is not about money anymore*, he told himself. *You don't have any money and you may never have it again. This is just one way to cope.* With these thoughts he focused as intently as ever on his diaphragm. Except now, instead of heeding the self-ingrained reflex that steered him away from "deep breathing," he intentionally aimed for it.

Once his heart was settling to a stable trot, he began to consider what had happened to him, what had happened to his eyes and ears. His initial impulse was to check online for articles about post-bankdeath audiovisual impairment or anything that might clarify his current condition, and he did the gestures to open FlexiPedia, using a bronze search engine of course because silver was too expensive. But the window never opened, and this reminded him that not only was his BodyBank deactivated, but that a web search would be impossible without sight and hearing anyways, an awful epiphany that brought dread quaking up from his gut. *No ImmaNet? With three senses? How the hell am I going to get to the District of Dreams?* But he defied these despairing, exasperated doubts and returned to deep breathing once more. *Innnnnnnn. Ouuuuuuuut. Innnnnnnnn. Ouuuuuuuuut,* he found himself humming in his head, and, with the help of this impromptu mantra, he soon summoned enough focus to return his attention to his predicament.

After entering the Death Codes into his BodyBank and committing identity suicide, the last thing Amon remembered was the overlay being torn away, and the blank patch in his memory that followed told him he must have immediately fallen unconscious. This was no surprise. In fact, he had been expecting to faint. From touch-crashing bankrupts in the course of his duties as an Identity Executioner, Amon knew that if you input the Death Codes into someone's BodyBank without nerve dusting them and shut it down suddenly while they were still conscious, this generated a cognitive backlash that knocked them out. That was why, before executing himself, he had sat down in a small side street, beneath the shelter of a balcony, away from the crowds and traffic and other dangers. While he would have preferred somewhere more private and secure, this was the best place he could find in a hurry when inflation surged and pushed him suddenly to the brink of bankruptcy. At least here, he was unlikely to be trampled or run over.

Yet although he'd been expecting to lose consciousness, he hadn't put any thought at all into what would happen when he awoke. He'd simply assumed that he would get up and find his way to the camps. But his job had never required him to deal with bankdead after they'd been cash crashed, and he realized now that there were gaps in his knowledge of the liquidation process. He knew how liquidation worked in outline of course, as he'd met many Collection Agents when they came to retrieve the inert bodies of bankrupts he'd executed. They were taken to the Ministry of Records for LifeStream upload and then to the Ministry of Access for surgical removal of their BodyBank, before being transported to the camps. He also knew a bit about life in the camps, how the donations of basic supplies were generous, how the bankdead were totally free (if not quite Free with a capital F), how the mysterious workings of the Market ensured that the District of Dreams was the best of all possible slums. Despite all his growing suspicions about the justice of the AT market, Amon still believed that this series of procedures was as humane as could be. But now he saw that his details on the transitional period between displacement and life in the camps were a bit spotty at best, and he wondered why it had been treated so cursorily in GATA's usually comprehensive seminars or why it had never come up in the InfoFlux. Was there something that GATA and the MegaGloms didn't want people to know? Could all bankdead go blind and deaf as he had?

Possibly. But if so, what would cause it? Being forced to perceive the world without any graphical overlay? No. Clearly not, as he'd experienced such moments before, like when he'd taken off his training bank as a child in the BioPen, when the activist called Makesh had hacked his eyes in Sushi Migration, when he'd accidentally clicked the wrong command in the Eroyuki bedroom . . . So then what about his being disconnected from the ImmaNet entirely? No. That didn't explain it either as he remembered severing his own connection—partially at least—in the elevator when he'd fled Shuffle Boom, which had been incredibly jarring, but hadn't taken away his vision or hearing entirely. So the reason had to be something other than losing the overlay or the ImmaNet, something at a deeper level . . . like the shutdown of his BodyBank maybe? Yes, that seemed to make more sense, as it was plausible that the cognitive shock that caused his fainting might have been related to his sensory problems in some way. But how exactly? Though Amon was no expert in cyberneurology or anything, he did have some common sense knowledge about how the BodyBank functioned, and, after a few minutes curled up on the ground breathing and thinking about it, this enabled him to muster a guess.

The biological sensors and chips of the BodyBank were, after all, networked into a seamless whole with his body. And along with the display in his eyes and the speaker in his ears, they had become an integral part of his perceptual system. The audio-video input-output loop that made the ImmaNet possible was ongoing even when no overlay was present, so that even naked perceptions would have been jointly constituted by his inherited sensory organs and the organic machines that were a part of them, in tandem with his brain and nervous system. This meant that his eyes and ears, along with their corresponding neural matrices, would have been habituated to receiving signals from digital devices connected to the ImmaNet, beginning when he was a child with a Training Bank and continuing for the last seven years since he received his BodyBank. Once the BodyBank had shut down and the artificial component of his senses was lost, the nerves involved would have been suddenly deprived of an information source that they had long grown to expect, which was woven inextricably into their regular function. This was probably what ruptured the awareness of people like him who cash crashed while awake. Then when they woke up still lacking the regular inflow, they would find themselves afflicted with blindness and deafness.

In other words, Amon, like every other Free Citizen, had perceived everything through a technological filter for his entire life. What he'd thought of as moments of raw, unprocessed experience, such as those moments in the BioPen, Sushi Migration and Eroyuki, had in fact been mediated by the calculating engine implanted within him. Now that his BodyBank was deactivated, now that he was perceiving for the first time without any manmade crutches, he was confronted with the naked world—the *actual* naked world—for the first time, and it was so unprecedented and alien to his consciousness that he was literally unable to see or hear it.

While this explanation did seem convincing to Amon, it was only a guess. And even if he was right, he had no way of knowing if it applied to all bankdead, only some of them, or just to him. For if he thought about it further, his situation was different from all the others before him. He, unlike anyone else in the history of the Free Era (as far as he knew), had committed ID suicide and so never had his data extracted or his BodyBank removed. Retaining his data shouldn't have been affecting his mind in a distinctive way, as all bankdead were unable to access them when their BodyBanks were shut down, but the fact that he still had his hardware might. Perhaps the surgery dust that removed BodyBanks in the Ministry of Access also repaired damage done by the disconnection, and he had missed out on this standard treatment. Liquidation had to work something like that, didn't it? GATA couldn't just let bankdead enter the camps in the same condition he was in, could they? They'd never survive a day! *So what about me then?* he wondered. *Am I going to survive the day? Or am I going to die like this, withering away in an alley . . . ?*

Isolated from his habitual network of information, he felt like a star in a black hole, his confidence cracked right to the core. And a glassdust flame of remorse seared gratingly through his flesh when he remembered that Mayuko too was lost to him . . . *At least you didn't go bankrupt before cash crashing,* he consoled himself. *At least you still have the information your enemies fear, not to mention your freedom. Yes, freedom.* Actually, he wasn't sure just how useful that information would be or whether he was indeed as free as he supposed, but telling himself this helped to surmount his sense of helplessness, and he reminded himself that this wasn't the first time he'd figured things out on his own. After his run in with Sekido and the recruiter in Shuffle Boom, he'd crouched in the Open Source Zone and woven the tattered fabric of events that had led him there into a story, without any help from the ImmaNet. Then as now, he still had hope, fragile as it might be, even if Mayuko wasn't coming to save him this time. Somehow he would reconnect, get back online, clear his unwarranted debt. Somehow, he would find Mayuko, make it to the forest, start his life over and live it right this time.

Reassured by such positive thinking, Amon pushed himself away from the foot of the wall, rolled over onto his back, and jolted to a sitting position. He then reached his left palm for the wall, leaned on it for support, and stood up. On his feet encompassed by a great, vacant unknown was profoundly bewildering. He could have been standing beside the edge of a rooftop or a roaring highway and he wouldn't have known it. If he was going to get something to drink, he would have to forge onwards.

But after two steps he stopped, a chill of fear freezing his spine. Which way to the Sanzu River? He didn't know. If he got oriented in the right direction, how was he going to get there? He couldn't say. Should he shout for help? That would only draw unwanted attention, possibly from his enemies, and likely no one would care. Was he going to grope his way along the alley or wherever he was? This would only make him sweat more and increase his thirst, wet beads already collecting along his hairline from the effort of standing up. And what if he made it out of this seeming alley? Then where would he rest? Where could he feel even remotely safe? Or if he did find another sanctuary, how would he recognize it? People could trip all over him, or he could walk out into traffic, or stumble off the bank and drown in the river itself. His dread of this silent domain, this uncharted ocean of muffled ink that surrounded him, was paralyzing. He wanted to go on, but found the trembling arising from his core with greater force than ever before and immediately sat back down on the ground. *Where am I? What's going on? What happened to my eyes and my ears? Am I going to be like this forever? Am I going to just die here? I need help. Who can help me? I want to text somebody. An ambulance. A taxi. A grocery delivery. Mayuko? Anything. Anyone. Please. Help me . . .*

Again, Amon gave in to his helplessness and curled up with his face against the wall to focus on his breathing. This was his only mercy, he realized, his respiration. But as calm gradually spread outwards from his diaphragm to the tips of his fingers, he started to feel weaker and weaker, the hard grit and dusty sourness and stench of the river growing dimmer and dimmer until his eyes slipped closed and the undark darkness sunk into slumber once more.

2
AN ALLEY? A STREET.
THE ALLEY?

Blink, blink, blink.

As the grog cleared from Amon's eyes, he recalled where he was and what state he'd been in before falling asleep, and a titillating thrill flared up from the pit of his stomach: *I can see!* It wasn't so much what he saw, just an encompassing gray blur, a single nethercolor that had consumed his world. But even this was so exciting he immediately tried to push himself to his feet.

Lying on his right side, he pressed his left palm hard against the concrete and managed to pop his torso just above the ground for a moment, but to his horror, his right arm refused to move or support his weight, and flopped back down with the rest of him, limp and senseless. *Have I traded blindness for paralysis*, he wondered for a terrifying moment, until his fingertips began to tingle and he realized they were asleep.

Apparently he had been using his right bicep as a pillow. He rolled onto his back to shake it out and get the circulation going, but found the light too bright now that he was facing upwards and turned his head left to avert his eyes. Pins and needles flooded down from his shoulder to his fingertips, and he noticed that the pain in his ribs had sharpened, two of them on the right throbbing with an almost harmonic agony like resonating xylophone keys. Sleeping all this time on concrete, he probably had bruises, sidewalk bedsores. But at least he could see.

And as he rotated his shoulder tenderly, he detected a faint noise. Nothing more than a kind of reverberation of a whisper. Still, it was something. *I can hear!* his thoughts cheered again, though this time his excitement was tempered by lethargy, a deadening weight that seemed to pool beneath his cheeks and the skin all over his body. He realized that the feeling had been there since the moment he awoke, but he had only just noticed. Now it had grown so heavy he thought he might faint, if not for the tingling in his arm just then swelling to an excruciating pitch. Then there was the pain in his chest. And his thirst too. His tongue pasty and grainy against the roof of his mouth, his thoughts frail and fuzzy around the periphery of his awareness as even his mind seemed to parch and shrivel.

Something to drink! Now! cried a voice inside him and Amon clambered to his feet, cautiously this time so as not to bang his head. It took him a few moments to straighten out his stiff body, his lower back sore now that his joints had thawed from slumber. But once he was upright he began to look around, trying to get his bearings.

On three sides of him were gray surfaces that appeared to be the walls and ground of an alley, though somehow he couldn't tell how far away they were. When he glanced at the two walls in turn, they seemed to draw away and return again rapidly, their distance from him constantly shifting. When he looked down, the ground played the same trick, his shoes appearing only a meter away and then stretching off on the end of his pant legs as though at the base of long stilts. The texture of the surfaces refused to resolve too, fizzling constantly like boiling champagne, so that he was unable to tell what material they were made of or identify the line that separated the walls from the ground, that is, the corner. While the noise in his ears might have been from traffic, it seemed to synchronize with these frenzied optical distortions as though the city around him was an instrument playing a dull dissonant song, or else the song was painting a flickering sketch of the city.

Dizzy, Amon lurched to his right, nearly losing his balance, and cast his gaze about in search of something solid to focus on. He found the walls approaching each other infinitely into the distance, forming a V-shaped pinhole horizon, and turning his head found the same on the other side. Then, following one of the vertical gray surfaces upwards with his eyes, past the blob-like protrusions he guessed were verandas, he saw a searing gray blaze above that he couldn't stand to look at for even a second.

Gray below, gray left, gray right, gray around. Everything as gray as the Liquidator uniform he wore. But Amon soon realized that "gray" was not the right word for what he was seeing just as the darkness of his blindness had not really been dark at all. Although he had never considered this until that moment, grayness seemed to exist only in relation to color or at least the possibility of color, as the colorless intermediate between black and white. With all such possibility banished from his experience, the metropolis had been reduced to light and dark gradations, like a jumble of shadows in various concentrations, some thick, some rarified, others in between. There seemed to be no word for this, any more than there was a word for "movement without duration" or "perspective with no angle." And his hearing was in a similar state. He wanted to say he was surrounded by "white noise," but his auditory experience didn't seem to merit the word "noise" at all. Some integral aspect of sound was missing; the wispy, gray hiss filling his ears too hollow and numb to qualify.

Although Amon wanted to start off and find something to drink, fear kept his feet pinned in place once again. He guessed he was in the alley he'd crashed in, or somewhere very similar, and that was somewhat reassuring, but still he was terrified of venturing into the vast unknown around him. Thirsty, drained, half blind and deaf, he wondered how much it would cost him to traverse this seemingly infinite alley. *Shit*, he caught himself immediately, feeling like an idiot for still calculating the price of everything he did. But he couldn't help himself. Even if he understood that his actions incurred no expenses, there was just no way he could accept this undeniable fact so quickly, not after a lifetime of believing and behaving otherwise. But if his doings lacked monetary value, he realized, then what value did they have? None, it seemed. All his actions were now equally worthwhile, so he had no reason to choose one over another. In other words, he might as well do nothing. It wasn't like he was going to achieve anything in his current condition anyway. He would be better off just lying down where he was and never getting up again, giving in to the quicksand of his—

Before these thoughts could decimate his will entirely, something substantial reached out from the vague formlessness around him and gripped his consciousness firmly: the smell of water. Thick and rank with a sweet hint of chemicals, it held him so much more firmly than the wispy ephemera that he saw and heard. The perception seemed to thread its way into him, thin tendrils of air reaching inside his nostrils and weaving themselves into his flesh and brain.

I have to cross the Sanzu River, he resolved. *I have to get to the District of Dreams.* And thinking of Mayuko, of the forest, of jubilee, Amon tucked his bunched-up dress shirt back into his pants, put his left hand on the wall beside him, and took a step down the eternally receding alley. Solidity under foot, and bare fingers brushing the plasticky wall, he lumbered gingerly forward on stiff legs. With each step, the hollow hiss grew louder, until, after a few more paces, the lines of the never-ending V suddenly split apart. And with that, his hand found empty air, his visual field expanding before him.

In front of Amon was an open space filled with a flux of dark movement. A torrent of charcoal blotches bubbled and blurred by in a constant stuttering onrush, distorted as though filtered through a warped fish-eye lens.

For some time, he stood transfixed by this dappled, colorless flurry, unable to comprehend or accept what he was seeing. Gradually, his eyes seemed to adjust, for slowly but surely he began to perceive its dimensionality and directionality.

The torrent was made up of four streams. The one closest to him rose to about his neck, with currents going left, some right, and others mingling or eddying back. The one behind this went right and the one behind that went left, both of them undulating by at varying heights like a landscape of Rorschach tests being reeled away. Beyond these was yet another multidirectional stream like the one right in front of him, and behind that a sheer wall rising into the bright gray blaze above.

Gazing at what could only be a busy street sandwiched between two bustling sidewalks, Amon remembered when he had crouched in the Open Source Zone on the verge of bankruptcy and tried to imagine what bankdeath would be like. He had pictured naked consciousness as something similar to a mirror with missing shards, reflecting existence incompletely. That was exactly how he felt now. The flowing, shapeless layers each emanated a different noise—a faint sibilant popping from the foreground, something more gravelly and gargling from the middle—as though his auditory experience were being sluiced through a fractal honeycomb, echoes of echoes colliding again and again with other echoes before finally reaching his ears. Until that moment, Amon never would have imagined that sounds could have shadows, but that was the best way he could think of it. Shadow sounds. Shadow things.

Although the thick breeze no longer carried the scent of the Sanzu River, its memory lingered in his awareness. It reminded him not only of where he needed to go, but conjured the image of water, further goading his already ravenous thirst. And he saw himself bent over the edge of the bank, lapping at the peaks of waves like a dog, though from the effluent-rich smell he knew this wasn't even an option. Instead, he would need to find something to drink before he went there, which meant, of course, that he needed a vending machine.

Amon wondered how he was going to purchase anything given that he had no money, but decided he would have to deal with that problem when he came to it. For the time being, his first task was to locate one, and he automatically did some finger-flicks to open Scrimp Navi and ask it for directions. When the program didn't respond, he felt a hot pulse of irritation, and even when he remembered that his access to the ImmaNet was totally cut off, his fingers continued to jitter of their own volition. They twitched out the command to pull up Career Calibration and ask his decision network for advice, then tried to access his inner profile to call Mayuko . . . Amon felt his frustration swelling at these failures and then got annoyed with himself for being frustrated about something he had no control over, his emotions and impulses at odds with his knowledge that what they sought was pointless. Only when the implications of his total solitude, his disconnection from any and all networks, set in, did his scuttling fingers finally relent and drop limp on the end of his palms, his chest quivering with dread. For if he couldn't get directions to a vending machine, how the hell was he going to find one? And if he couldn't message anyone for advice, how was he going to solve this problem, or any problem? He had never tried going to a new place without a navi, even in areas of the metropolis he was familiar with, but now he was on the edge of Tokyo—as far from the familiar as he'd ever been. Caught in the most bizarre, perplexing predicament of his life, he needed input from other minds more than ever, and yet he was severed from them all, even Mayuko. Survival seemed impossible. He might as well be on a desert island, though he stood in one of the most populous cities on Earth.

He couldn't feel any sunlight—if it was even day—but the summer heat was getting to him. Pooling moisture clung to the fuzz of his buzzed head, his skin sticky everywhere, his mouth itchy with dryness. Beginning to feel light-headed, his fingers did the gestures to open MyMedic, wanting advice on resolving these symptoms as though he was connected to such an app, and he was left to guess as a layman what diagnosis his sensations might signify. *I must be really thirsty*, he supposed, as if he didn't already know that, and started to worry that he might pass out if—

Ah. Out of nowhere an idea took form. From experience he knew there were vending machines somewhere on every city block, so what if he wandered around and tried to, well, look for one? Amon had never thought to search for something without an engine before. It struck him as an oddly inefficient way to do things, and in his present condition he wasn't confident he could safely cross the road or even recognize a vending machine if he saw one. But after pondering the issue for a few moments—his throat seeming to parch as he watched the insipid muddle froth by—he could think of nothing better.

And to his relief, he found the shifting silhouette of a street growing more definite before his eyes, spaces opening up to carve out shapes in the flow. Though every passing thing continued to blend and blur by so that he couldn't tell where one ended and another began, outlines were beginning to trace themselves around the loci of distinct swirls. At the same time, he started to catch spikes in volume and pitch as his ears learned to discern peaks and valleys in the mish-mashed soundscape.

Heartened by the apparent improvement in his senses, Amon shifted his will and attention to embarking on his search. Unsure of what lay ahead, he continued to waver at the threshold of the alley, hunching over with his hands on his thighs and watching the rush of the city. Could what his dysfunctional eyes and ears took for the sidewalk in fact be the road? Could it all be one big hallucination? *Only one way to find out! Courage, Amon, courage!* he rallied himself, and tentatively stuck out his arm. Immediately a passing lump in the flow knocked it aside and kept on going. Relatively soft and warm and covered in fabric, Amon had no doubt it had been a person, for touch didn't lie. But how much had the collision cost? *Nothing, you idiot. Nothing.*

His heart thumping in his chest, Amon took the first step. As he slipped into the rush going left, he was bumped from behind and heard a shrill, granulated whine radiating from that direction like microphone feedback through a cheese grater. A person's voice? Who could say for sure? All he could do now was walk onwards, following the direction of the current, and was surprised to find himself carried along smoothly, without any further collisions. Though he couldn't consciously see the obstacles he negotiated, some deeper part of him seemed to, guiding his feet with raw instinct so that he weaved fluidly along his course. Awed by the wisdom of his own body, he looked down at it and saw that he too was a splotch of molten nethercolor. His absorption into this mass of inscrutable beings was unnerving, like becoming a drop that could not quite dissolve in an ocean. But unlike everything else in his visual field, he could confidently sense where he ended and the surround began, feeling the air on his face and hands, the fabric of his suit brushing his skin, the pressure of his shoe-swaddled feet against the ground. With visceral rhythm, he matched the pace of the pulsating jagged blots around him, dodging and sidestepping oncoming forces until suddenly he bumped hard into the person in front of him. The entire crowd had come to a stop and Amon guessed the light must have turned red, though he could see no signal up ahead, just a square gap where movement had momentarily ceased. An intersection surely . . . leading to another block?

Suddenly Amon thought of the alley—the only place he knew in this vague baffling metropolis, the last link to his former life—and the idea of crossing when the signal changed was terrifying. For in his present state, he would likely be unable to find his way back and so would leave the alley behind forever. But was he ready to do that? Since any block was just as likely to have a vending machine as this one, shouldn't he stick close to his lone sanctuary until there was good reason to abandon it?

The crowd started forward but Amon carved his way left to a wall and began to follow it back the way he had come. Now the gray forms pouring past him were beginning to take on the contours of humans, though their forms were murky. Three-dimensional upright shades with four limbs, a torso, a head, and even a hat or hairdo on some of them, their faces still a frizzling blank, the digits of their hands webbed together like the blade of a spade or large spoon. *VREEEEEEr.* He heard the unmistakable whine of a motorbike accelerating, and looking to his left saw vehicles—cars, trucks, even a few bicycles—rolling and roaring by, one after the other. He was glad for this returning acuity, but as the intermerged liquid continuity of the city resolved into sharper focus, Amon began to feel ever more thirsty and light-headed. With a new burst of urgency, he trotted ahead, his right hand on the wall brushing across glass, then concrete, then glass, before reaching a gap. Looking to his right he saw two walls hung with rows of balconies bordering a narrow walkway. An alley to be sure, but was it the alley he'd started in? Either way, Amon wasted only a heartbeat before stepping into it and away from the crowd.

Sweat dripping from his forehead and down the back of his neck, Amon was feeling weaker by the second. He put his palms against the right wall with his head down and leaned there for a moment to collect himself. Wondering how much his walk down the street had cost, he glanced into the bottom right corner of his eye to check his AT readout. But obviously it wasn't there and this reminded him that he was no longer part of the market, that his actions had no value, that his existence— Best not to look at that area of his visual field anymore. What he needed to do now was find a vending machine quickly. And reluctant to waste any more of his waning energy venturing onto that busy sidewalk again, he wondered if there was some other way, not using the ImmaNet, to find what he was looking for.

For several minutes he leaned there, his hands on the plastic wall, drawing a blank on what to do next and frowning hard as if the force of his brow muscles would gestate a plan in his head. It was only when he sensed a headache coming on and gave up at last with a (somewhat guilty) sigh that he suddenly had another epiphany. *What if I . . . ask someone for directions?* He had never considered this wild idea before either, and now that he had, it seemed even stranger than searching for something without an engine—the navigational equivalent of rubbing sticks together to start a fire. Given the state of his hearing, he wasn't sure if he could understand the answers of people he asked, but he seemed to be gradually recovering and it was worth a try anyway. As his strength drained rapidly away, he felt the urge to lie down and knew he had to do something before he let himself sink into oblivion again, maybe never to resurface.

When Amon took his hand off the wall, stood up straight, and looked back to the street, he was grateful to discover that the bodies in the crowd now had hands with separate fingers and wrists on the ends of arms, which now had sleeves! He could make out outfits (mostly suits as far as he could tell). And faces, their mouths and noses taking shape. And eyes too, though their pupils and irises were indistinguishable from the speckled, buzzing patina that danced over their bodies.

Excuse me, he tried to say to the passing streetwalkers, but all that seemed to come out was a chinkling whir as though he were gargling with a blade-sharpener throat, and not one head turned to acknowledge his utterance. *Excuse me*, he tried again, this time fatty-cartilage-chunks-ground-in-a-blender flute stutters, but again he was ignored. A dozen more times he tried, raising and then lowering his voice, attempting polite singsong or barking abruptly, unable to tell how any of it sounded to others because all that accompanied the sensation of air rushing out between his lips was incoherent noise.

By about the twentieth time though, he began to recognize his own words. "Awckskyuews nmee," was all he could parse at first, the vowels and consonants bleeding into each other. But after repeating himself again and again, the syllables found their identity and cohered in relief against the background hum of the city. "Excuse me."

At the same time, human voices began to stand out as reverberating grunts, and the twanging grumble of each passing car bobbed up from the traffic. Given hope by these improvements, Amon rapid-fired his phrase, "ExcusemeExcusemeExcusemeExcuseme," and raised his hand over the sidewalk to wave for their attention. But while a few turned their heads to glance at him, no one stopped, and his mouth was so pasty now that forming speech with his tongue and lips was extremely uncomfortable.

Seized by a desperate impulse, Amon hopped into the middle of the sidewalk and spread his arms out to his sides to block the oncoming crowd. "Please!" he begged. "Can anyone tell me where to find a vending machine? I'm thirsty, you know?" But all he got from the passersby was a moment's confused pause, where they bumped and bunched up in front of him, before resuming their walking, some ducking under his arms, others sidestepping him into the gutter or alley. A few turned back the way they'd come rather than bother with him, and one man in a bowler's cap proceeded straight into Amon's right arm to shoulder past him. As if encouraged by this violence, several salarymen brushed by in the man's wake, buffeting Amon from both sides until he nearly lost his balance and stumbled back into the alley.

It was as he stood there with head bowed, stewing in exasperation, that he suddenly felt a strange tingle in the back of his neck, as though someone was watching him. Struck with fear, Amon swept his gaze around the street, scanning the crowd carefully. He could now make out the darker circle at the center of their gray eyes well enough to tell that everyone seemed to be focused elsewhere, all gazes averted as they marched by. *Could Sekido or one of the Birlas be hounding me?* Amon thought, looking to the faces floating past in cars and on the far side of the street, glancing up to scope out the windows and balconies above, crooking his neck to check down the alley behind him . . .

Wait! There. In the alley. Not the lurking spy he sought, but something else. Protruding from the wall just short of the busy street on the other side.

Down the alley he hurried and soon saw it clearly. A tall block. A vending machine!

The machine standing against the wall had a rectangular frame with a groove running down the middle. This divided it into two equal halves, each embedded with a bin enclosed by an opaque plastic flap around knee height. The frame was just slightly shorter than Amon, and as he went closer, he could see dust and grime accumulated on the flat top. If this was the alley in which he'd awoken, it had only been a few paces away, but he'd gone in the wrong direction. And Amon reflected momentarily on how an arbitrary choice, between say left or right, could transform a life, perhaps the future of a whole corporation or empire.

He was unsettled to find that no logos or vending attendants appeared upon his approach, as this left him no way of determining what the machine sold. For all he knew, it could be beer or corned beef or umbrellas. The left-to-right mirroring design did remind him of the all-purpose feeding machines he'd often used that provided beverages on the left side and food on the right, but he couldn't be sure. And as he stared at the vending machine, wondering how he might figure this out, the full severity of the even worse problem he'd been putting off began to dawn on him. While he'd meant to find some way to buy goods without money or the ImmaNet when he found a vending machine, now that he faced one directly—its hard, impenetrable shell seeming to confront him defiantly—he couldn't imagine what that might be. Promise to build its CPU a human body in exchange for freebies? Propitiate its algorithms with a song and dance?

Aw ssshiiit . . . he groaned with resignation and put his face in his hands, leaning the top of his head and elbows against the machine. *How the hell am I going to get something to eat and drink?* Vending machines were where food and drinks came from. If you were hungry or thirsty, you spent money and out came edibles and drinkables. Sure, he'd been to restaurants before, but most of them cooked with vending machines in the back or at least got their ingredients from them. About the only dish he'd ever had that tasted different than all the machine-printed ones was the sushi the Birla sister had treated him to, but that was gourmet cuisine reserved for the world's wealthiest. Regular people had to eat regular food and that meant vending machines. The idea that his access might be cut off had been impossible to entertain seriously. But by committing identity suicide, it seemed, he had unwittingly condemned himself to desiccate and die. With his head against the machine, he could feel it vibrating, the cooling mechanisms keeping (what was probably) his sustenance fresh, so close and yet unreachable.

"FUUCK!" he howled, jerking his head up from the hard plastic and slamming the surface of the left segment with his right palm. To his small satisfaction, a little dent appeared in the surface, but he immediately heard a strange hum emanating from inside, like a wine glass being rubbed around its rim, yet sharper, more strident. Warily he took one step back, but when the sound quickly faded his helpless anger surged again and he kicked the right side as hard as he could with the sole of his dress shoe.

Shwew, chrinkle. Without warning a cloud of tiny particulate enveloped Amon's face before instantly dissipating. He frowned at the machine in surprised horror, when suddenly the mere sight of it made him extremely nauseous. It was as though he were watching someone eat their boogers or lick infected wounds, but he endured the awful feeling, staring stubbornly at the dent left by his kick. It was deeper than the last, and he mustered his will to deliver another, to smash his way into this stockpile of wonderful refreshment as though cracking an egg filled with golden ambrosia, until he began to dry retch convulsively and had to look away.

What did that thing do to me? He tried glancing back and then away, hoping the nausea might fade, but it seemed to get progressively stronger each time and he gave up, resting his eyes on the wall. *It must have been revulsion dust*, he realized: nanobots that stimulated the precise areas of their target's brain to form an association between intense disgust and the first thing they beheld. Their liquidation coaches had gone over it briefly during training when covering the different types of psychosomatic security systems they might encounter.

Amon was stunned to find such an expensive weapon installed in a mere vending machine, as the AT market was supposed to make defensive measures like these superfluous. Anyone who broke into a vendor would be fined enough to at least fully compensate the company that owned it for any damage, loss of merchandise, or other associated expenses, a legal arrangement that discouraged such illicit behavior. So the companies that maintained the machines had no reason to invest in additional preventatives, since they made profits whether the crime succeeded or not. Unless vending machines were specifically designed to keep out bankdead, who could not be fined and therefore needed to be deterred by force, which made sense now that Amon thought about it . . . though it was still a difficult idea for him to swallow, after all these years believing their sole purpose was convenience.

Whatever the justification for keeping him out, Amon had to find a way to get in. From what he remembered, the neurological link between the visual stimuli and the reaction could last for hours. The trouble was that his thirst wasn't going to wait that long.

Staring at a point on the wall, Amon kept the vending machine in his peripheral vision, eliciting only the slightest edge of his nausea, and tried to guess where the deeper dent had been so he could deliver another kick. He hesitated, fearing another dusting. Then walls would disgust him, seriously compromising his ability to find his way through the city afterwards. He wanted to charge in with his eyes squeezed shut and blindly pummel the mechanical monster with the flat of his hands and shoes and elbows and forehead. But what if the sight of his own eyelids became revolting and every blink made him want to vomit? This prospect was too awful to even contemplate. And so Amon froze, his eyes twitching as his stomach churned, clueless as to what he should do next.

Though his body burned with wooziness after his violent exertion, Amon wasn't sweating at all, which was seriously scary—a warning that he really had to drink something and fast. While he might try to search for a different machine, it seemed reasonable to assume that they would all be just as well defended. If he couldn't bust in here, most likely he couldn't bust in anywhere.

If only I'd made it across the Sanzu River before crashing, he thought. If not for the flash inflation that took out the last of his funds, he might have already been enjoying the generous supplies doled out by the venture charities—the capriciousness of the market condemning him to the mortal choice he now confronted. Should he gamble it all on one last effort, flailing desperately against a booby-trapped box to remain in this vague, insipid world when he didn't even know for sure if there was anything to drink inside? Or should he lie down right there and give in to the downward spiral of broken dreams he knew awaited him the moment he closed his eyes? Were there any other choices than these, to either go down fighting or go down dreaming . . . ?

It was as Amon dithered over this question that he felt more strongly than ever that someone was watching him and looked in the direction he had come—to the far mouth of the alley. There he saw a man, static amidst the gray crowds and traffic streaming behind him, his charcoal pupils fixated unflinchingly on Amon. Startled by the man's intense stare, Amon unconsciously went to pat the nerve duster strapped to his belt for reassurance when he realized for the first time since waking up that it wasn't there.

His pulse throbbing rapidly, Amon stood up tall to face the man. His vision seemed to have improved considerably, for the man's features and attire came into clear resolution, if still without color.

A head shorter than Amon, he was exceedingly fat—mostly around the waist—with a great round belly and thick love handles, but also flabby biceps, hefty thighs, and hanging jowls. He had a broad forehead, made broader by a receding hairline that ate an S-shaped patch from the mat of curly frizz covering his pate, a wide flat nose, and the somewhat weathered skin of someone around their late forties. Amon found his outfit peculiar, a jumpsuit that seemed to be stitched entirely of pockets made from a dark fabric similar to that of a sports coat. From ankle to neck and all down his sleeves were openings of different sizes in the cloth, some thin slits the width of a playing card, others gaping circles able to accommodate a softball. The man stood there at the threshold to the street with his arms hanging at his bulging sides, his big eyes studying Amon intently, and Amon wondered how long he'd been watching him. Had he just stepped into the alley now? Had he witnessed Amon's struggle with the machine? Had he heard Amon's pleas on the sidewalk? Or had he been following him since even before that? And what did he want now?

Amon couldn't concern himself with such questions for long. They were important perhaps, but if there was any chance this man might help him, he had to forget his reservations and just try asking. There were simply no other options.

"Please. I need to ask your help with something," said Amon, his voice clear and crisp in his ears for the first time, albeit raspy with the dryness of his throat. He thought he could detect a slight nod of the man's forehead but he wasn't sure. "I'm . . ." Amon pointed to the vending machine, "th-thirsty."

Not showing any sign that he'd acknowledged or understood Amon's request, the man continued to stare at him impassively. Amon didn't think he had ever felt a gaze so unwavering. Even when fixed on one thing, eyes usually twitched or vibrated slightly, but his seemed uncannily still, like a car somehow rolling without spinning its wheels. No one on the street had paid Amon any attention, except to dodge or push him aside like an inanimate obstacle. Now this man was giving him far too much of it and Amon couldn't help but periodically look away for a split second, feeling as though he might wilt. "I'm not sure if there are any drinks in here and I don't have any money. But if it isn't too much trouble, would you mind getting me a drink? Anything will do, even the cheapest one."

His eyes still locked on Amon, though not seeming to quite meet his gaze, the man opened his mouth as if to speak, but it was another second or so before any words came out. "And . . ." The man cleared his throat several times as though he hadn't spoken in a while. "And after that?" His voice was quiet and gruff.

"Huh? P-pardon?"

Again the man's mouth opened and his throat and tongue quivered as though silently stuttering before he spoke. "After your drink. Where to?"

"Th-the river. I want to go to the Sanzu River."

"Know the way?"

"I . . ." Then it hit Amon that he would have to find his way there without navis. The smell of the river might lead him somewhere, but the lay of the streets wafted the breeze in odd ways, and although his vision and hearing were getting better, he'd had this much trouble just finding something a few paces away. *Imagine traveling a longer distance*, he thought, and the metropolis suddenly seemed to loom gigantic and enigmatic about him, an endless puzzle made glass and concrete. "No . . . not exactly. Still, I—"

"When you get there, what you going to do?"

"I'm going to—I'm going to cross. Into the District of Dreams."

"Got a boat?"

"A b-boat? There must be—I was planning to use the Bridge of Compassion."

"Got money for the toll?"

"Toll? There's a toll?"

"What about the barricade?"

"Well . . ." There was a barricade? On the bridge? For what? The bankdead were perfectly free to come and go, weren't they? "I'm sure I'll figure something out." Amon wasn't sure of this at all now and only said it so he wouldn't sound like a fool. "But for the moment I'm really thirsty like I said. So could you . . ." Amon indicated the machine with a quick flick of his eyes that brought up a flash of nausea. "Please?"

The man seemed to give another nod, though it could have been a trick of Amon's imagination. "Got something for the road?"

"Um, pardon?"

"Something to offer me for the journey."

"Oh. Like I told you already, I don't have any money I'm afraid."

"Forget money. We'll do a trade."

"But all I've got is this suit I'm wearing and . . ." Amon remembered that his duster was gone and wondered what could have happened to it. He was sure he'd had it when he lay down in the alley but couldn't recall whether it had been with him when he woke up.

"How about a story?"

"A story. You mean, you want me to trade you a story?" Was that slight vibration of his head another nod? "I . . . I don't think I have any stories."

"Everyone has a story. The one about your life will do fine. Understand?"

Amon thought he understood but paused anyways, thrown off by the oddness of the idea and of the person who had proposed it. Who was this fat, balding, middle-aged man, and why was he dressed like this? Surely he looked different to those who could see his digimake, but why have all the pockets? Obviously he wasn't sent by Sekido or those that backed him, because then he would have surely dispatched Amon on the spot, and Amon sensed no suggestion of a threat in his stare, though that still didn't mean he could be trusted.

"Of course," Amon said finally. "I'll tell you anything you want to know. But please"—he pointed in the general direction of the vending machine without looking at it—"something to drink."

The man gave a subtle flick of his chin that might have been another nod and stepped over to the machine. Reaching around his waist to a pocket on his lower back, he took out a strange bundle of wires and what looked like a piece of glass. Once he'd slipped this onto his left hand, Amon saw that it was a glove. The back was a tight weave of electronic substrate, wires and circuitry, the front a clear flexible display that stretched from the bottom of his palm to the tips of his fingers.

The man went up to the wall beside the left half of the machine and stuck one finger into a thin pocket around his thigh. From there, he fished out a device that looked like a small steel cylinder. When he put this against the sidewall of the machine, it clicked onto the surface like a magnet. Immediately images lit up on the flat of his hand, various alphanumerics and blueprint-like schematics that Amon took to be the specifications for the machine. The man then began to scroll through them by subtly moving the joints of his gloved fingers and brushing the fingers of his other hand on the palm display.

While it was nauseating already for Amon to stand so close to the machine and catch glimpses of it, this was only exacerbated by a raunchy smell that clung to the man, like a fermented synthesis of dirty toilet and filthy locker room. Nonetheless, as he was curious what the man was doing, Amon watched him with a mixture of fascination and disgust. After a few seconds of scrolling through the schematics and clicking in several locations to expand particular sets of numbers, the man plucked off the cylinder, returned it to one of his pockets and poked the fingers of his right hand into five separate narrow pockets to withdraw several tiny items from each one: two circular sheets of black plastic, a skein of thread-thin wires, half a dozen obsidian-like beads, transistors, diodes, an assortment of electronic components, and a tiny rubber hand.

"Hold out your hand," he said, and Amon did as instructed.

Using Amon's palm as a sort of worktable, the man then lay down one of the fingernail-sized plastic sheets and several other pieces. As he moved the fingers of his gloved hand the tiny hand began to move in synch, shadowing his motions. From a hole in the tip of each of its pin-sized fingers, even smaller tools popped out—a screwdriver, a blowtorch, a wrench, a key, a gluegun. Then the hand formed a sort of tripod with the base of its pinky, thumb, and wrist to stabilize itself and assembled the various parts together using these tools, the man stroking his palm display to manipulate them. First, it glued a substrate strip to the plastic. Then it began to glue the pebbles and components in various spots and soldered these to wires, crisscrossing and re-linking them into a circuit. As Amon watched, he noticed that the man's fingers were longer and thinner than his build would have suggested and worked with surprising speed and nimbleness. His gestures were fluid, the tiny hand never fumbling or faltering at even the most delicate of tasks, transitioning smoothly from one procedure to the next as its minuscule appendages rewired and reconfigured barely visible pieces inside the makeshift chip.

"What are you doing?" asked Amon, but the man ignored him and kept at his task. The man's behavior was totally inscrutable. If he was going to get him a drink, why didn't he just buy something?

Within less than a minute, the chip seemed to be nearly finished. The man did one last check—the little fingers tugging lightly on the wires and prodding the nodes to make sure they were secure—before dropping the hand back in his pocket and snapping the other plastic sheet over the first to seal everything. Finally, he took it from Amon's hand and reached into a tiny pocket on his left shoulder with his right index finger and thumb. There he pinched some sort of fabric and pulled it out as a magician might flourish a handkerchief, flicking it open so that it expanded into a plastic sack.

"Get set to unload," he said, handing Amon the sack and pointing to a spot just in front of the machine. Amon wasn't sure what he was talking about, but he took the sack and, keeping his eyes averted from the revolting machine, stood where the man indicated.

Once Amon was in place, the man put the device up to the side of the machine, where it clicked onto the surface as the cylinder had a minute earlier. Immediately there was a buzz and a clack, and then *cah-chunk cah-chunk cah-chunk* as the internal mechanisms engaged and various items began tumbling one after another into the two receptacle bins. Before Amon could blink, the man was kneeling in front of the machine, reaching into both halves and shoveling plastic bottles, rice balls, and sandwiches into his pockets. Amon fell to the ground to the left of him, where he saw the glistening bottles popping out. He dry-heaved twice in the presence of the machine but closed his eyes and probed greedily with his hands beneath the plastic flap of the bin, grabbing the first bottle he could find, snatching it out, twisting the top, chugging.

"Load up!" barked the man, but Amon ignored him and kept the bottle tipped back into his mouth. Whatever it was he hardly tasted it, only felt it. Like a cool, succulent waterfall of refreshment itself pouring through his gullet and being absorbed by his tongue and throat before it even reached his stomach. Amon then chucked the empty bottle over his shoulder and groped inside for another.

"Let's go!" called the man. "In case the CareBots come."

CareBots? They didn't sound so bad, and Amon was too immersed in downing his second drink in the same way, the rich moistness soaking into—

The man yanked him by the arm and the bottle fell from his grasp, splashing onto his suit as it spun to the concrete.

"Gwa!" cried Amon as he flailed pathetically for the bottle, which had already bounced well out of reach and was spewing its fizzy contents against a wall.

"Here," said the man, proffering a sack full of vending goodies. Amon took the sack and, when he felt its bulky weight in his hand, realized that the man must have grabbed it from him and filled it up while he was in his rehydration rapture. With all the drinks inside, he wouldn't have to worry about going thirsty for a while. But then he had to wonder. *Did I just aid and abet a robbery? And why would this man pay the fine for this blatant credicrime when buying the machine's whole inventory would have obviously been much cheaper?*

"Go go go!" shouted the man, pulling Amon along by his bicep, but Amon stiffened and resisted when he suddenly realized what this man was. His lack of interest in money, his disregard for credilaw, his bizarre attire, his curiosity about Amon's life in the Free World, his smell. He was bankdead, the first one Amon had ever met outside the line of duty.

When Amon stood his ground, the man gave up on him, let go of his arm, and stepped hurriedly out of the alley into the crowd. Realizing that he would soon be alone again, Amon swallowed his bewilderment and dashed onto the sidewalk in pursuit.

3
TOKYO NAKED

Slinging the heavy sack over his shoulder, Amon followed behind the man as he waddled through the crowd with incongruous agility and speed for his size.

He was relieved to find that he could see and hear reasonably well again. Though all remained colorless with a sort of fuzzy haze drifting about, and traffic noises were still slightly muffled and distorted, the vehicles whipping along the two-lane road to his left looked and sounded like vehicles whipping along a two-lane road, the people walking on the sidewalk around him like people walking on a sidewalk. Now he could move along without feeling bewilderment at every step, his weaving between pedestrians conscious once again.

But soon a new sense of bewilderment struck him, when, after tailing the man for a few blocks, the crowd came to a standstill at the next intersection, and Amon's gaze was untethered from the task of navigation for a moment, drawing outwards from what was right in front of his face and taking in the city all around him.

On the one hand, Amon knew that the street he walked along had to be part of Tokyo, for he had no reason to suspect he had ever left. The same cloying perfumes and exhaust fumes invaded his nostrils. The same hard concrete met his shoes. The same sultry air steamed his skin. The sweet, lingering tang of the vending beverage in his mouth tasted no less familiar. This was the metropolis he had inhabited his entire life. His touch and smell and taste left no room for doubt.

But his eyes and ears fed his consciousness a different tale. The first thing he noticed was that there were no images anywhere. No animated shop signs or winking billboards. No advertainment blazing walls or logos cruising airways. No rainbow promostrobe, trademark phantasmagoriflow, or talking-head kaleidoscopes. Without perceptual candy, commercial markings, or semantic adornment of any kind, a strange stillness seemed to envelope the streets and the sprawling skyscraper surround, matched also by the dampened sonic atmosphere. Engines droned by. A coptor chopped above. Stilettos and leather soles clacked around him. But there was no adverbabble, no character assassination jingles, no idol product placement debates. No variety show murder mystery theme songs, no mockumentary soap opera laughtracks.

For Amon, who'd never even thought to imagine the metropolis without information, the transformation was eerie. Yet what he found disturbing more than what was lacking was what had been added. In place of the InfoFlux was filth. All the windows, whether of shops or apartments or cars or buses, were encrusted with white sediments and dust, smeared with grime and handprints, some cracked or broken with rusted frames, as though they hadn't been cleaned or repaired in years. The sidewalk was speckled with gum spots, plastic wrappers fluttered about, and he glimpsed the faint sparkle of broken glass crushed into powder on the tarmac between the bumpers of the cars sliding by beside him.

The passing streetwalkers had changed as well, looking a decade older on average than the crowds he was used to, with wrinkled, sagging, lusterless skin; baldness, and gray hair; yellowing, crooked teeth. Then there were the asymmetries and flaws that had little to do with age: the off-kilter, bloodshot eyes; hairs twizzling out of mismatched nostrils on bent noses; flabby arms, bloated bellies, and jiggling thighs; birthmarks, moles, sunspots, scars. They were all slovenly too, with shirt collars invariably ruffled and askew; pants creased and stained; shoes scratched and scuffed; unibrows unplucked and bristly; nails long and grotty; bedhead, hathead, shag.

Altogether, they reminded him of the people he'd seen behind the overlay in Sushi Migration and the Shuffle Boom elevator, of the whore from Eroyuki . . . The difference was that this was not some fleeting window into another realm, not a brief peek through the slats in an existential veneer.

This drab, dirty, blighted city, along with the rickety worn-out cars and unattractive slobs that inhabited it, stretched endlessly in all directions and was undoubtedly here to stay. This realization about the spectacle, though obvious and undeniable, was almost as unsettling as the spectacle itself, and Amon looked up in search of a visual (and intellectual) respite, some seam in this all-too-encompassing new locale. There he found slivered gaps in the roofscape, but the glare of the sky was too bright for his still-healing eyes to look at, too distant for his discombobulated pupils to focus on, and he quickly averted his gaze streetward once again.

Immediately Amon realized that the man was no longer in front of him and frantically whipped his eyes about in each direction. *What if I've been left behind?* he thought. *I'm doomed.* Spotting him on the other side of the road as he made his way around a corner, Amon took one step to rush after him, then halted abruptly, noticing something perplexing: there was no signal at the intersection. Apparently that had been part of the overlay too. Since the cars were stopped and no pedestrians were crossing, Amon guessed that the light was probably in the middle of changing, which meant it would be safer to wait a few moments and make sure it wasn't turning red, though if he stayed he might lose the man forever and be left here all al—

Amon bolted across the empty road, the heavy sack bouncing its irregular contents against his back. Just as he was reaching the other side, a car leapt towards him and he bounded forward to clear the edge of its hood, the air of its passing brushing the back of his neck as he staggered to regain his balance, shocked that Mindfulator hadn't warned him of the danger. With his apps all gone, it was up to Amon to watch out for himself, and he hurried around the corner, where he was relieved to catch sight of the man just before he turned another corner up ahead.

Catching up with the man after a quick dash, Amon followed him down several side streets. This time he stuck close with his eyes glued to the man's back, partly for fear of losing sight of him again, and partly to avoid the sense of dissonance from looking at a place that was at once the Tokyo he knew and a very different city altogether.

The man moved at a brisk pace, showing no signs of tiring despite having to carry the large weight of his flesh and whatever he had stashed in his pockets, and Amon was soon running out of breath, sweat dribbling down his forehead, faintness rising to his head. When the man pulled some kind of pastry out of a pocket, unwrapped it and devoured it in mid-stride, Amon realized that he was hungry. Though it hadn't dawned on him until that instant, it had been either a day or days since his last meal, and the sudden throbbing of his gut now dominated his awareness. It wasn't long before Amon found himself lagging behind, and he used his last burst of energy to jog ahead until they were shoulder to shoulder. "Hold on . . . please," he panted. "I need to . . . take a break?"

The man kept going without responding, and Amon thought he hadn't heard him or had ignored him. But after a few more strides he made a sudden right and went over a small fence of dark metal bars in a single hop. There he stopped—in an alley paved with small stones—and took out what appeared to be a sweet bean bun from a pocket. Amon scrambled over after him hauling the heavy sack, and plopped it down on the other side, where he leaned over with his hands on his knees to catch his breath. When he lifted his head, the man had already finished his bun and was chowing on some sort of sandwich. Mouth watering despite the smell of the man, Amon bent over to rummage inside his sack for a rice ball, tearing off the wrapper and swallowing it down almost without chewing. He only realized after he was done that there had been fish flakes at the center.

From Amon's sack, the man withdrew a bottle of some translucent liquid, popped it and took a big swig. Amon imitated him by rustling a darker drink out of his sack and draining it in seconds like the last time. He watched the man chuck the bottle down the alley, where it hit the wall at the end and bounced to a stop on the rocky ground. Amon was about to do the same with his when he noticed something about it and his hand paused. It had tasted like a coffee chocolate sports drink but the bottle was unlabeled, with no brand name or logo. No list of ingredients or disclaimers. Just a clear plastic tube with a residue of shaded fluid at the bottom. It had been designed for Free Citizens who could see it on the ImmaNet. What it looked like to the bankdead or anyone else was irrelevant. If he thought about it, this was true of the bottle, of the vending machine it had come from, and of everything else in the city—from the gutters to the peaks of the highest towers—as though it all existed to say that his senses, his mind, his body, were not welcome. But then what was this man doing here, a lone bankdead far away from the camps that could support him? And this raised further questions, like how he had found Amon, why he had bothered to approach him, and what his reason was for offering to guide him now.

When the man scarfed down a rice ball of his own and started back towards the fence, Amon tried clicking on him but his profile failed to pop up. If he was going to get answers, Amon realized, he would have to ask. "Hold on a second," he said.

The man stopped with his hand already on the fence and turned his head to look at Amon.

"Can I ask your name?"

The man just stared back impassively, his intense gaze seeming to almost meet Amon's but not quite, their eyes just shy of contact. After a few silent seconds, Amon became nervous and felt he had to say something. "S-so how much farther to the Sanzu River do you think?"

"We're going somewhere else first."

"Oh. W-where to?"

Letting this question go as well, the man turned around, put his other hand on the fence, and bent his knees to jump.

"Wait!" Amon called out and the man gave him another off-target stare over his shoulder. The rice ball seemed to have merely whet Amon's appetite, and when he got the chance he wanted to eat more, much more. But now that his thirst seemed to be sated at last, a touch of relaxation had settled on him—his muscles looser, his pulse slower—and this feeling had awakened yet another long-neglected urge. "Before we start moving again, is there a washroom nearby?"

The man pointed towards the end of the alley with his left index finger and then bent it to the right. Amon hadn't noticed until then, but apparently the alley continued to the right, and stepping over to the far wall, he saw that it was shaped like an L. There was a door at the end that looked like some sort of service entrance, but he approached to find no handle. As he was trying to pry it open from the crack beside the jamb, he noticed a sharp, sweet smell emanating from around his feet and realized what the man had taken him to mean by "washroom."

The situation had grown too urgent for Amon to be picky.

"Um, do you have any . . ."

A roll of toilet paper bounced off the wall, skipping and tumbling over the rocks, before coming to a rest on the ground beside where Amon was already crouching.

Although Amon had been in Tokyo for as long as he could remember, he recognized nothing on the winding course the man was leading him along, turning down side street after side street into obscure corners of the metropolis. This area, the fringes of Tonan Ward, was unfamiliar to him, and he couldn't see any of the regular skyline landmarks, like GATA Tower or the headquarters of The Twelve And One. Just unmarked streets, bleak skyscrapers, unkempt pedestrians and weathered cars melting past one after another.

Since Amon had not caught a whiff of the river for some time, he suspected they were moving away from it. Although the man had already said they were taking a detour, this nonetheless made him anxious and Amon occasionally found himself twitching his index finger unconsciously to open his navi as they walked. At the same time, he couldn't help flicking his gaze repeatedly to one of the bottom corners of his visual field, either to check the clock on the left or his AT readout on the right, both of which he recognized weren't there but couldn't resist the urge to look at.

The stress and disorientation of not knowing the time made the empty space where his clock should have been too attractive to ignore. While he guessed it was day because the sky was still too bright to look at, he could determine nothing more precise and had no sense of how long anything took. Had they been walking for minutes or hours? Were they proceeding quickly or slowly? They seemed to move fast relative to the other pedestrians and cars, but Amon found their speed difficult to gauge. Sometimes a motorbike seemed to carve through traffic in slow motion, as though the gelatinous air hindered its progress. At other times a hobbling granny seemed to rip along the curb, like a lopsided comet. Clearly his mind was adjusting to the naked world, but there was still a long way to go.

Amon's AT readout, on the other hand, drew him in with the promise of purpose. Without knowing the cost of following this man, of putting one foot in front of the other, or of any other action, Amon couldn't tell whether what he did was important. And his eyes responded to this uncertainty by darting again and again to the information source that had always dispelled it.

Eventually, after Amon had given in to these compulsions dozens of times and they had taken more turns along small side streets than he could keep count of, the man stopped on a street lined with residential condos. Standing on a patch of sidewalk, he stared up at one of them, a building of around ten stories. While his legs remained still for a time, his hands shifted restlessly from pocket to pocket, transferring various things from one location on his person to another. They moved quickly and often palmed the smaller items, preventing Amon from seeing what they were, though he still managed to identify a few: a tiny wrench, a metal plate, an elasticked bundle of chips, a tangle of wires, an antenna, a soldering iron, bare speakers . . . The man would transfer something from his left shoulder to his left thigh, something in his paunch to the back of his shoulders, from his hip to his forearm . . .

He continued this pocket inventory shuffling for about a minute, staring up at the building with a frown as though pondering some fraught subject, until suddenly he stopped and cut straight down an alley between the building and the one to its left. Amon followed him to a small empty parking lot on the other side, where verandas were stacked up the rear wall.

"Stay here," said the man and began to gallop full speed towards the building. Half a meter short of the wall, he leapt and grabbed the floor of a second-story veranda. For a split second his rotund form dangled there, swinging slightly, until he did a pull up, bringing his chin level with the floor. He then swung his body to the right, put his right leg onto the floor as he grabbed one of the rails with his left hand, lifted his right hand from the floor to grip another rail, drew his left foot up onto the floor, and pulled himself to his feet on the edge outside the railing. Amon watched in rapt astonishment as the man performed this entire stunt smoothly and rhythmically, as though he had done it countless times before.

Without pausing, the man stepped on top of the horizontal handrail, withdrew a plastic bottle from a pocket around his lower back, raised it over his head, and slipped it between the vertical poles of the third-floor rail, where it remained standing on the floor of the veranda above. He then stepped back onto the floor on the outer side of the rail, gripped the poles, crouched down with his body arcing outwards from the waist, and finally hang-dropped back to the ground where he landed on his feet with a hard thud.

He did everything with such practiced ease he hardly made a sound otherwise. Nevertheless someone seemed to have noticed, for the door to the third-floor balcony opened and a boy stepped out. Wearing shorts and a golf shirt, he looked to be about eleven or twelve, his skin lustrous and clear, his cheeks slightly freckled and flushed with youth. Even at this distance, Amon instantly noticed the boy's resemblance to the man, with the same wide flat nose, big sharp eyes, and frizzy hair, though the boy was far from obese; his short, skinny frame appearing fragile up high above the ground.

The boy stepped over to the edge of the veranda and stood before the bottle. Then, glancing furtively over his shoulder to the open door, he picked it up before slowly scanning the parking lot with a peculiar look of sadness and excitement. His gaze drifted about, passing obliviously over Amon and the man as if they were no more opaque than the air. Failing to locate whoever had brought the bottle, the boy looked behind him again as if to check that he wasn't being watched from inside and twisted off the top. He raised the rim above his chin and began to pour it between his parted lips. At that moment, although his mouth was busy receiving the fluid, Amon could see the boy smile and flutter his eyelids as though he were viewing a video. Amon immediately recognized the well-known adverpromo the kid was reenacting and, though the bottle was unlabeled, knew he was drinking Cloud9 Nectar. He could almost see the golden mist pouring into his mouth and the approaching nimbus cloud that would carry him into the sky. Amon glanced over at the man and saw his hard, impenetrable visage broken. In the cracks was a heart-rending expression—his eyes glazed doleful yet proud—as he stared at the boy relishing the soft drink.

When the boy had downed about a third of it, he swept the parking lot one more time, his eyes gliding over them again without seeing. Then he tossed the bottle into the parking lot, where it bounced twice and spun under a car, the momentum of its final bound stifled into a burst of ricochets by the bottom until it came to a rest. He then went back inside, and once the door shut behind him, the man began retracing his steps into the alley, his face seamless and unreadable once more as Amon followed him off.

Watching the man walk just ahead of him, Amon thought he could detect something different about his bearing since before entering the parking lot. Though it might have been Amon's distorted sense of time, he seemed to be moving at a more relaxed pace, as Amon no longer had any trouble keeping up. There also seemed to be a subtle shift in his gait that made it somehow more ponderous, more absorbed, and his head was slightly bowed, as though he were lost in thought. Meanwhile, whenever they stopped at an intersection, his hands would launch into an agitated flurry of pocketing and reorganizing, now and then coming up with a packet of smoked squid, peanuts, chocolate, or some other snack, which he promptly tore open and poured into his mouth. Although the man's face no longer betrayed his emotions, Amon thought he could detect a new air of sadness about him as well. Surely these changes were related to his encounter with that boy. With his son? Most likely it was because of this relationship that he'd chosen to live outside the bankdeath camps and forego the generous supplies of the venture charities, not to mention the company of his fellow bankdead. His indirect gaze and curt manner of speech suggested that he wasn't used to fraternizing, and Amon doubted there were many other bankdead on this side of the river—if any at all. Most likely he had no friends here, though his apparent aversion to conversation suggested he wasn't exactly dying for someone to talk to. But if they were father and son, why did the man have to interact with him so surreptitiously? Instead of lurking in the parking lot, why not just go up and say hi?

Amon wasn't expecting answers from the man after his previous questions had been brushed off or ignored. All the same, when they approached a railroad intersecting the street they were walking along and the gate came down, forcing them to wait for the train to pass behind a group of pedestrians, Amon said, "Um. Sir."

The train creaked and groaned laboriously as it passed, and Amon supposed that it lacked the sound dampeners usually added to public vehicles so riders would think they were better maintained. The man turned around and looked at him with his off-aim gaze. "That boy . . ."

Amon gave up on what he was going to say as the man gave a slight frown, his eyes glistening with painful memories. They stood there almost looking at each other for an uncomfortably long moment, until the man shook his head.

"He likes Cloud9 Nectar," the man said, turning away from Amon to face the gate. "It's his favorite drink." And Amon stood there staring at his back, reluctant to pry any further, until the tail of the train went by, the gate lifted, and they crossed the tracks with the gathered crowd.

Traversing the naked streets at a more leisurely pace, Amon was now able to take in the surround more carefully, his focus no longer clouded by thirst and haste (though he was still hungry). Stripped of the InfoFlux, the metropolis had stopped crying for him to spend, for him to act, for him to believe, for him to enjoy. It was simply there, these great, gungy slabs of worn concrete, metal, plastic, and glass, not seducing or offering, cajoling or guilting. *But what does it want me to do?* was the question that remained poised on the surface of every wall and road and sidewalk and window that came into Amon's field of sight. A place that asked nothing of him, that failed to constantly stoke his desire, seemed like sheer waste—bleak, purposeless, impersonal—in clear violation of the most basic principles of marketecture. Because what were cities for if not to fuel the economy with their every fiber and atom? The sense of lack seemed to soak through his pores, ladening his blood with the pointlessness of his existence. Perhaps this osmosis of apathy had been happening all along, but the promoracket had deafened him to the hiss of its ceaseless seeping. So long as the cracks in the sidewalk were not so deep that someone tripped, the windows so old they actually broke, the doors so rusted they wouldn't open, no one would notice and the charade could go on.

Watching the pedestrians between which the man moved, Amon could see that they existed in the other city, the Tokyo Amon had always known rather than the one he now confronted. They talked to themselves, laughed to themselves, cried to themselves, argued with themselves, twitching their fingers and shouting out commands. Most unsettling of all were their eyes. Unable to see what Amon was seeing, they weren't looking at his spectacle but an invisible one, like mystic sages or madmen. Unable to hear what Amon was hearing, they weren't tuned to his soundscape but a silent one, like bats or schizophrenics. Their feet seemed to be aware of the hard ground they walked upon, but every other part of their bodies was oblivious to their location, not needing to touch anything around them as every vehicle or shop door opened automatically and every lobby elevator Amon saw through the front windows came to meet them. And they were just as removed from each other, avoiding physical contact whenever possible to maintain their comfort zone and save money, all conversation snippets blurted out by passersby addressed to someone far away or to no one at all, like an archipelago of islands floating together high up in the clouds.

Amon recognized that he was at a disadvantage here without ImmaNet access, as many happenings were simply incomprehensible to him—a woman blowing a kiss to a partner not there; an old man gazing with apparent wonder into a dusty, crumbled demolition site; the crowd of streetwalkers diverted around some invisible obstacle on a crosswalk; the tide of bodies shifting to secret signals. Nonetheless, it seemed tragic to him that only the wealthy could afford to see what he could, and even then only momentarily. Few would ever guess how filthy and neglected was the space in which they made their abode. Sometimes they looked simply ridiculous to him, like when a line of grown adults skipped along the sidewalk together. Apparently they were playing a game where they stepped on chains of related images to summon advertisements and earn rebates as Amon often had on his way to work. Surely he would have appeared just as silly to anyone who saw beneath the overlay as he now could. And considering how he might have looked to the bankdead when he was a Free Citizen led him to another thought that had been gestating in his mind since encountering the boy: How did he look to Free Citizens now that he was bankdead?

His reflection on storefront windows followed along beside him, but with the dirt on the glass and his ailing vision, it appeared merely as a gray, misty wraith of a man, faint and insubstantial. So he did a series of gestures to cast his perspective outside his body and look at himself, feeling a twinge of frustration in his gut when Teleport Surprise didn't open. With his manifestation apps gone, his once mobile viewpoint was shackled permanently to his eyes. But he did his best to resign himself to this fact. From now on, he would just have to look at himself from inside himself, and he raised his hands in front of his chest to inspect them as he walked, turning them over several times to check how they might have changed. They looked veinier than he remembered, the fortune lines more deeply etched, and there were a few moles he'd never seen before. Covering his wrists were the sleeves of his jacket and he glanced down at his uniform to find the gray all uneven, the fabric shiny and coarse, his fake leather shoes scuffed. He was no longer a Liquidator and the shabby state of his attire seemed to bespeak the sham of still dressing like one. Though he no longer felt allegiance to the Liquidation Ministry or to GATA, he suddenly found himself ashamed to be wearing it, desecrating this suit with his bankdead flesh, and the feeling only intensified when he imagined how ugly his exposed face must look without digimake to the men and women on the street. If their faces were anything to go by, his shame was well warranted.

Hold on. Just because this was how he appeared to himself, that didn't mean it was how he would appear to everyone else. Come to think of it, he hadn't noticed anyone react with disgust or horror towards him. No one passing him on the sidewalk seemed to take special notice of him despite his uniform. On the contrary, they hardly seemed to notice he was there at all. The only time their gazes paused on him was when he was directly in their path, and even then they simply stepped around him and moved on without even looking him up and down. *Perhaps they're just too distracted by the InfoFlux to pay me any mind*, he supposed, until he noticed that the crowd treated his companion exactly the same way, neither the streetwalkers nor the drivers giving him a second glance. There was just no way a fat, balding man wearing a jumpsuit made of pockets could blend in, even in a district like Akihabara or Harajuku where people often wore digiguises, let alone amongst this workaday crowd. The man's son had looked straight through them, suggesting they had been edited out of his feed, which was perplexing in its own way. But these people could see them and yet apparently not in the way that Amon and the man saw themselves, which returned Amon to his initial question: What exactly did they look like?

Amon had no idea, but he stared deeply into the eyes of the multifarious men and women blurring by, as if to dredge his figure from their souls. And although he succeeded at no such thing, his thoughts soon arrived at what seemed the most likely conclusion: that he and the man were digimade in the most generic way possible, probably as salarymen in typical business attire. If he was right, then the default settings of every Free Citizen's overlay digimade bankdead to be maximally inconspicuous, preventing them from either appalling or distracting. So while Amon was isolated from the meaning of the metropolis and the minds of the denizens who shared of it, he was being simultaneously incorporated into it, a thread of the wrong material woven imperceptibly into the same cloth. Never had he felt more lonesome and estranged despite the proximity of so many, and the feeling only worsened each time he and the man walked by one of the automated doors that fronted the street, for they steadfastly refused to budge only for them.

As the minutes went by, Amon's gaze drifted over the countless faces streaming past, and he was surprised to discover how many variations there were. Physiognomic diversity that had been eliminated by esthetic algorithms now appeared vividly before him. The location of a birthmark or a freckle, the angle of an akimbo jaw, the dimensions of an oversized ear, the intricate topography of acne craters and wrinkles, the detailed coloration of eye redness—idiosyncratic flaws were endless and ugliness was infinite, while beauty, it seemed, was a narrow set of possibilities. At the same time, Amon was surprised at the uniformity of their dress. They wore garments of different sizes to fit their bodies, and there were different types like jeans and chinos, blazers and vests. But without brand names, logos, and overlaid designs, there was little to distinguish garments of each type. The same was true of the cars, with sedans, jeeps, convertibles, and trucks that seemed almost interchangeable, except for slight variations in their dimensions and degree of wear. The same was true of vending cuisine and beverages. The same was true of all sorts of products surely, Amon realized. And while everyone believed their precious possessions were designed by product development teams just for them—in accordance with the finest breakdown and analysis of their unique preferences, personalized to their very essences—there seemed to be little difference between anything anyone owned. Some strutted proudly with their chests puffed out, like an elite executive or an emperor, while others hung their heads meekly, but to Amon all appeared equal in their unattractiveness and unimportance. It was only because of the job he had done as a Liquidator that the digital differences of more money and less money, better style and worse style, higher status and lower status became palpable differences. For without the threat of bankruptcy, it would all be so much specious nonsense.

At least that was how it looked to bankdead Amon. He questioned the validity of his own perspective, especially since he still saw everything without color and was now visited occasionally by other, more worrisome sensory disturbances. Like how a face would occasionally break up into a granulated enigma of shaded flesh. Or how the angles of the streets ahead would warp into spirals that corkscrewed into an endless horizon, the skyline collapsing into a flat, distanceless smattering of texture. Engine rumble melting into a woman's snore. Oddly enough, the most dependable aspect of his world seemed to be the strange man—his guide?—without whom his journey would have surely ended before it began, Amon fading away like the netherbeing that he was into this vague husk of a city called naked Tokyo.

4
THE NEAR SHORE

As Amon followed his guide to the ends of the metropolis, only the cityscape's transitions marked the passage of time, the streets growing wider and narrower, busier and calmer. Seconds or minutes or hours passed as unending tracts of chipped, crusty concrete passed underfoot. As sheer cliffs of smudged glass and metal reeled along on both sides. As countless identical cars blurred by on rattling, wheezing engines. The sloppy, blemished streetwalkers misting around him, their eyes and minds an infinite distance away. Tokyo's titillating buzz had been syringed from its veins, the bland hum of one-sided conversations, whine of motorbikes, and swish of automatic doors the only sorry excuse for stimulation it still retained.

Gradually the air grew clingy as a swirling, granular fuzz seemed to smother everything in sight. This thickened with every step, until Amon could smell a solvent sting and taste a sort of battery-char tang on his tongue, feeling as though he were being digested by the metropolis. When at last the stench of the river began to mingle with this smog, Amon identified a distinct time: it was twilight. With the sun now fallen far beneath the looming skyline, evening shade began to creep its cool over the concrete at his feet. And catches of a cloying barnacle-turpentine pong slipped on drafts through the alleys he passed into his nostrils, announcing the approach of his initial destination, the threshold between city and camps, between bank life and death: the Sanzu River.

Now that Amon was certain the river was near, his anxiety about where they might be headed settled down, but was replaced immediately by a jittery foreboding. For what would the best of all possible slums look like? Soon he would see with his own eyes, not the humanidocupromo images all Free Citizens knew, but the place itself. Soon he would cross over, perhaps never to return, and his jaw began to tremble at the very thought.

Every now and then the man would stop for a moment and scan the rooftops in the direction the sun had set, only faint traces of shaded swirls in the sky to show it had ever been there. Soon the air was darkening as the dregs of the day sank beneath the hidden horizon. By the time they arrived at the Sanzu River, night was beginning to blot out the streets. The roads and sidewalks sketched in pitch, the skyscrapers lining the road like monoliths of nothingness reaching into the sky. Amon could barely see his guide right in front of him, until they turned left off a broad, busy boulevard onto a narrow laneway and the view before them opened up like never before.

At the end of the lane, they stepped out onto a raised walkway that stretched in both directions above a concrete riverbank, beyond which was a massive watercourse glimmering faintly under light from the other side. Was that blurry, glowing mass way over there the District of Dreams? It was hard for Amon to make anything out in the distance with his still-healing eyes, but what else could it be?

The man had already taken a seat on the edge of the concrete ledge facing the river, his legs dangling down. Seeing that they were taking a break, Amon used this opportunity to go down the nearest of the stairwells running to the riverbank at intervals of about twenty meters. There he leaned against the railing that bordered the water's edge to get a better view of his imminent future.

Across the river, a dark, mountain-like mass towered, slight jagged irregularities at the top silhouetted against the sky in the soft white glow of what looked like lanterns. In various places—both high and low along this structure—these round lights wavered in the breeze, some fixed in one spot while others wandered slowly, appearing and disappearing, climbing and dropping, approaching and receding. Wherever their shifting, scattered circles of illumination were cast, Amon could see segments of the looming darkness carved out into skyscraper shafts and thin alleys past which innumerable figures melted in a steady stream. Particles of something kept fluttering down through these lit-up areas, almost like black snowflakes though it was the heat of summer, and a few of the lanterns seemed to break apart, like crumbling cookies of light, contributing radiant crumbs to the shadow flurry.

What awaits me on the far shore? wondered Amon, transfixed by the strange, baffling scene, this question summoning memories of the many sympathvertisements he'd seen. Scrubby men, women, and children in rags lining up before volunteers who doled out supplies from boxes stacked behind them. Mothers proffering babies to nurses who lay them gently in rows of little cribs. A preschooler sitting on the lap of a Charity Brigade freekeeper laughing with joy. Such images represented all that he knew about the District of Dreams, and only now that its border was nearly in plain sight did he realize how incomplete they were. While they displayed the good work of the venture charities, an important facet of the camps to be sure, details on the day-to-day life of bankdead were scarce. Yes, there were videos introducing the various slum tours, hikes, and safaris on offer, but they provided only glimpses so as not to give away too much of their product. Where were the exposés on the conditions residents faced? Where were the interviews with grassroots operators on the ground trying to make lasting improvements? Perhaps they were available on silver and gold search engines, but Amon had never been interested or rich enough to check and it was too late now.

He could hear the faint hiss of countless whispers drifting over the water and the swish of cars along a highway not far behind him as he traced the course of the river with his gaze. It ran right to left, curving itself away out of sight on both ends like a bow of flowing lead, the dull membrane of its surface distorting with the eddies and undulating sway. Wavering and warping with the waves and current, he could see a spatter of stars. Yet while his eyes could capture the reflection, they fell short of the reflected, and looking up into the cloudless sky all he saw were diffuse shimmers like sunbeams through a kaleidoscope smeared against the black curtain of space. This was his first time seeing the sky and river without the ImmaNet, he realized, and his mind was simply not up to the task of perceiving them.

When Amon looked back at the far shore straight ahead, his fingers began to twitch involuntarily again. Concerned, he raised his right hand and saw that he was doing the gestures for *zoom in*. Once again, he felt frustration rise in him at being trapped in his body, unable to turn on night vision and toss his perspective across the river, or even search for "District of Dreams" on FlexiPedia. But he knew such thoughts would only irritate him further, and as a cool sea breeze along the river stroked his hands and scalp, Amon tried to remember what he knew about this place. Immediately a map he'd once seen floated up into his mind's eye. A huge almond-shaped territory bordered on all sides by thin channels of water. The fresh water of the Sanzu River separated it from Tonan Ward to the east, where he now stood, and the saline Tokyo Canal from the Miura Peninsula to the west. These two streams wrapped around the shoreline and merged at the southern point of the almond, where they wove their way between an archipelago of smaller artificial islands and at last fed into the Pacific. At the northern tip, the Bridge of Compassion served as both a dam between these two bodies of water and as the main land bridge connecting the city to the camps. There had been no neighborhoods or municipal divisions of any kind on the map, just one contiguous landmass. For all the detail the map provided, it might as well have been one of the blots on the globe he'd found when searching with God's Eye for his dream forest. Already Amon could tell it was nothing like the spick and span city he had beheld from the window of the weekly mansion he and Mayuko had taken refuge in, just as he had suspected. The mystery of what lay ahead did fill him with a faint thrill of adventure and expectation, but this was overpowered by his dread. The longer he looked at the distant cityscape—with its crumbling lights, shadow snow, dim figures, and cluttered architecture—the more intense became the conflict between his desire to cross immediately and his urge to run in the opposite direction. Of course he could do neither, and the contradictory energy of these impulses soon became so intense that he had to avert his gaze.

But when Amon turned around and looked back the way he had come, he was struck by an even more disturbing sight. Whereas the far side was lit by the uncertain glow of those crumbling lanterns, the metropolis on this side was completely dark. Not a streetlight or a headlight, a flashlight or a candle. The city he had inhabited for twenty-seven years was completely blacked out, just a great inky mound looming before him. He remembered the darkening streets they had just walked through, but with all the bewildering experiences that day he'd hardly taken notice. Never for a moment did he suspect that the night could have eaten Tokyo whole. Where was the promoglow that had danced constantly on the walls and windows, the sidewalks and cars? He wanted to blame this on his eyes, but then he recalled his flight from Shuffle Boom. Inside the elevator, when he'd hacked the nodes that connected the space to the ImmaNet and the overlay had peeled off the naked things beneath, the light too had disappeared, ripped off into the shaft above. Could the entire city have been like this? Could all light have been a projection, every glint and glimmer, every shine and shimmer? Considering these questions, he imagined himself and the man stepping onto this riverbank a few minutes earlier, emerging from blank absence as though from a cave for the first time.

The idea that he'd spent his entire life in darkness was too tragic and absurd to contemplate, so Amon swept his gaze about for something to get his mind off it and found the man sitting on the bottom of the ledge. Facing the river with his back up against the wall, he was just then taking out various individual-size snack packets from different pockets, and arranging them on the ground around him. When Amon saw the man unwrap an apple Danish and bite into it, he suddenly felt his stomach clench up with hunger and sat down beside him, laying his sack at the base of the wall. He could smell the man's odor mingling with the smog and river fumes, and scooted about a meter away before eyeing the packets spread out on the ground.

"May I?" he asked, pinching a foil bag whose contents he couldn't see between his fingers and holding it up. Glancing at the packet for only a split second, the man gave Amon another one of those borderline nods and tore open a pouch of some sort of powdered nugget. Amon popped his bag and poured it straight into his mouth, finding deep-fried cheesy fish puffs. When he finished chewing, he rummaged in his sack for more and was soon gnawing on beef jerky while the man crunched on peanuts. One after another, Amon plucked unlabeled junk food from his bag or the man's spread and devoured them, tasting a sweet potato crepe, *umeboshi* kelp salad, pork cutlet roll. Containing mostly carbs, salt, chemicals, and sugar, it wasn't the most satisfying meal and Amon was eager for the better nourishment he would surely find in the District of Dreams. But it was enough to fill him up temporarily, and he washed it all down with an opaque drink, his tongue blazing with the unmistakable flowery, carbonated cream of Cloud9 Nectar.

Having fulfilled his immediate hunger, Amon felt a touch of calm sink in again. It was the first time he'd sat down in . . . in a while anyway, and it felt good to get the weight off his sore feet, which had been punished by walking in dress shoes for so long. He watched as the man continued to eat, packing in pastry after salted snack and alternating with a gulp of some soft drink until scraps of torn plastic litter and bottles surrounded him. Gradually the man's pace began to slow and after one last pinch of smoked squid he swept together all his litter with both hands, cradled it to his chest, and carried it to the river's edge, where he dumped it all in. He then returned to the ledge and, sitting beside Amon in the same spot, turned to him and said, "How about our deal?"

The question caught Amon off guard, and he paused before responding, "Right. You want to hear my story?" The man gave that nod that wasn't a nod. "Okay. Well . . . where should I begin?"

"The beginning. Where else?"

Amon considered this for a moment. What the man said made sense enough, but where was the beginning? He would have to skip to the very first seg in his LifeStream and did the gesture to open—

"But I've lost my . . . my ImmaNet. I mean, I can't get the video."

The man just gave him his off-target stare.

What does he expect me to do? Recall without assistance from my Body-Bank? The past scenes in Amon's head were so faded and dull in comparison to their digitally recorded counterparts that the work required to conjure them in his awareness hardly seemed worth the effort. And once they came to him, he would have to assemble them into a story himself, without the powerful banality filters he had always relied upon. Then there would be nothing to stop him from saying something incredibly boring. Recounting his life in a tolerably entertaining way without the sentence proposals and auto-correcting of VentriloQuick seemed like an impossible task . . . but the man had brought him to the Sanzu River as promised and if Amon wanted his help crossing he no doubt had to do his part. So he closed his eyes and reached shoulder-deep into the recesses of his unconscious, stretching and groping for the point where it all started. There he felt the trigger of diverse memories awaiting him, but most escaped his grasp, as though he were tugging off the tails of lizards hidden behind a curtain. Whatever he did manage to snag refused to stay in his private theatre, dissipating like a stale mist released from a cellar the moment he focused on it.

"Where were you born?" asked the man, his words cutting into Amon's tripped-up reminiscing.

"I-I don't know."

"Where were you in the first moment you can remember?"

"Green Ladybug," Amon replied without hesitation. "A BioPen called Green Ladybug. That's where I grew up."

"What happened?"

"That was when . . ." Amon trailed off, retrieving images slotted in a forgotten fold of his mind, "when I met Mayuko Takamatsu, my first friend. It's not much of a memory really. Just a few fuzzy moments . . ."

The man nodded without nodding, perhaps encouraging him to continue.

"So I'm on the roof of the BioPen, where we used to play sports. There's a mini putting range and a tennis court, except the nets are down and the equipment is away because it's not gym time. The air is kind of cool but pleasant, so it must be spring or early fall, I'm not really sure. I guess I'm not supposed to be there because I'm feeling kind of guilty and afraid. Then I notice there's another kid there, a girl, and she's hanging from this fence at the edge of the roof. She doesn't seem to notice I'm there but I'm curious to know what she's looking at, so I toddle over on my unsteady legs. We've got to be three or four I guess. I pull my chin up right beside her, so close that we're touching, but she doesn't seem to care and neither do I. Kids are like that about touch sometimes, you know.

"Anyway, there's this sea of skyscrapers below us. Just a typical patch of Tokyo, but it looks breathtakingly huge and mysterious to four-year-old me. The sky is stunning. It's this deep complex blue, with hints of red and ochre and other hues that only young eyes like mine can see, and there are these gorgeous streaks and dabs of cloud all linked together like the skin of a fruit peeled in one go, and the sun is behind one of them, blazing it all silvery-gold. And, like her, I'm instantly mesmerized."

Amon closed his eyes and pictured the scene. To his surprise, it appeared vividly before him, ten thousand times more vibrant and compelling than the frail colorless world he was in, as though his mind's eyes could view waking life while his body's eyes were stuck in a dream. Strangely, there were no images or adverpromo segs wriggling across the cityscape, and Amon realized that he must not have been hooked up to the ImmaNet. His first time viewing the naked sky had not been on the riverbank minutes earlier, but here on the rooftop years ago, though he'd forgotten all about it until now, as though only with this second viewing could he unlock the memory. Was it before he'd received a Training Bank or during a brief period when they'd taken them off? He couldn't remember, but found himself drawn ever more viscerally into this vision of the past as more words tumbled from his lips.

"We're hanging off the fence and our bodies sort of dangle together. I can feel the warmth of her shoulder and hip against mine. Then Mayuko raises her arm all of a sudden. She points up at this one spot above a skyscraper and cries, 'there!' It takes me a moment to see what she's talking about, but just fading into view is this single star, which is puzzling to my three- or four-year-old mind because I can't figure out what a star is doing in a blue sky during the day. I look over at Mayuko, and at the same moment she looks at me. Past the strands of her comet hair, I see her eyes fixed on mine and she looks just as confused. Then I look back up at the star and wonder how long it would take for more stars to appear. I start to hope that maybe we can just hang there all day until the sky is full of stars, and I kind of know that Mayuko is feeling the same way. Then out of nowhere I feel a hand grab my ankle and someone tugs me away from my perch."

Had it been Rick disrupting them to get their attention? That was Amon's first thought, but no, he decided, because Rick had been orphaned to the BioPen much later. So maybe it was the SubMom coming to discipline them for wandering off? But Amon wasn't sure and the memory stopped there. The abrupt ending left him with a feeling of nostalgia, for a simpler era when everything had been decided by the comforting educational protocol of Fertilex, and Mayuko was with him, and he hadn't hurt her yet . . . and with this thought his nostalgia turned to longing and his longing to fierce remorse. *I left her there with those men . . . I lost her . . . forever?*

To evade this razor-cutting, answerless question, Amon opened his eyes and found the man meeting his gaze directly for the first time. This was startling, but Amon could detect no menace there, and began to search his face to see how he'd taken the story so far, scanning for some indication of whether he'd told him too much or too little. He could find no suggestion either way, but thought he sensed the man's eagerness for Amon to continue, and accepted that he would just have to rely on his own judgment to sort out the mnemonic chaff as he went along.

As the words began to spill out, emotions bubbled up with them—rage, sorrow, joy, despair—sometimes bleeding into his voice, making it shake and quaver, lilt and grate. Amon's manner of telling could hardly be called eloquent, with its frequent starts and stops, digressions and regressions, non-sequiturs and abandoned threads. But the man's apparent interest unshackled Amon from his inhibitions and soon he was talking on and on without thinking, holding nothing back that might aid him in relating who he was.

Amon told the man about growing up in Green Ladybug with Mayuko and Rick. About how he and Rick became Liquidator partners working for GATA while Mayuko ended up as an in-house designer. About the night of his Identity Birth, when his boss, Sekido, had persuaded him to sleep with a prostitute and his relationship with Mayuko had ended. He told him how he'd scrimped and saved to visit a forest he saw in his dreams, how he'd worked at GATA for seven years and had been promoted to Identity Executioner, how he and Rick had fallen out after Amon became his supervisor. He told him how Mayuko and Rick had begun to date, how Rick had wanted to start a family with her. He told him how he and Rick had cash crashed the mad, flower-obsessed Minister Kitao, how the MegaGlom Fertilex and its partners had colluded with GATA to gain control over the Ministry of Records in his absence, how they'd forged records to fool Amon into liquidating Chief Executive

Minister Lawrence Barrow. He told him how Rick had disappeared, how even Mayuko had been unable to reach him, how his co-workers Freg and Tororo had said he cash crashed. He told him how an activist calling himself Makesh Adani had offered him a job and warned him of impending danger, how he'd been charged a huge amount for an action he hadn't performed called jubilee, how Fertilex and GATA had both refused to reverse the charge and provided no explanation. He told him how he'd visited the PhisherKing and received several files proving that Barrow's cash crash had been a trick, that jubilee was brought about by a Blinder who'd willingly chosen the BankDeath Penalty, that Rick had not been cash crashed but had committed train suicide. He told him how Minister Sekido and a GATA recruiter imposter who had been the spitting image of Makesh Adani had lured him to a fake job interview, how Sekido had infected him with a virus and delayed his incoming salary, how he'd done the same to Rick before he died, suggesting that he had in fact been murdered. He told him how the virus had nearly bankrupted him, how Mayuko saved him at the last moment, how they'd figured out that the lookalike activist and recruiter were the Birla sisters, Anisha and Rashana, quarreling over their inheritance. He told him how he'd taken refuge with her at a weekly mansion, how the virus had hidden in his finger and given away their location, how a hideous emoticon man and his goons had shown up with piranha dusters, how Amon had been forced to flee, leaving Mayuko to be beaten and hacked. He told him how he'd insisted she erase all records of him so her assailants would never know she had harbored him and made a deal with the PhisherKing to keep her safe, how he'd committed identity suicide using the Death Codes that only an Identity Executioner like him was privy to, how this had been the only way he could escape and hold on to his information about the conspiracy surrounding jubilee, since it allowed him to cash crash without going bankrupt and thereby keep his location blinded from Liquidators who would have otherwise apprehended him and removed his BodyBank. Finally, he told him how he'd woken up blind and deaf, how his vision and hearing had recovered only partially, how he'd been searching desperately for a way to get something to drink when the man had arrived.

While Amon spoke, the man stared off in the direction of the river, glancing at him only when Amon occasionally reached a particularly moving scene, and fiddled continuously with the things in his pockets. Although Amon hardly noticed as he focused on telling his tale, the movement occasionally caught his attention. It made him think of upside-down juggling: one thing always held in a hand while another fell into a pocket. Tiny wrenches, penlights, crystals, hooks; he could barely make them out in the dim glow that reached across the river. The man hardly seemed aware of what he was doing, as though he were unconsciously reorganizing his possessions, and Amon wondered how it was that he always seemed to know exactly where to find something when he needed it. Also, how did he fit all those things into his pockets? His clothes appeared snug around his bloated contours, yet there were no visible lumps anywhere. If not for the occasional glint Amon caught from the wider ones, they would have looked empty. It seemed impossible that there could be space beneath his clothes for all those snacks, tools, and components, as well as his ample flesh. At one point, Amon found himself imagining what might be going on beneath the fabric. He saw the fatty wrinkles of the man's neck continuing all the way down his torso, carving deeper and deeper into his flab to form capacious recesses, the pockets mere doorways to deposit valuables into seams in his flesh . . .

When Amon got to the end of his story and the sloshing of the river had reigned for several minutes, the man's hands came to a rest. "What now then?"

"You mean, like, my plans?" asked Amon, wondering what the man thought of him now that he knew all his secrets. He was exhausted and had a slight headache after so much talking, though he felt relieved to have fulfilled his side of the bargain.

The man un-nodded.

"Like I told you before, I need to go to the District of Dreams."

"What for?"

"What for . . ." The wheels of Amon's thinking caught on the question. What for indeed. He'd been planning to go to the District of Dreams before cash crashing because he'd simply assumed that that was where bankdead were supposed to be, and when he'd awoken the smell of the river had reminded him of that intention. But he'd never carefully considered why that should be his destination, and after that first eerie glimpse of the far shore, he wondered if it was the right choice after all.

Not that he had anywhere else to go. He'd vacated his apartment days ago and lacked the means to rent a room anywhere else. His only remaining friend was Mayuko, and part of him wanted to seek her out directly to make sure she'd got out safe. But the weekly mansion where he'd last seen her was all the way on the other side of Wakuwaku City and she would have surely vacated long ago. Her apartment was supposed to be somewhere near the mansion, but lacking access to the map in her inner profile, he couldn't narrow down its coordinates any further, and in all likelihood she would have gone into hiding after escaping anyway. Even if Amon could somehow learn her location, he had no navi with which to reach it, and could only wander the metropolis aimlessly on foot. This was obviously a hopeless task and, from what he'd seen of naked Tokyo so far, probably suicidal as well.

The whole metropolis seemed designed to exclude. The many devices and elements of infrastructure Amon had always thought of as enablers of convenience for those who'd earned it did double duty cutting off access to those who hadn't. The vending machines were locked boxes that kept non-citizens from food and merchandise, the automatic doors checkpoints to filter them out of buildings, and the elevators he'd seen through lobbies armored cells to keep them grounded. Something similar, Amon supposed, would be true of ticketing lines at train stations and airports, of shops and services of all kinds. And any bankdead that tried to defy these barriers would have to be kept out by force, violence if that was more cost effective, for they could not be deterred from behavior that caused damage or loss of property using fines and fees as with Free Citizens. Hence the security system on the vending machine, and the CareBots the man had mentioned. Only an electronics wizard like his guide would have any chance of surviving in such an inhospitable place, and Amon wondered for a moment whether he might say he'd changed his mind and beg the man to help him find Mayuko. But even if his pleas succeeded, and the man was somehow willing to stray from his son for however many weeks, months, or years it might take, allowing Amon to mooch sustenance from him all the while, in all likelihood they would never find her for all the reasons Amon had already considered and Amon would end his days a mendicant phantom, grown fat like the man on soda and junk food, or eventually splitting from him and wasting away alone in some alley . . . No, Amon's instincts had been right. His answer was clear.

"There's . . . There's nowhere else for me to go . . . nothing else for me to do . . . and I have so many questions. The District of Dreams seems like the only place I might find the answers."

Clearly he had to go to the District of Dreams. Not just because that was where bankdead went, where the supplies were, where the charities would give him shelter. But because of the promise he had made to the PhisherKing, to keep asking questions until all doubt had been vanquished from his mind. If he would have any hope of finding answers he would need to reach the Birla sister calling herself Makesh, as Fertilex seemed to be at the center of everything. And since he'd left her a message telling her to find him in the camps, going there was his only chance, as slim as it might be.

"What kind of questions?"

"Like what is this whole plot at GATA about and who's behind it? Why did they crash Barrow and Kitao and why did they choose me to do it? Why did they murder Rick and why are the Birlas involved? What is jubilee?"

"How are you going to get your answers?"

"I'll get in touch with Makesh. I'll learn the truth about what's going on, about the meaning of jubilee, and about all the connections between GATA and Fertilex, those two recruiters and Sekido. Somehow, I'll have to get my BodyBank working again . . . and . . . and I'll use my LifeStream to show the world that Barrow was assassinated, that Rick was murdered, and that my bankdeath was a sham! Then I'll take back my identity and my savings and my job. I'll find Mayuko . . . and one day we'll go to the forest, together."

In the silence after he'd said this, Amon was surprised by his own words. For going to the forest had always been a solitary ambition, but now he wanted someone else there with him, and a faint intuition gave him hope that it might actually happen some day, though how and in what form he could not fathom.

5
THE SANZU RIVER

C ome," said the man. "There's no time for sleep. We have to catch the drone window."

Drone window? At these words, Amon opened his eyes, dreams vanishing unremembered like smoke. He was lying on his side with his back wedged into the crook of the ledge, his cheek resting on the hard, gritty ground. Looking straight across a stretch of concrete under pale, early light from the sky, he could now see a smattering of bird shit, soybean rinds, cigarette butts, and shards of glass spreading to the railing of the bank. For a few moments, he lay there listening to the slosh of the river, the hiss of traffic, the whispering voices, and the *rakhaw* of crows, not yet grasping the meaning of the man's words. Though Amon had been up all night talking, somehow he didn't feel groggy, as though his fractured slumber in the alley had been enough sleep for days, perhaps even a lifetime. Yet his body was tired and he didn't feel like moving.

Only when the man started walking towards the river did Amon get to his feet and shuffle after him. The lingering cool of night still softened the heat of the sultry air even as a milky dawn glow seeped from behind a cluster of buildings downstream. The moment they reached the fence along the bank, a thin blade of light slipped over the rooftops, and Amon gasped as color bloomed on everything it touched.

A thick curtain of silver-gray smog hung above the river and draped over the surface, obscuring everything beyond a ribbon of brownish-green along the water's edge. Looking up, he saw through the veil of fumes that the sky was still fairly dark, a platinum blue that got lighter as it approached the sprawling roofscape horizon. Peering back over his shoulder, he saw grimy blighted skyscrapers leaning over the ledge where they had slept, its bare concrete dappled in brown and discoloration by ocean wind funneled along the river.

Green! Brown! Blue! Silver! And gray! Real gray! Whether this was the dawn of the city or of his own mind, Amon couldn't tell, but his skin thrilled with goosebumps. At the same time, his excitement was tainted with a certain jarring dissonance, as something about the scene seemed slightly off. The feeling was difficult to describe, but somehow the colors seemed unlike any colors he had seen before. Take the platinum blue. Patches of the sky were undoubtedly composed of this color. But what if what he now saw was blue, and what he'd seen before was "blue," or the other way around. If his memory could be trusted, "colors" in his past were more sleazy, whereas colors now were more tangy. These adjectives were the best he could think of to articulate the ineffable difference in his experience. Something integral that was once so prevalent it had been impossible to perceive was missing, as though he could no longer feel air on his skin, taste his own mouth, or smell his own nostrils. It wasn't like he was seeing a different part of the light spectrum as far as he could tell—not different shades or hues—more like a different spectrum altogether, as though he were adjusting to a whole new kind of light.

Rakhaw. Rakhaw. The calling of crows from across the river brought Amon's focus to his ears and he realized that the sounds (or "sounds") around him seemed out of whack in a similar way. The hum of cars, the whispers of the far shore. While everything he heard was sharply defined and crisp now, something in their tonal quality seemed off-kilter, as though his eardrums had been tightened or loosened ever so slightly. *But if these colors and sounds are different from before*, he wondered, *how do I determine which are the right ones?*

While Amon struggled to assimilate the new richness of his existence, the man remained by the railing, staring out at the river-fume fog. Finding no resolution to his quandary, Amon imitated the man, unsure what he was doing but hoping to learn what he might do next. Under the disc of light now swelling over the skyline, the hazy shroud began to thin and dissipate, nibbled away by a gentle ocean breeze blowing continuously from downstream. Amon watched as pockets and channels opened up, widening the visible strips of water through which various boats—freighters, trawlers, cruisers—were moving up and down the river. Then a gust of wind ripped the veil away, its yellowish-white strands rippling as they fled, until the whole width of the river expanded before Amon and the other side was revealed in the bright clarity of morning.

The far shore had no riverbank. Instead, rising straight from the water was a haphazard conglomeration of skyscrapers, as tall as the buildings elsewhere in Tokyo but packed together far more densely. And if they were skyscrapers, they were the strangest skyscrapers Amon had ever seen. Each shaft was built of cubes in different colors—burgundy, silver, avocado—and joined to its neighbors without clear delineation, the individual cubes spanning and connecting different buildings like toy blocks stacked out of alignment. Heaps of these interlocking structures tumbled along the length of the river and mounted back in layers to the serrated skyline, forming a terraced topographical jumble of jutting right angles and hard edges.

Nowhere could a level surface be found, with the cubes indenting and tilting at all possible angles, and many leaning shafts bowing their rooftops or distending their middle sections over the river. The only gaps in the tight press of architecture were slight cracks between shafts, no taller than a story and too narrow to accommodate two adults standing shoulder to shoulder, let alone a car. There were no windows either, just sporadic stretches of stairs attached to some of the walls, stopping for several stories and then starting again, or covering only one story on one side and then continuing on another. Numerous people climbed up and down them, or squirmed through the cracks, and Amon guessed these were the figures he'd seen passing the lanterns at night. The cookie-crumble lights were not visible in the daylight, but the shadow snow that had fallen with them was. He could now see these flakes drifting steadily from the buildings and fluttering down into the river. They seemed to originate in numerous jagged holes and pockmarks that glared from the faces of many of the cubes as though the buildings were coming apart. And it might have been his imagination, but Amon thought he could see the cityscape growing gradually, as new stories seemed to pop up suddenly among the rooftops, forming higher towers that rose above the others into the sky.

What mess is this? he wondered, standing there transfixed, *A place where people live?* the color, depth, unity, and texture that were returning to his vision only intensifying his bewilderment at the scene.

Prying his eyes from the far shore, Amon glanced to his side and found the man still standing there, staring out over the river. His gaze seemed to follow the boats, which continued to float by in both directions.

"Are you looking for something?" Amon asked, not expecting an answer but trying anyways.

"There," said the man, pointing downstream. A three-decker freighter was just then coming around the furthest bend in the river. It had a grayish-green metallic hull, perhaps 100 meters in length and 25 in width, with neither windows and portholes on the sides, nor cabins and railing on top—just sheer surfaces everywhere.

The man pulled out the same display glove he'd used before, slipped it onto his left hand, and watched the boat intently as it crept up the river towards them. Amon could sense a sort of tense determination in the man, a poised readiness.

The freighter grew bigger and bigger as it approached, passing other boats coming and going on its course along the shore about ten meters from the bank. When it was close enough that its huge bulk loomed over them, the man reached into his pocket, withdrew a cylinder just like the one he'd used on the vending machine, and tossed it with a soft underhand motion at the boat. It hit the side of the hull about one-third the way up from the water with a faint click as it attached itself there, and the man began to move the fingers of his left hand while stroking the palm display with the fingers of the other. For a few seconds Amon wondered what he was doing, when the boat began to decelerate and veer sharply towards the shore. Soon it was coasting gently straight towards them, losing momentum until it bumped the bank softly with its prow and rebounded to a stop. In response to more flicks and strokes, a column of horizontal grooves about two meters in length carved themselves down a section of the hull wall and the segments between them began to protrude, forming the steps of a staircase that ran down to the water, the bottom step half a meter from the shore. The man then climbed over the railing, hopped across, and bounded up the stairs by twos and threes.

Clearing his befuddlement with a shake of his head, Amon followed, going over the rail and timing his jump carefully to match the slight bob of the boat.

Atop the deck, the man proceeded to the bow and continued to stroke his display. Amon stumbled after him as the boat lurched to portside, the man now steering it towards the far shore. A humming sound came from the direction they'd boarded, and Amon glanced starboard to see the top step fold back into place in the hull. The retraction of the stairwell seemed to signify that there was no going back. And when the boat turned, Amon looked back to watch the blighted metropolis drift away. It then struck him that this was his farewell to the city, and his gaze flitted over the cluttered sprawl of dull blank buildings, as if it might find a last bit of visual dazzle—of promotainment and adverflomo—to feed his eyes. Yet the grimy windows merely gleamed a sickly dull blue in the dawn light, and he felt a stab of fear and sadness watching everything he'd ever known left behind in the white, frothing wake.

Turning around, Amon joined the man at the edge of the deck and watched as the heaping shoreline ahead loomed rapidly closer, the outer face of the District of Dreams growing clearer by the second. The cubes it was built from appeared to be about half a story tall and each had what looked like a sliding door. These were positioned to open onto a stretch of stairs rising diagonally from corner to corner. Few of the stairs had handrails or banisters and some were simply a series of escalating pegs or rungs. Given the doors and their size, Amon supposed that the cubes were individual rooms or shelters. Their exteriors were not merely in different colors as he had thought, but seemed to be made of different materials: turquoise stucco, white granite, persimmon tile. All were in various stages of dissolution, some looking brand new and immaculate, some letting off only a slight sprinkle of flakes from still-intact surfaces, some peeling away rapidly from shallow depressions, some spewing their fibers from multiple jagged holes that went straight through to the walls behind. Others were just perforated husks straining under the weight atop them and one was just rubble, the shaft it had supported now leaning upside down into the river, having toppled headfirst. It was as though the shelters were being eaten by slow acid, except instead of melting they came apart bit by bit. And with the breeze blowing the flakes into the sky or dispersing them in every direction, Amon suddenly recalled one day in the BioPen, an eduvidtrip to Ueno Park near the end of the cherry blossom season, when all the flowers came apart in a flurry of pinkish-white, a petal snowstorm. In a similar way, the flakes before him swirled down to the greenish-brown surface of the Sanzu River, coating it with specks of the buildings as though shattered reflections of the city were drifting rapidly downstream. All over this disintegrating crush of shelters, men, women, and children thronged, climbing up and down the intermittent staircases, crawling through fissures where the rooms didn't fit together cleanly, cramming the deeper layer of buildings that kept peeking in and out of view through thin gaps as his vantage shifted with the progress of the boat. Amon simply could not comprehend what he was seeing. Such precarious disorder, such crowding, such decay . . .

Thlop-thlop-thlop-thlopthlop. The sound of something hard and wet hitting the side of the boat reached Amon's ears. Dropping flat to his belly so as not to fall, he peered over the starboard edge of the deck, where forms hung submerged in the water around the hull. Though it was difficult to make out what they were beneath the brown-green waves, the freighter seemed to be cutting through a whole field of dark patches, and Amon watched as whatever they were smacked into the hull one after another with a *thlop*, before bouncing away to continue their journeys downstream. Then one of them broke the surface momentarily, and Amon caught a clear glimpse. *A face?* he thought with a shudder, *Was that a face?* wondering how that could be possible and—

Vweeeen. Amon lifted his head and perked up his ears as a whirring sound suddenly phased into hearing. It seemed to originate somewhere downstream and he spun around to his feet only to find himself immediately blinded by a searing light. The sun appeared to have emerged from the Tokyo skyline, because it was too painful for his still-healing eyes to look anywhere remotely near a particular cluster of buildings, the whole area a great white blot in his visual field. Instead, he tried to hone in on the whir, darting his gaze from the water to the sky to the cities on both sides while squinting to minimize the glare. For several seconds, he spotted nothing, the sound growing louder and louder, until an airborne sparkle around the edge of the blot leapt into view.

The strange glass creature he saw flying about fifteen meters above the water dazzled him as sunbeams refracted through its body, and he could only stand to watch it in his peripheral vision. From what he could tell, it had a torso like a housefly the size of a cat, its wings a glittering blur, its six legs shimmering lines that dangled below. But in place of the usual composite eyes bulging at the front, it seemed to have two small heads poking forward, one that of a horse and one that of an ox. Though Amon couldn't make it out clearly, obviously it was some kind of drone, and though it meandered slightly the way flies do, its flight path was straight enough that he had no doubt it was charting an intercept course for their boat. *An attack drone or a reconnaissance drone?* he wondered, thinking back to his Liquidator training, and remembered a word the man had used—CareBot—the pounding of his heart and electric tingle of his skin poising him to leap overboard if need be, floating faces or no floating faces.

"Look!" Amon cried, when the drone was about a hundred meters away. "What's that?"

"Ah!" the man exclaimed, his eyes going wide. Immediately he snatched something from a front pocket and chucked it in the drone's direction. Arcing through the air was what looked like a baton. It was sketching a trajectory wide of the target, but the toss hadn't seemed intended for a direct hit, and as the baton or whatever it was passed a couple of meters to the drone's right, the drone suddenly started to shake, its wings stuttering erratically. Then the palsied robot changed course and began to chase after the baton. *Splish-thwip-thwithwip-SHA.* The baton fell into the river and the drone plunged in after it like a dog chasing a ball, spraying the tips of the waves all about as its wings batted them. Then all was as it had been moments earlier, except for a slight sloshing around the entry point in the river. For several tense seconds Amon stared at the water, but thankfully the drone never resurfaced. He had no idea what it was or why it had come. *Good thing I have this guide*, he thought, looking at the man with a rush of gratitude, for without him he might have been dealing with the drone—whatever its nefarious purpose—on his own, assuming he'd even made it this far.

Soon the freighter entered one of the clouds of flakes that fell steadily into the river. As the air around them filled with specks of the buildings, the man steered right until they were moving upstream alongside the over-leaning, bulging shoreline. Suddenly there was a tearing sound like someone ripping up tape and a burst of screaming. Amon turned with alarm to see a shaft just behind the stern in mid-collapse, a cascade of varicolored room chunks sending up a puff of petals as they dropped into the water with a splash that rocked the boat. The heavily perforated shelters spat flakes into the air while they sank slowly out of sight. Moments later, several survivors surfaced from the wreck to begin swimming back and Amon realized with horror how many had not been so lucky. He now noticed the rubble of other fallen shelters littering the edge of the river just beneath the waves and saw that the man kept the boat just clear of these dangerous shoals. Soon enough, there was a break in the reef of debris and he turned the boat into a cove of open water, directing the prow towards the shore. Many of the people climbing the steep stairwells that hung out over the water stopped to glower at their approach, as the calling of the crows grew progressively louder, their ominous concert all that seemed to greet Amon's arrival.

The shore was nearing fast, only about a dozen meters now, and with a few strokes on the palm display the boat began to slow, then to coast. Amon could feel his his breaths quivering fast and his knees trembling in sheer terror. All that separated him from a new life in the District of Dreams was a rapidly shrinking strip of water. Just the sight of this bizarre formation of shelters had overturned all his expectations, and already he had witnessed a horrendous accident. He didn't want to even imagine what it might be like to set foot inside. But how was he to enter? The stairwells all ended several stories above and the base of the structures went straight into the water below, leaving nowhere to disembark.

The man guided the coasting freighter between shattered skyscraper shallows to a spot where the angle of the buildings over the water wasn't so sharp, leaving space for the prow to drift further in to the shore. As the boat came to a stop, it juddered under their feet and the man said, "Give me the sack."

Amon handed him his sack as instructed, and the man reached into his pockets to procure an armful of drinks and snacks, which he dumped into it.

"Take this with you," said the man, handing the sack back.

"Thank yo—"

"And this," the man interrupted, taking something else out of a pocket beneath his belly and profferring it to Amon under his palm so its silvery form was partially concealed. Amon knew it by touch even before the man took his hand away and allowed him to see it: his nerve duster. "How did—"

"Bring this to a place called Xenocyst." He handed Amon another item: five sheets of plastic rolled up together. "To a man named Hippo. Tell them Tamper sent you. And watch out for Opportunity Scientists."

Amon unloaded the drinks and food into his suit jacket's outer pockets, slipped the roll of plastic sheets into its right inner pocket, stuffed the sack into its left inner pocket, and slid the duster into his holster. He then glanced at the seemingly impenetrable mass looming over them and looked at the man called Tamper, confused. "But how do I—"

"Into the hole," said Tamper. "You'll have to jump." He pointed to a room with an oblong hole eaten diagonally from the right to left corners. It was about two meters from the edge of the deck and nearly level with it, though tipped back ever so slightly like a receptive mouth. Flakes of the grayish asphalt-like material of the room's exterior sprayed rapidly from the zigzag lips of the hole like a swarm of flies taking flight.

"You're saying I should—"

"Quickly, before the current drags us out of range and another drone arrives."

"But . . ." Tamper gave Amon one of his off-aim stares and Amon frowned back for a moment. "Thank you. I—"

Without warning, Tamper bent low and began to plow Amon slowly towards the edge of the deck. "Turn!" he shouted and Amon, instinctively accepting there was no point in resisting, spun around and leapt, his flailing arms outstretched as he flew through the spray of flakes into the crack.

6
THE FAR SHORE

hudwhack! Amon's ankle banged the bottom lip of the hole as he flew into the shelter and slammed chest-first into the floor. Taking most of the impact with his forearms and legs, he bounced once and flopped out prone onto a surprisingly soft surface. This cushioned his fall somewhat, though he was winded nonetheless and lay there huffing away the nausea for a while. When his breath was back, Amon rose to his knees and found himself in a two-meter-by-two-meter room with a ceiling too low for him to stand, the interior of the shelters out of which the whole District of Dreams seemed to be built. Twisting around from the waist to look back the way he had come, he saw sunlight pouring into the room from the hole. He searched outside for Tamper, but found only a stretch of greenish-brown waves covered in boats, with a smog-hazed sprawl of neglected skyscrapers on the other side, the freighter nowhere to be seen.

Twisting back around, Amon looked about slowly and saw that the interior was the same grayish asphalt material as the exterior, though if the floor was anything to go by, it was much more pliant than it appeared. Flakes swirled into the room from various holes in the walls and ceiling, all of which offered jagged windows on walls of other colors and materials. Only the several thin tears in the wall straight ahead of the crack let in additional light, though much dimmer than the direct sunbeams behind him, and Amon guessed this would be his way out. Careful not to put his hands or knees through holes in the slanted floor, he crawled in this direction and found a little knob in the wall that he guessed was a handle for a door, a crack running straight down the center indicating where it opened. Jiggling the knob in different directions, he discovered that it twisted clockwise and heard a click after one rotation, before sliding half the wall open to the left.

Directly outside was a staircase, and a meter in front of that the exterior wall of another room. Sticking his head out beyond the edge of the stairs, he found a vertical tunnel or fissure only about two meters wide. Below he could see a sort of flooded canal walled by the structure Amon was in and the adjacent one ahead, but an overhanging ledge blocked his view upwards and jutting shelters blocked his view left and right. There was little else visible from where he was. If he wanted to get a better vantage, it seemed, he would have to move.

Here we go, he thought, *into the District of Dreams.* And with trepidation, Amon stepped out onto the stairs. Running diagonally up to the right, they linked to the line of stairs attached to the wall of the next room above, forming a zigzag that went up half-story by half-story through the tunnel. As there were no connecting stairs below, Amon's only option was to climb. In three strides with his long legs, he reached the end of each flight before doubling back to the next one and continuing upwards. The steps were little more than flat nubs, like the blades of paddles sticking from the wall, and since there were no railings, he stepped with heightened tightrope carefulness, steadying himself by grabbing the bottom of the stairs above whenever they were in reach.

He could hear a muffled hum of muttering and whispers emanating from every direction, as though the buildings themselves were conversing, and a steady excretion of flakes gently pelted his head and arms as he ascended. For about a dozen half-stories, the stairpath continued upwards like this, until it wrapped around to another wall of the same shaft and he stepped around to the other side. Then a few flights up it shifted to a neighboring shaft separated by a small gap that he needed to hop. At one point the stairs ended entirely so that Amon had to stop and search for a moment before he found a new staircase starting behind his head and turned around to climb onto it.

He continued like this for several minutes—zigzagging, winding, turning, and climbing—until he guessed that he was fairly high up. Though with the tight enveloping walls built of misaligned cubes sticking out and leaning at erratic angles around him, and his only light a faint glow filtered through cracks between them, he couldn't see more than a few half-stories up or down at any time and had no way to determine his elevation.

The air was musty and thin in the fissure, and he was just beginning to feel short of breath when he heard someone slide a door open below him. Startled and afraid to meet anyone in this strange, constricted place, Amon hurried upwards panting as he went. Soon the encompassing murmur grew louder and he could tell he was approaching many voices above him. A couple more flights and the stairpath came to a roofway about eight rooms wide that was packed with bodies trudging from right to left. Immediately an intense reek, much like that of Tamper but ten thousand times stronger, struck his nostrils, and he hesitated on the top step, watching in awe as hundreds passed slowly by, his first up-close encounter with bankdead in a group.

Amon found them hideous, even worse than the undigimade Free Citizens yesterday. They were gaunt, pale-skinned, and milky-eyed. Many were missing teeth and those they had were brown and chipped, sometimes black and visibly rotten. Some had skin bright red with eczema or acne, dotted with warts, blotted with purplish discoloration. Some had black eyes and scabs, gashes and scars. Others hobbled along, hunching, limping or dragging a paralyzed limb. Though Amon found their ages hard to reckon, the majority appeared to be adolescents, teenagers, or early twenty-somethings, with few over thirty and none over forty. Many, irrespective of their age, carried babies sitting bundled to their chests.

Everyone wore a combination of T-shirt and shorts in plain, subdued colors that were in varying degrees of disintegration just like the buildings, from untorn to moth-eaten to barely clinging rags, flakes of fabric wafting in their vicinity. None of the women had bras, and glancing down, he saw that they were all barefoot, that no one in the crowd had shoes.

Suddenly Amon heard someone behind him yelling impatiently in words he didn't understand, and feeling their hand prod his back, he bristled and hopped forward, slotting himself in. The crowd's force began to shuffle him along and they immediately passed through a square tunnel. On the other side, Amon found himself in a trench cut two stories deep and four roofs wide into the floor of what looked like a cavern made out of stacked shelters. Narrow dissolving skyscrapers joined together into upside-down-stair-like structures that leaned inwards from all directions, meeting overhead to counterbalance each other and form an irregular dome of jutting sharp angles.

Looking around, he was taken aback by how seamless the city was. Though the metropolis that raised him was an endless swathe of tightly clustered buildings that blocked all horizons, there were always slivers through which one could see beyond to the InfoSky. Here he could see no such breaks, just a solid mass enclosing him, with some new layer of obstruction always looming behind any other. Even looking straight up yielded no vista but irregular arching shafts overshadowing all. Though the elevation was high, it almost felt subterranean and it was hard to tell how light from the sun crept in. There weren't even roads or proper walkways. The constant flow of bodies had to carve its passage through whatever spaces could be found, rising up start-and-stop stairs and along irregularly terraced rooftop ledges, spilling into crevices and squeezeways, cramping the open squares and jumping the gaps. Thousands squirmed along every available surface, entering and leaving the cavern along the tightest pathways, sometimes horizontal, sometimes vertical, sometimes sloping precipitously.

Viewed from in their midst, the staggered stages of disintegration for each room didn't appear to be the result of age or blight. Every wall, even on the heavily perforated rooms, looked newer than the buildings in Tokyo, without rust, dirt, or wear of any kind. They were simply coming apart for whatever reason, immaculate rooms atop brittle waifs, vice versa, and everything in between. The downward-drifting flakes they gave off filled the air, a motley assortment of rooms shedding a motley assortment of materials that fluttered over and around the heads of the crowd—tinted glass, aluminum siding, straw, cobblestone, split log, vinyl, clapboard, granite, limestone, off-white toilet seat, red brick—mingling with the flakes from their clothes, which seemed to be dissolving too. Amon held out his palm to catch one. Bringing his hand down to inspect it, the surface looked like wood. Except it had a jagged crystalline structure like a snowflake and was shaped like a flower petal. Less than feather-light, it was almost weightless and soon blew away, though he felt not the slightest draft.

With so many people crammed in this tight, unventilated space, the heat and humidity were like nothing Amon had ever experienced. The air seemed to hang so utterly still around his skin he felt as though it might solidify and seal him in while melting him into a new form, like the factory mold of plastic figurines. Now the body odor combined with other smells, the dominant one being a strange combination of gasoline and watermelon. Beneath this stench, he caught occasional wafts of something musty and eggy, like sulfur mixed with deep-fryer fumes and mold, and something earthy that was even worse. At the same time, droplets of fluid regularly fell *tap-drop* on his head, running down his cheeks and neck with his sweat.

While many plodded along silently around him, enough of them were talking in low voices to each other that a murmuring buzz echoed through the uneven contours of the cavern. Even when Amon could make out the sounds, he could understand none of it as they were speaking the camp dialect, pejoratively called Hinkongo. While it supposedly incorporated many Japanese words, the pronunciation was too unfamiliar for him to catch them, and he had no chance with the Korean, English, Mandarin, Tagalog, and Russian vocabulary mixed in. The buzz was layered with the crying of babies and the calling of crows: *rakhaw, rakhaw, rakhaw.* There seemed to be a whole flock of them above at any given moment, though Amon could never spot them.

Trudging along, Amon watched architectural formation after formation pass by—from deformed pyramidal alcoves to tottering tilted towers to petal-spitting heaps of rubble where whole sections had collapsed—and he began to catch glimpses inside rooms through jagged holes in walls and the occasional open doorway. There he saw lone residents hunched against walls or couples cuddling on floors, the spaces invariably devoid of furniture, with only a few small items he couldn't identify scattered in the shadows. In dark nooks left by oddly fitting corners, children huddled while adults crouched on elevated stairwell stoops with blank downcast eyes. Down cracks and tunnels here and there, he also caught the gleam of glass and steel, and supposed it was from the luxury condos that had been built there during the infamous construction debacle . . . or at least what remained of them after all these decades.

Amon couldn't think to describe how all these sights and sounds and smells made him feel. It was all too absurd for him to even accept, let alone articulate in his mind, his new abode like the dregs of countless dreams brewed again into an impossible new nightmare.

Soon the progress of the crowd began to slow, and beyond the bobbing headscape up ahead, Amon saw that the trench was blocked by a sky-scraper with only a narrow passage busted in its wall. With everyone in the trench apparently headed in the same direction, Amon began to wonder where they were all going.

"Excuse me," he said, turning to a gnarly dreadlocked woman beside him who looked around thirty. Her eyes went wide and she flinched slightly as though surprised and afraid. "Sorry to bother you, but do you know where this path leads?"

The woman frowned, apparently confused by his question, but after a few seconds, "Thez ez thah Rawd teh Delayvry," she responded in the accent bankdead had when trying to speak standard Japanese. *Road to Delivery?* Amon was about to ask more when the woman ducked her head into the crowd and slipped away.

Puzzling over her wariness, Amon realized how much he stood out here, just the opposite of how he'd blended in on the other side. Here was this tall man, with a buzzed head, relatively clean-shaven, the only blemishes on his skin scars from long-faded teenage acne, wearing (admittedly somewhat scuffed) dress shoes and a full suit, while everyone around him was shoeless, ungroomed, their plain summer clothes falling off their bodies. That would explain why he sensed eyes scanning him from head to toe, though when he looked around no one would ever meet his gaze, and why there always seemed to be extra space around him in the crowd, as though he were a glob of oil in water.

In his uniform before cash crashing, he had stood out even in the Free World, as Liquidators were generally feared and revered. But he could only guess what impression he made on the people here. Had they ever seen a Liquidator before? Certainly the crashdead had, though Liquidator dispatches here were extremely rare to Amon's knowledge, as bankrupts rarely tried to hide out in the camps, so most crashborn probably hadn't. They most likely mistook him for bankliving, whatever significance that had for them, but he doubted many connected his gray uniform with the profession it signified.

The earthy smell increased suddenly as the wall to his right ended, opening up into a gap between buildings where the rooms fell away to form the jumbled cube-terraced sides of a steep valley. Jostled by the crowd, Amon found himself pushed up to the edge and overwhelmed by an atrocious stench rising from the bottom, where he saw a pool of thick, mud-like liquid. Lining one side of this open sewer were several stairwells, from one of which stood three boys pissing over the side. Where their streams fell on the surface of the mire was a mound crawling with insects and rats. *Could those long whitish objects sticking out of the mud be human bones?*

To stop his gagging, Amon reeled in his gaze and saw that he was approaching the skyscraper hole into which everyone was pouring. Whatever extra room the crowd might have been giving him soon disappeared as the trench began to bottleneck. Suddenly the weight of bodies crushed in on him so tight the air was pressed right out of his lungs, and he felt hands groping and patting him from all sides. While the men and women encircling him all seemed oblivious, averting their gaze from him as before, their hands were touching him everywhere as if they had minds of their own, reaching into his pockets, between his armpits, down his shirt, into his pants.

"Off!" he wheezed, unable to muster enough breath despite the panic electrifying his whole body. "Hands off!" Even those closest to him didn't hear, or pretended not to, and he wriggled spasmodically as though that might brush them away, but the groping only seemed to grow more frenetic. Raising his arms, he put his hands onto two shoulders and used all his strength to push himself up, leaping out of the squeeze. The crowd closed in tighter, trapping his legs, and he relaxed his arms, letting his body ride them, so he could reach down for his holster. He found two hands engaged in a tug of war over his duster and wrenched it up from between them, before putting the tip of the barrel into the back nearest to him and screaming, "Back off or I'll shoot!" The man or woman—Amon couldn't tell in the melee—fought their way scrambling into the crowd away from him. Nearby onlookers soon spotted the gun Amon held over their heads and began to flee frantically. He couldn't tell where they found the room to get away, but the bodies soon evaporated from his vicinity, and with nothing to support him he plopped to his knees. Not wanting to be overtaken, he sprang to his feet and spun, wheeling his duster in a circle in case anyone dared to approach. Amon had never identified the faces of his assailants and had no idea who to trust, so he wanted to keep them all away. Voices some distance behind him were shouting out complaints as the scuffle had brought the procession to a standstill.

"Keep moving!" he huffed to everyone nearby, still panting, and flicked his gun towards the skyscraper hole. All who saw him obeyed his gesture and started forward, maintaining even more distance from him than before as he too continued on ahead.

With the duster still firmly gripped in one hand, he patted himself down with the other as he proceeded, discovering that the food and drinks in his pockets were gone, though the plastic roll was still safely in his jacket. Rolling it open on in his palm, he saw that the five sheets were sliced-open plastic bottles and found tiny etchings written in neat vertical lines down both sides. Some kind of strange script that he'd never seen before and couldn't read . . .

On the other side of the hole, Amon saw that the crowd began to diverge up ahead, everyone taking one of three separate routes. Some went up a stairpath to an elevated alley on the right, some climbed a series of terraced rooftops that wound up around a corner to the left, and some disappeared down a hole in the floor just before a dead end in the trench ahead.

Now that he was finally presented with a choice, not just bumped relentlessly along a fixed course, Amon remembered that Tamper had told him to go to a place called Xenocyst and find a man named Hippo. That, he decided, would have to be his destination and goal. He had no reason to distrust Tamper, who had been true to his word, and in any case, there was nowhere else to go. But which one of these paths was more likely to take him there? He had no idea of his location, so what hope did he have of picking the right one? It was so frustrating to be lost like this. The District of Dreams was far too crammed and convoluted to take in with his eyes, but one quick glance at a navi and he would grasp the whole layout immediately. Why did finding his way around have to be this hard? It wasn't fair! Suddenly he felt his hands begin to spasm. Raising them before his face, he watched as his ten digits snapped, flicked, pinched, tapped, strobing involuntarily through a series of gestures as though possessed. He wanted so desperately to cast out his perspective and explore the area safely without exerting energy; to click on the buildings and the attire of the people, check their material and learn why they were dissolving; to open a travel advice page and study up on the customs here, activate auto-interpreting; to ask his Decision Network for advice or consult with Mayuko . . . check the time . . . his heart rate . . . More than anything he wanted to know how much everything he was doing cost and how to reduce those costs; to reassure himself that his actions had value. For each of these frustrated desires, Amon's fingers shifted through commands that were supposed to satisfy them, twitching rapidly and inexorably, his chest tightening as a shudder radiated out from his spine to his restless hands.

It was all too much. He had to stop somewhere and gather his thoughts. What he needed was a quiet spot with less traffic. Searching around, he quickly found a half-story flight of stairs attached to one of the rooms that formed the left side of the trench. It was a short distance above his head, and pushing his way to the wall beneath it, Amon leapt up to pull himself onto the bottom step. There he sat with his eyes closed, his head hanging between his knees, his mind awhirl, his breathing rapid, his nerves buzzing in pandemonium.

Shock. That was the word for what he was experiencing, Amon realized. The constant barrage of hunger, congestion, excrement, disease, had left him perplexed, appalled, almost delirious. *Was this the "best of all possible slums?" Could the market truly provide nothing better for the world's poorest?* It was hard for him to imagine anywhere worse, and he felt like he had just scratched the surface. Sure, being without the ImmaNet was supposed to take away some of your options. The people here were not entitled to all the freedom they could earn, as they were incapable of earning at all. In other words, even if they were still entirely free, they lacked capital F Freedom. That was why the pecuniary retreats were so dreaded by all Free Citizens. But the conditions weren't meant to be this bad. The donated supplies and their custodians, the venture charities, were supposed to alleviate suffering for the bankdead and make life as comfortable as those who'd forfeited their right to be a part of the action-transaction economy could hope for. Yet where was there even a trace of comfort here? And this was where the people he cash crashed had ended up, the nerve dust scream he'd always hated to inflict nothing compared to—

Now was not the time for dwelling on what he might or might not be responsible for. Before anything else he needed to regain control of himself, and began to practice his new kind of breath reduction. *Innnn. Ouuut. Innnn. Ouuut.* Amon was surprised to find himself getting used to the smell, though there didn't seem to be enough air in here, and his suit was just too thick. He was tempted to strip it off, but didn't want to risk having it stolen. Hot, woozy, and thirsty, he keenly missed his stolen drinks and felt a twinge of helpless anger when he thought of what had just happened. It was awful. This place was awful. He couldn't stand it. He'd spent the last day or so trying to get in here, but now he had to get out. Return to the streets of Free Tokyo. Go anywhere other than here. But the breathing helped, his exhalations expelling his worries, his inhalations inflating a saving thought: *I'm here in this place right now, the largest bankdeath camp in the world, the District of Dreams, not somewhere else, here, and I need to accept that. I need to figure out where I'm going.*

Amon opened his eyes. The air had brightened a notch as though dawn had shifted to late morning. It felt odd to judge the time of day by changes in the light. High above, he saw a beam of direct sunlight angling down on distant rooftops, though the sun itself was nowhere to be seen. All he found was the tiniest of starfish-shaped openings containing a pathetic speck of sky, bleached and dirty like gungy milk. Silhouetted in the light, a room seemed to unfold out of nowhere like a flower blooming in an instant. Was this one of the pop-up floors he'd seen from the boat? On the ledge beside it children flew kites, catching drafts channeled between buildings. The kites too were dissolving. One girl tried to launch a rapidly flaking one with a hole right through it, but it fell immediately and dropped off the edge of the rooftop, swinging back on the string she held into the wall. Amon felt someone watching him again and, casting his daze down at the plodding crowd just below, saw eyes avert and heads turn away. Then an idea came to him: *Maybe these people can help me find my way. Maybe I can ask them for directions.* It might not have worked with Free Citizens but it was worth another try here. Unable to access navis themselves, bankdead were probably more accustomed to such behavior.

His plan decided, Amon unstrapped his holster from his belt and hid it in the left inner pocket of his jacket. This way he could reach his duster easily in case of danger but not scare anyone who might help him. He was about to hop off the stairs when out of the corner of his left eye he spotted something crawling along the wall just beside his nose. A cockroach! Startled, he pulled his head away, afraid it might fly at him. But then the strangest thing happened. It stopped right in front of him, and a circular flap in the center of its back slid away, revealing a blue eye, a human eye, that stared right at him. Terrified and revolted out of his wits, Amon crept back, slipping right off the edge of the stairwell. He barely managed to grab the top of a step, giving the crowd just enough time to react before he lost his grip, and dropped into a small gap they'd cleared for him. Bending his knees to take the impact, he managed to stay on his feet and bored ahead through the tight throng, looking fearfully over his shoulder at where the creature had been. But it must have closed its eye, for it now looked like a regular cockroach.

Before Amon knew it, the split in the path was approaching, and he began to ask those around him frantically for directions. "Excuse me," he said. "Excuse me." But they all marched onwards in step with him, no one even acknowledging that he had spoken. "Hey!" he shouted, cutting out the politeness after a dozen "excuse me"s had failed. "I'm looking for Xenocyst. Anyone know the way?" Still no one spared him a glance even by the time he reached the split, where, not knowing which way to go, he submitted to the crowd pushing him into the hole straight ahead.

Amon followed a stairpath zigzagging several flights down the hole. At the bottom was a slanted landing from which he poured with the crowd into a thin triangular gap between two leaning buildings. This lead to a tight chamber shaped like a many-sided warped polygon, that fed into a downward-sloping tunnel so low Amon had to crawl in line with the others on his hands and knees, brushing droplets of water off the ceiling with his back, the air even mustier and hotter here. Gradually a dim glow brightened until eventually the tunnel ended at an open square filled with sunlight and he could stand up again.

The square was a solid concrete slab, and Amon supposed he must have reached the ground level of the island atop which the shelters were built. About ten meters in each direction, it was the most spacious area he had come across since leaping off the boat a few hours earlier. Above, he could also see a decent patch of sky, about the size of his hand held out at arms length. Silver-blue with shriveled wisps of fluff. A damp breeze slithered over his cheeks and the ground swirled with varitextured petals, spirals dancing slowly on drafts.

Standing in the corner of the square to his right were two vending machines from which a lineup stretched diagonally to his left. The lineup was fed by bankdead coming from three directions—the tunnel he had just exited, an alley in the wall to his right part way to the machines, and a stairpath wrapping out of sight into a fissure on the far side of the square. Those at the front of the line, having concluded their transaction with the machines, all left by one of these routes with a bottle full of blue liquid and a rice ball in hand. In the distance, above the half dozen stories behind the machines, reared an immense architectural formation that looked like a twin-peaked mountain, the slightly taller peak to the right rising from the shoulder of the other to create a valley between. For a second Amon thought it might be his first ever sighting of Mount Fuji. But to his knowledge, Fuji was supposed to have only one peak, and the slopes should have been rutted from the numerous cave-ins that had happened since the MegaGloms had hollowed it out and filled the core with garbage. Instead, the surface of the slopes was a mosaic of squares, as though it too were built of rooms.

Feeling more and more thirsty, Amon decided to line up for the vendors. He had no money, but neither should anyone else, so surely he would be able to get a drink here. Over the heads of those in line the two plastic rectangles seemed to beckon. He watched as person after person at the front stepped forward, inserted their finger into a small aperture around shoulder height, and bent down to retrieve one of the bottles from a cubby below. They then repeated the same procedure with the other machine, retrieving a rice ball this time, and made their way out of the square. Amon immediately recognized that the aperture was a genome reader, as similar devices were common in the hospitals he had visited, and guessed that the venture charities used them to ration supplies fairly.

Reaching the head of the line, Amon inserted his finger, and felt a slight tickle in his fingertip as a pin-point-sized circle was taken from the top layer of skin for instant genome profiling. But instead of the clunking it had made for the others, he heard an urgent wine-glass hum, the same alarm sound preceding his revulsion dusting, and stepped back immediately. Those behind him soon pushed forward to get their share, and Amon was quickly bumped aside. As some of them gathered a short way off to the side, popped the lids and began to drink, chatting in low voices, Amon gaped with thirsty eyes. Why did they get beverages when he had been denied them?

He watched in confusion as they finished their drinks, ripped open clear wrapping around their rice balls, and after eating the rice balls, began to chew on the wrapping too. The empty bottles they didn't eat however, instead tossing them into a heap along the wall behind the machines. Some of the bottles at the bottom that had probably been there for a while were dissolving just like the clothes and buildings and kites, their transparent plastic petals joining the twisters of multifarious flakes spinning across the square. It was then that Amon realized what they were all made of. *Fleet*, he thought, *this material must be Fleet.*

Sometimes sold under the brand name Hakanite, he'd seen an adver-promo flick about Fleet several years ago. It was a nanomaterial released onto the market as a waste disposal solution. Not only could it imitate a wide range of other materials depending on how it was assembled, it could be programmed with an expiration date. After the designated time had elapsed, the molecules would begin to come apart in pre-designed formation, leaving no garbage. As he hadn't heard anything about Fleet for several years, Amon had just assumed it had failed to sell or that its products had been recalled for some reason, but apparently not.

When he thought about it, making disposable supplies out of Fleet (and some edible substance in the case of the wrappers?) seemed sensible to him, as it would be difficult and expensive to deal with the waste generated by the huge bankdead population. But it baffled him that clothes, shelters, and everything else would be made of the same ephemeral material. Shouldn't these be as long-lasting as possible so the bankdead could make continual use of them? His fingers twitched "FlexiPedia" and "bronze search engine" and "pecuniary retreat supplies" and . . . *damn it.*

He had to get to Xenocyst, whatever it was, and find Hippo, whoever he was. He needed someone to talk to and, as strange as it seemed to him, to ask about all this madness rather than look it up. But the path had split into three again—the tunnel behind him, the alley, and the ledge—this exponential ramification of options threatening to lead him nowhere over and over and over. And even supposing he did stumble upon his destination, how would he recognize it when he got there?

As Amon stalled, feeling lost and overwhelmed, he heard a man's voice calling out in a clear tenor projected for many ears.

"Step aside you giftless. Make way for one who has made the sacrifice. I am Marketable and yet I gave up my chance for a Job to liberate you all. In the name of the Giftnature, make way!"

For the first time someone was speaking standard Japanese, and even though it sounded somewhat stilted Amon was excited he could understand the words, if not quite the overall gist of it. Apparently the crowd could understand too, as they began to part and clear a path.

Walking from the direction of the stairpath through the aisle between bodies was a man who looked different from anyone else Amon had seen thus far. He wore a patchwork robe of various fabrics—navy blue, bright yellow, stripes—each with a different vibrantly colored symbol on it. These were composed of letters, distorted geometric shapes, or abstract icons, and Amon guessed they were logos, though they were static rather than animated as he was used to. Most likely, they were still images derived from the logos of venture charities, or perhaps the MegaGlom subsidiaries that owned them, though he recognized none of them. It was as if the man's outfit had been stitched from an assortment of brand name garments cut into strips. His skin was clear and his hair, instead of the standard disheveled tangle, was buzzed short with a pattern shaved into it that Amon couldn't make out from where he stood. Though fairly tall and lean, he had a healthy bit of flesh on his jowls, and a red glow to his cheeks, his light brown eyes sharp, his straight posture proud, almost haughty. In his arms he cradled a bundle wrapped in cloth, and as the man approached, Amon saw that it was a baby.

Is this someone who can give me directions at last? Amon wondered, encouraged by the fact that the man spoke his dialect and that he was responsible enough to be taking care of a baby. At the same time, something about his stern manner gave Amon pause.

"This little suckling was destined for the Cycle of ReCrash," boomed the man as he held the baby up for all to see, "but as is writ in the *Book of Jobs*, 'Let even the smallest be dedicated to Universal Giftnature.' With the blessings of the Free Market, his Delivery is near . . ."

The preacher hurried across the square as he spoke, but when he caught sight of Amon in his uniform, his tongue and step both faltered. Cradling the baby close to his chest, he began to slink away, eyeing Amon from the corner of his eye with a suspicious frown.

"Excuse me," blurted Amon louder than he intended, his fear of losing his only chance to get directions dissolving his caution. The preacher froze and looked Amon up and down. "Do you know the way to Xenocyst?" asked Amon. The preacher stared at him for a few seconds, apparently confused, his eyes twitching with fear.

"X-Xenocyst?" he replied.

"Yes," said Amon, feeling somewhat relieved that he had finally succeeded in asking his question.

"For what purpose do you ask me?"

"I'm lost. If you could just point me in the right direction, I'd—"

"Listen for the voice of the Web why not? But leave us alone."

After a few seconds staring at the man in perplexity, Amon guessed what he must have meant and said, "I don't mean to bother you, but I'm actually not bankliving. I'm disconnected just like you."

"I know not what schemes you contrive, but I won't be deceived."

"No, I swear. I just cash crashed a few days ago."

"Is that so? Your suggestion is that the Spider who schemes to bind the Market sucked out the little Web beneath your skin but left her clothes on your back? As if anyone would escape Er so quickly!"

"Look, I'm not familiar with how everything works here, but I crashed in a different way than usual so I got to keep my clothes. It's hard to explain. I . . . I was a special case."

Still frowning, the man inspected Amon carefully, as though truly seeing him for the first time "I view no CareBots in your vicinity. Have you ordered their vacation?"

"I . . . I really don't know what you're talking about."

The man's right eye squinted with suspicion. "So you seek what, according to your word?"

"I told you. I'm looking for Xenocyst. For a man named Hippo I'm told will be there."

"Bankdead or no, I advise caution of heretics and scoundrels."

Just then Amon heard a woman squeal. Turning towards the sound, he saw a man at the edge of the square near where the preacher had entered leading a woman by the nape of her neck, and another man soon stepped down the stairpath into the square behind him.

Like the preacher, both men wore outfits patched of variously colored and patterned fabrics, but these were stitched into shorts and a T-shirt instead of robes and had no logos on them. The man leading the woman was a compact bundle of muscle, the sleeves of his shorts and T-shirt stretched skin-tight. His scalp bald and shiny, he had large buckteeth that kept his lips pried open and a thick unibrow with deep furrows above wide eyes that gave him a look of constant bafflement. The man coming down behind him was big-boned and tall, his broad, thick shoulders and chest filled in with little muscle, and his arms disproportionately slender. His hair, a straight frizzy curtain to his shoulders, wrapped around all but his sleek, foxlike face.

The woman looked to be in her late teens, the area around her right eye swollen, the collar of her shirt stretched to reveal the flat of her upper chest, her forearms scratched. The hand of Bafflefrown was on the nape of her neck, his stubby fingers gripping her tightly as he led her limping onwards.

The Preacher called out something to Bafflefrown and Slenderarms, and they rushed over with the woman. An exchange of low-spoken words followed, with the men glancing at Amon now and then, as though discussing him. Then Bafflefrown pushed the woman onto her knees and growled something at her, before the three men stepped close to Amon.

"Tell us who you are once more," said the Preacher, as the baby began to cry, its voice muffled by his chest. "You say you fell from the Free World and the Web, but the Spider left you with your clothes and now you search for the Gene Sucker?"

"Um, if by the Spider you mean GATA and by Gene Sucker you mean Hippo, then I guess that's right."

"But the *Book of Markets* is clear: 'The crashdead stripped of all vestments, with no profit in him, his body made ready for the giftless garb that lasts but days.'" The Preacher pulled up Bafflefrown's shirt to expose his belly and pointed to some faint markings there as if that illustrated his quote. "How do you explain the contradiction with the teaching and experience? You must have proof!"

"I don't know anything about your teaching. And . . . well, I don't have proof of anything, but . . ." Amon caught the eyes of the woman. Still kneeling in the dust, she looked up at him pleadingly, her swollen eye beginning to darken. "I promise you that everything I say is true. If we had more time, I could tell you the whole—"

"No! Hold back your stories," demanded the Preacher. "If you are truly crashdead, your memories will defile our DNA."

"Okay," said Amon. "So can you just tell me the way to Xenocyst then? Then I can go where I need to go and leave your DNA in peace." These men were making him intensely uncomfortable and he felt a strong urge to walk away. He had approached the Preacher because he spoke Japanese and carried a baby, but his companions seemed to have assaulted and abducted a young woman, and the Preacher's words sounded like plain nonsense. When he noticed that the square was almost empty, with the lineup before the vendors disbanded and the few remaining bankdead now slowly vacating the area along the three paths, he knew he had to get away.

But he now realized that the three men had crept into a triangle around him. They stood in their places giving him hard stares, saying nothing.

"I've gotta go," said Amon, unable to think what would count as an excuse in this timeless, jobless place, and tried to step between the Preacher and Bafflefrown, but Bafflefrown pushed him on the chest, forcing Amon to take a step back.

"What was *that?*" Amon snapped with a perplexed, indignant stare, but the three men just looked up timidly at the sky as though searching for some angry god. Amon hovered his right hand just outside his jacket lapels, ready to draw his duster at the next provocation, his pulse quickening.

After a short time, the Preacher lowered his gaze to Amon. "So you speak honestly? The CareBots have truly forsaken you?"

"Yes. I've been telling you—fugah!" Amon yelled in alarm as Slender-arms sprang behind him, wrapping his arms beneath his elbows and locking him in a full nelson before Amon could get his hand to his duster. He bucked and twisted against the hold but Bafflefrown quickly stepped in and grabbed the breast of his shirt to hold him still.

"Or maybe you are a clever bankliving spy," said the Preacher, who proceeded to crouch so he could lay the baby face-up on the dusty, petal-swirling concrete, its cries louder now that they were no longer blocked by the Preacher's chest. He then reached inside his patchwork robe and took out a tool with a black metallic handle that resembled a magnifying glass, except in place of a clear circular lens was a parallelogram of translucent, orangish-red glass.

"What spy? Spy for who?" Amon squeezed out, straining hopelessly to slip out his right hand, his eye on his jacket lapel where the duster remained hidden. "I told you! I'm bankdead just like you!"

"Is that so? Well we shall see."

The Preacher stepped up to Amon and reached out with the tool to bring the glass closer to his face. Amon struggled with all his might against the limbs restraining him.

"Ohhh," Bafflefrown roared, his jaw muscle bulging, veins popping in the furrows on his forehead, his whole face turning pomegranate red, and booted Amon in the shin. Crying out as pain thundered through his bone, Amon looked up and saw that the parallelogram was now a finger's breadth from his face, the Preacher's eye up to the other side of it, inspecting Amon through the colored glass. Up close now, Amon saw that the pattern in the Preacher's hair depicted what appeared to be hieroglyphs and equations, and that Bafflefrown's face was covered in strange scar illustrations, like faint inkless tattoos, depicting the same. Amon could smell the Preacher's foul breath, like old broccoli and vinegar when he said, "A spy after all, precisely as is writ in the Book of Jobs, about the 'forking tongues of debt and delusion' that 'lure the unmarketable down ten thousand roads of mendacious poverty.'"

"I'm not lying!"

"But I have descried the Web's reflection in your eyes."

"Web!?" Amon wracked his mind to grasp the Preacher's words and could only suppose that the lens allowed him to see the fibers of the computer system still implanted in his eyes. "I told you already I'm a special case. I have a BodyBank but it's shut down."

"Ohhh!" shouted Bafflefrown again, flexing his muscles and popping the veins all over his body as though his very flesh would explode with rage.

"Blasphemy!" hissed the Preacher.

"What is?"

"That word. It is forbidden by the *Book of*—"

"What wo—"

"Ohhh!" bellowed Bafflefrown, and Amon stopped speaking.

"So the Web is 'shut down,' you say?" The Preacher peered at Amon closely through the glass again, the skin of his face and the whites of his eyes tinted orange.

"Yes!" yelped Amon. "It's all so complicated, I—" Amon almost said "went bankdead without losing my BodyBank" but corrected himself with, "the Spider cut my connection to the Web but left its reflection in me."

"That is impious and impo—" The Preacher's eyes went wide with wonder on the other side of the glass. "Wait! Just as you say, I see the tracery across your eyes but without the throb of color along each strand. Yet this cannot be, for . . . for . . ."

The Preacher tilted his head to the side in thought. Bafflefrown turned to watch him, looking as baffled as ever, and Amon felt Slenderarms's hold loosen slightly as though he were doing the same.

"A figure such as you appears in the scriptures. As is writ in the *Book of Opportunity*, 'A marked and tainted one draws near before the Last Crash, kindred of the Spider with an acid soul of debt.' If what you say is true, then you may be the subject whose appearance is predicted."

The words *Book of Opportunity* jumped out as Amon realized that these were the Opportunity Scientists Tamper had warned him about, though he was unsure what exactly was "scientific" about them.

"I don't know anything about that," said Amon. "Just let go of—"

"Can you promise you are truly bankdead?"

"Yes!"

"But you have been cut loose from the Web?"

"Yes!"

"So you can no longer pay the Charity Brigade for their protection or the help of their drones?"

"No! I'm totally broke. No money! No bank account! Nothing!"

"But you seek the Gene Sucker?"

"Hippo! I'm looking for Hippo!"

"Ohhh!" Bafflefrown roared again, but this time he seemed to be expressing his excitement rather than his anger.

"Then the divine kindling of the down between your eyebrows will fire up the Lighthouse of Opportunity and lead us all to Jobs in the Free World!

"Ohhh!" Bafflefrown seemed to concur.

"W-what are you talking about? I-I—"

Ignoring Amon, the Preacher said something to the other men. Bafflefrown immediately pressed down with his boot on Amon's toes, before grabbing the back of his neck with one hand and underneath his chin with the other to lock his head, while Slenderarms kept the rest of him immobilized. The Preacher then pointed the lens edgewise at Amon's face and he realized for the first time how sharp it was. It didn't look like glass, but some sort of transparent ceramic sharpened like a knife. The Preacher started to wave the blade from side to side, enacting some ritual as he hummed syllables that sounded neither like standard Japanese nor the local dialect.

"The Voice of the Market has spoken! All we require is a sample of your down for our Scientists."

"A sample? My—no! Off me! I'm—"

"Fear not. You will encounter no serious harm. Only your eyebrows will be enough."

Amon flinched as the Preacher lightly pinched his left eyebrow between thumb and index finger and pulled it outwards, bringing the edge of the knife towards the skin stretched from Amon's forehead.

"No! Let go!"

"This is the only path to Delivery."

"Eeh-yah," Amon rasped at the sharp touch of the knife on the side of his brow, gritting his teeth as he braced for more.

But he only felt the vibration of Slenderarms's voice on the back of his neck as he shouted out something and both Bafflefrown and the Preacher whipped their heads to the side. Over their shoulders, Amon saw that the woman had picked up the baby and had been crawling for the ledge from which they came, but was now frozen in her tracks, looking back in quivering terror under their stares. The Preacher released Amon's eyebrow and barked something at Bafflefrown, who let go of him to stomp towards the woman, who appeared to be the mother of the baby.

"GYAHHHHHHH!" she shrieked as the man approached. Putting down her still-wailing baby, the mother scrambled to her feet as if to run, but her ankle appeared to be twisted as she only managed to stagger a few limping steps before he grabbed her shirt from behind and smacked her in the back of the head, knocking her to the ground. There she lay on her belly, trembling and whimpering. With Bafflefrown no longer holding him, Amon thought to break out of Slenderarms's hold, but the nearby Preacher's knife made him hesitate. Before he could decide, Bafflefrown, apparently satisfied that the mother had been subdued, picked up the baby and lumbered his way back towards Amon. Once he'd laid the baby down a few paces away, the Preacher turned towards Amon and readied his knife as Amon felt blood trickling down his left cheek. Only then did he begin to writhe against the hold, ready to endure any punishment so long as he could stave off the grabbing hands and keep his eyebrow.

Gwah-aaahhh-gwah-aaahhh-gwa-ah-gwa-ah-gwa-ahhhh. The baby's wails grew louder and more urgent.

As Bafflefrown tried to get a solid grip on Amon's bucking neck and the Preacher's fingers fumbled at his brow, Amon saw something move rapidly in the edge of his visual field and Slenderarms let out another call of alarm. Amon and the other three men all looked to the stairpath entrance, from which a woman was sprinting across the square towards the mother at incredible speed. It was Mayuko.

Or so Amon cognized for a flash, until she stopped beside the prostrate mother and her blurred form stabilized into focus. She was too tall and muscular to be Mayuko, with broad shoulders and hefty calves showing from her shorts. Her face was also wider and rounder, her short hair lacking Mayuko's special luster.

"What insult is this?" shouted the Preacher in Japanese. "You dare to trespass on sanctified Opportunity land?"

"We'll only be a moment," the woman replied, bending down to put a reassuring hand on the mother's shoulder while glowering fiercely at the Preacher. "Just give us back her baby and we'll be off."

"Give YOU the—" The Preacher shook with such rage he couldn't finish his sentence, and squeezed the handle of the blade tight in his fist. He barked at the two men in camp dialect, spurring Bafflefrown to let go of Amon's head before pulling his fist back and slugging him in the stomach. Amon retched out all his air with the nauseating impact and went limp in the hold of Slenderarms, who released him and let him crumple to the ground. Amon had a split second to lie there unmoving before a blow landed on his side. Slenderarms began to kick him repeatedly in the ribs, pulsing spots and stars across Amon's vision at a steady tempo, his chest thudding with sharp, sickening pain.

"Ohhh!" The sound of Bafflefrown's roar, the ensuing cry from the woman, and the continuing wail of the baby reached Amon's ears muffled and faint, as though his hearing was insulated with fluff. Without realizing, he found himself curled up in the fetal position as the thunder in his ribcage no longer carried pain, the hard ground drifting away . . . *Do something or you're dead!* a primal voice called up from his depths, and suddenly remembering the duster holstered in his jacket, Amon reached for it, fumbling for the lapel twisted behind his back.

"Grahhhhhh!" the man above him yowled as Amon aimed blindly in the direction of the kicks and pulled the trigger. Slenderarms's unconscious body collapsed onto Amon, who threw him tumbling aside and pushed himself slowly to his knees.

The Opportunity Scientists had been so eager to take a sample of him they hadn't bothered to search him yet. Amon had been lucky. *The fools.*

Raising his head, Amon saw the Preacher staring at Amon's duster fearfully, his ceramic knife outstretched in his hand. Beyond him, the woman prowled slowly around Bafflefrown, poised to lunge with a surgical scalpel held beside her hip, while Bafflefrown warded her off with a white club that appeared to be a human thigh bone, which he held over his shoulder like a bat.

Amon raised the barrel of his duster to shoot the Preacher who had tried to mutilate him, but paused when he saw the infant held in his arms. While nerve dust might only cause pain in adults, it could cause neurological disorders in babies. Instead, he pointed the barrel at Bafflefrown, waiting for the woman, who for the moment at least seemed to be helping Amon, to circle around and give him a clear shot.

Fwoo-fwoo-fwoo-fwoo. Amon whipped his head towards the approaching whir just in time to see a spinning metal disc strike his wrist. Pins and needles shot through his forearm and the duster went flying from his hand, hitting the ground and skittering away, coming to a stop equidistant from him and the Preacher.

Amon looked in the direction the disc had come and saw a man standing at the foot of the stairpath, having just entered the square. As the man reeled in the disc on a wire and it rolled along the ground towards him, Amon saw that it was a small wheel and that the man had what looked like a yellow children's tricycle strapped to his back. Out of the corner of his eye, Amon saw the Preacher bolt for the duster and started for it a split second after. The Preacher had a slight head start but was hindered by the load of the baby and looked set to reach the weapon at the same moment as Amon, only two more steps until they collided, when the woman launched between them, her legs moving faster than anyone Amon had ever seen. Scooping up the duster, she spun to face them as they converged on her, raising the barrel and pointing it back and forth from Amon to the Preacher while jogging backwards out of reach. Amon stumbled to a sudden halt, transfixed by the weapon, and saw the Preacher do the same.

"Ohhh!" yelled Bafflefrown, and looking over, Amon saw him raise the thigh bone high above his head, the mother prostrate just below him. He stared at the woman with Amon's duster wearing a frown of the most intense bafflement, challenging her to make a move. But the man hurled his wheel overhand so that it spun in the air and began to roll on its rim towards Bafflefrown. He held two metal rods joined into a T-shape with wires attached like a marionetteer's control bar, and when Bafflefrown sidestepped the wheel the man pulled on two of the wires so that the wheel leapt up on its side like a hockey puck, whacking him right in the temple. Bafflefrown raised his arms to block the wheel after the fact and fell flat on his buttocks as the man pulled on two different strings to retract the wheel like a yo-yo. The woman shouted something to the prostrate mother and she began to scramble away from Bafflefrown who, abandoning his original prey, charged at the man. When the man hurled another wheel along the ground, Bafflefrown was ready this time and brought his forearms arms up to block it while his legs brought him charging almost within clubbing range. But before the wheel struck, the man pulled a wire to send it flying wide and pulled another so that it fired a spoke that impaled itself in Bafflefrown's shoulder as it passed. "Ohhh!" Bafflefrown roared and swung his club into the man's ankles, knocking his feet out from under him. The man pulled another wheel from the tricycle on his back and was about to throw it up at Bafflefrown as he raised the club again when the Preacher shouted, "Stop!"—the word identical in both dialects so that Amon understood it. The Preacher had the tip of his blade up to the baby's neck and everyone froze, Bafflefrown with his club aloft, the man with his wheel recoiled, the woman with Amon's duster aimed at the Preacher, the mother cowering in the dust. And Amon—disarmed and surrounded by enemies, his body a pounding cacophony of pains—wiped a dribble of blood from his forehead with the back of his hand as his gaze twitched between the four combatants, terrified and confused. *Gwah-aaahhh-gwah-aaahhh-gwa-ah-gwa-ah-gwa-ahhhh.*

"Vacate the square now!" snarled the Preacher in the standard dialect.

"If you do anything," said the woman, "I'll dust you."

"And risk ruining the gift value of this baby?"

The woman said nothing in response, keeping the duster trained where it was.

Amon had no idea what they were talking about, but saw that he was not party to their dispute and made a run for the tunnel by which he'd entered the square.

"Halt, or I'll shoot!" shouted the woman.

Amon stopped and looked back over his shoulder to see his duster aimed in his direction.

The Preacher shouted something to Bafflefrown and he began to back away from the man with the tricycle towards the mother, who had snuck halfway to a wall of shelters at the edge of the square.

"No!" the woman shouted, turning the barrel on Bafflefrown this time. "If you touch that woman I don't care what happens to the baby. You're both getting dusted and I can promise you won't ever wake up."

"You pretend to threaten us?" demanded the Preacher. "In our domain?"

"You kidnapped these two right from our doorstep. As if you—"

"War! You'll be lucky to escape war for coming here, you gene-sucking witch!"

Bafflefrown continued lumbering towards the mother as he'd been instructed, the shoulder of his patchwork T-shirt now dark with blood from where the spoke protruded.

"I don't give a shit about turf or war," cried the woman. "All I care about is this baby right now, and if he doesn't back off you're all just *done!*"

The Preacher and the woman glowered at each other for a tense few seconds. But the Preacher soon looked away and called out something in the camp dialect. Bafflefrown changed directions, still eyeing the man warily, and backed now towards the Preacher. When the two men were side by side, the Preacher looked over at Amon, hungry fervor in his eyes, then over at the woman as though he might persuade her to take him. But when his eyes drifted over to Slenderarms, his fallen companion, he seemed to rethink things. He said something to Bafflefrown, who sheathed his club into the back of his shorts, the top hidden beneath his shirt, and went over to Slenderarms to lift him up over his shoulder. The two men, each carrying a different person, then went to a stairwell in the corner of the square opposite the man, shambled up two stories, opened a sliding door, stepped inside the room, and were gone.

The pain in his ribs shifted into a deeper, duller ache, as Amon brought his gaze down to find the woman aiming his duster at him again and the man stalking over with a wheel poised ready to throw.

Fuck.

7
THE COUNCIL CHAMBER

1

Spirals of multitextured petals raised by the scuffle whirled slowly in the tepid breeze around the two figures that faced Amon in the empty square. They remained utterly still, with their weapons trained on him, watching him cautiously. Blood trickling from his eyebrow, his heart pounding against his sore ribs, Amon glanced fearfully back and forth between the two, awaiting their next move.

The woman was tall and looked to be in her early thirties, her body shapely and athletic with muscular legs and shoulders, and a narrow, curving waist. Her short hair was shaved on the sides and rose in unruly waves on top. With long, striking eyelashes and clear, golden-brown skin, her face was almost what would normally be called pretty, if not for her off-center jaw, which tilted her long chin to the right and revealed a few crooked teeth between the left side of her thin lips, giving her a horse-like appearance. While her brow was unfurrowed, her tired, light-brown eyes seemed to frown, as though she had little patience for anything she saw, and Amon wondered how he ever mistook her for Mayuko.

Her companion was built like a stuntman: short and slim with taut muscles, the veins sticking out on his lean yet toned forearms. His features were small and delicate, except for his forehead, which was broad and roughly hewn like the face of a boulder, his brown hair parted in the middle and clinging flat to just below his ears, a smattering of dark bristles on his cheeks and chin. Like the woman and most other bankdead Amon had seen, his expression was grim and stony, but unlike them he radiated a certain calm watchfulness, his sharp eyes shifting slowly about as though always readying him for the unexpected. From the metal cross he held, thin wires ran to the hubs, rims, and spokes of the two wheels on the chipped mustard yellow tricycle on his back and to those of the one he held in his hand, ready to throw.

"Who are you?" said the woman.

Amon—battered, thirsty, and exhausted, lost in an incomprehensible city, robbed of his food, drinks, and only weapon—wanted to run. But he had no illusions he might escape this pair with their long-range weapons and the woman's great speed. So he simply stood there dumbly, his lips quivering.

"Quickly!" snapped the woman. "Before they come back with more men."

"She asked you a *question!*" barked the man, drawing the wheel further back threateningly.

"My—please," Amon blurted. "My name is Amon Kenzaki. I'm—"

"We don't care what your name is," said the woman. "What are you doing dressed like a Liquidator and how did you get *this*?" She shook the duster she was aiming at him.

"I—p-please. I-it's a long story. You . . ." His intention was to stand proudly and face them, but his nerves were frayed and he cowered involuntarily, lowering his head.

"You think he's one of those *fuckers*?" the man growled.

"No," the woman replied. "They were sampling him when I got here."

"Doesn't mean anything."

"He nerve dusted one before I took this."

The man glanced at the duster in her hand. "He can't be bankliving?"

The woman shook her head. "No drones," she said, arcing her eyes across the empty air above as if to illustrate.

In his shock and fear, Amon found himself gesturing compulsively, and before he could stop himself, he clicked the man and woman to check their profiles. *Their anonymity is just . . . wrong*, he felt. *Who are they?*

As Amon twitched under their gazes, he watched the man and woman exchange looks.

"Crashnewb?" the man asked the woman.

"I'll take care of him," she said, tipping her head towards the mother trembling on the ground a short distance away. The man nodded, snapped the wheel in his hand onto the axle of the tricycle on his back, walked over to the mother, and bent down, starting to console her with whispers and a hand on her back.

"Get out of here," the woman said, glowering at Amon and giving the duster a flick in the direction the three men had exited the square. "Now!"

"Hold up!" said Amon. Only a few moments earlier he had wanted to get as far away from these people as fast as he could, but now that it was clear they weren't out to harm him he saw a desperate chance to seek help. "Let me ask you a—"

"Forget it. Get moving!"

"No. Please. I-I'm looking for a place called Xenocyst. Do you know the way?"

"We don't take crashnewbs. So off. Now! Before I dust you."

We?

"Please . . ." Amon dropped to his knees overwhelmed, droplets of blood dribbling off the end of his chin. "I have something for—for Hippo. A man called Tamper sent me with it." Amon looked up at the woman, begging her with his eyes. "Could you please just tell me where it is? I can't speak the dialect here. I've got no one else to ask."

She paused momentarily, squinting as though in thought, before calling out, "Ty. Have you ever heard of someone named Tamper?"

"Yeah, sure," said the man called Ty. He now had the woman on her feet and was helping her along with an arm around her waist. Her swollen eye had purpled darkly, though her limp seemed to be gone and she could almost walk at a normal pace. "He was an electronics engineer. Lived with us a while before you came. Weird guy but very useful to have around."

"What happened to him?"

"Went over to Free Tokyo a few years back. Wouldn't say why." While the woman spoke in perfectly natural Japanese, Amon detected a thick camp accent in the man's, though he was fluent enough. "Got some reports in the beginning, but no one's heard from him for months. We were startin' to worry."

The woman nodded and turned to Amon. "Take off your clothes."

"Excuse me? You want to see the p-package, right?" said Amon, reaching inside his jacket for the plastic roll. "I can—"

With one firm shake of the gun, "Hands away from your pockets!" Amon froze. "Your clothes off now or I'll rip them from your dusted body!"

"But—"

"You think we care about you? We'll leave you here for those OpScis when they come back with a whole gang of field priests. Is that what you want?"

Trembling, he stared into her fed-up eyes.

"Starting with the jacket."

After gripping the collar and pulling the sleeves off his arms, Amon folded his jacket and held it in the crook of his elbow to begin unbuttoning his shirt.

"Quickly!"

Jumping at her voice, Amon dropped his jacket on the dusty ground, the plastic sheet from Tamper still in the inner pocket, and hurriedly finished undoing the remaining buttons on his shirt. He then tore off his garments one by one—his dress shirt, undershirt, shoes, socks, belt, and pants—plopping them at his feet. When he was standing there in his underwear, feeling embarrassed and vulnerable, he paused, and looked questioningly at the woman.

"Slide them down and lift up your balls."

Amon was going to protest, but balked at the impatient look in her eyes and sent his shaking hands down to the elastic around his waist.

When his underwear topped the pile, he lifted his scrotum and the woman bent down slightly to look beneath, saying, "Now turn around and spread your cheeks."

Amon did as she asked, and could feel her gaze burning a spot he wasn't sure anyone had ever looked at before.

"Stay like that," she said, and Amon watched from beneath the dangling obstruction between his legs as she trotted over and picked the plastic roll from the pile of clothes.

"Okay. You can put on your underwear. Ty!" she called. "The cowl."

"You're not bringing him along?" said Ty as he helped the woman onto the stairpath.

"The Books should see this," she said, holding up the plastic sheets.

"Let's just take his stuff and go."

"He could have more information about Tamper."

"He could be one of their spies."

"I told you he dusted one—"

"We can't be sure."

"There's no time for this!"

Ty grunted with a shake of his head. "Alright, but this is your call. And if those fuckers catch up, we're leaving the dead weight."

The woman nodded.

Ty left the mother sitting on the stairs and jogged towards Amon. When he reached around his back towards his tricycle, Amon flinched, fearing an attack on his defenseless, sore body. But Ty merely plucked a piece of black fabric from where it dangled from the handlebars.

"Put this over your head," he said, handing the fabric to Amon, who took it and saw it was a sort of cowl with a zipper at the bottom.

"Why do I have to—"

"PUT. IT. ON," the woman demanded, giving the gun a shake.

With panicked hands, Amon fumbled the cowl over his head. A sharp stink hit his nostrils and he wondered how many people had layered their breath in it before him. Just enough light seeped in that he could see the texture of the fabric, though the world was completely cut off. Suddenly hands grabbed at his neck and when Amon shrunk back, "Hold still!" the woman shouted from a few paces away.

Quickly the hands closed the zipper tight, and something hard and intricate was wound around his wrists. When it was tightened and he could feel links digging into his skin, Amon guessed it was a chain made of plastic. In less than a minute, his wrists were tied together in separate loops in front of him. Then, cowled and bound, Amon felt a tug on both of them simultaneously.

"Move!" said the woman, and Amon trudged out of the square on his leash.

2

Amon found himself blind once again. Except now ruthless strangers were leading him like a slave or beast through an unknown space, full of unknown dangers, expanding around him like a great burrow of hidden scorpions.

They took him first up a stairpath that had to be the one his captors and the Opportunity Scientists had used to enter the square. The hard grating of the steps dug sharp squares into his soles. Following the slight pull of the chain on his wrists, Amon felt along the curving walls for reassurance, until they ended and his fear of falling increased at every unsupported step. If these paths were anything like the ones he'd climbed that morning, it could be a long way down . . . When Amon proceeded too warily, a strong tug came on the chain and he tripped, his right shoulder slamming hard into the next stair.

"Hurry!" said Ty. "We've got to move before those assholes come back."

Getting to his feet, Amon continued up the stairs, focusing intently on the chain now, speeding up when it grew taut while keeping his footing as best he could. Soon they reached a level path where Amon felt something hard and granular underfoot, perhaps gravel. People kept brushing and bumping past him in muttered conversation as wafts of sewage and effluent filled the air.

Beset with all manner of discomforts—his ribs throbbing individually at different frequencies of pain, his wrist sore from the strike of the wheel, his gut aching from the punch, blood and sweat pooling inside the cowl, nauseous, dizzy, disoriented, his thirst worsening by the second—Amon fidgeted the commands to activate MyMedic. Maybe he was just bruised as it seemed, but what if his bones were broken and needed to be set? What if he'd sustained hemorrhaging, or contracted a fever in these unsanitary conditions? What if he was about to die? Without sensors to scan his vitals and an analyzer to provide a diagnosis, he had no objective way to determine what was actually going on with his body. Despite his senses telling him that his injuries were not mortal, he anxiously repeated the same gestures in a loop, knowing that no windows would pop up in the darkness of the cowl but unable to stop.

Presently he heard the mother sobbing quietly just up ahead and the consoling coos of the other woman. Over the murmur of the crowd and the *rakhaw* of crows, fervent shouting echoed from the distance, the tone reminding him of the Preacher's when addressing the crowd. Who had those three men been? Opportunity Scientists, or OpScis as the woman had called them? Surely, but then what the hell were those? The shouting grew louder, soon accompanied by howls and drums and clangs and rumbles. Increasingly he was buffeted by passing shoulders as the crowd thickened, until he was squeezed in with other bodies, their coarse-rubbing fabric and heat on his bare flesh as the chain continued to tug him along. The ground against Amon's feet changed several times, from tile to more grating to soft cobbled foam. When he stepped onto what felt like flake-strewn concrete again, the space opened so that he was no longer touching anyone and he was brought to a near standstill. Only directed to take steps forward occasionally, he could soon hear a familiar *ka-chunk, ka-chunk* not far ahead, and knew they were lining up for vending machines.

"Alright pal," said Ty eventually. "Stick out your pinky."

"I'm not sure if—"

"Stick out your pinky!" snapped the woman.

Although Amon was afraid of getting revulsion dusted again, he was in no position to argue and let his chained hands be lifted up to shoulder height, his finger brushing the rim of the small aperture as it was inserted. Immediately he heard the familiar hum and tensed up with fear until Ty jerked his hand out.

"Vertical! Did you hear that?" asked Ty.

"Yes," replied the woman called Vertical. "What was it?"

"The alarm."

"Are you sure? How?"

"I dunno."

"Why don't you give it another try?"

Again Amon's finger was inserted into the hole in the same way. Again the machine hummed.

"What is this?" said Vertical. "Who sets off the alarm on this side?"

"Forget it now," said Ty. "Let's just get back as quick as we can."

The chain continued to tug Amon along, through all manner of cramped pathways, rooftops, and stairs that he could not see. After a while, the footsteps and murmuring began to reverberate differently, telling him they were now indoors. Presently he heard sizzling and a steady hammering, as the smoke of burning plastic choked his lungs. Then they were outside again and his soles kept splatting blobs of something wet and sticky on the spongy ground. Without his thick suit, he wasn't as hot as before, the faintest breeze now directly cooling his sweaty skin. Still, his thirst kept increasing. The hot moisture trapped in his cowl only reminded him of his dry mouth and throat, the serrated growl of hunger in the depths of his stomach almost forgotten alongside it. Soon the dim and quiet created by the muffling fabric around his head took on a keen, nagging edge. Before stepping into the District of Dreams, in spite of his efforts to avoid distractions for the sake of frugality, Amon had been accustomed to daily doses of advertainment—images dancing in the corner of his eyes, audio humming at the threshold of hearing. With his bankdeath, countless new sights and sounds, not to mention violence, in this harrowing labyrinth had busied his mind. Yet now this stimulation too was stifled and there was nothing to help him forget the awful present. His ears began to ache for theme songs, tear-jerking monologues, catch phrases, his eyes to burn for strobing colors, 3D starscape dramas, special effects. He would have even taken the pandemonium of the spammers if only they would be so kind as to swarm him again, his whole body atremble with pointless gesture after gesture and—

"Gyah." Amon let a sob escape in spite of himself when his restlessness and discomfort and terror became unbearable.

"WHAT?" said Ty, yanking so violently on his chain that Amon thought his shoulders would pop out of their sockets and nearly fell on his face. "What's wrong with you?"

"I just . . . I just want to . . . N-nothing . . . It's nothing."

"Come on!" Ty gave the chain another yank, so that it cut off circulation to Amon's hands and a pulse of numbness spread to his fingertips. "We're almost there."

"Should we leave him after all?" asked Vertical. "I doubt we'll get much out of him. Not with webloss this bad."

"We've already dragged him this far," said Ty. "Anyone this weird should tell us something."

"Have you ever heard of someone like this?"

"Never. Not once in my whole life here . . ."

After that they were silent.

Despite his shaking, Amon forced himself to continue plodding and squeezing and climbing along with Ty tugging him when he lagged behind. His inability to see through the cowl, to rotate his perspective and look down on his captors from above, to take snapshots of their faces and image search them, to research who they were and who they served, was maddening. His vision was not supposed to be bound by his eyes, his hearing by his ears, his thought by his brain. But with the satellites and sensors and spatial models that were once extensions of his body now severed, he was reduced to a mere hunk of itching aching dumb meat, lost and helpless, beaten and humiliated, wearing nothing except the cowl and his underwear—but why leave those on?

I ought to be as naked as this world, he thought. *I ought to touch the air directly, to be here without mediation.* That would complete the stripping away of his former life, the disrobing of his common sense, the peeling away of all the truths he had ever held dear.

Amon wanted to scream.

But fearing further reprisals from his new masters, he clamped his quivering jaw and followed their lead, in thrall to whatever unadorned destiny might await.

3

"Stop here." Ty put his hands on Amon's shoulders and spun him in circles before leading him onwards. He did this several times at intervals of about ten minutes, apparently to disorient him, as if Amon had the faintest idea where they were going. Soon they paused as Vertical briefly explained who Amon was to someone, and Amon guessed they were passing through some sort of checkpoint.

Up many steps they went, along narrow ledges, down the slanting face of leaning buildings, and into some kind of flat passage made perhaps of cracked tile. Sounds had that indoor reverb again and the voices grew more clamorous, less furtive and subdued. Soon Amon could hear babies—crying, gurgling, laughing—with mothers babbling to them soothingly. A woman's animated voice, apparently reading a children's story. More tiled passages and stairwells until, echoing faintly as though from a distant room, women were groaning and shrieking in pain, a bustle of chatter around them. Then several rises and turns later they took a sudden left and Amon felt hands undoing the chains. He gasped with relief to be unfettered but the moment they fall clittering to the floor, he was shoved down from behind onto a fabric-covered floor.

"Get dressed!" barked the voice of a woman that wasn't Vertical, and Amon realized he was on top of clothes.

Crawling off onto the tiles, he groped the garments and was disappointed to find the texture was not that of his uniform, but thinner and softer. It was a T-shirt and shorts, and the moment he slipped them on, "Come," the woman said, grabbing his left wrist to pull him along.

After traversing several more corridors and stairwells, Amon was led into a room where several people were talking, the echo of their voices suggesting spaciousness.

"Kneel," said the woman behind him, and Amon sank to his knees on a hard floor.

". . . background is the issue," said a man with a soft voice that was thoughtful and slow yet commanded attention. "While we acknowledge your skills, positions and resources are scarce and we simply cannot take the risk. We also have doubts about the truth of your account."

"But that was just a brief period in my youth," whined another man. "I haven't volunteered at Delivery in years and—"

"The official pronouncement of the council," interrupted a third man, with a deep nasally voice, "is non-admittance, and you will now be escorted out of the compound. Bring forth the next applicant!"

The shuffling of several feet receded out of the room.

Guessing he was in some sort of courtroom where he would soon be judged, Amon felt a pang of fear travel up his spine when hands reached under his armpits to lift him to his feet and guide him a few paces away. "Kneel," said the man who owned the hands right beside him, and Amon dropped back onto the wooden floor, sensing the breath and presence of various people around him. He flinched as hands touched the cowl, unzipping it and pulling it off.

Although the space was not particularly bright, Amon had to blink several times after being covered so long before his vision cleared.

He found himself kneeling directly on a wooden floor facing a line of people.

Glancing quickly around, Amon saw he was in a large empty room that resembled a dining hall cleared of furniture and fallen into disrepair, the floorboards scuffed, warped, and discolored. About a dozen people formed a circle with him at the center. Like him, they were seated with no pillows or rugs, either cross-legged or with their feet flat on the floor. Behind him were a woman and two men lined up with paddles laid horizontally on their laps. Everyone present wore the standard camp outfit and kept their eyes trained steadily on Amon. Ty and Vertical were nowhere to be seen. They must have passed his chain to someone else and slipped away without his realizing.

In the spot in the circle directly in front of Amon was a man he immediately guessed to be Hippo. The moment he saw him, Amon was reminded of a certain African mammal and remembered that "hippo" was the English word for it. Hippo looked to be in his late fifties or early sixties, with deep wrinkles in his forehead and radiating from the outer sides of his eyes. He had one of those squat, stocky builds that wasn't exactly fat but was never without a bit of padding, his neck, chest, waist, and fingers all thick. What particularly made him resemble a hippo was his large bald head, gray-brown leathery skin, large mouth and deep-set, small eyes. These seemed to regard Amon with penetrating attentiveness.

To his left was a lanky man, with skinny arms and legs but a slight paunch. It was difficult to tell his age. Though his black skin was smooth and seemed relatively youthful, his short Afro-textured hair was pure white and patchy, a thin crescent scar curving from the center of his forehead to the center of his crown. He wore large-rimmed, almost windshield-thick glasses with one missing lens, so that his right eye appeared enormous while his left was at regular magnification. He blinked frequently, and seemed to squeeze his eyes shut with the surrounding muscles rather than simply lowering and raising his eyelids, his long, bony fingers interlinked on his lap.

To his right was a boy who looked to be about ten. His skin was pale and speckled with moles, his hair sandy brown and arcing about wildly like flaccid porcupine quills, his eyes hazel. Balanced on the palm of his right hand he held what appeared to be a jade-colored tablet, the screen unlit.

In his left hand was a digital pen. Though his features didn't resemble the lanky man's whatsoever, the two shared the same hunched posture and distant, thought-filled eyes, which seemed to be taking Amon apart, component by component.

Stenciled in chipped black paint on the off-white wall behind Hippo was a sort of logo or emblem of a young girl inside a bubble or cell. The girl stood there defiantly with her arms at her sides as a pin poked towards her face into the membrane, the surface bending inwards, either resisting or about to pop.

"The initial inquiry for a new applicant will now commence," said the man with the broken spectacles, who was the owner of the deep nasally voice. "Do the councilors present wish to raise any comments or objections at this time?" The man's unevenly magnified eyes swept once around the circle. Then, apparently satisfied when no one stirred, he turned to Amon and said, "Kindly provide your name, sir."

With piercing gazes skewering him from all directions, Amon fought to subdue the cold jittery fear seizing his stomach and give them his name. But when he opened his lips to speak and the air slipped inside his mouth, he realized how dry and pasty it was, as of course it would be after all his exertion on the way here. Already the new T-shirt he'd been given was damp and sweat was dribbling down the back of his neck.

"First . . ." he rasped, reaching out his hands palm-up along the floor, "water . . ."

"Have you come here with nothing to drink, young man?" Hippo asked.

Amon gave a feeble nod, wishing he could explain about the vending machines.

"Well showing up expecting charity is hardly going to help your application," Hippo said, shaking his head. "Does anyone have a drink to spare?"

A bottle rolled gently from the right side of the circle and stopped just short of Amon's side. He shoveled it close to him with his elbow, picked it up with his other hand, sat up, popped the top, and chugged the fizzing sports drink down in one breath. Water, Amon was learning, was something that had to be taken in when you had the chance.

"Alright," said Hippo after Amon had gasped in refreshment. "Let us begin again. Book, please."

"Kindly provide your name, sir?" said the man with the nasally voice who was called Book.

"Amon . . . Kenzaki."

"Your age?"

"Twenty-seven."

"Your place of birth?"

"T-Tokyo."

"Free Tokyo or the District of Dreams?"

"Free Tokyo."

"What skills can you offer?"

"Skills?"

"All able members are required to provide their labor. If perchance the council were to grant you a hearing and issue approval of your application, what manner of valuable contribution would you be capable of?"

"Well . . . I-I . . ." Without his intending, it seemed, Amon was applying for membership. But to what? Since he had found Hippo, this had to be Xenocyst, which ought to be reassuring since Tamper had told him to come here. Yet he had no idea what Xenocyst was or what membership in it might entail. Here he was in these strange clothes, in this strange room full of strangers staring at him with strange eyes, in the middle of the strangest place he had ever been, and he was supposed to somehow convince everyone of his value to them? Still, as baffled as he was, Amon saw that he had to follow along. Otherwise he risked being dumped in the camps alone like the previous applicant, or suffering whatever punishment might go along with rejection. No one had threatened him yet, but after what the Opportunity Scientists had tried to do to him, anything seemed possible. "W-what sort of skills are you looking for?"

"Are you completely ignorant of our needs, young man?" asked Hippo. "You didn't even bother to ask around before you came?"

"S-sorry," said Amon, wracking his brain for something to tell them. "I-I used to be a Liquidator. Maybe my experience will come in handy here."

Amon heard someone click their tongue in disapproval.

"So you made a career out of banishing innocent people from the Free World? What use, exactly, might that be to us?"

I . . . Amon tried to move his lips in response to the question, but his jaw only moved soundlessly as a wave of trembling started at his mouth and spread down his body. Fear and anxiety had rallied together with his restlessness and confusion—the primitive ignorance of his time, place, temperature, vital signs, and names or even pseudonyms of these people. He didn't want them to misunderstand him. Though he had sincerely believed in his job for years, the events of the last week had awakened many doubts. But were his doubts enough to convince them he was a decent human being when there were people here who might have suffered at the hands of his colleagues? Would they ever recognize his usefulness? What if they dumped him out there again, with all the robbers and filth and chaos? What if those men cut him up? What if he ended up like those bones in the open sewer? As all the shocking memories of the day rose up into his mind's eye and he imagined the similar horrors that awaited him if they cast him out, he felt overwhelming pressure to somehow say what they wanted to hear and soon panic had fully hijacked his being, dominating every nerve in his body, until he could no longer keep his head up and bowed it to the floor, shaking and panting rapidly.

The room erupted into chatter that sounded like Japanese but none of which Amon's troubled mind could translate into meaning. "Answer when you're addressed!" growled a man's voice from behind as something hard jabbed into his lower back. Tensing with terror, Amon dropped onto his side and curled up into a ball. Out of the corner of his eye, he saw one of the guards standing over him with his paddle outstretched, the other two poised with theirs behind him.

"Relax, young man," said Hippo, the stir of voices settling when he spoke. "They're just here to maintain order. Back up on your knees and please do your best to answer our questions."

When the guards sat back down, laying the paddles over their thighs, Amon rose timidly to his knees and faced Hippo again, still shaking.

Hippo nodded to Book.

"The council returns to the previous question," said Book. "How might your experience as a Liquidator serve this community?"

I have to tell them something! Amon's thoughts screamed. *I have to show them that I'm not who I was, that I have so much to offer!* But his desperation to explain only summoned a stronger wave of shaking and his head dropped to the floor again.

Mutters went around the circle for several seconds until Hippo asked, "Listen, young man. Can you speak?"

Yes, Amon failed to say. He tried to nod his head but only managed a slight jerk and wasn't sure if it was distinguishable from his tremors.

Ta-tap, ta-tap, taptaptaptap, ta-tap . . . Amon heard a tapping noise coming from the direction of the boy. The sound continued even as Book said, "His symptoms of webloss are severe. We conjecture at least several days before he can communicate normally, on the assumption, of course, that he is capable of recovery."

"Then I propose we eject him without wasting our time with the hearing," said Hippo. "The council has heard the stories of numerous Liquidators in the past, and I doubt there's anything exceptional to learn from this one. Even if he were accepted in this condition, it would be *weeks* before he could contribute anything."

Tap-ta-tap, tap, taptaptap, taptap . . . The sound from the direction of the boy started up again, and Book said, "We are not expressing either support or opposition to this proposal. However, membership protocol states that due to limitations in resources and a lack of psychiatric facilities, adults who are not mentally healthy are not to be admitted unless the council finds special reason to justify their eligibility."

"Well, any special reasons?" Hippo addressed the circle.

A brief silence followed.

"Do any councilors wish to raise any comments or objections at this time?" asked Book. There was another silence. "Then let the voting commence. All in favor of ejecting the applicant?"

Looking around the room as his visual field quaked, Amon saw the nine men and women in the circle raise their hands.

"All against?"

The hands all went down and then there was stillness. Hippo, Book, the boy, and the guards had not raised their hands and did not seem to be participating in the vote.

Book nodded and turned to Amon with his mismatched gaze. "The official pronouncement is non-admittance, and you will now be escorted out of the compound."

Amon sensed the guards reaching for him from behind.

"PLEASE!" he shrieked, finally finding his voice and suddenly too much of it. "T-Tamper told me! Th-there's a package! Ask V-Vertical! A p-p-package!" He flung his hands out to Hippo beseechingly as the three guards began to shunt him out of the circle with firm hands.

"Hold on," said Hippo to the guards just as they were about to cowl Amon before the doorway. "This young man just said, 'Tamper and Vertical.' How does he know the names of two people very dear to this council?"

The guards gripping Amon stopped and there was a moment of tense silence before one of them said, "They're the ones that dropped him off in the holding room." From her voice, Amon guessed it was the woman who had led him to the council chamber.

"Well where are they then? They were supposed to bring him themselves, were they not?"

The guard said nothing and silence followed until the tapping from the boy began again and Book said, "Regulations require that the escorts of applicants report promptly to the council and remain available for subsequent inquiry."

"Then better bring him back and sit him down," said Hippo to the guards. "And can someone go call Ty and Vertical? I don't think we should throw him out until they've explained their reasons for bringing him. Unless someone objects?"

"Do any councilors wish to raise any comments or objections at this time?" asked Book.

The issue was decided by another moment of silence, and the woman who had brought Amon hurried out of the room as the other two guards led him back into the circle. Returned to his knees in the center, Amon let out a long, quivering sigh of relief and let his head down to the floor. Nothing had been decided in his favor, but the mix up might have given him another chance to express what he wanted to say if he could just get his nerves under control. So, closing his eyes while the council waited for Ty and Vertical, he took this opportunity to breathe deeply. The faint chatter around the circle and occasional footsteps in the hall made him anxious, but he did his best to focus on the sensation of his chest expanding and contracting, disregarding as much as he could what was going on around him. The cool wood on his forehead, the cold sweat coating his back and scalp and armpits, the toxic buzz of terror in his skin, the ache in his ribs that sharpened with each inhalation, the sting of the cut on his brow, the weight of his exhaustion pulling him into the floor, his warm breath rebounding onto his face, his heart pulsing a beat of blood into his temples. Amon lost track of time as everything faded into the shadows of his awareness except for his body reflecting on itself.

When his shaking was beginning to subside and his respiration slowly settling, he heard Hippo say in a clear, firm voice, "Let's get started." Only then did Amon finally raise his head.

Inside the circle in front of him, Vertical and Ty were kneeling and facing each other in profile.

"The inquiry will now recommence," said Book. "Vertical, Ty, it has been brought to the council's attention that you were the individuals who escorted the applicant to Xenocyst. Is this account correct?"

"Yes," "Yup," they said almost simultaneously.

"In consideration of these facts therefore, the—"

"Then why didn't you bring him yourselves?" Hippo cut in. "We almost ejected this man thinking he was applying on his own. We could have missed out on valuable information!"

Ty and Vertical glanced at each other before Vertical said, "I was attending to Shari, a woman we brought back earlier today. She's in shock after the OpScis beat her and took her baby. I wanted to make sure she was receiving the right care. So we asked one of the guards to drop him off in the holding room until we came back. I had no idea that someone was going to bring him in so quickly."

"Well it's true that council business is moving faster today than usual. But that doesn't mean you can leave it all up to the guards. Many of them are new to our procedures as you know."

"I'm very sorry," said Vertical with a bow.

"And how about you, Ty?" asked Hippo.

"I had to leave my supply crew today on an emergency, so I stopped by the warehouse to see they're all back okay."

"You abandoned a supply crew you were in charge of?"

"They kidnapped Shari and her baby from our crew. I had no choice."

"Well, we'll leave it up to the council to consider your decision once we hear what happened. Go ahead, Book."

"The council now requests your report on the events concerning the applicant, Amon Kenzaki, not excluding all background incidents such as the involvement of the aforementioned Shari. What is your reply?"

"You wanna take this, Vertical?" asked Ty.

"Yes, fine," said Vertical. Then, raising her voice to address the circle, "This morning, I was on a routine scouting mission into the southern buffers when I heard one of our alarm bells to the west. Rushing over as quickly as I could, I found a supply crew led by Ty en route to Delivery. They all looked battered and ruffled, and Ty explained that they had just been attacked by a group of OpScis. They'd managed to fight them off but a gifted woman and her baby had been kidnapped in the confusion. Ty and I decided that we had to try and rescue them, so we left the other two escorts to take the rest on to Delivery as planned."

"Would the other party present, Ty-kun, wish to add any testimony concerning the kidnapping incident?"

"What's there to say?" said Ty. "We tussled. Some of 'em went down, some didn't. When the flakes had cleared, we were one short, plus a baby. A few must have snuck in behind when we were busy busting the others up. I was raring to go after them but they were too tough for me to handle alone, and if I took either of my escorts the supply crew would be vulnerable. So I rang the bell and Vertical came in no time."

"Are you happy with that?" Vertical asked Hippo and looked inquiringly around the circle.

Hippo nodded. "Yes. That level of detail is fine. Please continue."

"So after that, Ty and I went to the edge of the nearest OpSci outpost. We started asking around with the locals. All of them either hadn't heard anything or were playing dumb. Then Ty heard a woman scream just across the border and I ran there ahead of him."

"You violated our treaty?"

"They kidnapped a woman and a baby in *our* buffer zone. That was already a violation."

"Yes, but OpScis don't often see the logic of tit for tat. You do realize this could mean retaliation?"

"You know I couldn't just leave a woman to be taken by *them*."

"Well they could have called in reinforcements. Then they'd have taken you."

"If they could catch me. We were on the outer edge of their territory anyways, too far for the mountain patrols to even hear us."

"You took risks and it's not clear what the repercussions will be on our relationship. If the situation escalates, are you willing to take responsibility for your actions?"

Vertical nodded. "Yes, of course."

"Good. Please continue with your story."

Vertical nodded again. "So I climbed up several stories and found three OpScis at a feeding station with the kidnapped woman, Shari. She was kneeling on the ground a few meters from her baby, who'd been left to lie in the dust. The OpScis were surrounding this man. Two research assistants held him while their field priest was cutting him with a Viewing Knife—you can see the mark on his forehead." Vertical pointed at Amon, who unconsciously touched his stinging cut. He also felt the caked blood all down the side of his face and realized what a mess he must look like. "I guess they were trying to get a sample."

Tap-ta-tap-taptaptap . . . With his head upraised now, Amon saw that the boy made the sounds with subtle motions of his pen behind the upturned tablet. His tapping continued even as Hippo said, "You have something to add here, Books?"

"Yes," said Book. "This behavior is anomalous for the Opportunity Scientists. Bankliving bodies are thought to be highly prized within the religion due to their scarcity and trace content of what the Quantitative Priesthood terms 'the Web.' However, we possess no records of their members collecting eyebrow samples, and all reported ritual excisions were performed on corpses."

Part way through the man's speech, the tapping stopped, though the boy's motions continued unabated. From what Amon could tell, he appeared to be writing, though what or why he could not fathom.

"Well he's living enough," said Hippo, "but is he bankliving? Vertical?"

"He says no and personally I believe him. As you can see, he doesn't have the Elsewhere Gaze. He never called for drones, even after the OpScis started cutting him. He's also suffering from webloss. At first, we thought he might be crashnewb who got rejected from Er, but now we're not so sure."

"Why is that?"

"Earlier, when we put his finger into a machine, the alarm started to hum."

"So he's already had his supplies for the day?"

"No. The security system reacted straightaway, on our first try."

"So he's blacklisted?"

"Maybe. But the food never even came out, so he's not a hungry ghost. And if he's a crashnewb he would have had to get blacklisted much faster than you'd expect."

"Well, if you're right, this man presents a unique case. The Opportunity Scientists must have clued in to this when they decided to sample him."

A whole conversation was revolving around Amon as if he weren't present, and he had little idea what any of it was about. Who were these people and who were the OpScis? What sort of qualms did they have with each other and what did any of it have to do with him? He wished someone would explain what was happening and question him directly.

"The way they treated him probably had something to do with what he was wearing," said Vertical. From a ragged sack at her side, she dumped out Amon's rumpled clothes into a pile, picked out his jacket, unfolded it, held it open by the shoulders, and displayed it to the circle.

Hippo's eyes went wide and Amon saw some members exchange perplexed frowns.

"He claims to be a Liquidator and that would corroborate his story," said Hippo. "Is it authentic?"

"I wouldn't doubt it. It's nothing like Fleet fabric. The texture is different and it's thicker than anything they give us except in winter. But the sure sign is this." Vertical unrolled something from Amon's undershirt and held it up: his nerve duster. "We confiscated this after he fired on one of the OpScis."

The circle shifted restlessly, in apparent surprise.

"Does it work?"

"Does it ever," said Ty. "You should have heard the guy scream!"

"Well that is all very puzzling. He obviously isn't involved with the OpScis either. Not if he's willing to deliver that kind of punishment to one of them."

"He's definitely not," said Vertical. "His taking one of them out helped

Ty and I drive the others away. But I'm sad to say we had to let the baby go. Their researcher had his knife to her throat!"

Cringing and shaking of heads.

"Well at least you managed to bring Shari back safe and sound," said Hippo. "That is a blessing amidst tragedy for which we should be grateful. So what happened after the men left?"

"I told this man to leave but he insisted we tell him how to get here. He told us he was looking for you and said someone named Tamper sent him. With his terrible webloss, I could see he's totally useless. But when Ty explained that Tamper's a friend of the council, I thought he might have information. So I decided in the end to strip him and bring him here."

"He mentioned Tamper and you two a moment ago. That's why we decided to call you in. I suppose that's the package for me?" Hippo pointed to the narrow tip of the plastic roll poking from the clothes.

"Yes." Vertical picked it up and unrolled it. "There are five coded sheets here. Can you read these, Books?" Vertical reached out and handed the sheets to Book.

"Certainly," said Book after a quick glance. "These documents have been encrypted with a cypher that we employed frequently until this past spring. In fact, it was I who instructed Tamper in its use."

"Well that speaks as strong evidence that this letter originated with Tamper as this man claims," said Hippo. "What do the sheets say?"

"As I no longer have the cypher committed to memory, I will delegate this matter to Little Book."

Book handed the sheets to Hippo, who laid them on the floor between him and the boy holding the tablet, apparently called Little Book. Only now that Little Book paused to pick up the sheets did he stop his slight pen motions behind the tablet. After briefly scanning both sides of each sheet, Little Book placed them back on the floor and recommenced his writing, as Amon watched his pen move. Until then his writing had been silent, but now each stroke on the screen was harder than before and made a rhythmic tapping.

Reacting to the sound, Book said, "The five sheets consist of two letters drafted by Tamper, one four-and-a-half sheets long and one occupying a single side of one sheet. The shorter letter is addressed to Hippo and concerns the applicant. The letter of greater length is addressed to Xenocyst as a whole and contains content of an entirely personal nature."

"Can we hear what the shorter one says? It sounds like the longer one can wait."

Tap, tap tap tap taptap . . . "The letter reads, 'Hippo, Spotted Liquidator running out Yume Station. Looked miserable. Followed to alley where he sat, command-gestured and blacked out. Searched sleeping body and found nerve duster. Checked back twice but out cold for hours. Returned next day. Saw him stumbling down busy street in bad infowithdrawal. Watched him attempt breaking into vending machine with bare hands.'"

At this the whole circle laughed, but Little Book was undeterred in his tap-decoding of the letter and Book in his simultaneous interpreting of the taps.

"Decided to approach and he asked way to DoD. Agreed to guide in exchange for story. So moving I gave back duster and told him to find you, Tamper."

Now Amon saw how Tamper had found him and taken his duster. A weeping Liquidator charging out of a train station would have been hard to miss.

"Well I have no doubt that this is indeed a letter from Tamper," said Hippo. "It uses one of our cyphers as Book pointed out and that brusque style is unmistakable." Hippo paused for a moment to think, before addressing the circle. "This is a very powerful recommendation from a man I respect. As most of you know, Tamper did many good works for us here. While I would usually advise against wasting time with an unstable man, just think what we have here: a lone bankdead Liquidator with a working duster who suffers from webloss but cannot use vending machines. Don't tell me you're not curious!

"Therefore, I propose that we offer him a hearing. If he's able to speak, then I'm sure he'll provide *some* amount of useful information. If not, we can always eject him as planned and none of us are the worse for it."

"Do any councilors wish to make further contributions to the discussion, either for or against?" said Book. "Then let the voting commence. All in favor of granting the applicant a hearing?"

Amon looked around the circle with desperate terror as several hands went up. He counted four.

"All in favor of ejecting him immediately?"

Another set of hands rose, and Amon counted four again. One of the nine councilors had abstained, making it a tie.

"The tie-breaking decision is awarded to our presiding chair," Book announced, looking to Hippo. "What is your vote, chairman?"

"You've heard my opinion already. I vote to hear his story."

"The official pronouncement, then, is that this man will be heard."

Amon sighed with relief again, and returned his focus to his breathing, praying that his nerves would hold out.

"Is the applicant ready?" Book asked.

"Y-Yes."

"Then bring out the mirror."

PART 5
NAKED STORIES

8
XENOCYST

1

Sitting alone on a thin sheetless futon, Amon watched hazy afterimages of the day dance and dissolve into each other in the darkness that enveloped him. Thousands of passing faces crowding narrow alleys and stairs, dawn sunbeams imbuing the river with color, a cockroach blinking its blue eye, crumbling heap of towers leaning over the approaching shore, the fervent eyes of the field priest as he touched the blade to Amon's brow . . . His mind was too exhausted to sort this jumbled stream into chronological order or contribute any thoughts to it. All he could do was blankly observe its flowing, trying his best to stay upright and awake.

Ribs aching, forehead stinging, wrist sore, muscles spent, Amon was so worn out he needed all his willpower to resist the weight of his body. He would have already laid his head on the mattress some minutes ago if not for the fact that Vertical was supposed to be bringing him food. He had been reluctant to enter this dark, hot, musty elevator when she and Ty had brought him here (about half an hour ago by his estimate) and told him this was his room, but had instantly given in when she promised him a meal. Having eaten nothing since the riverbank with Tamper the night before, his stomach throbbed so urgently with hunger her deal had been irresistible.

He was not happy about being locked up in this tiny space, no better than a jail cell. He was not happy about anything that had happened to him that day. But he felt some small relief because he knew it could have been worse. At least there were walls and a roof to shelter him from the horror outside for now. After all his baffling experiences since waking up in the alley, what might happen tomorrow or any day after was not for Amon to even guess.

"Before you is a conventional mirror," Book had said at the council after one of the guards placed a small easel with a square mirror set on it in front of Amon. "Do you perceive your reflection?"

"Y-yes," said Amon, aghast at the sight of his own naked face for the first time. Though all his familiar features were there—buzzed hair, blue-green eyes with double-folded lids, longish nose, thin line of mustache—without digimake his light brown skin was pocked, his jaw slightly crooked, and his lips too small, not to mention the greasy sheen of sweat coating him, the nick in his left eyebrow and the blood caked down his cheek. In a brownish-gray T-shirt and shorts, he felt as though the mirror were reflecting the wrong person by mistake.

"What the council requests," said Book, "is that you stare into your own eyes while you speak. You are permitted to look away at any moment you wish. However, at such times you must desist from speaking immediately. Do you understand and consent to the requirements?"

"Yes. But what is this for?"

"This is the method by which the council ensures your statements are truthful. There are specific eye movement patterns that I have been taught to identify. Insofar as you refrain from telling a lie, it will be unnecessary for you to fear us."

This reassurance only made Amon more nervous. What were they going to ask him? Would he be able to answer truthfully?

"The hearing will now commence. Is the applicant ready?"

"Yes," said Amon, staring into his own eyes as instructed.

"According to the letter, Tamper first encountered you in the vicinity of Yume Station. By what means did you enter Tonan Ward?"

"I took the train." Amon wanted to look around the circle to see how people were reacting but kept his gaze trained on his eyes.

"Access to a train would require monetary payment, unless someone bankliving escorted you. By what means did you cross the river into Free Tokyo initially?"

"I didn't. I mean, I crossed here, to the District of Dreams, for the first time this morning."

"To clarify then, you were shipped to Free Tokyo from a bankdeath camp elsewhere. Is that your claim?"

"No. I've never been to a camp before."

"But you are not bankliving as we have already discussed."

"Right. I'm bankdead just like all of you. No bank account, no apps, no ImmaNet. Nothing . . ." Amon felt his voice cracking as though he might cry at the thought.

"I think we need to take this interview back slightly," said Hippo. "So, Kenzaki-kun I believe it was. How exactly did you end up meeting with Tamper, bankdead and dressed like a Liquidator?"

"It's a long story," said Amon, remembering the hours it had taken to tell Tamper.

"Well the council is very busy," said Hippo with a curious smile. "We have several other cases to work through yet. But since your case is rather complicated, it seems we have little choice but to hear you out."

"O-okay . . . so where do you want me to start?"

"One usually starts at the beginning."

Amon thought of Tamper, who had said something similar—perhaps he had even learned it here.

"Make sure to tell us everything important," Hippo continued. "Especially the parts you regret, as those are always the most instructive."

As Amon began his story, he felt gazes searing him from all directions, as though many magnifying glasses were concentrating awareness on the one spot where he sat, his own awareness through the mirror among them. He meant to tell the council more or less the same story he'd told Tamper, but after what Hippo had said about regret he found his remembering guided in unexpected directions, following currents of painful emotion to their source. The incidents he related seemed to play like videos inside the light on his pupils and the moments that brought him guilt appeared there most vividly. It was as though the sins appearing in his reflected eye were reflected back by his eye looking upon it, and this reflected reflection was in turn reflected back ad infinitum, so that segments of his past layered over each other endlessly until their reality thickened into an event that seemed to actually be happening at that moment. Like the time in the Ginza club when he bowed to Sekido's demands and cheated on Mayuko. Or the time in Shinbashi when he refused to give Rick advice for the sake of his savings. Then there was his assassination of Lawrence Barrow, his hanging up on Mayuko in her moment of grief over Rick's death, his agreeing to accompany her to a weekly mansion where she would ultimately be hacked and beaten . . . Deep in his own pupils, Amon saw those he had hurt grimacing miserably—Rick, Mayuko, his many bankrupt targets—and he would cringe. Occasionally the guilt was so intense that he would have to look away, stopping his tongue as he'd promised. While it had been hard enough admitting to such mistakes in front of Tamper alone, now a whole room of people was listening, analyzing, judging his every word.

Partway through, another bottle of soda was brought to him, and he would pause occasionally to sip from it and gather his thoughts. Since this was his second time telling the story, the words came more easily. His audience remained silent aside from the occasional question when he faltered, and he puzzled over their attitude. From their bright steady gazes, they seemed rapt with attention, but how could something so dull as a mere story without music or visuals of any kind hold the interest of an audience so completely?

All the while, Little Book kept moving his pen over his tablet, starting when Amon spoke and stopping soon after he paused. Amon could only guess that he was taking notes, a practice he had only ever seen in historitisements and that struck him as preposterously archaic.

When at last Amon was finished after however many hours, the council was silent for a while, apparently immersed in thought, until Hippo spoke. "Thank you, Kenzaki-kun," he said, using the formal "kun" a second time. Then to Amon's surprise, he turned to the council and said, "I propose we make an exception to our protocol and offer him a trial period."

There was another pause, but now the councilors were frowning and exchanging looks.

The first objection was raised by a man on the left side of the circle. He had a gray-streaked beard on an otherwise young, smooth-skinned face, and sunken, dark-ringed eyes, which seemed to gaze off over the heads of the assembly as he spoke. "Are you joking?" he said. "This infojunkie wreck?"

"He is suffering from webloss, that's undeniable," said Hippo, "but the speed at which he's been recovering is remarkable. Only a few days ago this man cash crashed. Without any Er treatment he's already managed to come this far. Only last week he was a full believer in the PR-opaganda of the Free World and yet now he seeks justice and recompense."

"A Liquidator seeking justice!" the man scoffed. "Think of all the innocent lives he's ruined."

"You saw the faces he made when he talked about his missions. We need someone like this, a man with substance."

"If we can believe anything he says," said Vertical.

"Well I for one don't see how he could have come up with something so incredible on the spot," said Hippo. "And everything he told us is independently backed up. The document is in Tamper's code and he was found with Liquidator gear. His eyes also confirm that he was telling the truth. Am I correct?" Hippo looked to Book.

Little Book tapped once on his tablet and Book nodded in confirmation.

The man with the gray-streaked beard opened his mouth to speak, but Hippo preempted him. "Before the discussion opens up any further, I should be honest and tell you all that there's also a personal reason I support his admittance into Xenocyst. You see, I feel him to be a kind of kindred spirit. Because, like me, he chose to cash crash of his own volition without going bankrupt. And like me, he's bankdead but still has his BodyBank beneath his skin."

Amon found these words profoundly puzzling. *How could Hippo have cash crashed without going bankrupt?* he wondered. *Had he too been an Identity Executioner who used the Death Codes to commit ID suicide? If so, why?*

"So taking into account the objections, I'd still like to propose that we offer him a standard trial period. Does anyone wish to respond?"

A discussion followed, with the bearded young man and a woman behind Amon arguing to have him excluded, reiterating and expanding upon the man's original points about his psychological and moral inadequacy. Though Ty remained silent, Vertical seemed all too eager to back them up with specific examples of his uselessness from earlier that day. When the debate settled, Book held another vote and this time it was five to four in favor of giving Amon a trial period without the need for Hippo to break the tie.

Nodding his head in acknowledgment of the result, Book turned to Amon. "The official pronouncement of the council is that you will be offered a standard trial period at Xenocyst. In other words, you will be granted approximately six weeks to complete our treatment regimen, stabilize your psychological condition, gain proficiency at the tasks we assign you, and demonstrate that you can make useful contributions to our community. During this period, or until you become capable of obtaining your own supplies, we will provide you with the minimum of clothes, food, and shelter. At the end of this period, or at the council's earliest convenience, your performance will be subject to a second review, at which time the council reserves the right to promptly eject you if for any reason they deem it necessary. Do you accept the offer under these conditions?"

Amon still had no idea who these people were, what tasks they would expect of him, or even where exactly he was; for all he knew, Xenocyst could have been this one room floating in a void. Nor could he say with confidence that his mind would get better in the allotted time, if ever. But he had been accepted, and people would be taking care of him, and with their help he might be safe . . . at least for the time being. He could see little other choice

"I accept," he whimpered, bowing his head to the floor with another sigh of relief that transitioned into full-body shaking, tears coming to his eyes.

Hippo had suggested Ty and Vertical be in charge of Amon because "you two neglected to escort him yourselves," and in spite of their protests the council had voted unanimously for this proposal. So they had been forced to lead Amon out of the council chamber and guide him through the building. With his cowl off, Amon saw the interior for the first time. Although the hallways were high and wide, a clutter of various medical items—forceps, syringes, boxes of diapers—was heaped along the walls, leaving only a narrow passage. Along this, staff in white, lino-leum-looking gowns bustled, some wheeling metal trays cluttered with scalpels, gauze, IV packs. Amon and his two escorts tread on the layer of dissolving wrappers and packaging that littered the patches of open floor. Its discolored tiles, from which carpeting seemed to have been uprooted, the holes in the ceiling every few paces for absent chandelier fixtures, and the empty portals where apartment doors must have once stood suggested to Amon that the building had once been a luxury condo. After turning down numerous hallways and climbing similar stairwells, they had arrived finally in front of the closed elevator doors, which Ty had immediately opened with a hand crank before Vertical had coaxed him in with, "Be a good little recruit and you might even get some food," in a patronizing tone usually reserved for children.

Creak, creak, creak. Amon awoke to the sound of the crank. He lifted his lolled head from his chest and wiped the drool from his lips, realizing he had nodded off as a blade of light slipped between the doors. Blinking in the sudden brightness, he watched the crack widen just enough for something round to fly into the elevator and strike the back wall.

Food!

Ravenously Amon fumbled the flattened thing from the floor with a quick "Thank you!" and heard more creaks as he tore off the plastic and the doors closed. Back in darkness, Amon bit into his splat rice ball and crunched on a pickled plum at the center—or something that vaguely tasted like one. The texture was more brittle than any *umeboshi* he'd had before. The rice too had an odd, melty softness to it. But that didn't stop him from gobbling it in two bites and wanting more when he was done. Already his memory of being able to have as much food as he wanted whenever he wanted seemed distant and removed, even though it had only been a few days since this was possible. It was as though having his first meal in the District of Dreams had changed something inside him, nailing him to this bizarre, incomprehensible place, as though the carbohydrates and sugars now nourishing his cells were messages that said he could never go back.

But if I can't return, I'll never see Mayuko again, I'll never resolve jubilee, I'll... In his exhaustion, Amon felt bereaved. So much of who he was—his friends, his job, his beliefs, his city—had been ruthlessly hacked away, amputated from his soul.

Yet the moment he lay his head down on the damp, spongy mattress in the dark enclosure, Amon left these thoughts and feelings behind for a time as he plummeted into a deep, dreamless sleep.

When Amon opened his eyes, the bulky shadow of a figure standing in the slat of light from the open door fell on him. It was Ty with his tricycle's front wheel rearing from his back, there to fetch him for his first trial day.

2

Xenocyst was an enclave within the District of Dreams that offered various services to bankdead, especially mothers, orphaned children, and infants. Unlike the venture charities, it was managed and operated by the bankdead who lived there. Each member of the Xenocyst Council was an elected representative of one of its nine districts, while Hippo served as an unelected special advisor. They were in charge of deciding who was granted membership, adjudicating disputes, and setting citywide policies. Beneath each councilor were various subcommittees that dealt with local issues and put council resolutions into practice.

At the center of the city was the battered condo in which the Council Chamber and Amon's elevator were located. It was known as the Cyst—a solid cell of glass and metal embedded in the midst of thousands of flaking shelters. The windows, all of which had remained miraculously in one piece over the decades, were milked over with filth, peeking out in grayish-white patches from the dissolving architectural mass that encased the building. With so many structures glommed around, Amon could never tell exactly how large the Cyst was, but it seemed to be nearly eighty stories tall and might have covered an entire block in Free Tokyo. In addition to serving as the central administrative base for the whole community, it also contained several service centers, each of which took up one of the lower floors: a nursery, an orphanage, a library, and a hospital, with obstetrics, pediatric, gynecological, and emergency wards. Radiating from the Cyst in uneven patches were the nine districts. These were built of what everyone called "disposable skyscrapers," or just "disposcrapers" for short, all connected together into a dense, continuous reef of city with just enough spaces left between them to form a complex warren of channels and fissures that allowed passage.

Amon's job on his first day was to help with construction. Ty took him up many flights of stairs to the roof of the Cyst, a flat concrete square extending approximately half a kilometer in each direction. There they joined a construction crew of about twelve residents and greeted a landing supply centicopter, the hundred tiny rotors on its pale plastic body whining and whirling against a bluish inky blanket of clouds in the pre-dawn glow. Under Ty's instruction, Amon helped unload the crates before lifting one to his shoulder and descending to one of the Cyst's exits, from which he lugged it to a much lower rooftop an hour's journey away.

Inside the crates—Amon discovered after the crew had all unpacked— were roombuds. These were about the size of an adult's head but shaped like bullets, flat on the bottom and tapering up to a small, dull tip. With a sack-full slung over his back, Amon climbed almost a hundred half-stories and walked hundreds of meters across narrow ledges to a particular spot Ty had indicated. He had warned Amon repeatedly not to drop the roombud and on his first installation Amon immediately understood why, for the moment one touched the surface of a room it bonded there and immediately began to swell. Once the bud reached about twice its original size, it would burst open in various locations as hundreds of structures folded outwards like origami flowers. The roombud cylinders were all black on the outside, but flowers with petals of various colors emerged and the shell of the bud flattened out and disappeared beneath them as they expanded and joined, weaving themselves together into flat surfaces that formed the cuboid shape of a room. Though the pattern and imitated material of the façades varied from room to room—wood, marble, polka-dot—depending on the color of the petals, they always felt soft to the touch irrespective of how they looked, and lost the illusion of texture up close, appearing to be made from some sort of tightly latticed crystal fibers.

Ty explained that roombuds were 3D-printed starters for self-assembling rooms. Originally designed as relief shelters for refugees, they were now provided individually to each bankdead by the venture charities or, as was the case that morning, flown in by special arrangement to select enclaves. Once triggered by touching another room, the fuel cells inside began to pop, the fuel mixed with oxygen, and a chemical reaction was initiated. This sent the nanobots that composed it configuring into larger nanobots that configured into larger nanobots, eventually realizing a formation that accorded with their instructions. Though individual roombuds were relatively light, Amon had to scale massive towers in the hot, muggy air carrying a dozen at a time, his body still aching from the strain and punishment of the previous day. Once these were installed, he would return to restock before immediately heading off to a new location. The work was exhausting and, due to the short lifespan of the rooms, had to be constantly repeated, the disposcrapers they formed constantly rebuilt. Made out of Fleet as Amon had guessed, the rooms remained in "full bloom" only until their pre-programmed expiration date, which varied from a few days to a few weeks. At this point they would begin to dissolve petal by petal, at first slowly but with the rate of dissolution increasing daily until they imploded under the weight of other rooms and the building collapsed. It was the job of demolition crews Amon saw here and there to bash apart such precarious structures before they posed a safety risk, and Ty told him that he would soon assist them.

At around noon, the construction crew headed off to the nearest feeding station, a concrete square either on a condo rooftop or the ground level of the island that had food and drink machines often called feeders. There the crew lined up, though Amon was told he couldn't access feeders because he hadn't yet registered at a place called Delivery, where the venture charities were all concentrated. Still suffering from webloss, he wasn't deemed psychologically prepared to make the journey. In the meantime, Ty provided him with rice balls and sports drinks, which he said came from a common pool of bonus supplies Xenocyst received.

Amon devoured these eagerly and found them surprisingly filling for their size, though not quite enough after days with little to eat.

After lunch, Ty sent a guard to take Amon to the library for an interview with Book and Little Book. The library was a large room on the fourteenth floor of the Cyst, identical in dimensions to the council chamber but filled with shelves built from various scrounged up pieces of wood, metal, and plastic. The books and documents on the shelves were likewise of varied material, with an assortment of paper books, uncurled tin cans, concrete slabs, and plastic sheets like the one used by Tamper. Amon was brought to a round space at the center of the room where many shelves ended and the aisles radiated out in all directions. There stood a square table and four chairs of different sizes and designs. Amon was given the swivel office chair with wheels that appeared to be broken, Book settled in a holey armchair across from him, and Little Book took a plastic lawn chair. The guard left the folding metal chair empty, leaning instead on one of the shelf ends, paddle in hand.

Even though Amon had already told his story to the council, they apparently had many more questions and he soon found himself answering them for hours on end. Book asked him about all sorts of topics, from the personal (what he'd eaten growing up in the BioPen, how many people worked in his office) to the political (what the names of recent GATA ministers were, what policies affecting the bankdeath camps had been enacted) to the economic (what the values of certain currencies were, when the market crashes tended to happen) to the latest fashion trends and idols. Sometimes his questions seemed too obvious to take seriously (where GATA Tower was located, what the capital of Japan was, what fifteen times twenty-two was), and Book repeated them so many times that Amon began to question the man's memory, though he had little right to complain as he was having memory issues of his own. Often he was slow to answer, the faint threads he followed breaking again and again under his inner gaze, connecting to nothing. At the end of their frayed vagueness, he would sometimes find another thread, but this too snipped apart, his past forever like a word on the tip of his tongue, close and abiding but invisible and irretrievable.

Book was persistent with his questions, humming them out in his nasally bass, and Amon answered as best he could. The whole time

Book stared at him through broken glasses—one eye planetary in its magnification, the other small and pale—while Little Book looked up at him from the tablet now and then, both man and boy considering him with careful, clinical interest. Little Book took notes constantly, but only occasionally did he tap out a message with the strokes of his pen, prompting Book to follow certain lines of inquiry with Amon and supplementing him with facts. Amon marveled at how the boy was able to express two meanings with a single motion of his hand, the strokes on the screen recording the conversation around him and the taps initiating a separate conversation with Book, though as he never uttered a word Amon began to suspect he was mute.

Various people would come over periodically to browse the nearby shelves. It reminded Amon of the bookstores in Jinbocho and the manga library in the Tezuka, and again he thought sadly of the life he had lost. He was surprised to find the titles indecipherable. The spines of some of the books were close enough that he could make them out, yet the lines that formed the script seemed to scramble and blur together.

"What language is this?" Amon asked during a lull in the interview, as he squinted at the strange runes arrayed down the lanes about him. He had noticed them on his way into the center of the stacks and wondered now if Hinkongo had its own script.

"It is Japanese," said Book. *Tap-tapatapatap, tap-tap.* . . "We infer that you are experiencing perceptual processing difficulties as a result of your affliction with cogwither."

"Cogwither?"

Taptap, taptap, taptaptap . . . "Cognitive atrophy. If you wish to re-acquire your former reading capacity, habituation is the only effective strategy. For this reason, making an effort is highly recommended. This will, moreover, ameliorate the symptoms of your infoyearn and crowdcrave."

Amon nodded, though he had no intention of following Book's (and Little Book's) advice. While it was disturbing to find his vision still wonky, if getting better meant doing something as boring and pointless as reading he was almost willing to accept it. The measly amount of information that could be contained on each sheet of plastic, tin, paper, or whatever hardly seemed worth the effort to take down. Scribbling on a tablet was slightly more efficient perhaps, since at least everything would be saved in one place, but it still seemed like a painstaking way to record someone's voice, and the playback method—reading—seemed immeasurably inferior without the option of audio speech.

"What are you writing?" Amon asked Little Book eventually.

Taptap, tap, taptaptap, ta-tap . . . "We are summarizing the key points in your answers," Book interpreted.

"What for?"

Ta-taptap, tap, tap-ta-tap . . . "To produce a record of events occurring in the Free World and compile a report for the council."

"Why rely on me? Are there no better ways to learn what's going on outside?"

Taptaptap, taptaptap, taptaptap, tap . . . "It is a rare chance for us to query a relatively verbally comprehensible crashnewb, especially one such as yourself who was employed at GATA, as a Liquidator no less."

Amon wondered why they would go to the trouble of isolating the "key points" of his speech rather than copying it verbatim. By allowing this boy to decide how to distill Amon's message instead of producing as exact a representation as possible, individual bias was being introduced into the record. And why would they place their confidence in Amon, who depended on no more trustworthy a source than his own fickle memory?

Being subjected to this absurd method of information transfer irritated Amon. He just wanted to send segments of his LifeStream or links to appropriate websites and be done with it. As the interview went on, Book's odd voice and Little Book's occasional tapping grew increasingly annoying. The stickiness of his skin from the close, dusty summer air only made it worse. After about two hours, the silence, the simplicity of the room, was just too much for Amon to handle. His breathing quickened, his head began to ache, and jolts of stress tremored from the base of his spine to the tips of his fingers. He did his best to ignore these sensations and comply with the interview, but was inevitably overwhelmed. He tripped on his tongue, blanked on words, scrambled his grammar, slurred incoherently, rambled, and flew on tangents only to realize that he'd forgotten the question. Soon his desire for apps, for indirect connection, for promotainment, for a measure of the value of his actions became so strong that his hands jittered and tears came to his eyes.

When Amon's concentration completely broke down, the Books dismissed him and the guard took him down to his elevator. He had been saved by exhaustion on his first night there and fallen straight to sleep after waiting for only half an hour. But this time it was still mid-afternoon, leaving more than twelve hours of captivity before his construction workday began, and he found himself lying on the damp futon with his eyes wide open for hours.

The chamber was utterly dark and quiet. In the stagnant, moist heat his body felt as though it were evaporating and circulating back to be absorbed by his skin, a cycle of melting and regeneration, like the ever-dissolving slum. Surely there was a ventilation crack or hole somewhere—otherwise he would have suffocated last night—but the only stirring in the air was his own breath. This darkness was different than the partial darkness when he'd been cowled and the darkness that was not darkness when he'd been blind. It was more like the darkness when the wall-less elevator had plunged him into the PhisherKing's domain, deep within the bowels of Tokyo, and suddenly Monju was there with him.

Something tells me your search is leading you to our rejuvenation, he had said, gazing at Amon with his multicolored eyes as he floated on the mercury sea in the hard light of the metallic sky. *Can you swear to keep asking questions until no doubts remain in your mind?*

Of course, Amon replied. *I don't know if it will lead me to understanding jubilee or Rick's death or the meddling at GATA, but I'll do my best to learn about this place and . . .*

Amon shut his mouth, realizing that he was talking to himself. As time passed, it was becoming harder and harder to distinguish the black space around him from the spaceless arena of his mind's eye. As he lay shaking and groaning with intense boredom, the muddy depths of his consciousness were astir, lumps of sunken memory whirling up into the dim waters of his awareness. Long forgotten memories, like the time he and Rick and Mayuko had invented a coded language to secretly mock their SubMom. Momentous memories, like his first day of work at the Liquidation Ministry. Embarrassing memories, like when he'd mistaken a minister's title at a GATA function. Images and sounds began to emanate from his surround too—pet koala ice sculptures, soap opera aromatherapy brawls, a jumble of conversations and soundtracks—like several TVs flicking out of synch from one channel to the next, the advertainment that had made up such a large portion of his life refusing to go down without a fight.

It was as though the darkness had become the mirror but shattered, the narrative pieces of his life scattered into no particular order. Except some fragments resurfaced more often than others—the moments he regretted—as though his guilt had been summoned by the exercise Hippo had made him undertake. Instead of staying to be rewound and skipped and fast-forwarded and edited as he pleased, they came and went as they pleased—butterflies escaped from their pins to flit through a storm-filled sky. It was terrifying to watch his own mind slip from his control or witness for the first time that it had always been thus, while his mistakes revolved back to torment him, riding on the tumult he had unleashed.

Sometimes he found himself weeping, other times laughing, whimpering, clenching his fists and jaw. Rolling on the mattress, off the mattress, flailing his limbs against the walls, curling up in the corner, cycling through every emotion and concoction of emotion for which there was no name, sweating in the stuffy, dank air. He chattered to himself, chastised himself, recited slogans and poetisements, sang jingles that got stuck in his head. Although he hated the council for locking him in here, he could understand why crashnewbs would be isolated like this, as part of him revolted at the collapse of his rationality, while another much deeper part was delighting in this purge. Caught in a momentary delusion born of habit, he searched for the settings of his brain to turn off repeat, but it just kept on rolling.

When Vertical finally stood there in the slat of light, Amon had never felt so grateful for the arrival of morning, for the start of a new day.

Amon was awoken each day by either Ty or Vertical and escorted to a different area of Xenocyst for his construction duties. Although he saw no rhyme or reason to the placement of the rooms at first and simply followed orders, after several days he began to grasp how his efforts shaped the city. The Xenocyst council did everything it could to prevent the short-lived nature of the buildings from engendering the tumbledown chaos seen everywhere else. In areas where each bankdead laid their room to suit their individual needs, there were constant battles over location, with everyone wanting enough elevation to get sunlight, proximity to the ground floor feeding stations, distance from paths prowled by gangs, and so on. With no possibility for compromise, they all fought to set up in the best spot they could, and the end result was convoluted, spiraling pathways, dead ends, darkness, overcrowding, and structural instability everywhere. To maintain an orderly cityscape that avoided these problems, the council had established a complex urban planning system, though its implementation took a large amount of manpower and fine-tuning for localities absorbed much of the subcommittees' time.

While the population of Xenocyst was just as dense as elsewhere—its shelters able to house just as many people—careful planning had ensured wider pathways to facilitate foot traffic, straight-standing, evenly spaced buildings to maximize and equally distribute available space, better ventilation to reduce overheating and mold, isolation of sewers and sky-charnels to reduce smell and vermin, installation of disposcraper-to-condo suspension wires to mitigate the destabilizing influence of fractured or liquefying ground . . .

Since there was no way to tell what material would emerge from each black roombud, the skyscraper shafts were composed of as motley and incongruous an assortment of rooms as elsewhere. But buds picked up from the venture charities on the same day were stored together so they could be matched by expiration date. This ensured that each shaft dissolved at relatively the same time, preventing them from toppling due to premature room dissolution and allowing for rolling replacement.

On the fifth day, Amon was assigned to demolition. His crew was given picks and sledgehammers to smash apart buildings in which perforations had begun to peek through. The walls were almost crusty at this stage, and they beat them until all that remained was a pile of rapidly flaking rubble, which a cleanup crew hauled away in plastic sheets.

A construction crew then moved in to install fresh rooms in the empty spot, yet the new structures they put up were never the same ones as before. They would always have a different number of stories, relocated and realigned alleys, or would branch off into other buildings at a different height. This arrangement was intentional as well. One of the main reasons was to introduce an element of unpredictability so that—even though the thoroughfares, both elevated and grounded, were less meandering and the stairpaths had fewer interruptions than elsewhere—trespassers such as the Opportunity Scientists would get lost. Xenocyst was an ever-changing three-dimensional maze, a single intricate structure, the layout of which was altered periodically and systematically as part of the rebuilding process. Only residents knew the ways from one point to the next, and usually only along their own customary routes as they adjusted to the incremental alterations.

After Amon had completed his morning duties, Ty or Vertical would take him to a feeding station and give him a meal—if a single rice ball, sandwich, or mini-bento was enough to count. Although he never exactly felt satisfied, he was never quite hungry either. The feeders, he soon learned, were 3D printers that used meal-replacement therapy ink. Whether reconstituted and shaped into grains of rice, fish tubes, broccoli, or whatever, they were supposed to provide all the necessary nutrients for a healthy diet. Like the *umeboshi* rice ball he'd had on his first night, the texture was frequently off, with meat being too crunchy and the rice and bread being crumbly or crispy. In some cases there were even flavor simulation mixups, where what looked like egg salad might for example taste like kimchi, or cod roe like sweet chestnut. While such culinary surprises were disturbing and oftentimes disgusting, Amon had always eaten the cheapest vending fare in Free Tokyo and got used to it quickly.

The strangest part for him was the food wrappers. Every morsel came out wrapped in what looked like clear plastic, though really both were made of exactly the same ingredients synthesized through a different method. The printer just painted on layer after layer of the nutritional ink until a single unit of meal-inside-wrapping was produced, which meant that all packaging was technically edible and just as nutritious as what it packaged. Amon was grossed out by the idea of putting garbage in his mouth, but since he was always left wanting a bit more, he quickly followed the lead of his fellow bankdead and began to eat the plastic bowl for pastas, the transparent shell for rice balls, sandwiches, and burritos, the wood-like snap-apart chopsticks. The bottles for the beverages, on the other hand, were made of Fleet, and he tossed those into the designated heaps, which never seemed to change in size as the bottom layer flaked away and vanished as fast as the top was replaced.

Once lunch was finished, a guard took him to the library for more questions. After his second night, he fought with all his will to stay focused on the interview, afraid of being returned to the elevator. Anything but being shut away in that awful chamber, locked up with himself, with all that he had done. Inevitably his concentration would fail him and the guard would take him there, but he was able to remain articulate for a little bit longer each day. With all his work done, he always craved a shower, and had to content himself with a few squirts of PeelKlean soap (which—along with the disposable clothes and shelters that made laundering and cleaning superfluous, and the beverages that provided all hydration—was supposed to take care of all individual water needs).

Then, alone in the dark, he stopped thrashing about and crying and laughing as the visions gradually subsided. He wasn't sure if he ever slept, but he managed to remain on the futon, his attention on his breathing as he rolled restlessly from side to side, trying to imagine the forest that refused to visit him anymore, his nights forsaken by dream.

4

This routine went on unchanging for weeks. Ty or Vertical in the slat of light, the endless stairs, the unfolding flowers, the collapsing towers, the summer humidity, the questions, the darkness. All the while, Amon was expecting to fail his trial period and be tossed out into the chaos at any moment, as his performance was terrible compared to the other workers'.

Vertical and Ty, despite their distinct teaching styles, both displayed their impatience with Amon and seemed resentful that he was keeping them from their main duties. Ty was a supply crew leader, in charge of guiding Xenocyst denizens safely to Delivery where they could restock, while Vertical was a scout, roaming the camps to gather information about the movements of the Opportunity Scientists, Charity Brigade, nosties, and other groups of concern. Whereas Ty barked out quick orders in the fewest words possible, and then shouted at Amon when he misunderstood what was expected, Vertical gave detailed instructions for the smallest tasks and snapped at him if he varied from them even slightly or if something went wrong in spite of his perfect obedience. He had been doing his best to follow along without complaint, but he was clumsy and acquired the knack slowly—sometimes dropping his buds, installing them at the wrong angle, or accidentally denting walls not slated for demolition—as he found learning without step-by-step videtutorials challenging and unfamiliar.

When he had learned to hit a baseball in the BioPen, for instance, a voice had said "grip the bat on the bottom with your right hand" while a blinking hand had gripped it in demonstration, then "lift the bat" with an arrow pointing upwards and so on. The tutorials awarded points for speed and accuracy and repeated themselves until students could perform the task proficiently. But even Vertical, in spite of her efforts to micromanage every operation, only gave vague instructions like "hammer the wall" or "roll the cart," leaving the minutiae of motor movements, like how to hold the hammer and how hard to push on the cart handle, up to Amon to figure out for himself. To crashborn residents like his co-workers, these simple procedures were common sense and they had trouble understanding how Amon could possibly be struggling to pick them up. In moments of pity, the kinder ones would come to his side and try to show him by example, but with the language barrier between them their explanations always degenerated into gestures, and when these failed, they would walk away, often sighing or shaking their head.

Supposedly, standard Japanese was the official language of Xenocyst, to make it more difficult for hostile outsiders (like Opportunity Scientist grunts) to understand them, and to train residents for communication with the bankliving, including the venture charities with whom they had to negotiate for supplies. But aside from the councilors, Book, Vertical, Ty, and Hippo, Amon had never heard anyone actually speak it, as the vast majority of residents were crashborn, and almost everyone used the camp dialect in practice. Despite sharing its grammar and many of its words with the standard dialect Amon knew, the pronunciation of Hinkongo was radically different and his ears could still only catch about half of what was said after several weeks surrounded by it 24/7. Though learning a new language wasn't a totally alien process to Amon, as he'd studied a bit of English and Persian in his BioPen schooling, he had always relied on apps like InterrPet, which assisted comprehension through real-time translation, and VentriloQuick, which made culturally accurate suggestions for what to say in a given moment. The fact that most people could understand at least a bit of standard Japanese removed the necessity to try expressing himself without it, making it even harder to improve. So not only was he incompetent at work and showing little promise of improvement, he was unable to comprehend directions or communicate with his crew. This made Amon increasingly nervous and afraid, and he felt a twinge of self-loathing every time he made a mistake, always expecting that the next one would be his last, his feelings only further impeding his performance.

A break in his routine finally came one afternoon in the library, when Little Book's hand drew still on his tablet and Book sat there silent for longer than ever before. Amon had been sensing something changing in the interview for several days, as the two seemed to be struggling to find questions for him. He had taken this as a sign that they were on the verge of wringing out the last of his useful information and discarding him. So when Book said, "Our interviews have now reached completion," Amon felt his whole gut tense and looked around in confusion, as he could not find the guard waiting by the shelf-end to escort him to the elevator.

"There's nothing else you want to ask me?" In the beginning, the questions had been agonizing and Amon had wanted them over as quickly as possible. Now he wished that he could draw them out and extend his time in the safety of Xenocyst even the slightest bit longer.

"I repeat," said Book, "our interviews have now reached completion."

"So when's the guard coming?"

"Never at all. I have advised the council that your webloss recovery has progressed sufficiently for you to be released from supervision and they have granted me their approval."

"So I can stay in the elevator? You're not sending me out there?" Amon pointed to his right, unsure which direction led out of Xenocyst.

"Although your trial period is still in process, in our opinion, your confinement to the elevator is no longer necessary."

"So what do I do now? Where am I supposed to go?"

"Starting today, your movements will no longer be hindered within the Xenocyst compound once your daily duties are complete."

When the implications of this finally percolated through to Amon's mind, his entire body sighed with relief and he bowed his head low in gratitude. "Thank you."

Stepping into the hall outside the library, Amon made his way without thinking to the elevator. For the first time since his hearing, he could choose for himself how to spend his time and, as he was unable to think of any other options, habit immediately seized control. But when he stood before the doors half-opened on the dim vault with his moist futon and felt the musty air on his face, he paused for only a moment, before turning on his heel and walking back down the cluttered hall to the stairwell, remembering it was the last place in Xenocyst he wanted to be.

He wandered the Cyst for a while, climbing past the urban planning room and the council chamber, until he reached the rows of guards outside the storeroom and was turned back when they discovered he lacked the password. From there he went to the lower floors, felt like a nuisance for getting in the way of the medical staff hurrying through the halls on various errands, and finally decided to head outside through an exit on the third floor often used by his construction crew.

Apparently Amon had been much more deeply absorbed in the interview than he realized, because when he stepped out onto a raised alley the sun had just set. He had never been outside in the camps so late before, and he watched mesmerized as the faint twilight creeping down through rooftop cracks faded and artificial lights blinked on one by one at various elevations above. Clearly these were the crumbling cookies he'd seen the night he sat with Tamper on the shore of the Sanzu River. The dim circles they cast dappled the dark labyrinth that subsumed him, from the looming toy-block canopy to the alley he stood upon, some hanging from stairs just beyond his reach. Up close they looked like paper lanterns containing an undulating sphere of pure glow.

Once night had fully taken hold and the lights stopped coming on, Amon snapped out of his trance, realizing he was blocking the narrow thoroughfare, and proceeded ahead with the crowd. When a bend in the alley approached, he feared he might lose sight of the Cyst—the only landmark he knew—and so began to make his way around its perimeter. Spiraling up the stairs and ramp-like angled rooftops, winding along the various squeezeways and tunnels, Amon circled it several times. How many hours this took he could not say, but as the night progressed he watched the lanterns begin to dissolve from the inside out. Fragments of their core fluttered out through the hole in the bottom, like falling fireflies that winked out after only a second. These had to be fireflLytes, another kind of disposable supply provided by the venture charities that Vertical had said he would help to install in the near future. Sparkles showered down and vanished just above his head as he passed through one bubble of illumination after another on his meandering course, gazing at the steady stream of shadow figures and petals that emerged from darkness into other such bubbles all around and then melted into darkness again. Taking deep breaths and basking in the sense of liberation that graced him, Amon thought of what he might do tomorrow when the day was done.

5

Finding little else to do with his time, Amon took to exploring outside after work. Although he traveled the same counterclockwise course around the Cyst for the first few nights, he began to gradually widen the circumference of his circle, moving ever further from the only place he knew. It wasn't until a full week had passed that he rallied enough courage to let it slip completely from view behind the layers of other structures. He then gave up on circles altogether and began to strike out in a particular direction, only turning back when the journey felt too far for comfort and his anxiety became unbearable. When he did inevitably get lost, he would follow the current of foot traffic that flowed constantly to and away from the Cyst until he could he see it again, or, if that failed, find a passerby to tell him the way in a pidgin of words and gestures.

He'd never had to build a map of an area in his head before and found the process maddeningly slow, especially since it needed to be updated constantly as the city changed day to day. Being bounded by his body and the limitations of his senses was frustrating. The walls of the shifting labyrinth were not supposed to be opaque but transparent, his perception floating about unfettered by barriers of any kind. But learning this new skill was also rewarding in some ways. His understanding of each space, he found, was not merely visual but visceral as well—his memory of where to turn on a roofway or how far to climb a specific stairpath imprinted in his nerves—and he felt a slight flutter of excitement whenever he sensed intuitively which way he ought to go.

Occasionally he spotted Vertical and Ty on their leisure hours. Ty could sometimes be found on a particular enclosed rooftop designated for guard training, usually around dusk. There, he would be engaged in target practice, tossing up several chunks of rubble at once, hurling a wheel, and altering its trajectory with the wires to hit them out of the air one after the other.

Amon only ever saw Vertical in motion, a blur appearing suddenly from some hole in the slumscape and then tearing through it at unbelievable speeds. She sprinted straight along alleys and squeezeways, leapt hand over foot up the outside of stairpaths and along the surface of slanting roofs, dodging around bodies, springing off walls, bounding over the heads of crowds.

Whereas Amon had thought of his after-work hikes at first as an effort to get oriented and grasp his surround, they soon turned into wandering for its own sake. When he remained still, he felt the burn of webloss and was reminded of all the apps he craved. Without PennyPinch, Teleport Surprise, MyMedic, AutoBarter, Career Calibration, Distinction, and all the other digital crutches he'd depended on since childhood, he had been deprived of something that seemed fundamental, and wondered if his mind would remain impaired forever, like a broken bone healed crooked. The boredom was particularly painful. It made it difficult for him to remember new events, every dull unadorned moment blurring indistinguishably into the next. But on the move, the unending trove of immersive relations he could enter into with walls and stairs and roofs and people soothed his heart and soul, helping him forget his lingering debilitations and escape from the visual and auditory disturbances that still plagued him from time to time. The possible combinations in which the buildings could be constructed and laid out was infinite, the routes he traveled all replaced as soon as he came to know them, so that his attention was constantly engaged with finding his way, each step a discovery.

At the same time, Amon felt lonely in a way he had never before experienced. Due to his lack of fluency in the local dialect, he was excluded from conversation, a pastime the residents seemed to enjoy more than any other. Everywhere he looked people were walking and talking, sitting and talking, eating and talking, their voices punctuated with the *rakhaw* of crows from high above. Nowhere could he escape the sound of constant chatter. Not even the elevator provided insulation now that the doors remained half open, allowing in echoing voices that came steadily down the halls. And yet Amon was never included in what he heard. His crew clustered away from him at lunch and during breaks, avoiding all communication inessential to the job at hand. And, on the days they finished early, loitered about blathering in the heat before sauntering off somewhere together without inviting him. None of the people whose faces he remembered from his daily routes greeted him, though he saw them greeting each other. Only the bone-chillingly creepy roaches that blinked their eyes at him—some blue, some brown, some hazel—seemed to pay him any mind, and so days went by where he spoke to almost no one.

Not that Amon desperately wanted to speak with anyone face to face. It wasn't just that looking at them without digimake made him uncomfortable or that it still felt like a waste of money. It was bizarre to have someone stand in front of you, their voice reaching your eardrum directly through the air, their breath on your face, their body close enough to touch, rather than communicate at a distance by voice, video, or badly spelled text. If conveying his thoughts was going to require such crude intimacy, he preferred to keep them to himself and maintain his solitude in the crowd.

The other Xenocyst pastimes Amon witnessed during his wanderings were no easier for him to grasp or appreciate. He saw children play catch with shards of rubble from collapsed disposcrapers and fly kites made from strips of clear bottles and dissolving rags; saw them scamper after each other up stairpaths, leap across rooftops, and slide down angled alleys; saw them play hide and seek in buildings slated for demolition and wrestle with each other in the holes, as though the whole slumscape was one massive jungle gym. Their games of make believe were so unlike the ImmaGames he had grown up with, staged as they had been in elaborate digital domains that were fully immersive without requiring any imagination, and he wondered about their sanity, spending so much effort to conjure the vague unconvincing realities of the mind's eye for the sake of mere entertainment.

Adult pursuits often took the form of massive communal undertakings without any clear purpose outside the undertaking itself. They carved intricate reliefs into the Fleet walls of abandoned, crumbling towers; cut out sequential images and speech bubbles in the rooms of lined-up buildings to make gigantic architectural comics; converted vast complexes into jack-o'-lanterns by smashing patterns into the walls and installing firefLytes inside; huddled in wavering cookie-crumble shadows, tossing bottles at a wall to gamble with their food; sang strange songs while beatboxing, rapping, whistling, clapping, banging out rhythms on their laps. It was all so strange and unnerving. Some of the art and music was familiar from stock clips or soundtracks for infopromo he had seen. The bankdead were, after all, incapable of owning rights to what they created or to anything else for that matter, and Amon had heard of "art scouts" who slipped inconspicuously into the District of Dreams in search of the next "folk entertainment" hit. But marketers knew well what "samples" of the "content" would suit the taste of Free Citizens, and lacking their editing, placement, and sleek design, he found the works here too crude for media consumption. He couldn't understand why the residents wasted so much effort when it was all going to vanish without selling anything, their songs fading unrecorded, their etchings dissolving unauctioned, and the overall effect was to leave him feeling more lonesome than ever.

Being alone was of course nothing new for Amon. As part of his cost-cutting, he'd forced himself into solitude for long stretches of time and had grown accustomed to it. But here, his isolation felt different somehow, more complete. Even after drifting away from Rick and Mayuko, he'd at least talked with his co-workers, like Freg and Tororo, and his supervisors, like Sekido and the other ministers. He keenly missed apps like FacePhone and Instant Get, which had provided the option to contact anyone instantly, even if he'd rarely invested in using them. Without his realizing it, the potential virtual companionship that had always existed in the background—his friends, colleagues, Decision Network, paid conversationalists, date seekers, online therapists—seemed to have endowed him with a low-level sense of belonging whether or not he ever actualized it. And whereas before isolation had been a choice, willingly imposed for the sake of his savings, here he was excluded from social activities irrespective of his wishes, which somehow made the loneliness worse, watching the bankdead of Xenocyst from the outside, aware at the same time that he was one of them.

It was difficult for him to accept this, for he wasn't just one of them. He was the worst of them, unable to succeed at the simplest of tasks. He was glad to have graduated from the interviews and took it as a positive sign for his trial period that they continued to let him work. But he had once been a promising Liquidator—no, Identity Executioner—and believed he had a shot at working with the Executive Committee, the highest governmental organization in Japan. He was aware now that the inspiration he'd derived from his career had been based on denial, on lies he'd voluntarily accepted about his life and who he was—that Liquidation was a service to society, that the AT market was beneficial for everyone, that the bankdeath camps were the best of all possible slums—but that didn't change how inadequate he felt. Reflecting on what he'd been and where he was now while strolling circuitous routes or lying in the dark of the elevator after a long, hard, bewildering day choked him with shame, his former pride transmuted to its opposite in this land of bankdeath.

Nothing seemed to bespeak his change of fortune more vividly than his clothes. The disposable shorts and T-shirt he'd worn since the day Vertical forced him to strip had become dirtier and dirtier until they had started to disintegrate and Ty had provided him with a replacement. These too had begun to flake away, a few specks flying off with every breeze that touched him, and he found himself missing his uniform. It was the only outfit he'd worn in the past seven years, as he'd been too cheap to buy garments other than underwear and socks, and he knew it was presumptuous to expect enduring materials when everyone else made do with transient cloth, but wearing it had always made him feel like a somebody.

At the same time, he was glad to have an outfit that allowed him to blend in. With his former muscle thinning out from reduced calories, his skin losing its color from lack of light, his buzzed hair growing in, and a beard taking shape, he was rapidly beginning to look like the bona fide bankdead non-citizen that he was. His ignorance of the customs and language still set him apart if anyone spent a few minutes with him, but at least they could no longer identify him as crashborn at a glance and being able to meld into a crowd was comforting. In fact, he wished he could be more completely indistinguishable from the rest and craved for the seamless anonymity of a digiguise. Partly he wanted to have the total privacy in public he had once enjoyed while concealing what he perceived as his own ugliness. But he was also hounded by a faint fear that one of the bankrupts he had cash crashed might recognize him and wanted a surefire way to hide.

It was an irrational fear, he knew. Crashdead were few and far between in the camps, and screenings ensured they were even fewer in Xenocyst, so the chances he'd bump into someone that he'd personally taken out were incredibly slim. Even if he did, his targets would have only seen him for a split second before he crashed them, so they were unlikely to remember his face, which was slightly different than his face now due to digimake enhancement in any case. Still, as improbable as such an encounter was, being an ill-adjusted crashnewb, he was highly vulnerable and couldn't escape the anxiety that someone might one day wreak retribution.

6

Amon's confidence with navigation improved gradually and his curiosity overcame his fear of getting lost, driving him ever greater distances from the Cyst. Until one evening, just before twilight, he found himself approaching the furthest limit that he was allowed to travel as a non-resident: the Xenocyst border.

He first began to realize that he had strayed from familiar territory when he noticed a change in the types of buildings. Instead of motley shafts made of various faux materials, rooms here were stacked with those of their kind—brick on brick, aquamarine stucco on aquamarine stucco, white granite on white granite—and there were patterns he hadn't seen before like stripes, checkers, wood lodge, tiger. Each room of a particular kind had a logo on it similar to those he'd seen on the patchwork robes of the Opportunity Scientist field priest. These were emblazoned on the door of each room so that they lined up on shafts with aligned stairwells and faced different directions on those that were unaligned. These brand name rooms also appeared to be slightly larger than the generic rooms, reaching to three-quarters of a story rather than one half, and had wider stairwells with proper railings that looked much less hazardous than the separate steps, pegs, or rungs elsewhere. The feeding stations were more numerous in this area so that the lineups were shorter, and the vending machines had logos that matched those on the rooms, as did the clothes of the local people. Though their garments were otherwise similar to the standard outfit, they fit the bodies of their wearers better and appeared to be of a sturdier weave of Fleet fabric, including matching sneakers whereas most bankdead went barefoot. The food was of slightly larger quantities—with fatter rice balls and bigger noodle bowls—not to mention more variety of toppings—and the drinks were in colors Amon had not seen elsewhere. The packaging also bore the same logos, and in addition to tossing the bottles into a heap, as was common in other places, they flicked away their wrapping as though they scoffed at such piddling nutrition, which some of the regular bankdead passing by stooped down to pick up and eat if one fluttered into their path.

Though Amon remembered seeing roombuds with logos on them and guessed that was how the construction crews here knew to connect rooms of the same kind, he had never been assigned to construct such buildings and found it all exceedingly puzzling. What was with the better quality, quantity, and design, and the brand coordination between shelter, clothes, and food?

As Amon continued through this perplexing area, the slumscape opened up into a large egg-shaped space illuminated by numerous fire-fLytes. Countless tunnels and squeezeways terminated at this capacious nexus and fed a continuous torrent of foot traffic onto various stairpaths that wound around the inner walls of the egg. These paths invariably connected to two portals side by side in a solid wall of buildings on the other side of the gap, about ten stories above where he now stood. Half the crowd streamed empty-handed along one network of routes into the left portal and the other half poured out of the right portal with bags of supplies hung over their shoulders. These he supposed were supply crews heading to and coming back from Delivery. Surprised to find he could read again for the first time since cash crashing, he saw a slogan written in English on the bags of the ones returning:

The gift of a baby is the best gift for your baby.

It took Amon a moment to translate this phrase into Japanese in his head, and once he'd done so he wondered if he was misunderstanding it. While the phrase seemed to suggest that the venture charities were encouraging mothers to give up their babies for adoption, he couldn't imagine why they would want to do such a thing. Since the altruistic act of rescuing babies from squalor and poverty and granting them the opportunity to earn unlimited freedom was expensive, it ran counter to their interests if more mothers took advantage of their programs, and should have appeared as a boon to the mothers without anyone needing to point it out. So why the advertising?

As Amon watched the faces of the mothers plodding in and out along the paths with babies bundled to their bosoms, he was suddenly filled with an inexplicable sense of foreboding, a sort of nauseating dread that compelled him to turn on his heels, vacate the egg-shaped space, and return as quickly as he could to his elevator, though the path looked different now that night had descended and he immediately got lost, not finding his way back until dawn when it was already time to wake up.

"What does it mean?" Amon asked Book in the library several nights later, his tone of voice betraying more urgency than he intended. "Why would the venture charities print that phrase on their clothes?"

Ever since witnessing that baffling spectacle at the border, Amon's unease had lingered, and for several days he had lost his desire to explore. Instead, he had been dealing with such restlessness that he kept circling within the areas he knew, yet lacked the will or energy to leave the perimeter of the Cyst. As he trekked the same handful of courses night after night, he mulled over the phrase on their bags obsessively, sensing somehow that the meaning it represented was an aberration but unable to unravel enough of it to understand why. Clearly he would never decipher it without more information and soon hit upon the idea of asking the Books. While he might have tried Ty or Vertical, who both spoke Japanese and were in charge of overseeing him, they had shown little patience for any queries unrelated to tasks immediately at hand, whereas the Books had carefully answered all his questions so far.

So he was disappointed when he finally caught the two of them in the library and Book replied, "I cannot answer that question."

"Oh. O-okay. I'm sorry to bother you then, I guess."

"You are not bothering me," said Book. He was sorting a pile of massive tomes on a table in the lounge while Little Book stood just behind him watching. "Xenocyst has been compelled by agreement with the venture charities to eliminate all academic education programs. If I were to answer you in the present circumstances, then I would be violating our protocol."

"Ah. Well no problem then." For the first time, Amon realized that there was a huge omission in the Xenocyst infrastructure: schools. There were places to eat, sleep, void, give birth, recuperate, even a block of buildings carefully conjoined to form a sort of architectural gymnasium for physical training. Nearly every essential human activity was covered, but there was nowhere for higher learning, excepting the library perhaps if that even counted and Amon believed it didn't. "That seems like a strange rule for the venture charities to make. Why would they insist on that?"

"For precisely the same reason, I cannot answer that question."

"Is there someone else I can ask about it then? It's—I'm very confused, you know. Sometimes it's hard for me to sleep . . ."

"Anyone to whom you inquire who comports themselves in accordance with our policies will be required to provide a similar response." *Tap-tap-ta-tapatapatap* . . . "What we recommend instead, as we recommended to you previously for alternative reasons, is that you utilize our collection. No restrictions have been imposed upon self-study."

Amon glanced at the book-filled shelves and then back at the two Books. He had no intention whatsoever of reading, but under their urging stares he felt it would be disrespectful to ignore their advice after he had sought it out and they had kindly given it. So he thanked them with a bow and stepped towards one of the aisles.

In the lounge at the front of the library, men and women slouched over books around a central table, sat along the walls, or crouched on the open floor while many others actively browsed the shelves. Amon hadn't been expecting the library to even be open so late—why waste resources keeping such an inessential facility running after hours?—but it seemed to be the busiest area in the entire building.

Although he was skeptical that reading would be in any way beneficial to him, he didn't want to be rude to Book, and so began looping back and forth down the aisles, passing repeatedly through the sitting nexus where he'd undergone numerous interviews. Though he'd been able to read the English phrase on the bags, he was somehow still unable to parse the Japanese titles on the spines and shelf after shelf of inscrutable runes slid past. He was wondering how long he should keep up this act, pretending to be interested in what seemed to him a stodgy, boring place that housed useless junk and enabled an utterly pointless hobby, when a single title that seemed to make sense jumped suddenly out of the incomprehensible.

It was three rows from the top at about chest height, and Amon did a double take before he could properly read the title—*The Woman in the Dunes*—though the author's name was too blurry for him to make out. He paused for a moment, staring at the spine in befuddlement—this lone strip of signal amidst endless rows and columns of noise—before hesitantly picking it up. It was a *bunko* edition, just the right size to hold in the palm of your hand, and without even looking at the cover he flipped it open. He was greeted by words as scrambled as the titles, and as he scanned through page after page of text of which he could not read a single line, he began to feel dizzy. Immediately, he put the book back in its slot and headed straight for the exit.

A sort of queasy dissonance lingered with him as he climbed his way back to the elevator, like an out-of-tune minor chord that jangled with the shadows around him. This emotional disharmony clashed with the dread still seething beneath his skin so that he lay on the damp futon all night, kept awake by pangs of anguish in his spine and chest. Now his restlessness had left him, to be replaced by a sort of ennui. For when the morning came, getting up was a struggle, and when work was over, he went straight back to the elevator, where he lay about staring blankly at the ceiling, sleepless.

The feeling stuck with him day after day, night after night, and it became progressively harder to get up each morning. Soon his hallucinations returned—the jingles and laugh tracks, the service announcement survival marathons and mixed martial art beauty creams—now humming with a sort of diabolic vibration that made him want to throw up. He managed to push the enigmatic phrase from his mind, but found thoughts of those he had sent here filling the cognitive vacuum. He imagined a bloodthirsty gang of them swarming him while he worked outside, or creeping into the elevator to throttle him while he slept. Sometimes in the dark, he remembered their screams one by one, ten thousand distinct voices decrying the pain he had caused, and goosebumps prickled his skin all over.

By about the seventh day he still managed to rise from his floor, but the long plunge off the end of steps and ledges he encountered on his construction course seemed to beckon, the erasure of choices appearing so much more attractive than any other choice he might make. The forest dream had not visited him once since he'd crossed the Sanzu River, nor had any other dream, and the air seemed to fill with a sort of sandpaper heaviness so that each breath weighed him down while scraping him away from the inside. Everything he sought seemed destined for failure: his job gone, Mayuko lost, the answers forever out of reach. For what did a lowly bankdead in the pit of all humanity, brain-damaged and incompetent, hope to achieve? Did he seriously think he might get out of the District of Dreams and make a difference when he had to use every ounce of energy just to stay alive, just to climb across a wasteland and labor away for a few morsels before climbing his way back again?

Then one night, as he was plodding his way back to his room, Amon felt a breeze blowing from above that reminded him of something, though he wasn't sure what. It was a cool end-of-summer breeze carrying a sad hint of fall, and he stopped to let it stroke his skin in the steaming air, knowing somehow that he'd felt one just like it long ago.

The breeze touched him intermittently, channeled down a stairpath crevice from above to the rooftop where he stood, and he tried to connect the sensation to a fragment of his past. But every time he sensed the moment drawing closer the breeze ceased, forcing him to start the reminiscing all over when it returned. Minutes passed and soon the feeling of having a memory approach and yet always remain just out of reach became unbearable. So he began to climb in the direction of the wind, searching for higher ground where its mnemonic power blew more steadily.

He had passed this stairpath many times but had never once taken it because it always seemed too crowded. That night was no exception, as he was bumped and jostled by those going steadily up and down. The path first took him to the end of a crevice where it began to slant sharply and then spiral around several shafts, transitioning into zigzagging tall alleys and winding tunnels, the breeze growing stronger and more persistent with each step as he hiked higher than ever before.

Amon was beginning to wonder where so many people were going at this hour, when he stepped out onto a packed rooftop, glanced up, and immediately caught his breath. There, high above, was the night sky. A mere thin slice of stars in a crack in the roofscape canopy to be sure, but all the more powerful for Amon because it was his first sighting. During his banklife, the clear night sky had been obscured by InfoStars configuring themselves hypnotically into MegaGlom logos, and after his bankdeath his vision had been too damaged. Then he had been locked up in the elevator, and when he was allowed to walk around alone he was always overshadowed by the leaning, looming structures or the clouds overhead.

Now he was seeing the naked stars—unadulterated, untainted, unveiled but for the faintest haze of smog—and stood shoulder to shoulder with the other denizens, gazing upwards so intently it seemed like hours before he realized they were all doing the same.

Considering only its appearance, the night sky didn't seem like much—just a bunch of twinkling lights really. The digital light of Free Tokyo had had more color, more variation in shape and tone, fizzling and blazing in dazzling patterns. But even with the blinking satellites scrolling relentlessly by, there was no denying that it touched him in a special way. Although the stars were indistinguishable from the InfoStars graphically, there was something imperceptibly different about them, the wonder he felt in his bones banishing all doubt as though it rang the pith of his inner unknown like a bell. He hardly noticed the bodies shifting around him as people came and went, chattering voices kept low by the celestial reverence they all instinctively shared, and it wasn't until he was finally trudging drowsily to his elevator, well into the midnight hours, that he sensed his dread was gone and slept soundly for the first time in nearly two weeks.

For a while, the dissonance that one title, *Woman in the Dunes*, had left in Amon had driven him away from the library and part of him blamed the Books for giving him bad advice. Opening its covers had failed to increase his knowledge and had only seemed to succeed in triggering the worst of his malaise. But like one's first taste of a strong cheese or beer, his initial aversion to reading grew subtly and imperceptibly into a curious desire to experience it again. As strange as it was for him to admit, part of what lay behind this fresh impulse was an emotion he'd rarely felt before: nostalgia. He found himself actually missing the nosties of Jinbocho and the Tezuka, where he had lived for seven years. Before he might have been ashamed of this feeling, as when Rick called him a filthy nostie in Shinbashi, but Barrow's defense of nostieism that night in Tsukuda had had time to percolate into him, and those days seemed to be long gone. This was a new world, a naked world, and the prejudices of the old one no longer applied.

So inevitably Amon returned to the library and soon found himself there whenever it rained after work or he was too tired for wandering. Sitting with his back nestled in a dim corner, surrounded by the dusty caramel-like smell and shuffling sound of other readers and browsers, Amon would knit his brow at the garbled pages for hours and hope they would resolve into legible symbols. It was a tedious, unrewarding effort, but something told him to persevere as though by succeeding at reading this one book he might open the door to all the others and step into the house of clarity they seemed to promise.

"I am here to inform you," said Book, approaching Amon one night while he was crouching in among the stacks, pouring over the novel, "that the council has granted us permission to make an exception in your case."

"An exception?" said Amon, looking up from the page. "To what?"

"We reported your combination of difficulties with reading and eagerness to learn. After lengthy debate, the councilors concluded that it would be prudent to provide you with a series of orientation sessions prior to your first expedition to Delivery."

"Oh. Okay. What sort of orientation?" Amon stood up, closed the book, and returned it to its slot on the shelf.

"I am utilizing this term 'orientation' as a euphemism in case someone were to misunderstand it." Book turned his head slowly from side to side and swept his gaze around the room, and Amon understood that he was worried about being overheard.

"Thank you," said Amon with a bow, unsure exactly what all the secrecy was about but grateful for an opportunity to make sense of his situation.

"There is no cause for gratitude as we are simply facilitating the council's verdict." The two Books stared at Amon, their eyes twitching as though studying him carefully. "Do not forget that you are still on trial and that failure to memorize and comprehend the orientation content could serve as a factor in your expulsion."

"Understood. I'll do my best. So . . . when do we get started?"

"We plan to have you oriented by the time of your co-habitator's first supply expedition next week, as you will be required to accompany the crew. Provided, however, that you can accommodate in your schedule a visit to us each evening after your regular duties."

"Of course. But co-habitator? Is someone moving into the elevator with me?"

Book shook his head and Little Book began to tap. "Allow us to inform you also at this time, on behalf of the council, that after the Delivery expedition, you will be required to submit your roombud to our common supply pool and will be assigned to a disposable room. It is there that you will be co-habitating with another individual."

"I see," said Amon, who was delighted to hear he'd be moving out of the elevator, but wasn't sure how he felt about sharing his room as he'd lived alone for his entire adult life. "Do you know who my roommate is going to be?"

"I am not familiar with whom you will be co-habitating, personally. However, I can inform you that the council selected an individual who is crashdead like yourself." *Tap-tatapa-ta-taptap.* "Xenocyst prides itself on the egalitarian integration of our members, irrespective of which world they were born in or where they are positioned within the camp hierarchy. Nonetheless, we prefer to pair crashdead in the early stages of acclimatization and expect that you will assist with your roommate's training."

A pang of guilt and fear struck Amon anew, as he wondered whether it might be one of his targets. But not wanting to seem paranoid, he kept his worries to himself, and simply thanked the Books again, prompting them to walk out of the aisle without a word.

After his first stargazing experience, Amon never felt the memory-laden breeze again. And finding himself too busy and tired to climb that same stairpath after work for the following few days, he continued visiting the library instead. Yet he noticed that the sky was visible along his routine course much more than he had first realized. When some task brought him up high now and then, the overlapping shafts would sometimes open up in just the right way to expose a sliver in the distance above. Or if he was lucky there would be a sprinkle of sky, multiple little tears in the roofscape visible from a single spot. Often these small openings were shrouded in flakes and a smog-like mist, or filled with the careening black arc of crows, the only place Amon ever saw them. But beyond these obstructions, inside the jagged openings in the slumscape, the sky was invariably there behind everything in the world. And he realized that it had always been there, behind the InfoSky, revealing itself occasionally when the swirling surge of videos and images would die down for a moment, like the view through a curtain blowing in the wind. He simply hadn't noticed, as these ephemeral glimpses were rare and had never seemed worth attending to until now, any more than a blank screen.

He was surprised by how often he could see the moon. It traced a very particular trajectory in the sky and yet was frequently aligned with his elevated viewing spots. He soon learned that Xenocyst had been intentionally designed this way, the whole slumscape reconstructed in accordance with the seasons to allow in a healthy amount of sun to the upper levels during the day and to make the moon visible at night. Since few had calendars, this allowed the residents to keep track of the passage of time and connect with something that Amon was only just beginning to understand.

Once he felt a spike of light glance down upon him while he worked and followed it upwards, only to find a strange absence awaiting his gaze, a visual lacuna that was neither black nor white nor any color floating in a crack in the toy-block overhang from which the bright heat shining around him radiated. Then he had to look away, the sun still too much for his eyes and mind to handle. He was reminded of how little he knew, how many questions lay unanswered. Who was Hippo? Vertical? Ty? The two Books? What were they doing in Xenocyst and what was this community all about? Then there was Delivery, with its strange slogan and the OpScis . . . Gradually he was learning about different facets of the District of Dreams, but this solar anomaly seemed to lay bare his ignorance and filled him with a sort of jittery curiosity that nothing in his bounded routine could satiate.

In certain frames of mind, when he looked up at a particular shred of sky, sapped of all promotainment, he found it dismally barren and banal—just something to keep the eye busy while working or performing some other task, like the wallpaper in the Liquidation Ministry office. And without his forecast apps he found the weather annoyingly unpredictable, unable to see what the incessant changes of the sky could be for.

The haze covered its azure in the daytime without any personalization to his preferences or biometrics. The clouds formed and drifted off one after the other, without concern for his actions or his wants. The blue lightened and darkened and deepened without anyone losing or earning a single yen. It just changed according to its own inscrutable principles, completely irrelevant to human existence. Sometimes its pointlessness seemed so grave that Amon hated the sky and wanted nothing more than to somehow get it under his heel, to piss the pigment of his obsessions and neuroses all over it. But he couldn't forget the power of the stars that night and found his eyes drawn upwards at every opportunity, hoping for a reprise from the quotidian grind, however brief and incomplete it might be.

9
THE ROAD TO DELIVERY

1

s Amon gathered with a crowd early one morning at the intersection of many rooftop alleys to head for Delivery, he was suddenly attacked from behind.

Strong arms wrapped around his chest and pinned his arms to his sides. Instinctively, he began to writhe against his assailant, wriggling violently and pushing outwards to break the hold. Book had told him that he would be introduced to his crashdead roommate here, and Amon felt that his fears had come true, that one of his targets had recognized him and come seeking vengeance.

But to his surprise, none of the dozen women, some holding newborns, or the equal number of men waiting with him, seemed concerned by the struggle. They just stared at him, dull-eyed, some with bemused smiles. Amon felt the man's hips clamp against his buttocks and his hot breath wrapping around his neck. The closeness was violating, but something, perhaps the man's smell, made Amon's arms go limp, his urge to resist suddenly deflating.

"Tha fuck!" the man whimpered as though on the verge of tears. "How the hell'd you end up here?"

Amon recognized the voice immediately, and as the man's arms loosened, Amon shook him off to turn around.

There, standing before him, was Rick. In the flesh, for there was no other way for him to be in this naked place, his face contorted with doleful joy. The air between them stirred almost visibly with emotion as their locked eyes and their hands quivered with the desire to get closer to each other though unsure how to do it. Despite their long friendship, they had never hugged before—given the high cost it had not been something anyone they knew did—but after seeing Xenocyst residents do it many times Amon had grown used to the idea, and Rick must have too, for soon the tension became unbearable and they collapsed into embrace. Their arms shifted about awkwardly for a few moments until they figured out how to fit together. Several onlookers laughed at the sight but Amon hardly noticed. Here in his arms was his resurrected friend, substantial, warm, breathing. *Please don't let this thin breeze carry him away*, Amon thought, tears slipping from the corners of his closed eyes as he felt the warm drip from his friend's on the side of his neck.

After a bittersweet span of time, they extricated and Amon looked Rick up and down, as his friend did the same to him. He was still the tall, broad-shouldered man with the brooding eyes that Amon remembered, though he had lost a fair amount weight. He was bony and grubby. They were both bony and grubby. Seeing Rick, Amon realized, was like looking at his own reflection, something he hadn't done since the council when he still retained his bankliving plumpness and luster. Like Amon, his clothes were beginning to flake away, his beard growing in straggly, his hair a tangled mess, his skin greasy. The camps had changed them both, irreversibly perhaps. But how could Rick be alive?

"What are you . . ." A million questions scrabbled with each other to breach the surface of Amon's mind, a million stories he wanted to tell summoned from the depths.

"Yeah, you too."

"But . . ."

"They told me to come here this morning."

Before he could ask who, Ty sauntered into view from around a bend with two young men and stopped in front of the group. "Morning, everyone," he said.

"Good morning," the crowd replied in unison with a bow. The intersection was tight with similar groups gathering before heading for Delivery. Petals from the overhanging disposcrapers drifted silently over their heads on the faintest draft.

"For those of you who don't know, call me Ty. I'm in charge of seeing you all safely to Delivery today. Now that we're all here, lemme tell you the plan. Everyone here has been assigned to floor seven, gate twelve, for supply pickup this morning. That's excepting me and the guards." Ty glanced left to right at the young men on either side of him. "We're only here as escorts. And one of us"—Ty glanced at Amon—"who hasn't been assigned a gate yet.

"Now listen up. Our route will take us through one of the territories in Xenocyst's jurisdiction to a neutral area outlying Delivery. We may run into OpScis there, but we've agreed that the Road to Delivery and its branches are ceasefire zones, so we're not expecting any conflict. Still, there could be a few loose cannons. We don't fully get their religion and it's hard to guess what they might do. So we have to keep our wits about us and stick tight. You follow?"

Everyone in the group said "yes" or nodded in agreement.

"Good. So of our twelve women, six are bringing babies. Four of the fathers are here with their partners, but we have two without an escort. Amon, Rick. That's your job." Ty pointed from Amon to one woman and from Rick to another. Amon nodded his head in greeting to his partner: a tall, big-hipped woman with waist-length wavy hair, freckles, and a slight lazy eye, who introduced herself as Bané. Her baby boy of about six months sat hanging against her chest on a piece of flaking fabric tied around her shoulders, his legs dangling to her midriff as he stared wide-eyed at something over her shoulder. "Stay close to them the whole way and be ready to fight for them if need be. Issues?"

Amon and Rick shook their heads.

"Now until we get outside the compound, you're all welcome to travel as you will, but no wandering or straggling!" Ty swept a piercing, narrow-eyed gaze across everyone with his hand over his shoulder on a tricycle wheel, as if in warning. "Once we go through the checkpoint, we're gonna travel in a line of twos. I'm taking the lead and these two"—Ty pointed to the guards—"will keep a watch on our rear at all times. Once outside Xenocyst, you will obey our orders at all times. If there's any contradiction in what we say you listen to me. Issues? Anyone?"

Everyone in the group shook their head.

"Alright, follow me and let's go." Ty began to walk down one of the alleys and the group set off behind him, leaving Amon and Rick standing there.

Amon had caught only the basic gist of what Ty had said ("follow me," "watch out for OpScis," "protect the mothers") as his mind was overwhelmed by the reappearance of his friend. And he immediately turned to Rick for answers, finding him already looking in his direction with an expression of quizzical stupefaction.

"So wha—"

"I—"

"You—"

"But—"

In the ensuing seconds of silence between them, their lips trembled stupidly as they tried to catch the right moment to say something, but hesitated for fear of being preempted by the other. Then Rick laughed nervously, spurring Amon to do the same, and put his hands on Amon's shoulders.

"Amon, Cheapskate Extraordinaire, a.k.a. Ebenezer Scrooge gone monk, what the hell are you—"

"No! You first! I thought you were dead."

"*Dead?* Bankdead?"

"No! Dead dead! Those bastards, they . . ." Amon's voice cracked.

Rick looked tenderly at Amon, the brooding sadness in his eyes offset by a wry smile.

"Amon, my friend. It's so nice to hear you swear again." Rick squeezed Amon's shoulder. "Like fucking music to my ears."

A kind of doleful, bittersweet joy welled up in Amon's chest, and he put his hand on his friend's shoulder, locking eyes with him as they leaned on each other for a moment.

"Come on," Rick said, "before we get called out for straggling," and they jogged a few paces to catch up with the rear of the group.

Crowding along the path from the rooftop alley intersection by the Cyst to the nearest border checkpoint forced the group to proceed slowly, giving Amon and Rick a bit of time to catch up. Since both were excruciatingly eager to hear what had happened to the other since the last time they'd spoken, neither would agree to fill the other in first, and they decided to settle the matter with a round of rock-paper-scissors. Rick lost and reluctantly began to tell Amon his story as they plodded their way along with the party. Whether the alleys were wide enough for them to walk side by side or so narrow they had to walk back to front, Rick and Amon stayed close to each other, leaning in and speaking into the other's ear in a low voice to create a private space for their communion.

"So the day we crashed Minister Kitao, right after we . . . had that argument at Self Serve, Sekido-san FacePhones me up and orders me to crash Barrow later that night."

"No! That fucking . . ." Amon shook his head ruefully.

"What?"

"Nothing," said Amon, shocked that Barrow had assigned Rick to do the same job as him just a day earlier. "I'll tell you when you're finished."

"Don't tease me like that."

"Yeah. Sorry. You were saying."

"Well, basically, Sekido tells me that the ministry is about to fire me. They're pleased that we dealt with Kitao discretely and everything, but that was hardly enough to make up for all my slacking. So based on my performance with Barrow, the higher-ups will make their final decision. If I do really well, they'll forgive me for everything and maybe consider promoting me. If I fail, my chances of staying employed are slim.

"Even without all the threats and ultimatums I'd have probably done the job without question the way I always did. But something seems off when Sekido-san says I'll be going in solo and then orders me not to tell anyone, even you, about the mission. I mean, why would they want me to ignore protocol and go on a mission without a partner? If the mission is so important, me and you should be on it together, to do the job right. Then he tells me to wait for his go-ahead before moving in. But if Barrow is already bankrupt, shouldn't I be rushing in there as fast as always to stop his bad debt from building up? Keeping me on standby just doesn't make sense."

Amon shook his head again, disappointed with himself for not clue-ing in on such oddities when Sekido had given him exactly the same assignment.

"What?"

"Nothing."

"Come on. What is it?"

"It's nothing. Maybe later."

"Maybe?"

"Later. Definitely."

"Stop doing that."

"Sorry. I'm listening."

"Where was I?"

"'Standby just doesn't make sense.'"

"Right. So I voice my concerns to Sekido-san right away, but he reassures me that the ministry has its reasons for keeping this secret and waiting for the perfect moment to strike, but he can't explain any further at the moment because blah, blah, blah, blah, blah, and then goes off on one of his diatribes about 'faithful reliabilism.' Usually I'd leave it at that, but something just doesn't feel right and I start to push him for more details and some more convincing justification for his atypical and probably illegal approach to the mission. I'm sure you can guess how far that got me."

"He started rambling in meaningless circles and you got precisely nowhere with him."

"The guy should get a prize for saying the littlest in the most number of words."

"Do the sounds he makes even count as words?"

"Ha ha! That's it, Amon—what a douchebag—how come you couldn't say things like that when we were still working for him? I could have had someone to vent with."

"Your story?"

"Fine. Yeah, so not surprisingly, our talk ends inconclusively. None of my concerns have been answered, but through that pushy roundabout way he has Sekido has managed somehow to leave it that the mission is still in my hands. We're having this conversation as I walk around waiting for his instructions, and when it's over I get on the train home at Tokyo Station to go kill time before the mission. But when I go to transfer at Otemachi, this guy bumps into me in a really rude and careless way, and the next thing I know Mayuko is calling me on FacePhone. I pick up, and I see her there, but I can barely make out her face because she's in this really dark place, screaming like crazy. I ask her what's wrong, but she's all panicked and completely inarticulate, just shrieking and begging me for help. I can hear her MindFulator going crazy in the background, telling her a train is coming. Asking questions isn't helping anything, so I bolt for where it says she is on my map, right on the tracks of the Chiyoda Line in the very station I'm in. I'm thinking what a weird coincidence this is when the display tells me the next train is in one minute and I start running like I've never run before while Mayuko is screaming away in my ears for help. I get to the platform with ten seconds to spare. She's about ten meters inside the tunnel and I leap onto the track and dash straight for her with the train coming right at me. But when I get there, no one's there. I can see someone looking up at me on FacePhone as I approach, but on my eyes the space in front of me is just empty. I flatten myself against the wall of the tunnel just in time. The train blasts by the tip of my nose. When it's stopped at the station, I return to the platform and climb up. The suicide crew is already there with their vacuums and hoses and cleanup dusters and stuff.

"I stagger through the crowd of gawkers and back up the escalator, trying to put together what's just happened. A guy bumps me and suddenly I'm having a sort of digital hallucination. Obviously this isn't some random hacking because the image was carefully fabricated. Whoever it was knew Mayuko was my girlfriend and wanted to get rid of me. But BodyBank security is supposed to be impenetrable. Someone committed a serious credicrime against me and I need to figure out who. But when I get to the top of the escalator, two Liquidators are waiting for me, a man and a woman I recognize from another squad, though I can't remember their names.

"I was too panicked earlier, but I finally think to check my AT readout and see that I've been fined for *train suicide* and I'm deep, deep in the red. But the costs don't add up. I was in the red to begin with before I made the jump, but not *that* far in. And with my evening pay arriving a few minutes earlier, I should still be solvent in spite of my crime. I think about appealing the fine to the Fiscal Judiciary since I've been tricked into doing it by someone who's breached me illegally. That's when the nerve dust hits."

As Rick told his story, they hiked with the party down crowded alleys cutting through the dense disposcraper mounds that encompassed them. Ahead of them, the mothers marched along carrying their fabric-harnessed babies, the rest unencumbered. Ty led the way, striding purposefully with his trike carving through the clouds of petals falling all around like a shark fin through water.

"So who the fuck do you think did that to me, Amon?" asked Rick, a look of raw rage and hurt blazing in his eyes. "I guess it was Sekido. I just can't imagine who else it could be, but I can't see why he'd do it."

"It was definitely Sekido," said Amon. "Your story is just dripping with his MO."

"But why would he have me crashed? Because I was late for work a few times? Because I asked some questions about a mission that didn't make any sense? Fire me? Sure, I could see that. But this . . ."

"Hmm," Amon hummed sympathetically, seeing how wounded and bewildered his friend was by the betrayal. Amon had gone through more before his bankdeath, much more, and confronted mad bureaucratic tangles, but at least he'd had the opportunity to resist the incomprehensible machinations around him, as futile as that resistance had been, and in the end he'd even managed to dispel some of the mystery surrounding them. How much worse it must have been for Rick to be fooled into cash crashing without warning, to be taken advantage of by an organization he'd entrusted his life and career to, and to wake up in the camps without the slightest inkling why.

"I can make a pretty good guess what happened to you," said Amon, "but I think it'll be easier to explain if I tell you what happened to me first."

"Please," said Rick. "I know I was the one who said all that stuff about how the stress from your frugality would drive you insane and bankrupt you. But I was thinking 'eventually,' like maybe a few years down the road. Not even two months have passed since that night and here you are, already adjusted to bankdead life. You must have arrived here *weeks* ago."

"I guess I should start with the day you disappeared."

Amon told Rick what had happened to him the night after their argument in the bar, beginning with his assignment to crash Barrow and ending with his identity suicide. He tried to summarize all the events as accurately and honestly as he could, but he was too ashamed to admit what he'd allowed to happen to Mayuko and too guilty to relate their parting words—Rick had been her childhood friend and lover after all— so he found himself fudging the details of his interactions with her. To avoid describing how she saved him from a humiliating fate in the Open Source Zone, Amon omitted the fact that he was nearly bankrupt after the parasite infected him in Kabukicho, and pretended as though he'd reasoned out that the recruiters were the Birla Sisters without Mayuko's help. On this version, he'd gone to hide out in a weekly mansion alone, but the virus in his pinky had exposed his location and by the time strange men were coming for him he didn't have the funds to fight back. His only choice, to hold on to his information and escape, was to flee and finally cash crash himself. Then, trying to tell the whole truth this time, he briefly narrated his encounter with Tamper and how he'd found his way to Xenocyst, where they'd granted him a trial period.

About halfway through his story, the buildings around them began to change. They were entering the area built of logoed shelters, with logoed vending machines and residents wearing logoed clothes that Amon had seen the day he wandered to the border. This, he now knew from the so-called orientations the Books had been giving him, was one of Xenocyst's communities of "gifted" bankdead: select individuals who were entitled to brand name supplies and other perks, as opposed to the "giftless" who made up the majority in the camps.

By the time Amon had finished his story, he could see a wide, curving alley up ahead, and Ty told them that it would lead them to a border checkpoint. The narrow passage their crew took was the center prong of a three-forking path that merged into the alley so that other groups proceeding along the paths on the left and right streamed in alongside them, their progress slowing as the crowd converged.

"Now that you've heard what happened to me," said Amon, "I bet you can make a pretty good guess about how you were cash crashed."

"You're damn right I can. I replayed those last moments before I got dusted a million times in my mind while I was recovering in Er. I *knew* the guy who bumped me had something to do with it."

Rick supposed that the man had stuck a tiny parasite on him, since BodyBank security systems could only be compromised through direct contact and this was the same method Sekido had used on Amon. Once he was infected, they had tried to trick him into killing himself. When this failed, they shifted to their backup plan of bankrupting him. His balance had likely jumped slightly when he was compensated for the credicrime of hacking committed against him, but he hadn't noticed because the fine had been hidden from his readout as it had been from Amon's. The amount had been insufficient to save him from bankruptcy because Sekido had delayed the release of his salary, which was due around the time he was supposed to jump. In case he didn't go bankrupt, Sekido had ensured that Liquidators were waiting to crash him, likely by sending them forged reports saying he was bankrupt.

"It looks like Sekido or whoever he works for has a whole system worked out for getting rid of people like us," said Rick. "He even dangled the carrot of promotion to lead me along just like he did to you with the Barrow job. But I still don't get why they tried to kill me. What did *I* do?" Rick sounded so offended he was almost whining.

Amon considered this for a moment and said, "I think Sekido and his partners must have been thinking something like this: Here's Rick, this highly skilled Liquidator with a poor work attitude. He's probably capable enough to take on a difficult mission, but since he's a bit lacking in punctuality and diligence, no one at the ministry will care if he disappears. They must have known about your financial problems too, so Sekido figured you'd be easy to push over the bankruptcy cliff if need arose. Plus, they could use your concern about your job security to get you to do their bidding. But you didn't do their bidding. You kept asking questions and persisted even when Sekido implied in his messed-up rambly way that you really ought to lay off about it. You were clearly on high alert, and this got them worrying that you might expose sensitive information like the forged bankruptcy report on Barrow, or that at any point in the mission you might clue in that it was all a big ruse, like I almost did, and go to the media. Or maybe you'd complete the mission and make trouble for them afterwards. Whatever might have happened, your willingness to be vocal about your doubts showed them you were a huge risk, so they decided it was better to take you out even if it meant delaying Barrow's identity assassination.

"Once you were gone, they scrambled to find a new assassin and quickly settled on me. I wasn't as expendable as you in their eyes. I had a flawless record, and as full of shit as Sekido and the recruiter turned out to be—from everything Sekido told me about the job close to the Executive Council and everything the recruiter said at the meeting—I get the impression they really were grooming me for something big. Maybe assisting with their coup d'état in some other way? Who knows? Aside from being more valuable to them than you were, I was also much more solvent and so a bit harder to cash crash. But since I was even *more* desperate to get a promotion, they could count on my obedience and total credulity; I was exactly the sort of person they would have wanted after you let them down. Plus, since my partner had just gone missing, they would have a decent enough excuse for dispatching me alone in violation of protocol if I'd bothered to ask about it. So they decided on the fly to send me in your place. Then when I started getting suspicious, they did to me just what they'd already done to you. Those conniving pieces of shit got both of us in the exact same way."

There was one difference and Amon was ashamed to remember it, let alone admit it aloud. While Rick had picked up on the dubious aspects of the mission—the delayed start time, the solo order, the secrecy—and expressed enough suspicion that Sekido needed to crash him before he even went through with it, Amon had been so blinded by his obsession with success that he'd swallowed Sekido's lie that this was all necessary for the sake of political discretion. Then he'd walked right into the trap set for him at Shuffle Boom despite having every reason to distrust anyone and everyone—especially Sekido—at that point. Along the way he'd cash crashed a man he greatly admired and the end result was what happened to Mayuko . . . If not for the jubilee charge, he might still have been working for them, never knowing what they'd done to his best friend. He'd been a gullible idiot, but not Rick.

Now that they had worked out what had likely happened to Rick, Amon realized that, while he had explained how he got from Free Tokyo to Xeno-cyst, Rick had not spoken about what had happened since his cash crash or how he had ended up on the supply crew that morning. He was about to ask when Rick said, "So what about Mayuko then? You called her a few times to check in about me. Never heard from her after that, or what?"

After Amon's omission of her involvement, it was the obvious question to ask, but Amon merely sighed with resignation and gave Rick a troubled look as if to suggest he hadn't heard from her without committing to either possibility in words.

2

Before Rick could dig into Amon's ambiguous evasion, they stepped into the large egg-shaped space along the border that Amon had stumbled upon and were pushed apart by the pressure of bodies. Crowds converging from every direction and elevation trickled up and down the stairpaths that formed a net-like matrix along the concave walls, flakes sucked swirling down into the center like a slow twister on drafts generated by their motion. The space looked even more egg-like during the day as Amon could now see that it was built exclusively from gifted rooms with white, ivory-like façades.

"Go on ahead and regroup before the exit!" Ty called back over his shoulder. Amon worked his way towards the other members as best he could while they all trudged slowly up a wide stairpath that ran along the lower left curve of the egg to the exit portal in the wall above, connecting to many other stairpaths along the way.

It was Amon's first time back at the border since that disturbing night and he gazed about at the scene, feeling even more disturbed now that he had some inkling of how it all worked. As before, supply crews poured in and out through the two portals near the top of the egg. The clothes of those leaving spat flakes rapidly, mere days remaining before they turned to rags, while the clothes of those entering were brand new, and written on their bags was that same perplexing phrase: *The gift of a baby is the best gift for your baby.* This was the slogan of the Charity Gift Economy on the basis of which the District of Dreams operated, and Amon thought back on Book's explanation of it the night before, his mind still grappling with its implications.

The "orientation sessions" Book had mentioned turned out to be lessons about various aspects of the District of Dreams. Each night after the council adjourned, the Books met Amon in the council chamber to serve as his instructors. As Book explained at the start of their first meeting, they had selected this location as their classroom instead of the library because it was the only place in Xenocyst where they could be confident of keeping their conversations private from the surveillance apparatus of the venture charities.

The main threat to privacy was the blinking cockroaches scuttling about, a kind of drone that Xenocysters had taken to calling PanoptiRoaches. Apparently the origin of this nickname went back to the days when Tamper still lived in Xenocyst. Upon request from Hippo, he had dissected several of the drones to examine their internal mechanisms and discovered that the eye wasn't installed with a camera or any other recording device (though the sample was limited and he could not rule out the possibility that *some* might have vision capabilities). But the Books had observed the apparently random pattern of their roaming and determined that it was carefully calculated to appear like erratic insect behavior while allowing the roach to touch every point across a particular surface specified by a set of coordinates. Upon examining these programmed locations with his makeshift scanners, Tamper discovered that the roaches laid microscopic sensors at each location. The walls of disposable rooms were already filled with sensors of the same kind, an essential part of ImmaNet infrastructure that served as network nodes ensuring no jitter or lag for any Free Citizen that visited the camps. But the PanoptiRoaches were needed to install and replace them in condos, roads, sewers, and anywhere else not made of Fleet. In this way, the venture charities had realized a monitoring matrix of inescapable scope. Although the fines for mass surveillance were too great for them to monitor everyone all the time, residents had to live with the constant fear that they could still *potentially* be monitoring anyone at any moment throughout the District of Dreams.

Upon piecing this all together, Tamper had designed and installed a digital quarantine system in the council chamber. Its main component was a particular nanodevice sprayed in the doorway, ceiling, and cracks between the walls and floor. This sent erroneous signals to PanoptiRoaches, convincing them that the space didn't exist and diverting them to lay their sensors elsewhere. Once all the elements were in place, Tamper had made the council chamber into a sanctuary totally blacked out from the ImmaNet, allowing the councilors to discuss matters crucial to the community without the need to worry about remote eavesdropping.

Since Xenocyst had made an agreement with the venture charities to never offer education of the sort Amon was receiving, for reasons Amon had not been told, the council chamber was the only place the Books could safely offer him lessons. And so the three of them had sat cross-legged on the wooden floor, Amon facing his teachers, Book's nasally bass and Little Book's taps echoing through the large, empty room.

Tap-tapa-tap-taptatatap . . . "In preparation for your visit to Delivery tomorrow," Book had said the night before, "our topic is the origin of the bankdead, as well as the rudiments of the Charity Gift Economy that defines our essence. We feel it appropriate to begin with this lesson, as it will provide background on both your present milieu and you yourself insofar as you are bankdead. In our explication of this origin, we will proceed chronologically and then conceptually, beginning initially with the era of the Tokyo Roundtable and continuing to develop our story into the present day.

"We must preface this historical account, however, by cautioning you about its potential inaccuracy. Although some individuals, such as Hippo and myself, were alive during the Great Cyberwar that culminated in the Tokyo Roundtable, none are capable of confirming what actually happened in that period with any degree of certainty.

"Firstly, the sheer quantity of information was too sizable to sift. Every event that occurred or supposedly occurred instantly spawned an enormous number of reports that diverged widely depending on the angle of the countless media actors involved. These permutations and variations on alleged facts were subsequently subjected to ongoing alteration, as the corporate blocs provided highly lucrative incentives to fabricate narratives that favored their business interests and edit the records supporting those that did not. Consequently, it became all but impossible to establish the authorship and authenticity of any particular message, to say nothing of any given set of such messages or their contextual interrelations. Moreover, the situation has not been improved by hindsight as the process of profit-motivated revision has progressed unabated throughout the intervening five decades of the Free Era.

"What we present tonight, therefore, is the best hypothesis concerning our past that we could cull from a combination of our most credible sources, including gold search engine research conducted by Hippo during his banklife, crashnewb interviews, and bankdead oral lore. Although we lack the means to evaluate even the probability of its truth, this account is the most internally consistent and meaningful version we have been able to construct. This, we believe, is the best that can be hoped for regarding such a fraught and contentious moment as the founding of a new global political era . . .

3

At the top of the egg, the various paths merged into a broad series of roofs stacked incrementally higher into short steps, which led to a wide ledge bending along the curved wall to the exit. On the ledge, Ty and his two guards waited for Amon and everyone else to gather before proceeding to the squarish portal. Flanking it were two sentries with nightsticks holstered at their sides. Ty gave the password and the group continued through. Inside was a dim tunnel formed by the outer walls of disposable rooms with a row of guards standing along each wall facing inwards. Just in front of their feet was a line drawn in something similar to chalk running the length of the tunnel. Between these two lines, a steady stream of residents trudged out. The guards chatted to each other in voices too low for Amon to make out the words over the murmur of the crowd, their nightsticks flaking away along with their uniforms and the interior walls.

The long tunnel darkened and then continued to grow increasingly brighter until they reached the other side. There Amon found himself blinking in the glare of the biggest patch of blue sky he had seen in weeks—a solid line that stretched off to the right and left above a series of looming buildings straight ahead. Bringing his gaze down, he felt a thrill of fear as he saw they were on an open ledge only a few paces wide that dropped two dozen stories. Before them was a sort of canyon, walled by two uneven precipices of buildings—the one they stood upon and the one across the gap that was obviously too chaotic to be part of Xenocyst—the floor far below paved with craggy, busted asphalt. The gulf was little more than ten meters across but, compared to the tight enclosure he'd experienced since entering the District of Dreams, it felt enormous. From where they stood, bodies squirmed down many-branching stairpath zigzags and trekked their way across the bottom of the canyon to paths and holes in the disordered structure on the other side. This space, Amon had learned, was a defensive buffer between Xenocyst and the outlying enclaves that wrapped around the entire compound. Most of the disposcrapers forming the outer wall of Xenocyst on their side were around twenty to thirty stories tall, but every ten skyscrapers they were only three stories tall with the stairwells tucked away on the inside. Sentinels stationed on the roofs of these low buildings kept watch for intruders and unauthorized construction in the buffer.

As Amon and Rick made their way down a narrow stairpath single file, Amon studied the towering mass of disposcrapers on the far side and found himself disturbed by its random, haphazard architecture, having forgotten in just a few short weeks what the camps had looked like outside Xenocyst on that first day. The staggered dissolution, the scattered and discontinuous stair-segments, the gaps left by ill-fitted rooms. Motley-patterned, misaligned shafts rose to various heights, some as high as Xenocyst's barrier, some higher, some mere stubs of just a few stories. Though none reached outwards into the canyon over the line enforced by Xenocyst, no other principle seemed to order their arrangement, and they leaned at almost every possible angle in all other directions, leaving triangular spaces that were nothing more than dead ends or from which heaped shafts on jumbles of rubble poked almost horizontal. Whether oblique or straight, toppled or standing tall, crumbling or solid, the disposcrapers crawled with residents and passersby—climbing, lying prostrate on gently inclined walls, sitting in rows with legs dangling over rooftop edges, going in and out of sliding doors—a steady streamer-curtain of varicolored petals gently fluttering earthwards over their shoulders.

The sun was still behind the buildings of Xenocyst, keeping them in shade despite the bright sky, and with a slight breeze blowing, Amon relished the cool. When they reached the ground, the two guards corralled everyone onto a flat patch of asphalt and Ty began to speak.

"We're about to enter Saménokuchi, one of our proxy enclaves. The plan is to cut straight across to neutral territory, so we don't expect any danger for the first leg. But this place changes so quickly it's real easy to get lost—even for guides like us—and the last thing we want is to get separated. So we're all going to stay in single file holding hands with the person in front. Issues?"

Ty gave them another scouring look until they all shook their heads and began to link up. Amon held hands with Bané in front and with Rick behind him, while Rick also held hands with the mother under his care. Over Bané's shoulder, Amon saw her baby asleep with his ear against her chest, a bundle of such adorable peacefulness that he wanted to shush all the canyon's murmuring crowds. Once formed into a human train, they made their way across the buffer, stepping carefully around dissolving rubble and fissures that exhaled the hot, foul breath of sewage. Amon had rarely walked on ground level except when lining up at feeding stations and felt anxious when he saw the bottom stories they approached straining under the weight piled atop them. Soon the disarrayed heap of edges and right angles loomed over them, showering them with flakes, and Ty started up a pegway that cut through a rising crevice. Ducking and stepping around the corners of shelters that jutted into the space erratically like teeth in a shark's mouth, they delved higher and deeper into the sprawl until the sky disappeared once again . . .

4

Tap-ta-tap, taptaptap, ta-tap . . . "But to dispense with the preamble, we begin with a question: Where did the bankdead come from? It would be comforting to believe, as standard PR-opaganda asserts, that all individuals on Earth began as Free Citizens when the AT Market was born and that bankdeath camps are inhabited exclusively by those among them who subsequently went bankrupt. However, this is manifestly false because, if we take the bankruptcy rate into consideration, the bankdead population could not have reached its current level in this manner. One might suppose that the difference could be accounted for by bankdead who are descendants of those conscientious objectors who refused to participate in the AT Economy from its inception, including extremist nosties, activists, academics, and community organizers, as well as violent renegades of various ideological persuasions. However, such dissidents in fact represent only a negligible minority. Few possessed the unshakeable convictions and courage required to willingly opt out of the new economy, as the potential rewards for joining were too promising and the risks incurred by doing otherwise too great.

"Rather, it was practically impossible to include most human beings, largely as a result of what is often called the AutoPoetic Revolution. In this subset of the Digital Revolution, developments in automation, nanotechnology, and self-assembly reduced the cost of production for most items almost to zero and rendered the majority of jobs obsolete in the process. Only certain types of technicians, researchers, creatives, sex workers, healthcare providers, and similar professionals that provided services not replaceable by robots and applications were required. The homeless, the stateless, the criminal, the racially or culturally margin-alized, the mentally ill, the handicapped, the unpensioned elderly, the victims of natural disaster, the orphans, and the refugees who already filled our planet's numerous slums were joined by even larger crowds of those who were simply unemployed and now forever unemployable. Whether outsiders by choice or circumstance, all became bankdead. As such, they would have no money, bank account, citizenship, official identity, access to information technologies, or jobs, and by design never would . . .

Since exiting the north-west checkpoint of Xenocyst, the supply crew had maintained a roughly north-westerly course. Amon knew this because of the radiant blankness that to his still-recovering vision was the morning sun. He always noted its position whenever it peeked into view as the Books had taught him, and saw that it remained at their backs. Navigating using directions still struck him as primitive and strange, for one's orientation with respect to the North Pole was irrelevant if you had a program to tell you the shortest distance from any point A to B, as he always had. But he was grateful for the skill now because it reduced the sense of aimlessness that traveling in the District of Dreams brought, making the labyrinth feel traversable if still beyond fathoming.

After climbing out of the buffer canyon through the crooked maw of the crevice, they had stepped out once again into light from the sky, a jagged scrap of white-streaked blue in the jumbled-toy-block canopy above. There, on a square platform that was the bottom step of a series of terraced rooftops, Ty called a break and had the guards hand out fizzy-sweet drinks. He explained that they would soon move from a proxy enclave into a neutral one and should be on the lookout for Opportunity Scientists.

Setting off a few minutes later, they scaled ledges from rooftop to rooftop, snaked down squeezeways, wound up stairpaths, as Ty guided them up and down within about a dozen stories' range. Occasionally Amon had to duck through holes in rooms, reach around shafts to shimmy up steps that didn't quite connect, or leap over yawning cracks of indeterminate dark depth. Few local residents showed themselves, aside from those occasionally slipping furtively in and out of distant rooms, and dim figures huddling in tight passages far below, their murmurs echoing eerily up the misformed walls, though several times Amon spotted other supply parties disappearing into slumscape holes or around bends up ahead.

Wherever he went, Amon was discovering, it was difficult to find a good vantage on the District of Dreams. He had seen its exterior on the riverbank with Tamper, and its underbelly on the way to Xenocyst. Now he was trekking its middle reaches, but nowhere on their undulating journey could Amon see the asphalt of the ground level, making it difficult to judge their elevation. His view never extended more than a dozen meters in any direction, with buildings ever leaning close around them like tidal waves made of cubes crashing together, Fleet petals falling like spray from their crests. Whether outside or in, high or low, it was all just as cluttered and confusing, the constricted routes intersecting and ending with no logic, the immediate shelters forming vast, intricate structures that he could never take in as a whole. Occasionally Amon would hear the crackle of unfolding Fleet as disposcrapers around them grew taller, or as a stack of rooms popped up in their way, forcing them to backtrack on a circuitous detour. Once there was a crunch, crash, and tinkling cascade as a room buckled, the stories above it toppled, and an entire expiring shaft crumbled on impact with an adjacent wall, the lay of the slumscape gradually being replaced as they traveled it.

When they reached a high roof-patch where strong winds blew between narrow gaps in the towers looming around them, Bané's baby—who she told Amon was named Arata—began to cry unconsolably. As though this were a signal to the other babies, two more began to wail and Ty was forced to call another break. The two other mothers rocked their babies softly and repositioned them in their makeshift harnesses while Bané pulled up her shirt and gave Arata milk. When they had eventually quieted down, the four fathers unburdened their partners by taking a turn carrying their babies and, feeling likewise obligated, Amon offered to take Arata for a while. Bané thanked him and showed him how to hold the boy, as it was Amon's first time, before tying the fabric around his his shoulders. Then, with a warm ball of well-behaved curiosity staring eagerly up at him, Amon followed Ty's lead along a narrow ledge at the edge of a long drop, where he had to lean into the bluster to keep his footing and worried constantly for Arata's safety. Thankfully, the trend soon shifted to descent, and before long they were sliding down a crawl-alley slope. There were no longer any flat surfaces to walk upon. Everything had a slant. Moving forwards or backwards always meant moving up or down. It was exhausting, especially with the added weight of the baby, and Amon felt new admiration for the mothers, as Ty never let them slacken their pace, trying to minimize the time they spent exposed.

Rick too was carrying the baby under his care, looking as scared of slipping and hurting the fragile new life as Amon felt. Amon wanted to ask him how he had ended up on the supply crew that morning, but it was impossible to talk in single file while keeping his attention on the unfamiliar, precipitous course. Though it felt condescending to be forced to link hands whenever they could, as if they were all children, he was glad for Rick's hand. Its lower grade of warmth compared to the baby against his chest and sultry air around them seemed to imbue his skin with reassurance, leaving him no doubt that his best friend was indeed back, as substantial and enduring as he could hope . . .

6

"However," *tap-taptaptaptap-taptaptap*, "the exclusion of the bankdead from the AT Economy cannot conclude any meaningful account of our origin. That is to say, we cannot adequately understand ourselves merely by indicating who we necessarily are not, namely Free Citizens. In addition to this negative account, it is incumbent upon us to also develop a positive one and outline who, or rather what, this denial of legitimacy forced our kind to inevitably become.

"Our identity is clarified when we consider the problem confronted by the Tokyo Roundtable, and the MegaGloms who wielded the most influence over it: what to do with all of us? No resolution was forthcoming at the Tokyo Roundtable and all proposals offered subsequently at numerous conferences were rejected. Exterminating us was not a viable option because a holocaust would be expensive to implement and potentially create a PR disaster for all the parties involved. Leaving us to decide our own affairs was no more feasible because we might organize and create black markets to rival the legal economy or form financially destabilizing hotbeds for dissent and terrorism. Perhaps in another era we might have been made slaves, forced workers, illegal migrants, serfs, proles, concentration camp inmates, or some equivalent underclass. However, there was no longer any demand whatsoever for unskilled labor and this presented a unique conundrum elites had never before confronted. The bankdead were a kind of anomalous byproduct of the action-transaction market that stood outside its usual mechanisms of organization and control. We could not be categorized as property the way dead matter and concepts could and yet we could not be charged for acting the way living citizens could either. Despite input from the whole gamut of relevant experts, the problem was proving intractable until a second problem was discovered that led the MegaGloms to a solution to the first . . .

7

After several hours of trekking, the style of the buildings began to change, as they entered another gifted community. It resembled the one on the edge of Xenocyst, with larger rooms in consistent designs that matched the outfits of the residents, though the pixelated propeller logos and orange, brown, and yellow Aztec-style patterning were distinctive. This enclave was also much more expansive, blending into neighboring sections of slum with shelters in other styles.

This was the Gifted Triangle, a huge isosceles tract of land with its tip pointing dead south and the opposing side running along the front of Delivery. It was heavily concentrated with a variety of brandclans enjoying proximity to Delivery and its supplies.

When the design of the slumscape had shifted twice—from Aztec to the whitish stone of English cottage to art deco steel and stained glass—they reached a platform overlooking a road of shoulders and bobbing heads that snaked along a cleft in the buildings. The cleft was bounded about five meters away by an irregular wall, and over the heaping layers of jutting corners that extended far beyond its upper lip a mountain reared into the sky. This Amon had seen the day he entered the District of Dreams and knew it was called Opportunity Peaks, the holy center of Opportunity Science. Having a closer vantage this time, he could tell that its two great peaks were landscaped out of thousands and thousands of rooms, dropping in slopes pleated with cube-built valleys and veined with crowded staircases.

Ty called another break and the guards handed out more refreshments. Amon—who had given Arata back to Bané a short while earlier when he had begun to cry again—sucked his blue sports drink down eagerly as the others drank theirs and Ty stood to face them on a rooftop elevated slightly like a stage.

"Here we are at the Road to Delivery," he began, pointing diagonally down to conduct everyone's gaze into the cleft. The crowd about three stories below them was denser than any Amon had witnessed before in his life. Nowhere did a pocket open up even momentarily, those with babies holding them protectively above as though offering them to the eclipsed eye of the sky. Without space to fall through, the flakes accumulated on shoulders like snow. Aside from a slow swaying, the only movement Amon could detect was a slight drift in different directions, the far side creeping south and the near side north. Though no visible markers indicated the division between the lanes of this two-way thoroughfare, a sort of equilibrium formed with curving spillover on either side of the middle.

"It's easy to get pulled apart by the force of the crowd, and some robbers will form currents to drag you away on purpose. But lose your grip for one second and you'll never make it back to us. I promise you that. So if you wanna return to Xenocyst in one piece, bunch up tight. Hold on to the shoulders of two others, and if anyone outside the group grabs you, shout 'pervert' and we'll do what we can. Okay! We all refreshed?" Then, without waiting for an answer, "In you go!"

Ty and the guards led them stepping along a spiral of pegs in a rounded wall to where they ended just a meter above the heads. The two guards brandished their nightsticks and Ty took one of the wheels into his hand, shouting, "Make room!"

At first there was no reaction, so Ty signaled to the guards, who crouched down to club a couple of the nearest men on the shoulders. "This is a supply expedition from Xenocyst. Make room NOW!"

As the men who had been struck yelled out in pain, Amon winced. They appeared to be unarmed and were jammed in so tight they could only cower as the crowd's startled eyes went to the guards. Everyone looked exhausted, overheated, and afraid, and Amon didn't know where the space came from but a wave of jostling spread, opening the narrowest rift in the bodies. Immediately Ty leapt into it and spread his arms to hold it open with the flat of his palms. The guards waved the other members past them to the final step, from which they began to hop in one by one, prying apart the crowd inch by inch as they filled the wound Ty had started. After hesitating momentarily at the edge, Amon dropped in too, his hips propped up on a bed of shoulders and heads for a moment before they moved apart and he plopped in with the rest. Once Rick and the two guards had dropped into their midst, they all held on to each other, forming a tight cross-stitched bundle of bodies on the Road to Delivery . . .

8

"This second problem that eventually guided the MegaGloms towards an answer to the bankdead problem was a particular threat posed by Fertilex. They, the MegaGloms, had to discover a means of acquiring human resources in spite of the fact that Fertilex had seized all life properties immediately following the outset of the Free Era. In the case of other essential resources, joint ownership arrangements and mutual inter-investment provided the MegaGloms with a share in each other and kept each member of the Twelve and One in check. For example, although R-Lite is commonly said to own energy, in actuality it only owns a majority of energy-related properties. A certain share in each stage of the production cycle, from patents on generation technologies to transmission and operation of plants, is owned by other MegaGloms, with their combined share exceeding that of R-Lite alone in some areas. R-Lite, therefore, could not unilaterally wield its influence in energy markets to dramatically increase prices to the detriment of other members. Fertilex, by contrast, not only possessed complete ownership of all life properties—including sex, inception, procreation, and birth—but the entire MegaGlom was in the hands of just two individuals who cooperated consummately, Shiv and Chandru Birla. This provided Fertilex with enormous profits from all reproductive efforts while threatening to drive the other MegaGloms into complete dependence on it for their entire workforce.

"Thus the MegaGloms recognized that if they allowed Fertilex to expand without hindrance, it would gain leverage over them in a variety of ways and thereby guarantee its market hegemony. Firstly, by engineering order-grown babies and rearing them all in Fertilex BioPens, it could regulate the quality of resources produced and decide where particular workers were distributed. Then it could keep talent to strengthen its organization relative to the rest and intimidate other MegaGloms by threatening to cut off supply, or destroy them by only divvying out the incompetent. Secondly, it could control prices not merely for all actions related to reproduction—from natural impregnation and artificial fertilization to cloning and synthesization—but additionally for the introduction fees that prospective employers were required to pay to access eligible adult profiles in the BioPen databases. The profits accumulated in these areas would fuel Fertilex's growth and allow it to buy an increasingly larger share of properties outside its traditional sector, until it was only a matter of time before it subsumed or subdued all competition.

"This production and supply monopoly would also endow Fertilex with the capacity to sculpt the market more generally. Through its adjustment of BioPen curriculums, it could instill the populace with particular preferences such as loyalty to Fertilex products. These preferences would influence their actions, which would decide the allocation of profits and losses, and therefore which companies succeeded or failed. Moreover, it could adjust the rate of population growth and thereby manipulate the size of the economy, since fewer people entailed fewer actions and transactions. This essentially translated into control over the quantity of available Freedom itself, as a smaller economy would result in reduced opportunities to earn.

"To prevent the imminent Fertilex dominion such powers would inevitably facilitate, the MegaGloms considered an alternative. Within the bankdeath camps there appeared to be an enormous supply of untapped human resources. Thus if Fertilex controlled all production, then perhaps they could instead rely on extraction. Unfortunately for the MegaGloms, however, this option too was precluded by GATA policies that outlawed economic exchange with bankdead. Simply purchasing babies from bankdead or employing them as SubMoms and SubDads might seem to be the obvious solution. However, since bankdead have no account with which to receive money, and barter exchanges are considered valid forms of compensation only insofar as they represent action fees—which bankdead cannot receive—it is impossible to pay them for any goods or services. Therefore, such arrangements would need to be labeled as expensive credicrimes such as *forceful appropriation*, *kidnapping*, *theft*, *enslavement*, *extortion*, *exploitation*, and *duress*, and the costs of hiring bankdead would far exceed that of acquiring all resources through Fertilex. More coercive means, such as fertility penitentiaries, were obviously financially precluded as well for similar reasons.

"Although the MegaGloms certainly considered pressuring the Executive Council to have these rules overturned, this, in fact, would have worked against their advantage because excluding bankdead from the market is one of the conditions that makes it possible. If exchange was allowed with those who were not monitored by BodyBanks, this would amount to accepting transactions that were not technically actions and the line between the formal economy of the Free World and the non-economy of the bankdeath camps would collapse. Since MegaGlom influence rests upon the system these status quo delineations support, this approach could have potentially destroyed them. Therefore, Fertilex appeared to be the only viable supplier after all. While all other natural resources could be synthesized and manufactured or mimicked on the ImmaNet at virtually no cost, the resource at the center of the action transaction economy—the actor itself, the human being—was set to be under the sole management of a single family, and the danger of a global monocorpocracy loomed . . .

9

What followed in the northbound lane of the Road to Delivery was a hot, slow grind. The absent circle of noon roasted their heads and their torsos trapped its heat, magnifying the warmth of communal blood that Amon could feel pulsing all around him. Their hearts all beat off rhythm, like a thousand metronomes out of synch, as Amon's flesh blazed. The sweat ran from his forehead to his tightest point of contact with the crowd around his diaphragm, where it pooled with the sweat of others, his body making a hopeless effort to cool this conglomerated being that had asborbed him, their combined stench so thick Amon thought he could almost see it. Despite the presence of so many, there was little conversation. The supply pilgrimage on the Road to Delivery was a solemn affair, everyone too focused on withstanding the discomfort and danger to do anything but breathe through it, sigh, and occasionally groan. Bare feet pattering, and a thousand babies crying, as crows *rakhawed* constantly out of sight. Amon and the companions he clung to took occasional steps when the pressure from behind forced them to keep their balance. But minutes passed without him noticing any progress and he became somewhat woozy, as though he would march in place until this corporeal inferno consumed the thin air of his consciousness.

Bané did her best to lean over her precious bundle and shield him from the light as he sputtered and sobbed, but the shade her head offered was only partial where he hung above the press, until the sun eventually shifted its angle and Amon felt the cool respite cast by the buildings to his left. They had inched far enough north that he could now see two ramps of concrete up ahead. From the ramp on the left, people laden with sacks of supplies were descending into line on the road. On the other ramp straight ahead, nursing mothers and the empty-handed were ascending. These two ramps slanted gently up to a bridge about one story off the ground, split by a concrete barrier about waist high into two lanes, one for each line. At the top of each ramp, another ramp looped back up to a bridge one story above the first, where yet another ramp looped back. This structure continued up for twenty stories, with twenty loops of ramp spiraling up to connect a twenty-decker bridge running straight ahead to some massive building of mirrored glass that was mostly blocked from view. Something flitted glittering in the air around the bridge, though Amon wasn't sure what.

When the crowd bottlenecked approaching the ramp, Amon felt bone-crushing pressure and had to forcefully pump his lungs to fight air into his constricted chest. He was reminded of his first day in the camps when he had been robbed on the Road to Delivery. He knew now that, despite its name, it was in fact a network of roads that split from this central terminus at Delivery into increasingly thinner and more numerous branches as it ran south to a region called the Tumbles. But Hinkongo didn't always distinguish between plural and singular, and many residents seemed to conceive of its many divergent paths as one.

"Hang in there!" called Ty. "Just a bit further till it clears up."

Mustering all his will, Amon drove ahead as one stitch in their bundle, compressed to the limit, taking baby steps forward, until sure enough they were soon at the foot of the ramp.

"There's no space to keep together anymore so let go of your partners once you're on the ramp. Up and around we go to floor seven. Careful not to let anyone push you over the edges. And remember: we convene at the exits of Delivery."

When Amon released Bané and another woman's shoulders, he felt the grip of Rick and someone else fall off his as he stepped onto the ramp. The speed immediately began to pick up, with the entire weight of the crowd launching him forward. He found himself twizzlering up the spiral ramp, his shirt peeled up by the twisting forces around him, his waist scraped against the rough concrete of the barrier he was using as a banister.

Reaching floor seven, he elbowed his way off the ramp and was carried across the bridge with the crowd. His lane, between the barrier running down the middle and an identical one to his right, was only wide enough for about four men shoulder to shoulder. It made up the seventh floor of the twenty-decker bridge, of which there were dozens parallel to his left and right at intervals of a few meters. Like every other floor of the bridge, Amon's lane led to a square portal in a mirrored glass complex shaped like a distended cube with rounded, convex outer walls: Delivery. This mall-like structure loomed a dozen stories above the top of the bridges and extended about half that distance below their bottom level. Over the side to his right, Amon saw a sheer drop to water far below. He almost couldn't tell it was water because there were so many soggy flakes swimming in it, continuously fluttering down on breezes channeled by the contours of the surrounding slumscape. The Delivery building, it appeared, was surrounded by a moat of sewage, the faint mist from its evaporating petals buoying a scent of nanochemical sweetness along with the earthy stench of shit and piss and rot. Crowds streamed from the roads along each ramp in through the right half of the portals, and others carrying supplies streamed out from the left side. On the adjacent bridges, Amon could see all sorts of people. Some were dressed in OpSci patchwork, others in brand name clothes, most in the generic outfit, and almost everyone in clothes well towards expiring, tiny patches of skin peeking through holes in the cloth.

In the space between the bridges flew a multitude of translucent creatures. Hummingbirds, dragonflies, bees, wasps, and moths made of what looked like clean, clear glass but filled with a faintly visible grayish fiber like ramified nerve tissue. They hovered, cruising and looping around each other in what appeared at first glance to be random patterns. Though Amon quickly noted a certain harmonious but threatening coordination to the way this swarm moved in tandem—the different species remaining evenly distributed in a given area with each member sticking to a set of fixed flight vectors and velocities—mimicking natural spontaneity while somehow managing to convey the impression of "patrol." These, Amon had learned, were known as CareBots, though many bankdead called them RiotDrones. Their shape and movement were seamless simulacra of the creatures they imitated, except that they had been programmed to do occasional jerks and twitches that were incongruously mechanical and therefore somehow intimidating, a wave of short-circuit motions passing from drone to drone. As Amon watched their shifting sparkle and listened to their air-whipping flutter in awe, their group reached the portal and he was nudged over the threshold into Delivery . . .

10

"To summarize then, the MegaGloms were confronted with two problems. The first was what to do with the necessarily disenfranchised masses now that there was no demand for brute labor. The second was how to acquire skilled labor and consumers now that Fertilex monopolized production of human life and CrediLaw made extraction unfeasible. The solution to both was worked out by a group of six MegaGloms that would come to be known as the Philanthropy Syndicate. Since neither the official market nor the black market would fulfill their needs, they created a new kind of market that was not a market. In other words, an economy that existed in a legal and regulatory gray area. In cooperation with the Absolute Choice Party at the helm of GATA, they would establish the Charity Gift Economy based on the principles of plutogenics.

"An outline of the justification for the CG economy is as follows. Firstly, although payment of fees, wages, and salaries to bankdead was illegal, magnanimous charitable donation was not. Similarly, although receiving goods and services from bankdead was illegal, accepting voluntarily offered gifts from them was not. Thus venture charities could provide supplies out of compassion and good will while bankdead parents could gift their babies, hoping to allow them better chances in the Free World. There is no explicit connection between these two actions; therefore, they do not count as transactions. Everything is coordinated by the vending machines, and the genome check is merely a way to guarantee supplies are distributed efficiently without demeaning chips or tags, ensuring also that parents only gift their own offspring.

"All PR-opaganda aside, in actuality the genome check performs additional, more crucial functions—and this is where plutogenics enters the discussion. In the past there was eugenics, various ideas, practices, and processes aimed at making a stock of living creatures 'good,' and dysgenics, ideas, practices, and processes that make them 'bad.' Plutogenics, however, falls into neither category, as it assumes no goal, good or bad, for any individual genome or gene pool. For example, a eugenics project might aim to create individuals with quicker reflexes, mathematical aptitude, visual creativity, or some more abstract trait such as intelligence or enlightenment. Those with genes more likely to be expressed as such traits would be encouraged to reproduce and those who lack them would be discouraged. Alternately, desirable embryos can be designed or discarded prenatally. However, the Free World obviously lacks any such stable, universal conception of what is good since each Free Citizen is left to choose their own dream and how to allocate the freedom they have earned. Instead, therefore, it is the objective and impersonal demands of the Market that decide which genes are preferable.

"As you are aware, individuals raised in BioPens have their Identity Birth Ceremony and are hired for their first job when they are twenty years of age. Hence, what the MegaGloms need to determine when acquiring or, in the case of Fertilex, growing stock for their BioPens is what kind of babies are likely to be in demand in twenty years. If they can successfully predict this, they can auction the profiles of these marketable infants to competitors or keep them for their own workforce.

"Thus to decide which individuals are worth acquiring, the MegaGloms must attempt to calculate how the totality of actions performed by the citizenry will distribute profits to specific sectors and change the economy over the following twenty years, what job openings these changes will create, and what abilities these jobs will require. In other words, a forecast is generated for the ideal applicants to predicted future positions and the task is then to acquire those resources in the present with the genes and epigenetic structure most likely to become such applicants given a specific rearing and education program. The MegaGloms must be careful to avoid all other genotypes because once a baby is adopted into a BioPen from one of the infant brokerages, they are legally responsible to pay for all their actions over the nearly two decades they are unable to work, in addition to the fee for genome registration with GATA. Largely for this reason, investment in human resources is the single largest operating expenditure for all MegaGloms. With such high risks, securing a skilled workforce while remaining solvent depends on accurate prediction, and highly sophisticated algorithms are deployed at Delivery to achieve this . . .

11

Inside Delivery was a long corridor with walls of black, glossy rectangles. Through their clear shell Amon could see rows of glass boxes stacked one on top of the other, each containing a naked baby. Through the glass walls at the back of the front row, he could see other babies lined up with the first, and others behind those, receding into the depths of the machine. Bright lights in the ceiling cast glare on the glass so that each receding baby was more difficult to see than the former, until they became a blur of flesh about four babies in.

Upon entering, everyone in line went immediately to one of the machines on either side and put their pinky finger into a hole. Children too small to reach had to be lifted and Amon watched as Bané inserted Arata's finger into a smaller hole below the first one. A crib with bars two centimeters high came sliding out of a thick slot in the machine and she laid her baby inside without hesitation. A dozen fine robotic limbs attached to the interior of the crib began to prod, stroke, squeeze, and scan him with various medical diagnostic tools, performing a total health check in seconds before the crib retracted inside the machine. Amon froze and watched Bané as she stared at the slot into which her baby had disappeared, saw her hold her hand out longingly towards it, grimacing with heart-rending sadness. But with the crowd steadily pouring in, she couldn't stop there for long and soon continued down the lane.

From Book's orientation the night before, Amon knew he was supposed to insert his finger into one of the machines like everyone else. But remembering the security system this had triggered three times before, he hesitated and stopped in the middle of the lane, watching the line move through. When the men and most of the women inserted their fingers one by one on either side of the corridor, they continued ahead without pause and their chosen machine never responded. But when the dozen or so mothers carrying babies interspersed in the line inserted their fingers, they stopped to look at the machine expectantly. Usually nothing happened, and their expressions showed a strange mix of disappointment and relief before they continued ahead. For two of these mothers the crib came out and they placed their respective babies on it, but once the diagnostic was finished it didn't retract for either of them. Instead, the machine began to emit a high-pitched bubbling sound that prompted the mothers to retrieve their babies and continue on, looking distraught. Only for Bané did the baby disappear inside.

The babies on their soft little beds inside the cubes all looked as happy as could be, the sleeping ones breathing slowly with perfect tranquility, the awake ones smiling or staring curiously upwards. This was in contrast to the babies outside the machines, most of whom were crying or cringing after so much time in the hot, packed lineup, and one of the three placed in the crib who had wailed in terror the moment they left their mother's arms. The universal happiness of the infants inside was so conspicuous that Amon found himself frowning suspiciously at these cells, wondering if he was in fact seeing a glass wall or a 3D display designed to mimic one.

The bankdead mothers were supposed to be offering their babies for a new chance in the Free World while the venture charities accepted this offer with reluctant but kind understanding. That was certainly how it had looked in the docutainment and compassipromo he'd seen in the InfoFlux. There, doctors in clean white clinics, wearing clean white robes, had delicately and meticulously examined all babies before taking them from their mothers, and nurses had been there to put a warm hand on their shoulders to comfort them for their loss. Never had he heard of machines that absorbed infants with such callous efficiency. Of course automation would reduce labor costs, he now realized, and pragmatically speaking this sort of system might be necessary given the huge population. But it seemed too industrial, too calculating for such a momentous, life-changing juncture. Using the genome readers to make sure no one received double supplies or to study the migratory patterns of bankdead was already a violation of their privacy. But based on the result these readers gave, some parents were given the option of putting their babies in the crib for the health scan while others were not, and some babies were rejected when, as far as Amon was concerned, their being unhealthy was all the more reason to take them in. Where was the humanitarian spirit he had come to know and, in a sudden rush of guilt early in his career, had personally donated his money to support? Although the Books' orientation suggested that no such spirit had ever existed in the Free World, part of him still expected it to be there, the countless images he'd consumed in his youth still holding strong against his recent, naked experiences . . .

12

"Whenever a bankdead adult inserts their finger into a gift receptacle or vending machine, their cell samples are processed through an algorithm that determines how likely their genome is to produce offspring with the right kind of genotype to become an adult who is optimally hirable for a particular range of predicted jobs. The algorithm raises and lowers the score of particular combinations of genes and epigenetic structures depending on how likely they are to produce long-term health, concentration, motor skills, creativity, frugality-versus-impulsivity balance, diligence, susceptibility to promotising, obedience, pattern recognition, and whatever more precise features are required. Each trait is subsequently weighted in accordance with the predicted contours of the market and the applicants it will demand.

"Once marketable candidates are identified, the next step is to secure them. Those whose hereditary qualities are judged likely to produce marketable offspring, the gifted, are administered bonuses to ensure that they are slightly more likely to proliferate and produce healthy babies than the rest, the giftless. As you have already observed on your visit to the border, what we signify by 'bonuses' is a differential in supply quantity and quality. The gifted are provided more supplies that are longer lasting, with superior design and comfort, as well as better-tasting, more nutritious foods. Moreover, they receive some limited medical services, such as obstetrics clinics for pregnant women, simple inoculations, treatment for STDs, antibiotics for mortal infections, and the Er program for crashnewbs.

"Additionally, the algorithm checks each individual's genome and epigenome against a database recording the genetic pool for the population of that bankdeath camp, which is shared between the MegaGloms operating the various machines. This is to ensure there are sub-populations in which there are mates with whom a marketable embryo is likely to result. Members of these sub-populations are donated the same brand of clothes and shelter. This helps them identify marketable mates and encourages the formation of brandclans, which are better organized to defend themselves from outsiders. Ideal pairings within these sub-populations are assigned a number or unique symbol that is printed on their shirts to facilitate their locating each other. The brands also help the MegaGloms keep track of which babies are marked for which BioPens, since each one funds the venture charities that service a different vending machine brand and expects to reap the rewards thereof. If the algorithm of two or more MegaGloms identifies the same individual as gifted or the same infant as marketable, an instant auction is automatically initiated to determine which one is allowed to provide their brand of supplies, with each MegaGlom deciding its bid on the basis of the probability of marketability assigned by its particular algorithm. In this manner, the MegaGloms of the Philanthropy Syndicate compete with each other. Firstly to develop algorithms that predict profiles in demand most accurately. Secondly to secure the individuals their algorithm recommends.

"When an infant is designated as marketable, the algorithm immediately identifies the parents from the gene pool—with the exception of relatively rare cases in which the sire is bankliving. The precise moment the infant is accepted into the receptacle, they are both upgraded to gifters and entitled to a bonus for one year as a reward for gifting. Whichever parent gifts the baby, they will both be issued their upgrade the next time either of them collects supplies. The infants are subsequently taken as wards by the MegaGlom, transferred temporarily to infant brokerages, and shipped to a particular BioPen to be raised. Similar algorithms will continue to be applied to calculate the hireability of the gift as it matures, with the expression of their genes at each stage of development being additionally factored in. Moreover, their profiles will be packaged and sold in advance to other MegaGloms as futures or other speculative derivatives with their value based on these calculations."

Little Book stopped tapping as Book stilled his lips for the first time, both of them locking their gazes with Amon's, their eyes twitching like switching transistors as they analyzed his response to this information.

"This has brought us now to the end of this account of our heritage and its relation to our present identity. Since technology has rendered brute labor obsolete, the poor have now become the pig iron of the global workforce. In the most literal sense of the phrase, we are human resources. That is our sole raison d'être."

Amon was impressed by the clear and articulate way the Books had explained such complicated ideas, as only accomplished scholars who'd spent years tangling with them could. But it was a lot to take in all at once and he was feeling lightheaded.

Perhaps detecting Amon's confusion, *ta-tappa-taptap*, Book added, "You will undoubtedly require additional clarification on the detailed lesson we have provided. Therefore, please collect your questions before our next meeting, as I am certain your expedition to Delivery tomorrow will provide illumination as much as it stimulates your curiosity."

Amon thanked them with a bow and the three of them left the council chamber, the Books heading for the library and Amon for his elevator futon, where he dropped to sleep instantly, his mind worn beyond its limit.

13

Still staring at the babies in their cells, Amon remembered Book's point about pig iron the night before and was reminded of something the

PhisherKing had said. He had spoken of balancing the cost and benefits of future generations and the "perverse industrial inertia" that kept humanity going. Only now were these words finally starting to make sense. *Can you swear to keep asking questions until no doubts remain in your mind?*

"Hey! Get going!" snapped Ty, who had just stepped inside Delivery and spotted Amon straggling in thought. "You've got a mother to take care of!"

Startled from his reverie, Amon looked ahead and saw that Bané had proceeded about ten spots in line. "She doesn't have the baby anymore," said Amon, glad he had a good excuse for spacing out on his duty.

Ty frowned for a second, registering the change. "You still can't just stand around like that. Go get your supplies so we can get out of here!"

Bowing slightly in apology, Amon hurried over to the nearest machine and inserted his pinky, feeling the tickle but thankfully hearing no alarm. These machines, located exclusively in Delivery, were called Gift Receptacles. Aside from intaking infants, their readers were the only ones in the camps that registered the genomes of crashnewbs like Amon. Now that he was on record, he would have access to the regular feeding stations and would no longer need to mooch off Xenocyst for everything.

As Ty followed behind him, Amon noticed that he wasn't interfacing with any of the readers. "What about you?" he asked.

"Like I said, today isn't my pickup day. Me and the guards are just here to see you back safe. Now keep moving!"

With another meek bow, Amon proceeded ahead and realized that he'd lost sight of Rick. Soon a gap of about five meters opened in the walls of receptacles on both sides. When he reached this gap, he saw that it was an intersecting hallway. Immediately to the left was a corridor parallel to his down which the outgoing line headed to the exit for the bridge. Over their heads, the hallway continued for hundreds of meters in the same direction, intersecting pairs of identical incoming and outgoing lineups for all the other bridges, and glancing to his right Amon saw that it continued in exactly the same way.

Equidistant between each pair of lines in the wall of the hallway was a steel door. Each door was flanked by two Charity Brigade freekeepers. These men and women stood stock still, holding assault dusters and wearing head-to-toe skin-tight uniforms that looked like clouded plastic, so that only their blurry skin color could be seen while their features were obscured. To the right of each door was a table behind which two people in generic, casual, bankliving outfits sat: Amon supposed these were career volunteers. Along the wall behind them, near the door guarded by the freekeepers, were stacks of black plastic supply crates.

Two more freekeepers stood just beyond the outgoing line and Amon watched as they occasionally waved over bankdead from his line. Once beckoned, the bankdead would obey without hesitation and head down the hallway, crossing the curtain of exiting people to line up in front of the table with a couple dozen others. When the bankdead reached the head of this line, they put their pinky into a hole in a small black cube resting on the table that Amon recognized as a standard genome reader used in hospitals in the Free World. A career volunteer man then took bags pre-filled with supplies from the crates and handed them to those at the front of the line, who slung them on their shoulders and peeled back to the exit line. One of the bankdead put the finger of her baby into the reader and a career volunteer woman took the baby from her to place it in a diagnostic crib like the one that popped out of the receptacles. When the diagnostic was complete, she then inserted the baby through a plastic flap into the foam-cushioned interior of a nursery crate and handed the woman a bag of supplies, while the other volunteer stacked the nursery crate behind them. There were three different piles of bags that seemed to be of slightly different sizes. Two of these piles Amon supposed were for people in one of the plutogenic categories—gifted or giftless—and the third a bonus for those from either category who had gifted their baby within the last year.

At first, he thought the Brigade was siphoning off people in his lane to alleviate crowding, until he noticed a reporter and his sousveiller standing beside the table. Although Amon couldn't see the immaculate suits they were surely digimade in—only their casual shirts, jeans, and sneakers—he could tell what they were from the way one man gestured towards the supply table in full view of the other, whose unwavering eyes could only be in ultra-definition recording mode. Between the bodies of the outgoing line, Amon could hear snatches of what the reporter was saying to his online audience through the eyes of the sousveiller:

"The sacrifice for mothers is tremendous, but they know that Freedom for the next generation begins here . . . the triumph of compassion . . . freekeepers here as neutral observers to maintain freedom between the bankdead gangs and factions . . . rags to Opportunity . . . equal gender rights in the best of all possible slums . . ."

Amon could imagine how this would all appear in the edited pitypromo the bankliving would see: the diagnostic box a doctor and nurse giving the babies a careful health check, the nursery crates the waiting arms of a warmly smiling parental guardian, the mother thanking the volunteers for taking her baby with a deep bow, the freekeepers—

The scene was cut off when Amon's line moved ahead and he continued past the hallway intersection. On the other side, the glossy gift receptacles were replaced by walls of black vending machines. Imitating those in front of him, Amon pinky-interfaced with each successive machine, and picked up whatever dropped into the bins. First a shoulder bag, then a T-shirt, then shorts, and finally the large heavy cylinder of a roombud. He put the last three items into the bag and spotted Bané up ahead taking a pair of sneakers from a bin. Amon tried interfacing with the same machine, but this time nothing came out. When he withdrew his pinky and tried again, the wine-glass alarm sounded and he quickly moved along. He tried four consecutive machines after that—out of which Bané got a toothbrush and toothpaste kit, a small tube of PeelKlean, a fireflyte, and a nightstick in a holster—but was rejected each time. All of her items, he noticed, had the same Mobius-strip-shaped logo on them, whereas his and those of most others were unmarked. And beside the logo on her white bag, in a silvery gray font, were the words, *The gift of a baby is the best gift for your baby.*

He thought then of Arata, and could almost feel the patch of warmth on his chest where the boy's weight had rested only a short time ago as he remembered him slipping away into the machine. It surprised Amon how sad he was to think that the cute, little baby would never return, though he had only met him that morning. How much harder it must be for Bané, who had carried him inside her body and out, and he wondered what drove her and other parents to make that heart-rending trade.

It was now clear to Amon that he was giftless while Bané was gifted, for although she would have received a supply bonus for gifting her baby, only gifted got branded gear. This perplexed him for a moment, as she was wearing a plain, tattered giftless outfit like everyone else in their crew. Then he remembered that not a single person in any of the supply crews wore branded clothes and realized that this must be a Xenocyst policy to disguise gifted as giftless and throw off OpSci kidnappers looking for chattel to milk.

Amon imitated the other giftless in skipping all the machines until the final one in the row, into which everyone, regardless of their plutogenic category, inserted their pinky. When Amon interfaced, a high-pitched granny voice said, "Please come to gate 12-16 in the morning two weeks from today." The recording repeated three more times as Amon continued to the end of the lane.

"What was that number?" Ty asked from behind.

"Gate 12-16."

"That's your floor and bridge. When are you going there?"

"The morning two weeks from today."

"Make sure to remember that. If you're hoping to get any supplies."

Amon nodded and continued ahead, reciting "12-16 morning two weeks, 12-16 morning two weeks," under his breath.

At the end of the dispenser row was another gap of a few meters with a sheer glass wall on the other side. This formed the border of another left-to-right hallway, along which he could see the backs of all the lines. Drawn by the pleasant sunny glow from the window, Amon stepped up and looked outside. Above, cloud wisps wavered like mirages in azure. Below was the city—not the slums, but the sprawling condos and office towers of Free Tokyo. Strangely, this area appeared to be in much better shape than the blighted stretch of Tokyo he had seen on his way to the Sanzu River. The walls of the skyscrapers looked clean and new, the windows polished, the roads swept. But if so, what for? Since this area would appear tidy to Free Citizens on the ImmaNet either way, there was no more reason to actually maintain it than anywhere else in the metropolis . . . unless this isolated pocket of tidiness was for the sake of the bankdead who looked out the rear window of Delivery just like Amon was doing right then . . . ?

Down below, running left to right along the base of the nearest buildings, was a body of water spanned by three identical suspension bridges. The bridges had two levels with four lanes each—all jammed with traffic—and were joined together by steel scaffolding into a single massive structure. Amon recognized it as the Bridge of Compassion: the only land route connecting the District of Dreams to Free Tokyo. This meant that the sliver of water on its left was the Tokyo Canal and on its right the Sanzu River, as the bridge also served as a dam that separated the metropolis's seawater from fresh. Several enormous pipes ran across alongside it. These pumped in the ink, both Fleet and nutritional, which was diverted through Delivery to a matrix of smaller pipes supplying every vendor and feeding station across the island. The vehicles coming and going across the bridge seemed to be a mix of charity personnel trucks, slum tour buses, and private cars, taking a highway on the Free Tokyo side and a ramp on the island side that curved around a gardened square to the lower levels of Delivery just below the window.

As Amon stared in a daze at the sole link between the city he'd inhabited since his memories were born and the one he inhabited now, thoughts flashed in his head like lightning on a black sky. He remembered the promoguiltumentaries and docucharitisements like the one he'd watched with Rick in Self Serve. Just a few steps away, at that very moment, a reporter was creating such programming, and yet everything Amon had experienced cut through the credibility of what the man asserted like a dull knife through fatty meat, slow and snagging.

"Amon!" barked Ty from behind, beckoning down the outgoing lane. "Time to go home."

Home. Now seemed as good a time as any to go there, whether that meant the BioPen, his old apartment in Jinbocho, his elevator in Xenocyst, his dream landscape, or somewhere else entirely. But could any place built on a foundation of lies ever merit the word?

It was in the lineup on his way out that Amon saw her.

The reporter kept interviewing the career volunteers and approaching bankdead as supplies were handed out and the freekeepers continued to conduct the line. But now, in the midst of this, was a woman Amon hadn't seen there before. She was surrounded by a group of men and women carrying assault dusters and wearing skin-tight armor like the Charity Brigade except their plastic was tinted gold.

Even though Amon was certain he'd never seen her before, she somehow seemed familiar. Wearing black chinos and a dark brown shirt with cuffs and collar unbuttoned, she was beautiful, though in a somewhat boyish way, with silky brown skin, short hair, and a small lithe body. Her movements were graceful but purposive, her features delicate and distinctively Indian, her expression calm and confident with a certain hint of unpliable fierceness. It wasn't until she blinked though—her long, sharp, scythe-like eyelashes rending the air in the naked world just as they had in the Free World—that Amon realized who she was . . . or at least narrowed down the possibilities of who she had to be to two.

Her build and complexion and face were more feminine and soft, her torso more curvy, the line of her lips and jaw more gentle, and her hands slightly smaller. But if not for the difference in gender, she would have looked exactly like both the activist and recruiter that had interviewed Amon—exactly like the Birla sisters in their digiguises as men.

But which one is she? he wondered with cold fear as she strode confidently across the open space, the box of mercenaries seeming to shield her from all imaginable threats. *Rashana or Anisha?*

If the woman was the activist called Makesh who'd warned him of coming danger in Sushi Migration and who he'd contacted on the verge of bankdeath, then she could be the key to his salvation—the only person who might scoop him from this ephemeral wasteland and help him find justice. If she was the recruiter who'd helped Sekido infect his left hand with that sinister virus, then she was his greatest threat, surely eager to snatch him, extract his incriminating information, and dispose of him however she might desire. But how could he tell the difference when they were twins who looked almost exactly alike?

Amon kept his eye on her in an unfocused way, searching for aspects of her presence that would answer these crucial questions without catching her gaze. He wanted to hang back and avoid moving any closer until he could be sure he was safe, but knew this would cause a disturbance in the crowd around him that would only draw her attention more assuredly, so he shuffled his way slowly and inexorably ahead as she approached his line.

To his surprise, she called out to someone ahead of him and began to talk with them. There were a few tall people ahead of Amon that blocked their face at first, but soon the crowd shifted and between their parted heads he saw, to his amazement, that it was Rick. The Birla sister said something, and then Rick replied, giving her a sour look as if to express his disappointment about something. *They know each other?* Amon thought, wishing that there had been some way to hear the rest of Rick's story before this moment.

After exchanging a few more words, the woman swept her gaze around the room as though searching for someone. Amon bent his knees to duck down as slowly and inconspicuously as he could, trying to give his face cover behind the head of a tall man in front of him. To his relief, she seemed to overlook him and soon turned to walk away, her guards parting for her and doing an about face so they could follow her in box-like formation. She then led them around behind the supply table, went through the door between the freekeepers, and was gone.

10
BETWEEN SLUM
& STARS, DUSK

Keeping his shoulder pressed against the wall to feel like he was grounded to something, Amon ascended the banister-less stairpath. He'd never been afraid of heights to begin with and scaling disposcrapers daily to reach his new room or fulfill his construction duties had diminished what minor fright he had initially experienced. But they were now approaching one of the highest peaks in Xenocyst and more than two dozen stories above the rooftops below he felt a churning rush of vertigo whenever he glanced down. The fact that the gray rectangles of about a dozen embyrbrycks were stacked unevenly on his cradled forearms only increased his worry that he might lose balance. Best to hug close to the wall, lean back slightly to make sure the load fell against his stomach and chest, and stay focused on the ascent. One foot after the other, stair by stair. It only took four or five steps to reach the top of a flight on the narrow skyscraper shaft, and Amon felt his breathing stop for a split second every time he reversed direction.

Just ahead, Vertical and Rick were carrying a small table together, with Rick facing forward in the rear and Vertical backing up above him. Both seemed completely relaxed, and although Amon wanted to stop for a moment to settle his jitters, he forced himself to keep climbing, not wanting to admit his fear. *Just a few more stories.*

It was the autumnal equinox, and Vertical was taking Amon and Rick to the rooftop of the Cyst to attend Xenocyst's fall festival. Helping out with the preparations after a full day on reproductive waste duties was turning out to be exhausting, but Amon was looking forward to the extra supplies he had heard would be distributed as part of the celebration. When at last they reached the top, he breathed a sigh of relief, but this seemed to release the pent-up jangles from his nerves and he began to shake, spilling the embyrbrycks onto the rooftop.

"Better pick those up before someone else does," said Vertical, steadily receding across the bustling rooftop with the table, "unless you want to lose all the credit for lugging them up."

Rick glanced over his shoulder as Amon knelt to gather what he'd dropped and chuckled, saying, "Lucky timing there, Amon. I'd hate to have been down there when it started raining bricks because of your butterfingers," before the two of them and their load melded laughing into the crowd. Amon began to restack the bricks, thinking how he would have been annoyed if it had been anyone other than Rick who had mocked him. But he wasn't annoyed. He couldn't be annoyed. He was simply too glad to have his friend back.

It had been only two weeks since Rick had reappeared suddenly before the supply pickup, and Amon reflected back on their conversation after the visit to Delivery when Rick had finally explained how their reunion had come about . . . or part of how it had come about. As with everything else in Amon's life, unanswered questions still obscured his story, like globs of oil in an aquarium.

By the time their crew made it off the Road to Delivery, they were trekking through gloom as the sun had long since fallen below the slumscape skyline. Ty warned them to watch out for Opportunity Scientists and unaffiliated bandits skulking along the highways, hurrying them along with their new loads of supplies so they could reach the outer walls of Xenocyst before nightfall. It wasn't until they entered a proxy territory that Ty allowed them to slacken their pace and Amon and Rick were able to walk side by side again.

"So who was that woman back there in the lineup?" Amon asked the first moment he could. "Do you know her?"

"You saw that, did you?" said Rick. "Yeah, I know her. Kind of. Actually, she was asking about you."

"Oh. Okay. What did she say?"

"She wanted to know if I knew where you were, but I wasn't sure if it was a good idea to tell her so I lied and said no. Was that the right thing to do?"

"Um . . . maybe. I don't know. I guess it depends on who she is."

"Rashana Birla."

"That's how she introduced herself to you?"

"Yeah. But not at Delivery. I met her before. In Er."

"I keep hearing about this place. Some kind of rehab center or something, right?"

"Yeah. For webloss. I lived there a few weeks until I came here."

"Why do they call it Er?"

"I think they said the guy who developed their system was named Er. Something like that."

"Okay. So you met the Birla sister there?"

"Yeah, she came to visit me while I was recovering. But let me back up a bit. It'll be easier to explain that way."

"Why don't you just pick up where you left off?"

"With the train station?"

"Please."

"Well, like I told you, I got dusted there. The next thing I remember was waking up soaking in this bright tank. No one explained anything, but I figured out pretty soon it was Er."

"What's it like in there?"

"Kind of like being back in the BioPen, except it's full of adults instead of kids and everyone's a bit crazy. They give you rehab banks, like training banks but with limited features. That way you can see the overlay, but no one can personalize the way they look or send messages or anything like that. A lot of the time, you're in a LimboQuarium. We just called it the tank. It's filled with this stuff that's the same temperature as your skin, but you're not really sure if it's a liquid or a gas, though it's kind of soft and burning in a cool sort of way. Like some kind of . . . menthol feather goo? It's hard to describe . . . you just sort of float there in stillness while doctors or addiction technicians or whatever have total control over what you see and hear. As time goes by, they gradually adjust your audio-video feed so you get less and less information each day. At first the images and music were on twenty-four hours straight, but soon it started to go off for one minute each hour. Then two minutes. Then four. Without warning, the ImmaNet would just die and the naked world would appear—then suddenly it would switch right back. It was shocking in the beginning, but they gave us lectures, and training seminars, and cognitive exercises on how to use our minds in place of apps, like for navigating around this complicated obstacle course. We did everything outside the tanks as a group, so I got to know the other patients a bit. In the last couple of weeks they started to teach us about the District of Dreams and how the supply system works at Delivery. Also how to use roombuds to build our own homes.

"I won't go into all the details right now, but it was a really carefully worked out recovery program. They kept telling us how lucky we were to be getting in. Supposedly not all crashdead are accepted. The rumors say only about 10 to 20 percent. No one ever told me what happens to the rest. I figured out eventually that my Er facility was a special one for 'giftless crashdead.' You have any idea what that means?"

"Yeah, but it's too complicated to get into right now," said Amon, realizing that Rick hadn't heard about the origin of the bankdead—or at least not in the way Book told it. "So when does Rashana Birla come in?"

"About a week after I cash crashed. Some secretary tells me that a big shot philanthropaneur who's the patron for the facility is coming to see me, and then Rashana Birla shows up. The first thing she asks after introducing herself is 'if Amon were bankdead, where in the camps do you think he'd be?' This surprises me. You bankdead? As far as I know, you're still scrimping away in the city. And I've never been anywhere but Er since crashing, so how the hell am I supposed to guess where you'd be? But the way she stares at me, I can tell she's not playing around—is it just me or are her eyelashes terrifying?"

"Her eyelashes are terrifying."

"So I think about it and say, 'Somewhere he could get promoted and live a quiet, orderly life.'"

"That sounds kind of like Xenocyst."

"Not bad, right? I guess I know you pretty well. But she didn't seem impressed because then she just nodded and left without even saying thanks, and my routine went right back to normal."

"How did you get to Xenocyst then? They told me I'd be getting a roommate and all of a sudden you show up! It almost seems like a miracle that you would end up here, with me, on the exact same crew. Don't you think?"

"I know. What a shock. I have no clue how it worked out this way. But it was Vertical that brought me here. About a week before my discharge. I was expecting to get kicked out like all the other patients. Then she came and brought me to the Cyst. I went through the council, told them my whole life story just like you did, and for the last week, the Books have been questioning me in the library every afternoon. Then, just yesterday, the interviews wrapped up and they told me I was going to Delivery. Said my pickup time was tomorrow. Then I joined the group this morning and that's when I saw you."

"Wow. Okay. So you've been here for over a week? Did anyone tell you why Xenocyst went to the trouble of picking you up?"

"Naw. No idea. The people at the clinic just said that someone had come to get me and I followed Vertical here and that was it, no explanation or anything."

"Hmm . . ." Amon considered this question for a moment, but no answer was forthcoming and a different query soon bobbed up from the turbid waters of his mind to bump it aside. "Um . . . so just returning to Rashana Birla again. What exactly happened at Delivery? What did she say to you?"

"She asked me if I knew where you were. I said no because you'd just told me how the Birlas were involved with what happened to you. It seemed dangerous. Was that what you wanted me to do?"

"Yeah . . . maybe. I don't know, but thanks. I think you were right to be cautious. If I'd wanted to meet her, I could have tried to wave to her from the line or something. I just wasn't sure . . . But did she say anything else?"

"Um. She said that you'd asked her to meet you here, in the District of Dreams, and that if I saw you I should tell you she got your message."

Amon felt a glowing trickle of excitement and hope, but it quickly congealed into anxiety and regret. "Shit . . ."

"What?"

"I left a message for the activist. If Rashana knows about it, it must be her."

"Better safe than sorry, right?"

"Yeah. I guess . . . but how do you think she knew you'd be in Delivery? There's no way you two would have just happened to meet by coincidence, and on the same day that we met. The chance of bumping into one person in this big, crowded maze is small enough."

"The Er staff were the ones who told me my first gate and pickup time, so she could have easily heard it from them."

"Okay. So that means she could be waiting for you at your next pickup?"

"Um, yeah, sure. If she can figure out what the supply scheduler told me. But just because she has access to information from Er, that doesn't necessarily mean she can get it at Delivery."

"You don't think someone with her kind of resources could find out when you'll be there?"

"Money's not the problem. From the way her guards acted all cautious around the Charity Brigade, I got the impression she's not welcome there. But if I see her again, do you want me to tell her you're here this time?"

"I . . . I'm not sure. Let me think about it and see what else we can figure out."

Soon after their conversation finished, they stepped out of a tunnel to the edge of the canyon surrounding the outer walls of Xenocyst. Amon remembered feeling a brisk wind blowing, that end-of-summer wind carrying a melancholy hint of fall, and looked up at the jagged patch of gray-blue evening sky far above them, sensing the memory that eluded him closer than ever.

Now the fall presaged by that wind had arrived and a chill breeze crept steadily beneath his clothes, as Amon finished stacking his embyrbrycks on the rooftop and stood up to look around. He was in the north-west corner of a wide square formed of many rooftops, a solid field of small room squares assembled around the large condo square of the Cyst at the center. A dense throng milled about on top, making various preparations for the festivities: stacking embyrbrycks in equidistant piles, assembling packaged food and drinks into orderly ziggurats, setting up enclosed fences so toddlers and young children could play safely, anchoring poles for personal hammocks with bags of Fleet flakes, setting up huge telescopes salvaged from who knows what anadeto hoard, doing last minute rehearsals of acrobatics and drama, lugging various items up the stairs from below. The residents performed these activities with visible anticipation and excitement, filling the air with a buzz of laughter, shouts, and chatter, though the tiredness that underlay each of their motions was clear to see, if not from the day's labor and inconveniences then from having to climb over two hundred meters to get here.

Bending down to cradle his stack of embyrbrycks, Amon stood up with their weight in his arms and was about to carry them into the crowd, when he felt the urge to look down. Curiosity had been building on the way up as he restrained himself to stave off the vertigo and now, he realized, was the perfect chance to take a broad view on the District of Dreams while keeping a safe distance from any dangerous falls. So he turned and stepped over to a few paces from the edge of the wall he'd just ascended, gazing west.

The precipice dropped away into a vast expanse of shadow dappled at different heights by the dim wavering circles cast by crumbling light cookies. Inside each circle were the right-angle layers of tilted rooftop clutter, and the black speckles of petals passing ceaselessly through. Above the silhouette skyline of hunched tower-mounds trickled a white-gold splash of fading radiance from the fallen sun, as the purple-black of evening bled into jagged cloud gaps and flushed out the lingering cobalt of twilight from the sky. Just to the south of this afterglow, two great segments of sky were blocked out by the twin horns of Opportunity Peaks, the twinkle of lights arrayed across them inserting the night's first constellations over the tumbling horizon. To its north was the bright mirrored bulk of Delivery, from which fresh stable lanterns radiated along each of its many bridges and connecting roads that carved through the slumscape, all paths a-shuffle with shadow hordes of bankdead, a darkly glimmering cloud of CareBots swirling above. Rearing behind all this and wrapping around to the eastern rim was the second layer of sprawl added by Free Tokyo—stripped of its digital clothes, those shifting neon fabrics woven of rapacious commerce—a slumbering behemoth of utter darkness nothing like the metropolis Amon had known, and yet from which he could still sense emanations of his past, like the outline of a shining jewel seen through the palm of a fist closed around it.

Is there some way back? he wondered. *Is there some way for me and Rick to return and find our old friend?* If there was it had something to do with Rashana Birla, but whether it was safe to approach her he couldn't tell, and either way they might have already missed their chance.

Upon returning to Xenocyst, Amon and Rick had delivered their supplies to a collection station and received a roombud to bloom in a spot not far from the Cyst. Their room turned out to look like off-white corkboard, and with the two of them stretched out on the rubbery floor-cum-bed of the tiny, insane-asylum-like chamber, it was tight and sweaty. Still, Amon felt infinitely relieved to be out of the elevator and reassured to have Rick by his side, falling immediately into another dreamless sleep.

The following day, Rick was assigned to Amon's disposal team and Amon was put in charge of training him. Soon they were spending almost every moment together. Waking up together, heading to work together, eating all their meals together. Rick even accompanied Amon after work to the stargazing rooftop where they jointly partook of the universe and the calm, soothing late-summer air. Only on supply run days, for which they were always assigned a different gate, were they ever apart.

For the first while, Amon couldn't believe that Rick was actually alive and with him again. But watching his friend carry roombuds, scrape waste off concrete, crush the Fleet rubble of skyscrapers into powder day after day, his existence became undoubtedly palpable and gradually Amon's disbelief turned to simple joy at having him back.

Now that Amon had someone who could relate to his struggles, adjusting to life there suddenly seemed easier. He could turn to Rick for advice whenever he was feeling indecisive, and share with him in the sense of pride that came whenever he mastered a task he'd once relied on a program for. Though Amon still occasionally succumbed to fits of restless gesture-twitching and spaced out on what his supervisor or co-worker was saying, it was heartening to know that Rick, even though he'd been through the Er program, did the same. Soon the pale, unedited, uncleanly faces that surrounded them no longer repulsed him, and he stopped worrying about the way he looked. He was still anxious that one of his targets might recognize him, but with Rick there he almost felt confident enough to face them, and when he saw how cheerfully his friend seemed to accept their new position, he could almost forget the shame of thinking how far he had fallen.

At night after work—wandering, lying in his room, or gazing at the sky—Amon's thoughts often turned to that moment when Rashana approached Rick, and he wondered if hiding from her had been the right thing to do. At first he regretted his decision, as it seemed clear that Rashana was the activist—not the recruiter. After all, she had received the message Amon sent to the activist, and her support for Er was in keeping with what the activist had said about wanting to help bankdead. Perhaps she had come specifically to find Amon and would be willing to do what she could to help him? But as he rehearsed the memory of the lineup beneath his eyelids night after night, he began to think that avoiding her had been wise. He remembered how the guards protected her—tracking her every movement with regimented ease—and it reminded him too much of the *tengu* who had accompanied the emoticon man when he broke into the weekly mansion. The recruiter had been with Sekido when he infected Amon with the virus that gave him away to the emoticon man, so the recruiter and emoticon man were most likely the same person, or at least in close cooperation. But what Amon had seen still left open the possibility that the vicious asshole who abused Mayuko might have been the activist all along, or else had intercepted Amon's message for the activist to now impersonate her. In either case, that would make Rashana, or more accurately the Birla sister calling herself Rashana, his greatest threat.

By the time Rick's next supply pickup rolled around, Amon had been unable to make up his mind about Rashana and, by default, his decision was to not have Rick approach her. His undecided decision turned out to be irrelevant, however, because she wasn't waiting for Rick anyway. Apparently, she didn't know where Rick would be showing up or thought it pointless to talk to him when he had failed to find Amon, or maybe had just lost interest in Amon altogether. Now Amon was back where he'd started before she appeared, trying to make sense of his new abode but holding onto hope that she would return and be the one he sought, whether deluding or guiding him towards salvation only the future could teach.

Returning from his reverie, Amon became aware of the weight of the embyrbrycks in his arms and turned from the rooftop edge towards the bustling center to look for where he was supposed to bring them. On a nearby roof, he spotted three women tending an embyrbryck pile and decided to ask them. They were rubbing embyrbrycks in their hands to activate them and laying them in a pyramid configuration where they gradually began to glow orangish-red dappled black. The faint light of each brick combined into a barely visible aura around the pile, and as Amon approached, he felt infrared heat radiating him, glad for his first taste of the lurid warmth these new fall supplies gave.

One of the women said that they already had enough and told him to take his stack over to the Cyst rooftop. So he made his way there, stepping across the makeshift plastic plank walkways laid over the cracks between shelters, careful not to bump anyone and drop his load. Already embyrbryck piles were going at the center of every cluster of ten rooftops or so. At the center of everything, atop the Cyst helipad where Amon had unloaded many a centicopter, was a square stage made of salvaged Fleet walls layered atop each other, flaking away and decaying before his eyes. Embyrbrycks were piled in an L-shape snug to each corner, with an open laneway between their tips allowing for access to the stage from all four directions. A dozen men and women clustered on top tuning treadle turntables, standup basses, and other instruments.

Once Amon put down his embyrbrycks in front of the men tending the pile at the nearest corner of the stage, he stood a few paces away, unsure what to do next. With many beginning to crouch in conversation around each warm pile, the bulk of the work seemed to be done. Realizing that his duties for the day were over, Amon felt the tension begin to drain from his body, his eyes drifting upwards.

He had been looking forward to a full view of the cosmos instead of the patches and slivers of stars visible between obstructions below. Sadly, the tattered blanket of clouds and haze overhead was denying him that pleasure. Yet after gazing upwards for a few minutes, he discovered a certain beauty in its pattern, like a gray fruit peel interspersed with pockets of darkening indigo, his mind drawn in and consoled by the sheer immensity of the sky reaching from horizon to horizon.

"Kenzaki-kun! Kenzaki-kun!"

Bringing his gaze down towards the voice, Amon saw a man waving at him from the opposite side of the stage. His focus resolved on a head in a seated crowd: it was Hippo. Sitting around him were Book, Little Book, Vertical, Ty, Rick, and a few councilors he recognized from the day of his hearing.

Amon stepped carefully through several huddled circles to round the stage and found Hippo beckoning to the spot beside him. "Come take a seat," he said, as everyone stared up at Amon expectantly, their faces yellow-gray under the warm glow.

Over the last few weeks, Amon had seen some of those present regularly: the Books continued their evening lessons, now with Rick in attendance; Ty sometimes enlisted them in brute tasks like righting tilting disposcrapers, or filling in liquefying craters in the island ground with debris; and Vertical still showed up occasionally to provide meticulous but impatient instructions for some seemingly sadistic reason, even though they could work independently with their crews now. But this was his first time seeing Hippo and the councilors since the day of his hearing.

It was strange to him that these elite denizens, the brains and brawn of the community, were paying him such special regard. Though Amon thought he had been just another insignificant case for the council, it had made an exception so that he could receive a secret education and had arranged specifically to reunite him with Rick. Now their special advisor had singled him out to join them and Amon couldn't imagine why. So he approached the company with trepidation, doubting his worthiness to join them as he sat down beside Hippo.

"Welcome," said Hippo. "Quite a long day, wasn't it?"

When Amon had settled cross-legged on the ground—Hippo to his right, Ty to his left, and Vertical, Rick, and the two Books on the other side of the circle—Hippo patted him on the back, and Amon felt the muscles along his spine flinch slightly. He still wasn't used to all the touching people did here—holding hands, giving massages—as the high price back in the Free World had discouraged it, and the contact of the man's hand filled him with an awkward, tender feeling.

Amon nodded. "Yes. Long and surprisingly chilly. But the breeze feels great with the embyrbrycks around and those clouds are wonderful."

At these words, Ty, Little Book, Vertical, and a couple others turned their heads to gaze upwards.

"Look what's happened to Kenzaki-kun here," said Hippo. "Just a few weeks ago he was in convulsions for his lost info. Now here he is, just another stargazer like the rest of us."

Everyone except Amon and Rick laughed at this, and Hippo proffered the open tip of a clear bottle filled with a liquid that looked golden-brown in the faint light. "Care to imbibe?"

Amon looked into Hippo's gleeful but somehow serious eyes and then down at the bottle. Although Hippo was not the first old person Amon had seen—there had been others in naked Tokyo before he crossed—he had never talked to one before and it felt strange to have his wrinkled face up close. He could smell alcohol wafting from the bottle and guessed it contained *suposhu*, a special moonshine made primarily of sports drinks that was much vaunted by the residents. The Charity Brigade seemed to have cut off all drugs, but they could do nothing to stifle secret brewers. Now Amon could explain Hippo's sudden friendliness. Partially at least.

"Ye—"

"Do you think it's safe to be offering him intoxicants?" Vertical cut Amon's yes please in half. "Don't forget, he hasn't been to Er like him." Vertical turned her head to indicate Rick, who was sitting beside her.

"Definitely best to be cautious," said the young man with the gray-streaked beard who had spoken against Amon being admitted. He glared at Hippo with a skeptical frown from the other side of the circle. "His mind is fragile. Maybe for good."

"Oh, he seems alright to me," said Hippo, looking Amon up and down. "What's your professional opinion, Books?"

Taptaptap, ta-tap . . . "From what we have hitherto observed and gathered from the reports of his supervisors, Amon Kenzaki's recovery from digital deprivation has been rapid and robust. Due to his inability to enter the Er program, he has not had the luxury of promowean or digidetox. Nonetheless, he has largely overcome perceptual fracture as far as we can determine from rudimentary sight and hearing tests, though his visual cortex is still adapting to naked inputs and it is yet to be seen whether he will regain the ability to read. His capacity to answer questions about the past demonstrates that he has made significant progress with naked oblivion and that his memory *retrieval*, at least, is functioning appropriately, though we have been unable to determine the state of his memory *production*. The severity of his affliction with other forms of cogwither is difficult to assess as the task set we assigned him was limited. Although his fasciculations appear to have gone into remission, he still shows other signs of focusburn, crowdcrave, marketitch, and promohunger. However, until he is able to obtain doses of deep stim from books, we believe the best remedy for him is to spend time outdoors, stay busy, and socialize as much as possible, speaking of course as non-specialists in infowithdrawal treatment."

While he was listening, Amon remembered the trivial questions Book had asked him repeatedly during the interviews and realized that they must have been cognitive tests.

"So it sounds as though he's in passable shape then, both physically and psychologically, eh?" said Hippo, eliciting a nod from Book before glancing at Vertical and the still-frowning councilor as if to check they were convinced, and proffering the bottle to Amon again. "A little sip then?"

Amon accepted the bottle and took a big swig. The taste was awful, like some combination of molasses, cumin, and bastard wine, and he coughed several times. Still, it did the trick, as a brain-numbing warmth floated up from his stomach almost immediately.

"How's my potion?" asked Ty.

"Foul," replied Amon between coughs. "But just what I needed."

The group laughed.

"Honesty isn't always the safest policy," said Ty with a playful sneer.

"Are you sure you didn't use to work in marketing, Amon?" said Hippo. "That would make a great motto for Ty's *suposhu*. 'Foul, but just what I need right now.'"

Everyone laughed again.

"That's a compliment, right?" asked Ty, reaching around to his tricycle.

"Of course, of course," said Hippo, smiling and raising his palms towards Ty in a gesture of mollification.

While several bottles of *suposhu* made the rounds, Amon listened quietly as they all traded stories about the events of the day, interspersed with plenty of silly banter. To his surprise and relief, they spoke in the standard dialect. Though Ty, Book, and a few others had accents, he could have mistaken Vertical and Hippo for bankliving, and everyone present was fluent enough that he could at least catch the gist of what they were saying. It was the first time he'd ever joined a group of people for no other purpose than to fool around and he had trouble getting involved, as though his mind was not quite tuned to their frequency. He began to feel anxious that he was failing to contribute in the way others expected, but soon noticed that Vertical behaved similarly, looking towards whoever was speaking and occasionally nodding or shaking her head, though rarely adding anything of her own. And Little Book just kept scrawling on his tablet, silently recording the happenings around him. The booze also seemed to melt Amon's inhibitions and after a few more swigs he was laughing at the jokes along with everyone else.

"So Amon, Rick. Book has told me that you two are learning quite quickly here," said Hippo in a low voice while the group was focused on a heated though not so serious debate surrounding Ty about the relative merits of different *suposhu* batches. It was clear to Amon that Hippo was referring to their orientations.

"I have no idea if we're learning quickly," said Amon. "There's so much we still don't understand, but we're doing our best."

Rick nodded in agreement.

"Well, do you have any questions for us now?" Hippo asked. "As I'm sure you've noticed, the Books are very knowledgeable, but they may not have answers for everything. Of course it would have to be something that's appropriate to talk about *here*."

By "here," Amon knew that Hippo meant "outside the digital quarantine." While Amon was knitting his brow with the effort of sifting his many questions for an appropriate one, Rick said, "There is one thing."

"Yes," said Hippo.

"So, um, I've been wondering about your names. I guess every place must have its own customs. But I can tell from your accents that some of you aren't from here originally. And I don't mean this in a rude way, but from the perspective of someone who grew up in Free Tokyo, your names seem pretty, well . . . creative."

When several people laughed at this, Amon realized that the group's attention was shifting to their conversation, the debate fizzling out.

"Very diplomatic way of saying 'weird,'" said Ty with a grin.

"I guess they think we should have boring names like Free Citizens," said the young man with the gray-streaked beard, giving Rick and then Amon a sharp glance.

"Perhaps now is a good time to tell them our name stories," said Hippo, preempting further quips.

A moment of silence filled by the chatter of the other groups around them followed. Amon could feel tension in the air as the councilor shot Hippo another skeptical stare, though Hippo seemed unperturbed.

"The council gives a new name to everyone on the day they're granted membership," he explained to Amon and Rick. "They're chosen on the basis of the tale each person tells at their hearing."

Then, addressing the group again, "So what do you think? They had to relate the events of their lives in detail at the council. It's only fair that we at least give them our name stories in return, even if they're ultimately to fail their trial periods."

Another silence came as Amon's festive calm was disturbed by the cold teeth of fear in his gut. *Fail our trial periods? Just as we're starting to adjust?* Only one week remained until the council was scheduled to consider their membership, and he couldn't imagine what they'd do if they were ejected. *Throw up a shelter on a precarious mound in one of the other enclaves? Convert to Opportunity Science?*

"I can go first if you like," said Ty eventually, drawing all eyes present.

"I was born in the District of Dreams from crashborn parents. A couple of bike nosties. And the collective we lived with hoarded all kinds of parts and tools.

"We kept trying to build a disposcraper, one big enough for all of us to live together. But we were all giftless, so some of our roombuds were defective or incompatible. They just wouldn't stick. The venture charities, they make them like this on purpose, to break us up. They know there's power in numbers. But all this does is play us and our gear right into the hands of the OpScis." Ty frowned with his roughly hewn forehead, starlight glimmering on his fierce eyes.

"I don't remember how old I was then—no more than six for sure—when they swept in at night. Toppled our building. By the time I crawled out of the rubble my father was a mess on the ground and they were dragging my mother away by the hair. I was the only one that got away." He patted the frame of the tricycle on his back affectionately as if it were his beloved steed. "I rolled into a tunnel too small for them to follow. Hid deep inside until they were gone.

"After that, I was on my own. I was just tall enough to reach the vending machines, so I could stay fed and watered. So long as I avoided the robbers and the orphan shepherds. But I was too little to find my way to Delivery for a room and clothes and all the rest. Doubt I would have survived the winter if Xenocyst hadn't taken me in."

Ty cast his gaze about to make a quick round of eye contact with the group and looked down to take a sip of *suposhu*.

"Anyways, about my name, I don't remember the incident myself. How the adoption scouts tell it, I was curled up in a deep, dark corner all alone when they found me. Almost naked with just the tiniest scraps of clothing still on me. They say I was so weak from hunger I was talking to things that weren't there and could barely keep my eyes open. But when someone tried to touch my tricycle, I snarled and attacked them like a wild beast. People grow up, but some things don't change, I guess."

As Ty explained, everyone at Xenocyst called him "Tricycle" in the beginning, which was pronounced *toraishikuru* in Japanese and eventually shortened to just "Tora." Since Tora sounded the same as the Japanese word for "tiger" and this matched the stories about how he reacted to his rescuers, the nickname stuck for years. Eventually people started to call him by the English "Tiger" for variation, and this in turn was shortened to just the first syllable, hence "Ty," which was the name the council settled on when he reached adolescence and was accepted as a full member.

★

Amon watched Ty intently while he was speaking, finding himself surprisingly rapt by mere words, the images they conjured paler than those of the ImmaNet but somehow rich in meaning. Beside Ty, Book had kept his ear tilted towards him, nodding thoughtfully. Not long after Ty was finished, he began to speak.

"I am a second-generation descendent of book nosties who refused to take part in the action-transaction system and were consequently driven to reside here, in the District of Dreams. My clan administered an analog academy in a condominium that we had secured, where my parents were the resident experts on our psychology and criminology literature. We expanded for a number of years as we received a steady influx of new books and scholars. At its peak, when I was approximately twenty years of age, our library had nearly ten times the inventory currently housed in the Cyst. Moreover, although our stacks were primarily for specialized research, we offered reading instruction and primary education to local youths in addition to advanced programs for individuals who demonstrated academic talent.

"However, we were informed one winter day that the condominium was substandard housing and would therefore be demolished as one component of an 'End Slums Forever' campaign. When our petitions to the Charity Brigade to cancel the initiative were rejected or stalled indefinitely, our only remaining option was to take up residence in disposable skyscrapers. However, constantly relocating our academy on a bi-weekly to monthly basis rapidly became a significant strain on the community. An increasing percentage of our members began to vacate with their books, resulting in the gradual depletion of our library. It was at this crucial juncture that I received news of Xenocyst, which had only recently been established, and learned also of the council's desire to provide educational services. With a stable condominium still under their administration—not to mention a variety of equipment, supplies, and expertise—they seemed far better qualified to archive our books than we were. Therefore, after conferring with the council, I persuaded my clan for permission to transfer a large selection. Initially, I designed the curriculum for Xenocyst's various classes. Ever since we became unable to conduct them, I have served as librarian and inquisitor. I do not believe it is necessary to explain how the council chose my name."

After a pause of only about one second, *tap-ta-taptaptap, ta-tap* . . . "I have received a personal request to relate Little Book's story on his behalf as he has no memories prior to his living in Xenocyst." The tapping stopped and Book continued.

"I was serving as inquisitor on the day that an undertaker crew carried into the council chamber a hearse. Prone atop it were five injured individuals dressed in the unbranded patchwork uniform of lower caste Opportunity Scientists. According to the head undertaker's report, her crew had been called to a rooftop on the border between one of our proxy enclaves and the outer foothills of Opportunity Peaks to assist the locals with disposal of an unauthorized sky burial. However, when they arrived, they observed several of the alleged corpses in the heap tossing and turning. Rather than ruthlessly disposing of living people in the local charnel grounds as duty recommended, they decided to transport the survivors to the council chamber for official consideration.

"I recall the discussion in detail. The council inferred, firstly, that these were victims of a ritual lynching and excommunication by the Quantitative Priesthood, most likely because they had been downgraded suddenly by plutogenic algorithms from holy brandclan member to giftless and were now believed to have DNA that could infect the marketability of others. Some councilors argued that Xenocyst should not be responsible for any superstitious brutality the religion inflicted on its own believers. However, others responded that it would be unconscionable to simply allow the injured to perish, and the council judged that those who convalesced might provide insider facts concerning their esoteric cult.

"Two of the five had died en route, and one was ejected after recovery and interviewing. The remnants were a woman and a boy of approximately eight years of age, both of whom were unconscious due to concussions. When the woman regained awareness, she repeatedly asked for information concerning her son and was granted access to the bedside of the still-comatose boy. Although Xenocyst policy forbids membership to any individual with connections to Opportunity Science, her doctors negotiated with the council to allow her to reside until the boy recovered.

However, several days before he did so, she attended a supply run and did not return, presumably to beg for absolution at Opportunity Peaks.

"When her son opened his eyes, he made no mention of wanting to see his mother as one might predict of a boy that age. In fact, the nurses discovered his inability to produce verbal speech, although he seemed to comprehend it, and he was sent to me for assessment. Whether his condition was congenital or resulted from the head trauma, I immediately recognized that he was a cognitive outlier. The precocious boy read at remarkable speed, displayed fascination with codes of all sorts, and developed a highly efficient tap code that he taught me so as to facilitate our communication. With the council's permission, I have personally overseen his education ever since and his knowledge in my areas of expertise already surpasses my own. After Tamper observed the degree to which he enjoyed writing, he designed him this tablet and Little Book has since assumed the roles of official record keeper, historian, and cryptographer.

"As I am certain you can deduce, the council named him after myself. However, he is sometimes referred to as LB, and when I am in a condescending mood my preferred appellation is Puchiboo, an abbreviation for 'petite book.'"

Apparently not at all pleased with this cutesy nickname, Little Book began to tap furiously on his tablet and Book said, "I refuse to interpret that part." So Little Book stopped his writing for the first time, breathing heavily with apparent indignation as he continued staring at the tablet, and the group laughed.

After Little Book, they went slowly around the circle in no particular order and the other six odd members told Amon and Rick their names, and why they had been given them. Despite their drunkenness, everyone was surprisingly courteous, cutting off all tomfoolery and giving their undivided attention when someone was speaking. Storytelling, Amon was learning, was something the bankdead took very seriously. Eventually they all went silent, and Amon noticed that everyone was looking towards one person who had not yet spoken.

Under their stare, Vertical shook her head. "No. I'm not getting into that here."

"Feeling embarrassed in front of these handsome new recruits, is that it?" said Ty.

Vertical glanced at Rick and then Amon before her eyes settled on Ty. "Believe what you like. Just leave me alone."

"Come on Vertical, we—"

"In the spirit of fairness," interrupted Hippo, "I do believe it's our turn to hear your story, Vertical."

"Fairness?" she said as though in disbelief. "You only told your stories for the crashnewbs. Do you really think *I* wanted to hear them *again*?"

"What's this—" "Oh, so she thinks—" "Ha! And you—" Several protests trundled in at once until Hippo's voice stopped them short with authority. "If not for us, Vertical, then for these two," he said, glancing at Amon and then Rick. "They bared their souls for all of us at the council, including you, and they may leave Xenocyst with no other reward than what they learn here."

Leave Xenocyst? Amon's mind echoed, the cold teeth of fear digging deeper.

"The least you can do is give them another story for the road."

"I would, but Ty was right from the start. The embarrassment . . ." Vertical's excuses were drowned out by fed-up calls of agreement with Hippo and Ty. She kept her mouth shut as the clamor continued, merely shaking her head. But the group was persistent in their cajolery, and when she eventually rolled her eyes, letting out a big, shoulder-sinking sigh of capitulation, they cheered.

"In my banklife I was a world-class sprinter. I'd placed well in several global races and was selected to represent Japan in the next Olympics. But just when I was reaching my peak as an athlete, massively multiplayer online sports began to take over and the popularity of traditional analog games hit a new low. I was one of the best in the world but even for someone like me sponsorship funding had almost completely dried up. Though I might have found work as a coach, the pay was pathetic and I had no interest in that. So I kept up the same training routine as always and attended every competition I was invited to at my own expense, just coasting along on my savings for as long as I could. The turnouts were small, but I'd spent my entire life running and I literally couldn't imagine doing anything else.

"I guess it's not surprising that my husband disapproved. He wanted me to balance my passion with practical financing and compromise on a day job. When he saw that I'd made a clear decision and wasn't willing to budge, he offered to support me. I refused. Yes, I was terrified of bankruptcy, but he was a law student living mostly on a scholarship. I wasn't about to drag him down with me. Not for my own selfish goals. As time passed, he worried about me more and more, until he got so tense I couldn't bear to tell him about my debt. I knew he'd try everything to stop me if he thought my situation was serious. In the end, I went bankrupt before we could say goodbye.

"After Er, I eventually found my way to Xenocyst and was accepted into the community. I'm grateful to be here. I feel like my abilities are valued and respected. The whole District of Dreams is my personal gym and the nutritional bonus the council provides allows me to train as much as I like. I may not have the chance to compete with anyone at my level and there's hardly any space for open running, but I've learned to direct my momentum in vertical directions."

As Vertical told her story, she kept her eyes half-closed with her gaze downcast, as though she were summoning memories from deep in her body. Only when she was finished did she finally look up, open her eyes wide, and take in the gaze of her audience. Immediately Ty said, "Vertical directions? You're not going to pretend that's how it ends?"

Painful emotion quivered momentarily across Vertical's face before she glared at Ty with a look of pure vitriol.

"What?" said Ty, grinning his raucous grin again. "That's not how I heard you got your name. You're leaving out the best part!"

"Ty is right," said a middle-aged woman with a white ovular face that reminded Amon of a clam shell. Her name, he had just learned, was Jiku. "I remember the day of her hearing well."

"I wasn't on the council then, so I wanna hear it too, if there's more," said the man with the gray-streaked beard, whose name was Yané.

"Come on." "Just give it—" "Yeah!" Others called out in support.

Vertical just shook her head repeatedly, mouthing the word "no." Although it was too subtle perhaps for the more inebriated members to catch, Amon thought he saw a moist glaze of sadness glitter in her eyes despite the affronted scowl as they pressed.

"Let's stop this now," said Hippo, apparently noticing the change in Vertical too. "I think she's given us enough."

"Half a story enough?" said Ty. "What about when you tried to go back there with him? It's only fair."

"Ty!" barked Hippo. "Let her be!" But before he'd finished the sentence, Vertical was on her feet and skipping rapidly from gap to gap in the tight knots of seated bodies, vanishing before they knew it.

"Vertical!" called Ty as the eyes of the group stared at the spot in the crowd into which she'd slipped, all of them looking startled and guilty. With a loud "tsk," Ty slumped forward, shaking his head with his face in his hands.

11
BETWEEN SLUM & STARS, NIGHT

The group went silent for a time, but they were too drunk for the incident with Vertical to spoil the celebration and gradually broke up into separate conversations in twos and threes. As Amon sat there bathing in reddish warmth from the nearby embyrbrycks, he watched several men hauling a sack through the crowd and handing out the vending grub inside as more bottles of *suposhu* made the rounds. The kites of children were sliding bird-like shadows over a skyscape of scattered cloud, blinking satellite, and concentrate of star as the crowd chattered and swayed around him. The sack of food approached, and when a man passed Amon a burrito, he imitated those around him in rubbing it between his palms just like the women with the embyrbrycks earlier. Soon he felt it begin to warm in his hands and chomped it down in two bites without removing the wrapper.

All the while, his thoughts were caught in a loop on what Hippo had implied earlier about him and Rick failing their trial period. Amon remembered the harsh eyes of the councilor after he'd cut him off to question his mental stability. Then he recalled moments when other councilors present had met his gaze with what he now imagined was similar disapproval in their eyes too. *Has the council already decided against us?* he fretted. *Are our days here numbered?* They would starve out there. Or die of illness. Or be crushed. Or attacked. But Hippo had said . . . and that man had cut him off . . . and the other councilors . . .

The same worries cycled again and again, until the band was finally set up on stage and music, the likes of which Amon had never heard, washed them from his awareness. Turntablists sat on chairs before treadle performance record players with attached amplification horns and built-in cross-faders. Behind them was a choir of singers, beatboxers, and fluteboxers, and on a raised gazebo-like platform several zither players. Over the clambering, jerky tit-tatter of a vocal drum ensemble and the eerie hum of the zithers, two choirs separated by three octaves sang bullfrog overdrive throat-bass and buzzing gospel-laser as the fluteboxers layered on pulsing, sorrowful ululations. The turntablists embellished it all with fade-in-and-out waves of improvised scratching, their pumping feet modulating the pitch of each warping sound as their hands jumped in skittering blurs over the vinyl. The result was a sonic tapestry of amelodic transharmonies in low tempo polyrhythms, reminiscent of traditional DIY dubstep, but with an otherworldly *gagaku* flavor, the beat seeming to celebrate a sort of persistence amidst oppressive monotony.

A few young couples started dancing beside the stage and the crowd cleared a circular space around them. To Amon's eyes, it was old-fashioned—a sort of pair dance that involved synchronized movements like videotape functions while holding hands. Their bodies appeared to flow together in slow motion punctuated by jolts of fast-forward, sudden pauses, and occasional rewinds. The skilled pairs timed these temporal shifts so synchronously they might have been controlled by the same remote. They also had this way of angling their bodies and breathing that made them appear two dimensional, as though they existed as flat images on a screen that was the sky behind them.

With so many novel experiences coming one after the other, Amon soon forgot his troubles and found himself in silent thrall to his surround. If they weren't performing or dancing, the participants were chatting, holding hands, smiling, frowning, cringing, laughing. The babies cradled in sheltering arms stared with all-absorbing wide eyes, smiled delirious baby smiles as they were rocked to the beat, or wailed as their mothers cooed soothingly. Children gamboled in the in-between spaces, darting beneath the arches of men leaning close for drunken conversation and receiving smacks when they tumbled onto the dance floor or made sudden movements anywhere close to the outer edges.

Without exception, it was the most bizarre spectacle Amon had ever beheld: people just being together bodily and sharing the night in celebration of the changing seasons. He thought he could almost sense the grinding hum of their souls, their struggles and needs and little joys in every gesture and vocalization, not released into the public for anyone's personal enjoyment but given over to all others in attendance fully and completely, the gathering itself a work of art for the sake of nothing but itself. The lines between entertainer and entertained seemed to blur and break so that even though he sat silently on the rooftop as dazed with curiosity as the infants, he felt as much a part of the performance as the audience—as though he were a viewer sucked inside a movie that they were all creating together.

Glancing around at the group, Amon saw everyone looking as absorbed and ponderous as he felt, their eyes capturing the moment yet somehow removed from it. Above them all, a rift had opened in the center of the cloud peel, as though a wedge of densely clustered stars were splitting the sky asunder. There, traced out in twinkling lights, Amon thought he could see Tamper giving the drink to his son on that balcony, just as the InfoStars had once animated logos. It was a sad vision, the gulf of light years separating these star-figments seeming no more traversable than the digital gulf separating the people Amon's imagination had made them from. He wondered then about the coded letter that Book had described as "personal." What did it say? Had Hippo read it?

Just then Hippo was sitting there watching the stage in silence, his chest rising and falling with long slow breaths, listening. He wore such an intense and serious look of absorption, Amon had to move his lips several times before he worked up the courage to say anything and interrupt him.

"Hippo-sama."

Drawn by his name, Hippo turned to Amon. There was a split-second pause before he returned to the present, saw who Amon was, understood his words.

"Just Hippo is fine," he said. "That's what everyone else calls me."

"Hippo."

"Yes?"

"I was wondering . . ."

Hippo met Amon's gaze, waiting.

"Just now I was looking at the stars . . . and . . . I started to think . . . I-I remembered about Tamper. I mean, what about his name?"

"That's right. You met Tamper, didn't you?"

"Yes. Does anyone here know that story?"

"Well, several of us could tell it, I suppose, if there was anything to tell."

"What do you mean?"

"Who would like the honors?" said Hippo, glancing around the circle. "Anyone?"

"This one's yours if it's anyone's," said Ty, who had been sitting up straight for a while now, no longer moping about Vertical.

"You could help me out, couldn't you Ty? I do believe you two were friends."

"Tamper was a good guy. I liked his work. But he wasn't exactly a talker. You knew him better than anyone, I bet, though that's not saying much."

Hippo closed his eyes, nodding thoughtfully. "Yes. Fine. I don't think I've told this one before but I suppose there's no better time than tonight."

Then Hippo raised his head and opened his eyes wide, taking in the attention of the whole circle.

"Several years ago, the council heard rumors of a bankdead man who had an incredible talent for electronics. It was said that he could build almost any device if given the proper materials. We thought he could be useful in Xenocyst, and decided to have our scouts seek him out. They eventually found him in the Tumbles, where he was living in a sort of burrow. He had dug a hole in a heap of Fleet rubble at the base of a disposcraper and lay curled up inside, surrounded by various tools and electronic parts. The walls around him were literally shaking with the strain of shelters piled on top, being nearly on the verge of collapse. So our scouts offered him a place to stay in exchange for his services, to which he accepted.

"After no more than two weeks, the council was already so impressed by what he could do that we fast-tracked his trial period and invited him to a membership screening. He agreed to attend of course, but when we asked for his story he refrained from telling it. He didn't explicitly refuse or even shake his head. He simply maintained his silence no matter what anyone said to him while his fiddling with all the doodads in his pockets grew faster and faster. Obviously this man had been hurt by something in his past about which he was unable to speak. So in order to keep his skills within Xenocyst, we voted on an unprecedented exception and waived the requirement of a hearing. Since we never learned who he had been, we named him after what he seemed to enjoy doing.

"Tamper ended up working here for several years. LB's tablet and the transistor radios we use are his handiwork, as are a few emergency lights and the digital quarantine devices installed in the council chamber. Being a man of few words, no one ever learned much about him. He used to come to my quarters at the end of the day and join me for an evening walk, but he rarely spoke even to me. Then one day about two years ago he said he was leaving for Free Tokyo, though he wouldn't say why. We occasionally received coded reports with information he had gathered from the other side—usually carried back by crashdead escapees who realized they couldn't survive outside the camps and had to be boated back by Tamper in exchange for a story—but those stopped a few months back and we imagined the worst.

"After what I heard from you, Amon, I think we should have called him Ghost. It's sad to hear how he haunts his son. If only we'd known how troubled he was by their estrangement, we might have been able to give him advice. Now it seems he's overweight and his fiddling is much worse than before. It worries me particularly that someone as private as Tamper was willing to open up the way he did in that letter. It's almost as though he's expecting something bad to happen and wants to clear his conscience before the end . . . I suppose that's what you get for trying to start a family in this world. But let's leave this heavy topic for now. It doesn't suit the occasion."

Hippo stopped and took a sip of *suposhu*, tilting his ear towards the stage as though listening carefully to the music, and the other members went silent, lost in their own thoughts. Amon glanced at their faces one by one and reflected on their various stories. Although relating memories by speech still felt alien to him, there was something comforting, he realized, about knowing what brought them here. He sensed intimacy between them now, even more so in some ways than he had with Rick before cash crashing, as they'd mostly shared LifeStream segs whereas there seemed to be something more binding, more . . . communal? about the act of narration directly through the air from tongue to ear.

Amon's gaze paused on Rick, and seeing that he was staring down at his lap with brooding, sad eyes, he immediately perceived what he was thinking. Rick's greatest aspiration had been to start a family with Mayuko and he'd been determined to achieve this in spite of all the financial obstacles. Now that possibility had been taken from him by Sekido's betrayal, and Hippo's closing words had surely reminded him of this hard, irreversible fact. Amon wanted to go over and put a comforting hand on his friend's shoulder, but felt awkward approaching him when he thought of the lie he'd told about Mayuko, floating between them like an invisible barrier. And when Rick sensed Amon watching him and looked up to meet his gaze, Amon couldn't help but avert his eyes.

"I'm going to the toilet," Rick muttered to no one in particular as he stood up, and began to carve his way slowly through the crowd with his head slightly bowed. He paused momentarily as he waited for a line of men to pass in front of him, his shoulders rising and then falling visibly with one great sigh, before he entered the gap in the standing bodies they had left and stepped out of sight.

Strange movements caught Amon's eye and he glanced to the stage, where a dance troupe of a dozen or so was putting on a show. The beat thrummed on continuously as it had the whole time, leaving no clear line between songs. The musicians just kept adjusting the phrases they repeated, subtly and incrementally, so that the soundscape was ever in transition, shifting so seamlessly Amon hardly noticed the changes until suddenly there was a whole new groove. Beside the band, the dancers intertwined their bodies into branching tree-like formations that ticked incrementally into new configurations, strobing their limbs to the beat like choppy cartoons. It struck Amon as strange that the people here, most of whom had never seen projected images, nonetheless imitated them in their art, like some distorted reflection in the mirror of progress.

Bringing his gaze back to the circle, Amon saw Hippo talking with a young couple. They had been waiting not far from the circle and had approached the moment he finished his tale to ask for advice. Amon was listening to the three of them discuss how to stop a leak in one of a condo's basement floors when he realized that Hippo hadn't yet told his own story. Vertical's dramatic exit, it seemed, had interrupted the rotation and wiped the fact that one person had been left out from everyone's minds.

Here, holding together the whole group, like a hidden pillar supporting the structure of their interconnected lives, was a gap, a narrative lacuna. Each one of them had been drawn to this community and it had embraced them, providing order, security, and health—a better life than they could have hoped for elsewhere. From orphans and pregnant mothers to outcast crashdead like Amon, Rick, and Vertical, Xenocyst helped all sorts of people. Yet Amon still didn't understand how it worked, who funded it, what its relation was to the venture charities or the Charity Gift Economy. All these questions and many more seemed to circle around Hippo, about whose past Amon knew only that he was bankdead but kept his BodyBank like Amon, an enigma that roused his curiosity like nothing else. He was working up the nerve to ask Hippo another question, when, as soon as the couple was finished, a man came over to discuss the spread of an infection in one of the birthing rooms.

Presently a group of about a dozen kids surrounded Ty and began to pester him, tugging at his collar and pleading until he reluctantly stood up and they all cheered. With the little ones swarming around his waist, he made his way towards the northern edge of the square and stopped on a somewhat less crowded roof. There he detached the wheels from his tricycle and began to do tricks with them—spiraling and ricocheting them off each other in complex patterns in the air—as the children pointed upwards shouting excitedly, pushing each other to gather close and grip his shorts.

Soon Book and Little Book got up and made their way to a lineup in front of a telescope standing in a far corner. One by one, the members of the circle wandered off—some to the palm reader who had just set up a table nearby, some to dance, some to who knows where. Eventually the advice-seekers too were gone, leaving only Amon and Hippo. Finally, it seemed, the moment had come to ask for his name story, but before Amon could open his mouth, Hippo turned to him and, in a low voice, asked, "How's it all going, Amon? Are you adjusting to life in Xenocyst alright?"

"Yes . . . I'd say so. I'm doing fine, I think."

"So there's nothing bothering you that you'd like to get off your chest?"

"Not really . . ." Ten thousand worries frothed up all at once but none seemed worth raising, and Amon left them to bubble away.

" . . . "

" . . . "

"Don't be afraid to speak openly with me, Amon. I know from personal experience just how hard it can be to settle in the District of Dreams, and I've watched many others go through it. It's overwhelming to suddenly be learning a million things at the same time. But your transition has been particularly tough, I think. Although many are denied Er treatment as you were, they at least have their BodyBanks removed safely."

Hippo paused, waiting for Amon to speak. But Amon froze under the penetrating attentiveness of his gaze, unsure what to tell him, his jaw quivering slightly though no words coming out. When a few bars of the beat had passed, Hippo put his arm around Amon and leaned in close, as Amon had seen others do when having a private conversation.

"There's no need to worry. Nothing you tell me now will reach the council or hurt your chances at membership. For my part, having some insight into what you're actually going through will only speak in your favor."

Again Amon felt the cold teeth clench in his gut as he was reminded of the question about his and Rick's future at Xenocyst. While he didn't want to lie and pretend everything was perfect when it definitely wasn't, he was worried his private thoughts and feelings might offend Hippo in spite of what he'd said. Yet being honest had taken him this far, earning him a trial period after his hearing, and something in Hippo's steady gaze seemed to unravel his fears. Up close, his dark brown eyes appeared infinitely receptive yet troubled, as though trying to embrace the whole world but failing again and again, his warm arm around Amon's shoulders and the stroke of his booze-tinged breath on Amon's cheek somehow adding reassurance to his words.

"Well . . ." Amon began. "I'd say that . . . yes, there are a number of challenges I'm still working through."

"Such as?"

"Hmm . . . Like . . . I've been having *some* trouble bonding with my co-workers and neighbors and everyone . . ."

"I'm sure. In fact, I'd find it unbelievable if you weren't. What else?"

"A lot of the symptoms Book mentioned earlier, I guess. Craving for apps and information and the boredom of having no video stimulation here. Then there's the different working style and finding my way around without any assistance. It's uncomfortable how everything is always changing. Not just the outer layer, the way it looks and sounds—the overlay changed like that too—but physically . . . Nothing lasts, so it's kind of hard to find your footing, mentally, if that makes sense. I mean, I've only been here for about two months, but even if I stayed for years I don't know if I'd ever find a stable enough place to put down roots . . . Don't take this the wrong way, but I'm also feeling disappointed with myself in the way I guess a lot of crashdead maybe feel disappointed in themselves. Because I used to have a job that I saw as important. Here I'm a nobody . . . But all of these problems, as much as they get me down sometimes, they feel manageable, like in time I'll be able to get over them."

Especially with Rick back, he thought, looking in the direction his friend had gone and wondering where he was. Some of the embyrbrycks were beginning to dissolve, red-hot specks drifting off with each gust of wind like cinders popping off a fire. These joined in the air with flakes detaching from the stage and fluttered up on drafts to form double helixes of shadow petals swirling around dots of tangerine glow before dissipating into the star pockets above. While the pairs continued their slow-mo, stop and rewind moves on the dance floor, the troupe were tangled together in a heap on the stage now, moving at double speed to the beat, limbs weaving through each other like a swarm of ticking robotic snakes, as the intensity of the music surged. Although the tempo remained steady and slow, the layered waves of rhythm shifting incrementally, a disjointed, mesmerizing force emerged from the interfusion of nether-notes, seeming to draw Amon's awareness into the depths of the continuous song like an undertow. A surging hiss of appreciative gasps rose from all around them, washing away all other sounds but Hippo's voice.

"I admire your positivity and have faith that what you say is true," he said, drawing back Amon's gaze. "With continued effort, I'm sure you'll succeed in surmounting those problems eventually. But I sense that you have other problems on your mind about which you are less optimistic. Am I right?"

"Yes . . . well . . . I'm lucky, I guess, though I never planned it this way—not by a long shot. I'm lucky that I forced myself to live frugally before, because I'm already used to doing with less apps and luxuries than most crashnewbs. All the habits and restraint I cultivated are giving me the strength to get through this.

"But . . . but this same training I made myself go through also feels like a weakness. Like I'm so used to calculating the cost of everything I do that I feel the absence of the market more intensely than I imagine others would. Every time I do anything, even little things like taking a step or licking my lips, I feel . . . indebted, not to anyone in particular, just to someone. And I have so much trouble making up my mind about even the simplest things. Like I'm always wondering whether I should blink now or wait a few milliseconds. Bite my rice ball or nibble it. Ask one of my co-workers a question immediately or wait until later. There's no price tag on any of these options, so they all feel as good as any other. But if I accept that, then there's no more reason to get out of bed in the morning than to lie there all day . . ."

No more reason to climb down a stairwell to work than to leap off it to the hard rooftops far below, he thought, but kept the depths of his despair to himself.

"I see. Yes, I sympathize with your conundrum," said Hippo. "I wish I could tell you where to find meaning in your choices, but that itself is a choice that only you can make. All I can suggest is to give it time. With sustained effort and reflection, the answer is sure to present itself."

"Thank you for your advice," said Amon, bowing slightly to Hippo, though he felt an inexplicable pang of doubt in his chest and turned away from him. As Hippo's arm slid from his shoulders, Amon spotted Rick. The dance floor had thinned out somewhat, and a group of thirty-somethings were accosting younger people chatting around the edges and tugging them into the center. One was emerging from the crowd hauling Rick and Vertical by their wrists. They were shaking their heads and protesting but nonetheless following along. The man deposited them in the midst of all the dancers and pushed them together, smiling and cajoling until they reluctantly took each other's hands, before hurrying off to find more victims. The music had settled temporarily into a quieter, more mellow groove, and the two of them merely stood there for several bars looking around self-consciously, until Vertical took the initiative and they began to sway. Vertical's mood seemed to have recovered. She smiled her horse-like smile as she taught Rick the steps and techniques, and Rick followed along with an embarrassed grin. Watching her graceful movements, Amon felt titillated for the first time by her beautiful, athletic body, with its tight curves and hard, shapely breasts. If only she wasn't so prickly. Then Rick's eyes met Amon's for a moment and, seeing simple joy in place of the earlier sadness in his gaze, Amon somehow found words for his doubts. He turned back to Hippo, and, leaning in close, said, "Still, to be honest, I'm not sure it's that simple."

"How so?" asked Hippo, putting his arm around Amon again.

"I mean . . . I don't know if I should bring this up, especially not at a celebration like this . . ."

"No, please. I can tell we're just getting to the core of your concerns."

Amon nodded. "Well, what I'm thinking relates to this one discussion I had with Rick and the Books the other day."

"What sort of discussion?"

"It started with a question that Rick asked." It had been Rick's first time joining Amon for one of his lessons in the council chamber. Although Amon never had the nerve to interrupt the Books, instead concentrating his attention on absorbing the complex ideas he was hearing, Rick had shown no hesitation in cutting in for clarification from the very start. "We were talking about the Charity Gift Economy and he wanted to know something about the marketability of the gene pool in the District of Dreams."

"Yes."

"Well, basically, the Books were in the middle of telling us how the Philanthropy Syndicate has set up this elaborate system to collect marketable human resources. He wanted to know, if marketable babies are all given to the charities and the unmarketable ones remain, why doesn't this lead to a decline in the marketability of the gene pool over time? It seems that the venture charities should be handing out condoms to the giftless or something, but they're not."

"And I suppose they explained about the variability of the standard of marketability," said Hippo.

"Yes," said Amon. "Their answer to Rick was a definitive no. Since what's considered marketable is constantly shifting, those who are giftless now could become gifted later. And because giftless sometimes produce marketable babies by chance, the more of them the better from the perspective of the Philanthropy Syndicate."

As Book had explained, the fact that a baby was marketable—that they were likely to be the ideal applicant for a possible job in twenty years—did not necessarily mean that they were likely to produce a baby upon reaching maturity who would themselves produce such an ideal applicant twenty years from their birth. By that time, the demands of the market would have drastically changed. In other words, marketable babies were not guaranteed to become gifted adults because what the plutogenic algorithm of each MegaGlom defined as marketable shifted frequently. This was due to developments in the theories underlying these algorithms, variation in factors fed into the algorithms (such as the availability of appropriate mates), the growth of technologies, and revision of educational methods. So while there were slight fluctuations in the average marketability of the gene pool, the loss of marketable babies caused no steady decline over time.

Rather, what might cause such a decline, contrary to Rick's suggestion, was the culling of the giftless population through the use of contraceptives. This was because giftless adults were occasionally upgraded to gifted or produced unmarketable babies who turned out to be gifted as the standard of marketability (and giftedness) changed. Moreover, due to the random manner in which hereditary traits from parents are passed on to each embryo, giftless couples also occasionally produced marketable babies, while gifted couples frequently produced unmarketable but gifted or simply giftless babies. Since the gifted were more likely to produce valuable resources, cost-benefit analysis recommended providing them a slight bonus to raise the statistical chance of their success in reproducing, and each MegaGlom invested in its own vending machine brand to distribute this bonus, cultivating a brandclan over which it had claim to resources. But allowing and even encouraging the giftless to proliferate was preferable as it tended to increase the size and diversity of the population, which raised the probability of their occasionally producing a baby who was marketable, gifted, or set to one day become gifted according to one of the algorithms. To this end, therefore, the Philanthropy Syndicate jointly operated the generic vending machines and maximized the likelihood of an increase in total yield at minimal cost.

"Right," said Hippo. "And how exactly does that relate to the issues you're facing, Amon?"

"It led me to ask a question of my own. It seemed to me that their explanation raised a number of moral issues. The way they described the Charity Gift Economy made it sound like people were cattle or show dogs or something. I couldn't see how GATA could call hiring bankdead to provide babies exploitation and charge MegaGloms credicrime fines for that, but allow them to basically initiate a collective breeding scheme."

"And how did the Books respond?"

"They said that according to the standard line taken by the Philanthropy Syndicate, the Charity Gift Economy is not comparable to breeding because there is no connection between the parents choosing to gift their babies willingly and the venture charities providing supplies out of pure kindness. Instead it is the ultimate expression of freedom."

While the gifted had learned over time that remaining together in their brandclans and mating in their designated pairs improved their chances to be able to gift a baby and earn more supplies, no one was ever forced or even asked to breed and no one forcibly prevented from doing so, either through the threat of violence or by any other means. The bankdead had never even been taught explicitly that there was any connection between the genes of the parents, whether babies were accepted, and the category of supplies disbursed. If anyone were to teach them this, the CG Economy could potentially be mistaken for a black market arrangement, requiring GATA to issue fines. Instead, bankdead had simply learned over the years through experience how the machines operated and decided of their own free will to accommodate their lives accordingly.

The whole process was automated, systematic, and objective. The Philanthropy Syndicate generously provided charity and the bankdead provided gifts of their own volition. The MegaGloms might decide sometimes to adjust that charity according to their own business models or not take in some babies depending on certain abstract standards, but this did nothing to change the essentially compassionate nature of their giving. Already they provided a basic minimum for everyone, which some even referred to as welfare corpocracy. If they decided to provide more for certain individuals, that was their own prerogative, and where was the fault in giving more? If the bankdead were influenced to behave in a certain way by such adjustments, that did not alter the fact that they were making voluntary choices. The venture charities simply operated drop boxes for babies, similar to the foundling wheels of Europe in the Middle Ages though sealed with temperature controls to protect their contents from the elements and vermin. This was a service for unfortunate parents who could not adequately take care of their offspring, and for their unfortunate offspring who were granted Opportunities and Freedom as a result. So if there was even the faintest trace of pressure on the bankdead, it was to encourage generosity towards the next generation. In the words of the MegaGlom human resource PR manuals that the Books had quoted, the level of scarcity and quality of supplies were the main 'humanitarian pressures' adjusted in a process of 'charitable selection' to ensure marketable genes would survive and the overall marketability of the gene pool would gradually increase, or at least remain in equilibrium, depending on what the market demanded.

For all these reasons, in the final analysis, the Charity Gift Economy was a process that arose spontaneously from the interactions of free individuals all pursuing their self-interests in accordance with laws—not from some imposition of any will over another. To call it 'breeding' was simply a misnomer. Rather, it was in keeping with the ideals of liberty and individual autonomy that made the free market possible.

"I'm still unclear about how this relates to your original concern, Amon? Could you elaborate?"

"Well, I didn't find the answer of the Books particular satisfying."

"I would certainly hope not."

"No, it's obviously a partial, self-serving picture of the situation here. But I couldn't come up with any follow-up questions. Instead, it got me thinking about the idea of freedom and the different kinds of meaning it can have."

Amon glanced up at the sky as if to summon inspiration from the patches of stars, but a thin gray film had bled from the interlinked cloud blots into the pockets between them, hazing and dulling their light.

"Even though I'm learning a lot from the Books, figuring out the terrain from my trips outside Xenocyst—my Hinkongo is good enough that I can ask questions of my co-workers now too—there's still a lot I don't understand about this place. So I could be totally wrong about all this. But, I mean, in some ways I almost agree that we do have a certain kind of freedom here in the District of Dreams. Free Citizens supposedly get all the freedom they can earn, but this means they *must* earn all their freedom, every bit of it. Here everyone has their basic needs met—something to eat, a place to sleep—without having to earn any money or serve the market. In a certain way, this allows us to be free or ensures that the freedom we have is in some sense truly free. In theory, it almost seems too good to be true, like the District of Dreams really is the best of all possible slums. No one is compelled to have a job or do anything in particular, so, in principle, we can do whatever we like with our time. Often this means just lazing about, but it could mean trying to better the situation, as it does at Xenocyst. Though we may not get paid for what we do here, I feel like we're helping people that really need it, with the hospital for mothers and the orphanage and everything, and we all contribute to maintain order and security for the whole enclave, which benefits everyone. Also, I can't say all the art is to my taste, but it's starting to grow on me and I can see how much it uplifts not just the regular residents but the artists themselves."

Amon paused for a moment to think of all the creativity he had witnessed, from the architectural comics to the children piloting make-believe spaceship kites to the band and dancers performing right beside them.

"So what I want to say is . . . it amazes me how much we're able to better ourselves and the community through our own efforts with so little. But at the same time, there's a limit to how much improvement we can make because life here is a tough slog. We may not need to work, but to get bare subsistence—the minimum nutrition, shelter, and clothes designed without any thought for comfort or style—just to get that, we have to use up all our energy on pointless tasks. We're always exhausted from constantly rebuilding our homes, climbing these insanely tall buildings to sleep each night, and descending to the feeding stations again the next day. Then there's the supply pickup, which is a long and dangerous trek whatever route you take, and everywhere you go, even in Xenocyst, it's packed and hot and suffocating and falling apart constantly . . . People like you and Book over forty are a rarity, right? I think that says a lot . . . Have I gone too far?"

"No," said Hippo, keeping his embracing eyes on Amon's. "Please go on."

"I mean, I see all this and I look back on my former life. Rick and I were Liquidators as you know. We dedicated the better part of our adult lives to banishing people here. We even felt pride in our work. That's how deluded we were. So many people condemned to misery by our hands. Losing the pricing on my actions isn't the only thing that makes it hard for me to get up, to get moving . . ." *to go on living*, he thought.

"I wish someone could give me the answer. I mean, I just don't see what we're supposed to be achieving here. We may not have to earn any of our freedom, but without the freedom to earn it seems like we can never be free at all. Instead, we labor away just to maintain conditions that are barely tolerable and nothing seems to improve. Despite being exempt from paying for our actions we're basically trapped doing the same things over and over. Don't get me wrong. Xenocyst provides a lot of great services, but so do the venture charities, right? And in the end, we're basically supporting them by providing them with human resources. Not only that, but we depend on them for the most basic necessities to stay alive. That means our fates are decided by the same plutogenic algorithms as everyone else in the camps. Our choices are limited by the same humanitarian pressures. So why don't we just let the venture charities take charge of us? What are we all striving for when it's obvious that nothing we do changes anything? Aside from our instinct to survive, why do we make any effort at all? Why do so many people get up off of their floor each morning?"

The moment Amon uttered this last sentence, he immediately regretted it. It felt so good to express the doubts that had been festering inside him for weeks that he had let too much slip. He couldn't believe what brutal criticism he had just leveled at a community that Hippo seemed to firmly believe in. Yet to his surprise, Hippo showed no signs of anger. He simply looked away, hanging his head, as though he couldn't bear to confront Amon's words. As Amon's focus shifted from speaking to his surround, he suddenly became aware of the music again, stuck on repeat as the band played the same complex refrain again and again. The fluteboxing and zithers spiralled rhythms over the disjointed pounding of the beatboxing while the singers wove in trance-like throat-vibrato punctuated with stabs and chirps of scratching. Gradually, almost imperceptibly, each successive loop had been growing softer and softer, until finally the music was too quiet to hear. A pause followed as the whole crowd, startled by this unexpected silence, seemed to hold their breath. Then everyone—from the dancers to the seated audience to the scampering children—began to cheer and stomp on the rooftop.

Despite cries of encore, the musicians began to clear away their instruments and disperse, as a new art form immediately took the stage. Now that the embyrbrycks were beginning to expire, they turned a bright orange, like molten glass, and began to release a constant spray of cinders that fluttered up and away on the breeze. Apparently, at this phase of their decay, the bricks were soft and malleable, like luminescent clay, for men and women worked together squeezing and molding and mushing them into new shapes—delicate ferns, birds, demons, stern-looking men, enigmatic women, skyscraper temples, gods. Depending on the contours of the sculptures, the cinders flittered off on the breeze in different formations, and cinderworkers standing behind the embyrsculptures waved paper fans to channel them on precise courses. Usually the cinders formed glittering rivers or abstract cloud-like patterns, but sometimes they took recognizable forms—Saturn, four-leaf clovers, hearts, open palms, constellations, mushrooms—appearing momentarily in the space and then disintegrating into nothing. Amon looked around for Rick and Vertical but spotted them nowhere, and turned back to Hippo to find his gaze waiting.

"Those are poignant and incisive concerns, Amon," he said. "In fact, they cut right to the heart of the most urgent issues we face here. I might have had answers for you once a time long ago. Unfortunately, my thoughts on this matter are no longer clear."

Hippo drained the dregs of his *suposhu* and laid the bottle on the ground. "I called you and Rick over here tonight because I wanted to show the council how much improvement you had made. I also wasn't one hundred percent sure about you myself. But I appreciate your honesty. Just promise me this."

"Yes?"

"Never repeat anything you told me to anyone. I understand the subtlety of your points, but the council might mistake it for crashdead arrogance."

"Has the council already decided?" said Amon with a sudden pang of anxiety. "Are Rick and I going to have to leave?"

"I'm doing what I can."

"Thank you so much," said Amon with another bow.

"I wouldn't get excited. I'm only an advisor. I don't run this place."

"But I really appreciate all your support. Can I ask you a question?"

"Asking never hurts. About what?"

"About the council . . ."

"Yes?"

"I don't know. I mean, you said you were arguing in my favor because you kept your BodyBank like me. What did you mean? Is that why you're helping us now?"

"I won't be talking about that tonight. If you'd asked about my name, that would have been easy. I received my name before the council existed, so I never had a hearing and it has no connection to my story. They call me Hippo because of the way I look." Hippo smiled wryly. "Not even I can deny it.

"But I cannot tell you much more than that. Because, you see, I am the founder of this community and Xenocyst *is* my story. It is the culmination of my life's work. I would need to tell you about the history of this community for you to understand who I am. But that would count as education. So forget about me. Let's concentrate on you. What can you do to show the council that you're worth something to us?"

"I—I don't know. I'm already doing the best I can just staying on top of everything."

"Well I'm afraid it's not good enough. Find something exceptional to impress them with or, I'm sorry, you and Rick may only have a week left."

A week, thought Amon, frowning into Hippo's embracing, troubled eyes. *What could useless crashdead like us achieve in—*

Suddenly there was a great cackling laugh from the direction of the stage. There, a man in a rapidly flaking black cloak stood raising his arm to the tatters of starry sky as a cloud of cinders billowed around him. He spoke in a high-pitched, dramatic voice, and Amon caught enough of the Hinkongo to know he was telling a story. The storyteller was accompanied by a fluteboxer, who provided background music and sound effects. Children were gathered at the storyteller's feet, sparkle-eyed and entranced by the lurid performance in voice, flute, and light. To his right now stood a massive embyrsculpture creature, with the head of some bird of prey on an elephantine torso; arms, claws, and tentacles jutting out from all sides; the whole motley body propped up on a dolphin fin curled between its small, stubby legs. Other sculptures smaller but no less exquisite, spanning styles from the surreal to the abstract, were arrayed across the stage around him. When the storyteller began gesturing to these, Amon realized that they formed a tableau of a scene from some famous myth. The material was too fragile to handle now and the sculptors had stepped away to calmly observe their redly glowing creations as they dissolved quickly. This was the cue for the cinderworkers to step in and begin to fan away with greater speed and focus than before, dazzling dot shapes and images taking form in the air so briefly Amon's mind could only register a pulse of the sublime before they were gone and his fear returned.

12
THE RESORT,
THE GIFTED TRIANGLE

1

Beneath a clear, late-morning autumn sky, Amon crept along a curving rooftop ledge behind Rick and Ty, looking up at a cylindrical glass building that loomed before them. The ledge was the upper edge of disposcrapers built of cream-colored, brand name shelters that circumscribed the lip of a huge crater in the roofscape sprawling endlessly around them. It was a drop of about thirty meters to the bottom of the crater and only about ten meters from the uneven wall atop which they stood to the sheer, see-through surface of the fifty-story structure that rose from it. Inside the cylinder were thin walls of what looked like plaster that divided its interior into high-ceilinged suites. These were shaped like triangles with a rounded outer face, resembling deep-dish pie slices viewed from the crust side. There were eight such slices on each floor, and the building rose far over their heads, making for hundreds of suites, each with a Jacuzzi by the floor-to-ceiling window and then plush rugs leading to a king-sized bed.

On a mission to settle a dispute with upstart Opportunity Scientists, Amon, Rick, and Ty were passing through a brandclan enclave built around a slum resort.

"Those rooms aren't much to look at for a resort," said Rick, when Ty halted to survey the crater.

"Maybe not to you crashdead," said Ty, "but I wouldn't mind grabbing a few winks in one of those beds."

"You don't think they're meant to be seen with an overlay?" Amon said to Rick.

To Amon's naked eyes, the interior of the rooms definitely appeared more shabby and plain than their size would suggest, with carpet stains, patches of discoloration on the walls, glass smudging, and a total lack of patterning. Though as Ty had implied, they were still lavishly furnished compared to what camp denizens were used too.

"Oh, for sure. I'm just calling it like it looks. You'd agree?"

"Um yeah, but—"

"I don't think this one is for looking at anyways," cut in Ty. "More for looking out, like peeping."

"You mean people come here just to stare at a wall?" said Rick.

While the upper suites above them looked out over the slumscape, the lower ones faced straight at the disposcrapers encircling the resort. There were no curtains on the windows or barriers of any kind between the hotel and the shelters, though a murmuration of glassy butterflies, bees, hummingbirds, bats, and other CareBots sparkled churning formations in the sky above its roof, their fragile beauty and grace somehow only emphasizing the threat they posed.

"Not just walls. Take a look at the sand garden." Ty pointed down below to the floor of the gap between them and the glass façade where it was ringed by a thin patch of sand. "At the other resorts you'll see a wider space with grassy golf hills, gardens, sculptures, maybe some hedges. Usually big walls for privacy too. But I don't think this one's designed to be pretty or exclusive. It's designed so the guests can get a view of who's living here."

"I don't see what's so interesting about them," said Rick. "Just look at them now."

Only two residents were visible inside the crater, a man and a woman, both sprawled out on different stairwells napping.

"I guess this resort is part of one of those educational charities," said Amon, vaguely remembering a humanidocupromo he'd seen years ago, "eh, Ty?"

"Yeah. We'll be crossing paths with a tour guide in a minute, so just listen close to what they say."

From what Amon had heard about slum resorts, a certain percentage of the fees for all actions performed in them was donated to venture charities, so the visitors could let loose with conscience soothed. They played sports, took seminars, glutted themselves on gourmet foods, knowing they were making a difference while enlightening themselves about the plight of the world's most unfortunate. It was a chance to experience actually living in a slum, without, of course, actually living in a slum.

Though most of the guests were supposed to be out on tours at this hour, Amon could see a few still lounging in their rooms. A young man soaked in his Jacuzzi, gazing out the window with an apparently forced frown of concern despite his relaxed eyes. An elderly couple sprawled naked on their bed, not moving, at least not right then . . . Amon supposed that many of the guests were exhibitionists of one sort or another, whether sexual or pecuniary, though the windows could be tinted to satisfy those who preferred privacy, unaware it was an ImmaNet setting the bankdead couldn't see. Further down in the crater, Amon spotted a bankdead mother and child in cream-colored brand wear stepping out of a shelter onto the side of the matching cream wall. Holding his mother's hand as she led him up a railed stairwell, the child looked up curiously at the hotel and Amon wondered what he saw.

"For a place designed to look out, they sure do a good job of showing off," said Rick, apparently following a similar line of thought. "Fuck, what I wouldn't give to join that buffet line."

On the fourth floor was a restaurant serving brunch, with rows of steaming trays surrounded by rows of tables with patrons chowing on colorful heaps of food.

"Oh yeah," said Amon. "Then we might have energy for a workout." He pointed to the gym occupying the floor above the restaurant. There, overweight tourists worked machines and, in one corner, lay on mats for a stretching class.

"Not me," said Ty. "Let me into that restaurant and I'd never leave the trays. Not for one second, I tell you, until they kicked me out of there."

"Yeah. You have your workout, Amon. I'm right there with Ty, packing it in till I'm about to explode and waiting for the moment a space opens up inside me again. Then I'd scoop some of that sweet, juicy whatever they've got right into my mouth. Eat just a bit faster than I digest so my stomach learns to keep pace."

Amon sympathized with both of them, though he said nothing. The hunger panging away in his stomach—and no doubt in theirs—said it all for them.

2

Several weeks had passed since the supply reductions had begun and Amon had first learned of the problem.

It was the day after the equinox festival while he was on an expedition to Delivery. He and Rick were serving under Ty as supply crew guards for the first time and had reached Delivery uneventfully, when, halfway through the entrance lineup, they heard a disturbance up ahead. A group of about ten gifted men and women wearing identical houndstooth outfits were banging on the dispensers and shouting angrily that their supplies weren't coming out even though it was their scheduled day. When they refused to proceed in line until someone gave them what they deserved, a handful of freekeepers moved in with assault dusters raised. To Amon's surprise, the freekeepers quickly decided to bring them to the supply tables. Talking on the way home later, Amon and Rick would suppose that they had been ordered by Charity Brigade higher-ups on the basis of calculations that it would be cheaper to appease them with a few cheap items than to pacify them violently with tear dust. Satisfied with this offering, the group left, the lineup unclogged, and Amon's crew moved through to the exit without further issue. Except that, for some reason, when each member reached the end of the dispensers, the scheduling machine assigned them a date two weeks later instead of one week as usual.

This was perplexing, but Amon didn't let himself fret about it until, returning to Xenocyst that evening, he went with Rick to a feeding station for a dinner rice ball and was rejected. Rick got the same treatment, as did many others in line, so that an indignant crowd soon gathered around the machines to gripe. Amon saw similar crowds at the feeding stations on the way back to their room.

Then, the next morning, the centicopter had failed to show. He and Rick ended up standing with the construction crew on the rooftop of the Cyst beneath the gold-blue autumn sky, waiting to unload roombuds and listening for the hum of the craft's one hundred rotors, hearing only crow-call and their own chit-chat, until nightfall when at last their super-visors accepted that it would not be coming and sent everyone home.

All these changes, Amon soon learned, were here to stay. Xenocyst received reports that disturbances similar to the one Amon witnessed had occurred on the same day in multiple supply corridors throughout Delivery. The council would later reason that the cause of these incidents was one of the MegaGloms, R-Lite, deciding to push the pickup date for one of their brandclans to a week later than originally scheduled. But the disbursement delay was not limited to this lone segment of the population. Apparently everyone was being invited to Delivery half as often, though the other members of the Philanthropy Syndicate were informing them on their next scheduled day rather than shifting the date forward without warning—a strategic error by R-Lite that presumably cost them more in consolation supplies and freekeeper labor than they might have saved on the cut. Feeders too, which previously provided three modest meals per day, now rejected their third meal every other day, though thankfully the quantity of beverages remained the same.

The timing of the supply reductions was particularly worrisome because they coincided with a drop in temperature. For a couple of weeks after the equinox, the sweltering humidity of summer had lingered inside Xenocyst despite the crisp air that had fallen on the island, and aside from the occasional cool breeze that carved its way in through tight squeezeways, the dense slumscape seemed to keep the season at bay for a while. Yet by the time of Amon and Rick's next supply pick-ups, autumn had penetrated every crack and corner, and the sneakers, pants, light jacket, thin blanket, and insulated roombuds they received became indispensable to fend off the increasing chill—especially at night. While these new supplies kept them warm at first, with expiration dates unchanged and yet invitations to Delivery less frequent, every item was intolerably worn out by the time they received replacements. Their clothes dissolved into tatters as though devoured by moths and their rooms sprung drafty cracks days before they got new ones, so that the cold remained a constant source of discomfort and danger. The heat of rub-warmed meals and hot coffee-like goos the machines now dispensed offered little relief, and with even smaller portions than before Amon was now afflicted constantly with a faint hunger.

Though the gifted were not as badly affected, since they had larger quantities and more durable items to begin with, most residents were in the same position as Amon and Rick. Everyone could see that if pickup times were pushed back even a few days further, many would be left naked and homeless. With coptor visits reduced, medical supplies at the Cyst were beginning to run low. Already, everywhere Amon looked, he saw hordes of sickly, gaunt figures in dissolving rags, crammed between precariously crumbling buildings, their heads bowed with exhaustion, their downcast eyes clouded with want.

He'd heard the middle-aged residents call these reductions unprecedented and no one knew for sure what might be causing them. A donations lull? A distribution mix up? A factory malfunction? Every explanation had its strengths and weaknesses, and with no reliable information to decide between them only confusion held sway. That and fear, for all in all, life in the District of Dreams had turned much tougher, and there was no guarantee it wouldn't get worse. With winter approaching, prospects were looking grim as grim could be.

As a result of all this, the council's time had become completely occupied with the crisis, and Amon and Rick's membership screening, scheduled for a week after the festival, had been postponed indefinitely. No new applications for membership were being accepted as they were short on resources even for present members, and while the discussion concerning those currently on trial periods had ended inconclusively, according to the Books the most likely policy would be to dismiss them automatically. On the bright side, these delays resulted in Amon and Rick's sojourn at Xenocyst being extended by default. But their days of safety seemed numbered—especially since their chances for acceptance were already slim, as Hippo had warned at the festival—and anxiety gnawed at Amon from morning to night, as visions of his imminent future in the worsening pandemonium outside haunted his waking life, if not his dreamless nights.

As he struggled on top of this to cope with the shortages, he recognized that his one blessing was Rick's company. Ever since the fall equinox, Rick frequently went off on his own in the evenings, either saying he wanted time to walk and think or just slipping away without explanation. But they still spent most of their time together, heading to work together, taking their meager meals together, sleeping in their room crammed shoulder to shoulder on cold nights when there weren't enough embyrbrycks to go around, rubbing PeelKlean into each other's backs and scraping away the dirt, listening to each other's groans with keen empathy.

Recently, Rick had been complaining of his discomfort more frequently than Amon, and Amon began to see how his frugality training gave him a slight advantage in adjusting to the deprivation. Surviving in the District of Dreams required the ability to get through one's daily exertions—climbing up and down huge buildings, squeezing through crowds, lining up, traversing circuitous labyrinthine pathways—all while operating on only a limited intake of nutrition, and most crashborn possessed a kind of languidness that kicked in whenever they had a moment to slow down. This skill Amon acquired faster than Rick, who still seemed to be operating at his city pace. Before, Amon had monitored every urge and impulse, to authorize or suppress them in accordance with the cost of the action they aimed to initiate, and whether the result of that action would bring him closer to his dream or to bankruptcy. Now he did so in accordance with how much energy they would expend, how much water and calories they burned, and whether they fulfilled a need right then and there. During breaks at work, while Rick chattered on with their co-workers, Amon often remained entirely still and slowed his breathing—as much to find calmness as to reduce his metabolism. Nevertheless, as his hunger grew stronger, it began to dominate his thoughts and challenge the limits of his conditioning. His first few weeks at Xenocyst had not exactly been luxurious, but they had been bearable. Now he felt like he would do anything for the chance to eat.

Meanwhile, another threat had arisen. At first, rumors floated around that Opportunity Scientists were becoming more active and ignoring traditional boundaries. They had always been known for occasional raids into Xenocyst-allied territories in the name of spreading their message, and for the occasional kidnapping of gifted Xenocysters to "purify" them. But now there were frequent reports of skirmishes, and the general consensus was that the scientists were out seeking plunder because their supplies were decreasing as well. This was a shocking development as the Quantitative Priesthood were supposed to be the Philanthropy Syndicate's darling, increasing yield at relatively low cost with their placating ideology.

Now that Rick had adjusted to his construction and demolition duties under Amon's instruction, and Ty trusted them to serve as his rear guards on Delivery expeditions, they were slowly becoming familiar with the different routes, rapidly dissolving and changing as they were, and with the intervening allied territories. The supply paths seemed secure thus far, as Amon and Rick had yet to encounter OpSci guerrillas. But based on Vertical's stories from her scouting missions, it wouldn't be long before they did. Already the Opportunity Scientists had set up a hidden missionary outpost in one of Xenocyst's neutral buffer territories and were using it as a base for robbery and abduction. An expulsion plan was under way, and the council was expecting quick success since most residents wanted the OpScis out, even as some were beginning to succumb to their proselytizing. Still, such incidents raised worries of a permanent supply blockade, and in the escalating maelstrom, Amon sensed a new kind of tension radiating from his fellow denizens as their anxiety and deprivation were now laced with vague premonitions of war.

With an ebb and flow of successes and defeats in the fighting, more and more guards were needed to assist in defense, though with their usual nutritional bonus no longer available, morale was dwindling. This forced the council to recruit residents for patrol who were inexperienced in the field, not to mention expendable non-residents like Amon and Rick. Since the council had returned Amon's duster to him and Ty had lent Rick a scary-looking rusted pipe, they were well armed, but being novices, their overseers kept them in friendly proxy communities close to Xenocyst. Until today that is, when Ty had been transferred temporarily to patrol as well and had chosen them to accompany him to the edge of Xenocyst-allied territory: into the Gifted Triangle. The venture charities built most of their brand name feeding stations around Delivery so that brandclans would all cluster in this area, making it less tiring for gifted to pick up their supplies and more affordable to manage them. It was also a neutral zone between Xenocyst affiliates and Opportunity Peaks. Here, at the southernmost tip of the triangle, where the two rival territories were closest, they had come to confront an Opportunity Scientist gang who had co-opted a slum tour formerly partnered with Xenocyst.

In general, bankdead shunned or avoided bankliving, being awed and afraid of them largely due to the way drones seemed to magically shield them from all harm. But slum tour operators forged relationships with bankdead and encouraged them to interact with bankliving tourists in exchange for supplies. In the enclave they were visiting today, a local group had been assisting for years with a particular tour run by Kindness Beyond Credit, the largest venture charity in the District of Dreams and the one rumored to have the most ruthless Charity Brigade unit. This group had always given a percentage of the supplies they garnered through this arrangement to Xenocyst as part of their security pact. But recently, Xenocyst had received a coded letter complaining of OpSci encroachment. Then all contact with them had been lost, and a colony run by Quantitative Missionaries that popped up inexplicably in their place had taken over the tour while also dominating the original inhabitants.

The supply tithe had been small in quantity and more symbolic of Xenocyst's authority than truly indispensable, but Xenocyst nonetheless had to respond. When OpSci attacks had been occasional, random, and not too severe, Xenocyst policy had been to ignore them rather than being drawn into a prolonged conflict. Now that insulting incursions were frequent and destructive, the council was under increasing pressure to send a message that this would not be tolerated and ensure that the lines of their territory remained clearly etched. With the local residents calling on Xenocyst to intervene, there was simply no way this could be overlooked, whatever the risks.

3

"As you can see, the donated shelters are designed to stack. This design enables the limited space of the island to accommodate its large number of inhabitants."

Ty, Rick, and Amon all crouched with their backs against up-jutting rooms, furtively peering over the edge of the rooftop onto a blacktop road ten half-stories down, along which a woman was guiding a group of about a dozen tourists. All three of them kept their heads tilted slightly to the side to catch her voice carrying from below.

"Each one has a stairwell leading to sliding doors, through which the residents enter and exit on their daily . . ."

The guide was short and red-cheeked, wearing a shapeless, baggy sweater of some course navy material that obscured her pudgy body except for the side-bulge of her hips, her lusterless crimped hair easily ruffled in the slightest breeze. The tourists all wore loose pants, thick boots, and light jackets as though on a hike. Some followed close behind the guide, eager to catch everything she said. Others stayed a few steps back to look around at the disposable skyscrapers and do click-gestures, probably tagging certain images for their photo journals. Parked in a little alcove on the far side of the road was the small bus that had dropped the tourists off a few minutes earlier, the driver inside staring with a look of boredom at the wall in front of him. Even from this height, Amon could see that everyone had the Elsewhere Gaze, their eyes glossing over their surround with a certain jittery excitation.

Over top of the buildings across the road Amon faced, just above the group, a handful of CareBots fluttered—DazzleMoths and OvenDragons—their sparkling forms unobtrusively tailing the tour, so as to remind all nearby bankdead to stay away without alerting the tourists to their presence and ruining the authenticity of the experience. West, beyond the ridge of these buildings, rolled the jutting corners, right-angle mounds and tumbled roof-plains of slumscape, through which the winding veins of several supply roads carved north to the mall-like cube of Delivery. These roads marked the border to Opportunity Land, and further west beyond them room-slopes rose higher and higher to the base of Opportunity Peaks reaching for the clear fall sky. From his vantage, Amon could see that the thousands of rooms composing this architectural mountain were a combination of brand name and generic ones. Usually impossible to attach to each other, they had been built together into an intricate pattern of concentric circles and lines that resembled an abstract mandala, like pixels forming an image. Flakes rose constantly from the mountain's every level in flurry patterns, blowing and swirling into ephemeral cloud shapes with the changing winds at different altitudes. It was the closest Amon had ever been to the home of those that had tried to "sample" him so violently, and his skin tingled with wariness, his eyes buzzing constantly with alert for approaching strangers.

"The shelters are moderately insulated, but because the weather can turn fairly cool in this season, Kindness Beyond Credit and our partners provide them with special supplies. These include bricks for heating and clothes of a thicker cloth than usual. There are also . . ."

Another small bus cruised slowly along the road behind the guide, the whirr of its tires drowning out her voice. Through the windows Amon could make out the faces of the tourists, their eyes absorbing the world outside the glass with visible wonderment, as though on a safari. From what he had observed of the buses coming and going over the hour or so they'd been perched here, none of them unloaded their tourists more than a couple hundred meters from the resort—the glass cylinder of which poked above the roofscape just a hundred meters south—and Amon wondered why they didn't just walk. Perhaps the ostensible reason was to ensure safety, though residents of privileged communities near Delivery like this one were not nearly so desperate as to harm bankliving, especially not with the CareBots poised ready to swoop in and offer protection for a fee to any bankliving confronted by someone without a BodyBank. More likely, the tour operators wanted to control what the participants saw, for going any deeper would introduce them to conditions more representative of the camps at large, and make their claims for the positive impact of donations less persuasive.

As part of their "open educational services" to help Free Citizens "observe poverty in proximity" and "raise awareness up close and personal," the slum tour operators promised that nothing would have any touch of overlay. Allowing naked viewing of the District of Dreams was possible because the Philanthropy Syndicate shared the image rights to it. The sky would still appear as a patchwork of advertisement, the tourists as digimade, and so on, but the slums and their residents would look as they did to those without ImmaNet access. Since the tourists were paying luxury fees for this service, it was essential for the operators to secure the cooperation of the more comfortable gifted in putting on a hopeful face and avoid leading their tours too deep to where the more depressing giftless enclaves could be found. Even with the overlay, there were certain aspects of the camps that could not be hidden, such as collapsing shelters, the smell of clogged sewers, and the threat of theft or violence. Without it, a momentary glimpse might be enough to eliminate a potential donor's faith in the power of their money to create positive change and so care had to be taken to curate the experience.

The tour turned left down an alley cutting through the structure Amon, Ty, and Rick stood upon, squeezed into double file in the narrow space as the woman's voice muffled into an unintelligible echo. Ty then led them through elevated squeezeways that sloped up, curved, and rounded back until they were in a crack over the alley. There they lay flat on the floor of the roof and peered over the edge, bringing the tour back in sight.

"There in front of the wall," whispered Ty, pointing down the tight alley to a dead end, before which eight or so bankdead men, women, and children sat. "The trespassers."

". . . to bring your attention now to this family," the guide's voice carried up to Amon's ears, as she raised her palm towards the same group. Two teenagers, a pre-adolescent boy, and another boy of about eight were the ostensible kids of a young man and woman. A grizzled old man meant to be the grandfather stood hovelled before them. They all clung to each other in a tight knot and looked wide-eyed at the tourists, their expressions and postures so timid and forlorn they were practically cowering, the young boy literally trembling.

Though they weren't wearing their patchwork uniforms, but instead shiny, faux-polyester kimonos presumably seized from the local brandclan, Amon didn't need Ty to tell him they were OpScis and that this was all an act. Their clothes were tattered but there was no sign of flaking, indicating that they had likely ripped them themselves, and the charcoal-like dust coating their hair and skin was not commonly seen in the camps and had surely been rubbed in intentionally. The members of this "family" hardly resembled each other at all, and the thick muscles of the young man and teenager, who had probably been included to stack the gang for self-defense and battle if the need arose, belied their supposed hunger. The adult man had telltale words and equations scarred into his hands and face. These were sacred texts, perhaps the Book of Jobs, Book of Markets, or Book of Opportunity, often tattooed onto the skin of believers (some living, some preserved in holy chambers of the Peaks). So here, just as the reports had stated, was a so-called "missionary expedition" entertaining the busloads of tourists and pleasing the venture charities by day, while banding together into a single force to raid the area by night.

"As you can see, some of their makeshift shelters are beginning to deteriorate," said the guide, waving her arm up and around at the flaking disposcrapers lining the alley. "With the help of your resort fee and the additional donations you may *kindly* offer, Kindness Beyond Credit will provide members of the local community with new clothes and shelters so that they can live in greater safety and comfort without leaving footprints on the poverty ecosystem. So we invite you to please join us in eliminating poverty through profit and turn a digital divide into a digital dividend by bringing development to the bottom of the pyramid."

The tourists gawked in silence and, from the way their eyes panned slowly around, Amon could tell they were trying to capture a clean recording for their LifeStreams. Several of them clicked on everything in sight—rooms, people, the ground—no doubt searching for additional info to supplement the tour. From what Amon had heard, many were investitarians who received discounts on the resorts due to their generous donations and who joined the tours expecting a report on what good it was doing. The rest would be a mix of less committed donors, personal growth seekers, travelers, researchers, nostie anadeto dealers, art scouts, sex tourists out to satiate their illegal tastes at half the price, and other less savory visitors.

All of them wore expressions ranging from sour grimaces of sympathetic consternation to faintly unsettled frowns, as though witnessing some abominable injustice, though to anyone who lived in the District of Dreams the area looked sumptuous. The particular brand of room stacked in this alley was designed to mimic traditional Japanese styles, with dark wooden exteriors and sliding paper doors that opened onto *engawa* porches. A slow emission of flakes did flutter around them, but this was normal after a few days of use and none had yet sprung any of the drafty holes so common in every other area. In actuality, this was one of the most privileged communities in the District of Dreams, and it was clear that the tourists had no idea.

"The unemployment rate here is one hundred percent, so there is little for the residents to do but wait for a helping hand and . . ."

"Looks like we're not the only ones watching," whispered Ty, and flicked his head with a sweep of his eyes at the opposite side of the alley. There Amon saw other eyes peeking out from shadowy crevices, nooks, cracks in doors, around squeezeway corners, at various heights across the adjacent wall, their owners in Fleet kimonos and yukatas like the OpSci faux-family. Most of them were watching the tour furtively, though a few glanced occasionally at Amon and crew.

"Those eyes don't look too friendly," Rick whispered back. "Do they know we're here to help?"

"Hard to say. Our scouts let their organizers know we were coming, but we don't know how far word has trickled down. Since we snuck in here to stay under the radar of the converts, some of them might misunderstand our intentions. Means any of them could be enemies until they give us reason to trust them, so watch out."

Although the locals had sent a coded letter to Xenocyst expressing their desire to resist OpSci dominion, Amon knew that some of them likely had faith in the religion, as was the case throughout enclaves outlying the Peaks. He remembered the Books telling him and Rick that the basis for the doctrine's widespread popularity was the ingenious way it resigned the bankdead to their role in the CG Economy. The poor had historically been reconciled to their position in part by the belief that anyone could achieve any goal they set themselves and acquire anything they wanted if only they had the talent and worked hard enough. While this whiff of possibility continued to instill Free Citizens with faith in the principle *all the freedom you can earn,* it had stopped drifting down to the bottom ever since it became patently impossible for the poor to possess the bank accounts and identity required to land jobs, earn money, and find career success. Opportunity Scientist dogma offered a substitute vision of salvation for have-nots in the Free Era. If infinite opportunity was no longer available to those who deserved it in this life, then it had to be available in a future life. Individuals with impure DNA—regarded as a code recording each person's accumulation of past good or bad deeds—lacked the innate talent to ascend to the Free World and escape from the Cycle of ReCrash, where one was reborn in the camps repeatedly. Yet even the giftless could unleash the underlying GiftNature that all human beings shared and one day attain rebirth as a marketable baby by adhering to tattooed prayers, rituals, and precepts. Included were rules emphasizing that passive, non-resistance to the Charity Brigade, reverence for the gifted, and multiplying fruitfully helped to purify one's genome.

This comforting metaphysical doctrine helped believers accept the conditions created by the venture charities, portraying them as the harsh but inevitable result of the Market's ineluctable turnings and as a temporary phase of financospiritual development to eventually be transcended, either personally or vicariously through one's offspring. The Philanthropy Syndicate was pleased by this since it need not invest in its own educational programs to induce complacency and had traditionally shipped extra supplies and weaponry to the Quantitative Priesthood in return, increasing resource yield at relatively low cost. At the same time, the doctrine earned the religion numerous followers. So much so that it had become part of camp-wide folk superstition.

Since missionaries had been in control of the enclave Amon, Rick, and Ty were visiting for at least a week, it was possible that even more had converted here than in other areas. Some locals might then accept that Hippo was the Gene Sucker and the Xenocyst rescue crew his DNA-vampire minions. Thus their presence would be seen as an inauspicious threat to karmic marketability, and it was impossible to know who to trust as Ty had cautioned.

"Is it alright to feed them?" Amon heard one of the tourists ask, drawing his gaze. It was a middle-aged woman holding an unopened bag of mixed nuts.

"Yes," answered the guide, "but certain foods can be hard on their digestive systems because they're accustomed to the food here. So we ask that you offer only certified bankdead feed, which can be purchased from our driver."

The driver, who'd apparently crept up behind them, stepped forward with a basket full of rice balls, bento boxes, sweat-bean buns, and other snacks wrapped in colorful bows like presents. Several of the tourists were already lining up in front of him to buy their feed and the remainder, having apparently brought their own, were approaching the bankdead.

"Be careful not to overfeed them because a sudden rise in calories can cause indigestion and other more serious health problems. Also, please refrain from direct contact. Most of them are harmless, but many prefer not to be touched."

The "family" held out their hands, still kneeling, and put their palms together in thanks before taking the proffered foods from the tourists and unwrapping them. As they ate, the family members exchanged looks of apparent ecstasy to show how delicious they were. Amon could see a firm-lipped expression of self-congratulatory relief on the faces of the tourists as they watched. One lanky woman even had her arms crossed and was nodding in satisfaction. The visible gap between their perceptions of the difference they were making and the actual result filled Amon with immediate revulsion, as much directed towards them as himself. For he knew he would have reacted much the same way only a few months earlier, if he'd even bothered to care about the plight of the bankdead, which, caught in his frugal obsession, he hadn't. On the contrary, he'd banished thousands here in his denial and never made efforts to help any of them. These tourists at least seemed genuinely intent on alleviating poverty through donations, even if they didn't realize or acknowledge how it merely supported the system that gave rise to the problem in the first place.

The family had finished their snacks and were coming back to ask for more when suddenly, out of cracks in the alley walls, other bankdead began to pour into the alley. The bus driver reached for the duster holstered at his side and the CareBots gave a simultaneous twitch, diving a notch lower in the air. But when the bankdead stopped before the tourists with hands outstretched, the driver settled back into standing there blank-eyed, the drones fluttering about as before. The adult men swarmed to the front, the women squeezed their arms in from behind, and the children crept in between legs, forming a dense tangle of bodies in the alley that blocked out the OpScis. The tourists soon went back to the bus driver, bought everything in his basket, and began to take turns handing the foods out. One by one the bankdead stepped forward and snatched whatever was offered from whoever was offering it. They then pushed to the back and either ate their food immediately or put it into their kimono sleeve pockets and snuck up to the front before a different tourist to get a surreptitious second helping. Some were successful, but the tourists quickly caught onto this trick and began reaching their arms into the crowd to offer food directly to children too small to push closer.

The tourists didn't bother to interact with any of the bankdead other than by feeding them, or try to make conversation even with the guide there, who Amon had overheard was supposed to be equipped with a Japanese-Hinkongo interpreting app. Perhaps this was partly due to the rushed itinerary of the tours, but Amon thought it had more to do with their perspective. The tourists hadn't come here to meet *people*, to hear their stories, to engage in dialog. Rather, they saw the bankdead as instantiations of "poverty" and "overcrowding," as mere elements in a spectacle they had come to absorb for the satisfaction of feeling later that it had changed them, unable to grasp what palpable challenges they faced in their quick visit no matter how well-intentioned. As far as intentions went, these tours certainly beat the other businesses that had found loopholes to operate within the Charity Gift Economy, such as the Kansha Hotels, where bankdead attended banquets full of generous investitarians and accompanied them to their rooms out of spontaneous gratitude. All the same, Amon hated everything the tours stood for—the insensitive blandishment of wealth, the self-assured feeling of doing right, the ignorance of what the bankdead needed and who they were—and to him the solid glass sanctuary of the resort amidst the Fleet structures seemed like a sentient tumor killing a body it wants desperately to heal.

Although the newcomers had completely shut them out, the Opportunity Scientists wore hopeful, needy expressions, but Amon detected hints of the anger they were hiding from the tourists in the tightness of their jaws and the venomous glares they directed at any resident that glanced at them. The guide, temporarily caught off guard by this break from the script, looked around at the milling group in confusion for a few seconds before finally deciding how to respond: "Alright, everyone. We'd best get back to the buses. Some of the new arrivals may be mildly contagious, and we have an appointment for an energy healing class on the observation deck after our tour of Delivery."

With that, she started back down the alley towards the road, the driver a few paces ahead. Then with a wave to the bankdead that was reciprocated only with blank stares, the tourists peeled back and began to follow her.

4

As the tour continued down the alley, the residents began to vanish into the cracks from which they had come. Then, the moment the last tourist stepped around the bend and the drones above them had flitted away, the supposed father clapped three times and the sliding doors of several shelters on the three lower floors opened. Out stepped men in patchwork OpSci outfits holding various blunt or spiky objects. These they quickly handed out to the erstwhile unfortunate family, whose visages of pleading desperation had hardened into merciless deadpans. Together they assembled into a crew of about twenty and began to confer in a huddle around a man in the multi-logoed robes of a field priest, making angry gestures in the directions the residents had fled. It was obvious even to Amon, who had little experience with such conflicts, what was going to happen next.

"Come on," whispered Ty, pointing to a stairwell that led down a dark, winding cranny. "We can't let this happen. Before they get organized, you two head down there, get in position to fight. I'm gonna get their attention."

"Hold on," said Amon. "Why don't I stay here and pick them off with my duster?"

"Because you'll only get a couple from up here. The rest will just scatter and we want to deal with them once and for all."

Amon thought about it and realized that he wasn't confident of his sniping from this distance, since he no longer had the marksmanship app he always used and hadn't practiced firing the duster since it had been returned to him.

"Other issues?" asked Ty, giving them a piercing stare.

Amon and Rick shook their heads and, as Ty set off creeping along the ledge, Amon started down into the cranny with Rick close behind. They stepped quickly but carefully into the dim, Amon's heartbeat picking up and his breath short in anticipation of the coming confrontation.

"Oi! OpSci assholes!" Amon heard Ty shout in Hinkongo from somewhere above. "Yeah! Up here! M'name's Ty. I'm in charge of Xenocyst border security for this area and I order you to vacate immediately! All trespassers must return to the Peaks! I give you ten seconds to comply!"

"Oh yeah, this shit—"

"Hah!"

"Comply? You—"

Amon could hear muffled shouts of anger in response as the cranny ended at a tunnel cutting horizontally through several rooms, the walls lined with the tiny baby cribs only found in gifted buildings. In the wall to their right was a zigzagging vertical crack that opened into the alley, where Amon could hear the heavy footfalls and yells of the OpScis. To their left Amon spotted the shadowy forms of several residents watching them warily with backs up against another wall. Turning to face them, Rick put his finger to his lips and did a swinging motion with his pipe towards the racket outside to indicate he was on their side. As they approached the crack, Amon heard the shouting grow louder and flinched nervously at several plosive clatters as Ty's wheel went into action. The upper body of the "father" popped from the crack and, as he began scrabbling his way frantically in, Rick dealt him a quick blow to the collarbone and he toppled backwards into the alley with a howl. Amon drew his duster and kept it trained on the opening until a man's face peeked in and he pulled the trigger, a hoarse shriek echoing at ear-splitting volume through the tight chamber as the dust did its work on his nerves. Amon felt a flash of guilt as he was reminded of the many bankrupt screams he'd elicited but was too tense and afraid to indulge it. In the taut moment of silence that followed they waited, Rick standing to the side of the crack with his pipe held back, Amon keeping his aim steady, ready to dispatch any other intruders but afraid to step out now that the OpScis were surely alerted to their presence, when one of the men behind them said, "There's another way out. Up there!"

Rick and Amon tilted their heads up to where the figure was pointing and saw a narrow opening in the ceiling above the crack that led to a low crawlspace.

"G-go out that way," blurted the man. "You can catch them by surprise."

Rick grunted his assent, jumped up to grip the ledge with the flat of his arms and shimmied onto it. Amon trained his duster on the crack a few more seconds to make sure no one burst in, before leaping up and climbing after him.

He found himself crawling behind Rick's buttocks until the ceiling ended and they both got to their feet, crouching in the still-low chamber. They were on a ledge overlooking the floor of the alley one story below, but rooms jutting around sheltered it from view. The only opening was a half-meter gap between where the floor ended and the base of the wall in front of them. Rick leapt into the gap brandishing his pipe, and Amon, taking a deep breath to settle his fear, hopped down right behind.

They landed on their feet in the alley beside two supine bodies, one inert from Amon's dust and one twitching on the tarmac from Rick's pipe blow. There was a crack and a groan as a man with a stake leapt at Amon from behind only to take Ty's wheel in his temple and flop to the ground. Ty stood on a balcony about three stories up, near the entrance of the alley, behind and to the right of Amon and Rick. Below him, two more bodies were sprawled unmoving on the ground. Before the dead end in front of them stood about a dozen men and women, the teenagers, kid, and older man in the rear. The young men and women held a mismatched assortment of weapons: shards of golf clubs, chunks of concrete, a jagged hunk of steel slag, whips of coiled wiring haphazardly fused . . . but the field priest, standing front and center, had become the locus of everyone's attention, for in his outstretched hand was an archaic weapon: a double-barreled machine pistol. He was aiming it at Ty but, seeing Amon's duster, now brought it down to aim at him just as Amon aimed on the crowd.

"This is a paraplegic duster set for wide dispersal," Amon growled. "Shoot me and I'll incapacitate every last one of you!"

Amon was lying—only assault dusters, not the Liquidator standard issue hand duster he carried, had such a setting, and it could only fire nerve dust—lying because he could see they were in trouble. If they'd merely been outnumbered, Amon's duster combined with Ty's tricycle and Rick's brute force would have tipped the confrontation in their favor. But the field priest's gun, if it wasn't merely for show and actually had ammo, gave the clear advantage to their enemies, for its bullets would be lethal. They had not been prepared for this. Neither Ty nor the security planners who briefed them seemed to have considered the possibility. It was rare for Opportunity Scientists to have long-range weapons like this, aside from perhaps the occasional slingshot or makeshift bow, and the three of them would never have done something so foolhardy as trying to take on twenty if they'd even suspected.

"Back up and stand with me," shouted Ty, and Amon did as instructed with Rick following, edging backwards while facing the OpScis until they were just below Ty's ledge. The angle of the barrel pointed at Amon seemed to beam terror into his chest, the field priest eyeing him with mortal uncertainty, neither shooting nor averting his aim. When they were far enough away, he barked something and a woman and two men broke off from their group to approach the two nearest of their fallen comrades.

"What do we do?" hissed Amon up to the ledge.

"We try to find an opening to run and retreat back to Xenocyst," said Ty. "But for now, we wait. The next move is theirs."

The two men began to drag away the one with the broken collarbone despite his groans of protest. The woman bent over the one Amon had dusted and slapped him in the face, eliciting no response. Then, after checking the man's pulse, she went over to the gunman priest, who kept his eyes and aim on Amon, and whispered in his ear. Several OpScis then huddled around them and, after exchanging a few muttered words, they all began to stalk towards Amon, Rick, and Ty. They formed two lines three men deep, the priest on the left in the middle pair with his wrist on the shoulder of the man in front, taking cover while keeping the barrel pointed at Amon.

"That wouldn't happen to be a nerve duster, would it?" asked the priest, his eyes and barrel boring into Amon. "Eh, gene suckers!"

His heart pounding, Amon kept all his attention focused on the priest, trying not to show his fear lest the bluff be exposed definitively, ready to shoot the moment he heard the trigger click. He was hoping that Rick or Ty would shout some order that would get them out of this mess, for he could think of nothing. There was no way to run before the bullets ripped through Amon and Rick standing side by side, and firing preemptively now that the priest had cover would only produce the same result. The best that they could hope for was that Ty might manage to flee with his life, though his success too seemed doubtful as he had several stories to climb to the roof and all it would take for the priest was to change the angle of his arm.

Just then, there was a thud and a clack as the priest's head and pistol slammed into the left wall. Four hands had reached through one of the cracks and jerked the man towards them in a rapid, barely perceptible motion. A few shots went off, but the bullets ripped into the Fleet wall against which the barrel rested and never emerged. Hearing this sound, Amon fired twice and heard shrieks as two men fell limp-limbed in front of him, before a hunk of concrete arcing from the back of the group whacked into his hand, knocking the duster from his grip and richocheting into his chest. The impact toppled him onto his back as the duster flew over his shoulder behind him, the hunk now pinning him down. Quickly, he rolled the weight off his ribs just as a man lunged down at him with a badly chipped machete. With no time to get out of the way, Amon mindlessly flailed his legs towards the man just as Rick piped him in the jaw. The glinting blade fell spinning erratically towards Amon's shins but chanced to strike the ground with its tip just between them before leaping up to his right with a twang and clattering against the wall, the piped man crumpling atop the flat of it. Amon sprang to his feet as Rick blocked the swing of a dented aluminum bat with his pipe, a dull metallic clang followed by the bat redirecting into his hip. Amon punched the batter square in the cheekbone as a wheel whirred over the man's head, cracking into the forehead of an approaching woman, bouncing back to crack the batter in the back of the head like a pinball, and then shooting down to smash someone's knee before Ty reeled it back in. Amon picked up the bat and lifted it over his shoulder, ready to wallop the next person who crossed his path—but saw all the remaining OpScis now flattened to the floor and walls of the alley. He watched as the priest's ankles disappeared into the crack he'd been grabbed from, wailing as he was yanked out of sight, and the woman who'd clued in that Amon carried a nerve duster was beside him being held and throttled by the three right hands of unseen assailants. One man lying on the ground was being slowly dragged by other hands into a crack between the floor of the alley and the base of a building that seemed entirely too thin for someone to fit—at least without breaking a few ribs. Another man was being choked by hands reaching from a jagged hole in a sliding door while a different pair of hands held the man's ankles in place from a lower hole as he writhed about and tried to pry the fingers from his neck. Yet another was being gripped in various places by child-like fingers, and a mouth was biting his ear as kicks rained down on him through holes from different directions. The residents, it seemed, had been itching for the chance to do this, and Amon, Rick, and Ty just stood there panting as their pent-up rage unfolded, until Amon remembered his duster had been knocked away and picked it up, as though it might shield him from the shock and horror of the scene.

Once the OpSci men and women had been pacified or hauled away, residents in kimonos and yukatas began to emerge from unseen nooks to strip the fallen ones of their clothes and weapons before carrying them off the way they had come. Amon hated to imagine what would happen to the prisoners next, even if they had brought this on themselves. The child too was nowhere to be seen . . .

There was only one man left, the grandfather of the family, who was curled up in the fetal position in the corner of the dead end. Three residents were creeping towards him with clubs and chipped spindles seized from their victims, wary as though his apparent defenselessness might be a ruse, their eyes wide and vengeful.

Ty, who had now climbed down to the ground floor, said, "Tell them to keep off him," flicking his eyes towards Amon's duster. "We need one to question and send back to the Peaks so they'll hear what happened and learn to fuck off."

Amon held his gun out so it was clearly visible and called out in his sternest Liquidator voice, "Step away from that man immediately. We're here from Xenocyst to restore our alliance with the residents of this community. Everything you can scrounge from the survivors is yours, but we need him for questioning."

The three residents paused and stared at Amon defiantly, but made no further moves towards the old man.

"Please!" Ty cried. "Remember it was thanks to us these guys came out in the open and you had a chance to get them off your back. So would you kindly turn that man over to us."

After another pause, the older of the three, a man who appeared to be in his mid-thirties, nodded to the other two, and they all melted into the walls.

5

When they reached the man, he was crouching with his torso between his knees and his head bowed, his long gray matted hair hanging over his face onto the ground. Scrawny, ragged, and dirty, flakes of cloth fluttering off him on the slight breeze, he trembled as their footsteps neared.

"Hey old man," said Ty. "We're here to have a word."

At the sound of Ty's voice, the man's back bristled, but no response came.

"Your friends are finished, but we've got no plans to hurt you. So long as you talk."

No response.

"Eh!" barked Ty, grabbing for the man's shoulder, but the man knocked Ty's hand aside with a swift forearm parry.

"Watch it geezer. If you don't—"

"Please leave me alone!" bellowed the man. For such a grimy, pathetic creature he had a shockingly clear voice, a voice that Amon immediately recognized. "I haven't done anything to anyone."

"Look!" shouted Ty, baring his teeth. "We're not—"

"Barrow? Chief Executive Minister Lawrence Barrow?" Amon interrupted. At the mention of this name, the old man's shoulders contracted visibly as though he were trying to squeeze himself into a tiny ball.

"Wait! You sure? Because of his voice?" said Rick. Then to the man, "Hey, you! Say something! Anything!"

"Who cares who he is! This old lump of shit out here pretending to be Gramps so he can rob these people of a bit of fucking food!"

Ty stamped one pace towards the man but Rick put his arm in front of him, saying, "Let me take care of this," before putting his palm on the man's forehead and giving it a sudden push. The man spasmed too late against the force and toppled backwards onto his side, the curtain of gray strands falling away from his face, leaving Amon and Rick no doubt.

"Once you said it, I knew it was his voice," said Rick. "And there he is."

Though he looked like he'd aged ten years since the last time Amon had seen him, whether from lack of digimake or from the tribulations of camp-life, this was indeed Lawrence Barrow, Chief—no, ex-Chief Executive Minister. His lustrous ponytail degenerated to ratty shag, his forehead deeply furrowed with wrinkles, he was at least twenty kilos lighter, looking withered and frail, though he still had his broad shoulders and impressively commanding nose below those husky-blue eyes. Rising up onto his buttocks, he sat there propped on his hands as his eyes twitched back and forth fearfully between the three men until he seemed to realize something and then honed in on Amon.

"You!" said Barrow with a frown. "It *must* be you."

"I . . ." Words failed Amon.

"Alright. Chief executive shithead, whatever your name is. We've got some questions for you, and if you can answer them you'll go free. If not, well . . . take a look at the mess they're cleaning up behind us!"

Ty began to ask Barrow various questions about the movements of the Opportunity Scientists in the Gifted Triangle: how many groups there were, when they operated, where they gathered at night for the raids, what plans they had over the coming weeks. Barrow answered everything clearly and in detail without hesitation. Occasionally when he said he didn't know something, Ty would threaten him with spit-flying fury, delivering a few boots to his thighs when he insisted on his ignorance. But since everything Barrow denied knowledge of appeared unimportant to the overall OpSci strategy and he revealed a number of useful logistical facts, it seemed clear that he was being forthright and honest. The whole time, Amon and Rick stood by passively observing the exchange, confused about how to involve themselves. From Rick's slight frown and squinting eyes, Amon guessed that his friend was almost as stunned by their stumbling upon Barrow as Amon was. Rick had likely never met him in the flesh and was surely stricken with the dissonance of encountering a celebrity he remembered as exceedingly successful suddenly reduced to a despicable nothing in the service of a pseudoscientific cult. For Amon, it was their second meeting and he'd witnessed unsavory sides to Barrow that colored his perception of the man in a different way, but that made the encounter no less bizarre for him. Though he'd known Barrow would be down here in the District of Dreams, somehow he hadn't prepared himself for this moment. Here was his old idol, the man he'd been deceived into betraying and identity assassinating. He'd tried to shoot Amon with a crossbow, understandable under the circumstances perhaps, yet this had nearly taken Amon's life. Should he apologize? Contribute his own kick for the trickery in the spa?

Over the course of Ty's interrogation, they learned that Barrow, like Rick, had graduated from the Er facility run by Rashana before joining with a nostie collective in the Tumbles, a vast region that took up the southern half of the island. Living far from Delivery at the northern tip had been tough and when his collective had tried to build new dispocrapers slightly closer to the supply road, an OpSci proselytizer militia had swarmed in and issued the ultimatum to convert or face their wrath. Barrow was made a slave at first but managed to talk his masters into emancipating him after a few weeks and had since served as a baggage carrier for various patrols and missionary expeditions. Listening to his smooth, masterful Japanese, Amon wasn't surprised his tongue had gotten him out of his predicament—or at least elevated him above the worst of it. Even though his Hinkongo would not yet be perfect, there would be no missing the mellifluous rhythm, with its entrancing pacing and carefully timed pauses, or the purity and richness of the voice he seemed to summon from the core of his body.

Eventually Ty went quiet and stared at the man for a few moments. Then, he turned to Amon and Rick. "Anything I forgot to ask before we send him back to the Peaks?"

"Well, actually, yes. Sort of . . ." said Amon. "I mean, there are some questions I—we need to ask him, though I don't think they'll help us much in this conflict with the OpScis."

"What kind of questions?"

"You heard Amon's story at the council, right Ty?" said Rick, who had heard about the hearing from Amon. "So you know that this man was at the center of everything that happened to us before we cash crashed. He might be the only person in the whole District of Dreams who can give us any clarity."

"So you want to ask him about your lives in the Free World? How long is this gonna take? Another OpSci gang could show up any second, and as the Xenocyst agent in charge I can't let them catch us just standing here."

"I do think we'll need a bit of time for this," said Amon, "so maybe we could try to find somewhere out of the way?"

"Like where? This place is crawling with all sorts of people we know nothing about. Some will be OpSci traitors."

"Can we try asking one of the residents?" Rick suggested. "They might know a good place."

"If it helps at all, I promise to answer as quickly and completely as I can," said Barrow. "For personal reasons, I want to speak to these two, but I don't want to be held up here any longer than I have to either. Not with those vindictive locals around."

The pleasing harmony of Barrow's voice humming in their ears, Amon watched as Ty looked back and forth between his, Rick's, and Barrow's expectant eyes, until at last he nodded. Then Barrow stood up to face them, raising his head and broad shoulders into an upright posture that reminded Amon of the imperturbably confident politician he had once been.

6

After Ty had strip-searched Barrow, he asked one of the nearby residents for a private place to talk. They were led by two men into a rift between buildings, up several half-flights of stairs, along a winding squeezeway, and finally into a tatamifoam room. Lit by direct sunbeam pins through tiny punctures dotting the ceiling, it was spacious enough for all four men to sit in conference.

"So, as you seem to have already realized for yourself," said Amon, "I'm the Liquidator who dispatched you. This here is my old partner, and this is one of Xenocyst's key security operators." Amon omitted their names though Ty had shouted his out earlier, as Amon had been trained not to give information unnecessarily to the OpScis.

"Pleasure," said Barrow with a slight nod to each of them and no detectable sarcasm. "What is it you'd all like to hear from me?"

"Well, my first question," said Amon, "is why you were identity assassinated. How exactly did that come about and who do you think set it up?"

"What a question for the assassin to ask of the assassinated! Though the key question, I suppose. I'll answer to the best of my ability, but I can't guarantee you'll be satisfied because my knowledge is far from complete."

"All we ask is what you know," said Rick.

"Yes. Well, let me start with the day before I had a run-in with this young gentleman here. It was early in the morning while I was having breakfast. A message suddenly appeared on my eyes. It said simply 'accept our offer within twenty-four hours or lose it all.' The moment I had finished reading it, the text burst open like a balloon spraying confetti and instructions popped out. These consisted of two statements, expressed as facts about the future as though their occurrence was already predetermined. First, I would admit to being the owner of the house full of analog detritus in Tsukuda, accept false evidence that showed I had siphoned public money to buy it, and bow out of office in shame. Second, I would accept the transfer of a massive amount of money and the deed to a warehouse full of high-quality anadeto after retiring.

"Naturally, I assumed this threat and bribe were coming from my political enemies. The Absolute Choice party obviously wanted me out, as my leadership and dare I say charisma threatened to keep them from power while my policies were anathema to their lobbydeology. But the more serious threat was a radical faction within my own Moderate Choice party. Although they had been opposed to me for some time, we had managed to keep them muzzled in the interests of holding our unified government together. I had already fired up this faction's animosity with my nationalization of urination and defecation, because they were fiscal conservatives and opposed the increase in credicrime fines required to implement it. As I'm sure you two know from following the news over the last few years, I managed to appeal to their punitive leanings by convincing them that the rise in fines would provide stricter retribution for those who violated the law, and this kept them quiet for a time. However, they became vocal again when I announced my plan to nationalize blinking as well, and the situation worsened when someone in my cabinet leaked other plans they were sure to oppose. I'm talking about the further nationalization of breathing and swallowing."

Amon knew it. Although he'd always been ashamed to admit to his extremist left-wing belief that breathing and swallowing didn't really count as volitional, he had sensed somehow that Barrow agreed with him on this point. Now he had confirmation from the man himself and felt a pang of guilt for what he had done to him.

"Was that the only reason for your downfall?" asked Amon. "I mean, I can see that those policies are controversial and the faction could have put up a big fuss, maybe even brought Moderate Choice down. But assassinating your identity strikes me as extreme. The costs are too great and the risks of failure too high, don't you think?"

"Absolutely. I completely agree. But there is a deeper layer to my plan that concerned them even more—or so I thought at first. You see, all of these different nationalization policies, as much as I agreed with them, were primarily just smokescreens for another, far more important, piece of legislation I was secretly preparing. To gather enough funds to compensate the owners of blinking for their losses caused by its nationalization, I was forced to raise credicrime fines across the board and I was planning to ratchet them up again for the nationalization of swallowing and breathing. I pretended that these were just temporary fiscal measures, but even after the deals were all concluded I intended to keep the fines high and maintain the increased inflow of government income. The faction acted as though they were opposed to these measures in and of themselves, but someone must have leaked the actual plan for which I enacted them as well, because that's the only way I could think to explain why they might threaten me. I was going to divert the extra funds to set up a GATA-run venture charity that would provide supplies to the bankdead unconditionally, that is, irrespective of whether they were suitable to provide babies or not. Moreover, the supplies were to be more plentiful and of a more durable kind than usual to ensure that everyone here had a more respectable quality of life."

"Government redistribution!" cried Rick in exasperation. "In the Free Era! You're joking?"

Amon was just as stunned. Though it seemed reasonable enough now that he'd lived in the District of Dreams for a while, anyone in the Free World would see it as just plain barbaric. The government's only roles were to make sure that Free Citizens always paid for their actions and that owners got their due. The ideal of justice was to have everyone getting the freedom they had earned, nothing more, nothing less. Magnanimity and social planning could only be a hindrance to its realization since they would decrease the freedom of those who had earned it for the sake of those who had not.

"No, of course not. I would never joke about something so serious and integral to the good will of humankind. I was doing what I could for the sake of those poor souls who, as I saw it, needed help the most. Though undoubtedly I was going against the grain. So no surprise that the opposition and the right-wing faction in Moderate Choice were just sizzling in their own vitriol to eliminate me when they caught word of what I was thinking. They lacked the evidence to go public and black-mail me because I'd been careful not to create any official documents or records that could link the plan back to me. But through certain information channels—I had my own spies placed within the faction you see—I intercepted messages expressing apoplectic disagreement with the redistribution and I knew they were biding their time for an opportunity to oust me.

"So after the message had exploded, I assumed it was either this faction or Absolute Choice that was responsible. But for several reasons I wasn't particularly concerned. First of all, I had accumulated enough inconvenient secrets over the years to devastate my opponents in both parties and had communicated to all of them that I had arranged for a close aide to disclose them should anything happen to me. And even if I did accede to their demands, coming out as a nostie was not incompatible with my strategies. In fact, I had already considered organizing such a scandal myself. Someone would leak a tidbit to the media that suggested I was a dandy nostie. I would deny it at first, until the location of my separate residence in Tsukuda was 'discovered' and the report would show footage of the exterior, which as you know looks so much like a nostie lair the public was guaranteed to demand a tour of the interior. Eventually, I would organize a press conference and admit that I was a nostie. My election strategists had determined that my ratings were high enough in the polls that the scandal would do little harm and my plan was to use my celebrity status to extol the virtues of analog detritus. If several other idols owned by lobby groups that support Moderate Choice also came out of the nostie closet, the media would be forced to have a discussion about anadeto's place in society and gradually it might become accepted, even rebellious and cool. At least that was what I hoped, and I'm still confident that it would have worked if not for what happened to me . . ."

Amon remembered how eloquently Barrow had defended anadeto and nostieism in his spa and imagining him doing the same on the news in the simpler, more accessible register he used in public, he could see that Barrow was probably right.

"So I was confident that I could out-duel my opponents with scandals if it came down to it. However, my strategists warned me that the timing wasn't right for me to come out. It was more prudent, they said, to do it after winning the election, not during the run-up, and voting day was only the following month. Losing the election was not merely a matter of sacrificing my own personal political victory, no." Barrow's voice gained an emotive lilt that seemed to trill warm sympathy through Amon's ear and into his chest. "By stepping down at that particular time, not only would I be giving *up* on my chance to help the bankdead through my policies, but I would be giving *in* to an Absolute Choice plan to harm them."

"What's this?" demanded Ty. With his tricycle laid on its side, he had been polishing it with a flaking rag, keeping one ear tilted towards the conversation, but now turned to scowl at Barrow, his craggy brow creasing. "You expect us to believe this bullshit? Since when do politics have any connection to us? Everyone knows it's the MegaGloms who decide how everything goes."

"Absolutely. Much is decided by the corporations backstage. But whoever was behind the policies I tried to combat, you are feeling their effects. For example, the supply reduction that has indirectly led to your being here in the Gifted Triangle, talking to me right now, is no doubt a direct result of them. As you know, Absolute Choice wants to make all autonomic processes—from heartbeating to heat regulation—chosen and commodifiable. That is their stated platform. However, my agents happened to intercept a video compilation outlining their unstated agendas, promoted especially by their current leader, Sawano Yoshinoi. The most worrisome of those were the segments describing a bankdeath camp 'clean up' to realize a 'slum-free world,' though there was no discussion of alleviating poverty. This proposal, veiled as it was in technocratic euphemism, suggested some sort of atrocity was brewing, and as I could not conscionably allow it to happen, whatever exactly it was, there was no way I intended to admit to embezzlement for the sake of my nostieism or to resign from office. If I stepped down at that particular juncture, Absolute Choice was guaranteed to take GATA, especially considering that my preferred successor in Moderate Choice—Thierry Kodama—is like me disadvantaged by being ethnically non-Japanese, but lacks a certain way with words that, not to be braggadocio, I'm sure you agree I possess.

"I came to this conclusion fairly quickly after my eyes were hacked and I had discussed the incident with my closest advisers. I immediately ordered some of my bodyguards to search my residence and then left for a conference, feeling confident of my decision to reject their demands and well prepared to outmaneuver the perpetrators if it came down to it. But I was soon given new reason to worry. It was a busy day so it wasn't until around noon that I had a chance to read the message from my guards about what they had discovered. It seemed there was a tiny parasite clinging to my bedclothes and this had facilitated the hacking into my BodyBank at short range."

Amon immediately exchanged a disgusted look with Rick that shared the thought, *just like the parasite that infected us.*

"Arranging to have this parasite snuck into my bedroom and onto my person was no cheap operation. A sophisticated illegal device would have had to be designed and given to one of my aides, who would have had to be bribed. I was clearly up against people who were on a different level in terms of funding and power compared to the politicians I was used to grappling with, and this started to make me feel incredibly vulnerable.

"Now, as you may know, the two main political parties derive about 99 percent of their funding from the MegaGloms of the Twelve And One and another 0.9 percent or so from private donors who work as executives at these MegaGloms or their subsidiaries. Most citizens in the bronze search class are unaware of this, but the SpawnU Consortium, made up of six MegaGloms plus Fertilex, tends to support Moderate Choice, while the Philanthropy Syndicate, made up of the remaining six MegaGloms, supports Absolute Choice. With politics almost exclusively funded by corporations, elections are dramatized proxy disputes between competing lobbies. Political positions disadvantageous to all, or at least most, industries are eliminated from public discourse by default, and only those legislations beneficial to some but not other industries are debated. This of course pushes all discussion to the middle of the road where the various interests can compromise and controversial policies can be decided by negotiation between the lobbies behind the scenes. If there was opposition to my plan from powerful interests, I would have expected campaign contributions to flow into Moderate Choice's coffers and for one of our members to tell me we had decided to give it up. That is standard procedure. Hacking and intimidation are simply not how the lobbies choose to influence legislative process, mostly because the fines are just too expensive to make it worthwhile. So this didn't seem like any lobby I knew and if it wasn't then I had no idea who I was dealing with or how to deal with them. Furthermore, if they were willing to spend this amount of money just to frighten me, then clearly they saw me as a significant obstacle and would be willing to go much further to get rid of me. The threat, I could be sure, had not been an empty one.

"I wanted to give a face to this monster that was emerging, but my usual information sources were either proving useless or too slow, so I decided to contact the PhisherKing. He and his Phishers were able to trace the hack to a group calling themselves the Gyges Circle. Their details were sketchy, but apparently this was a highly secretive partnership between top-level MegaGlom executives. A number of such associations exist where powerful individuals cooperate to advance their personal objectives. However, the strange thing about this one was the combination of its members; apparently, it was composed of execs from the Philanthropy Syndicate together with Anisha Birla. The conundrum here, as I'm sure you see, is that Anisha was the heir to Fertilex, which is the leading member of the SpawnU Consortium, and the interests of the SpawnU Consortium, not to mention Fertilex itself, are at direct odds with those of the Syndicate. The SpawnU Consortium depends for its human resources on Fertilex's order-made babies, while the Philanthropy Syndicate works actively to resist the Fertilex monopoly by extracting resources from the bankdeath camps. The idea that execs on opposing ends of the lobby spectrum would band together was impossible for me to accept. What could the alliance possibly be for?

"Now I could understand why the Philanthropy Syndicate would be opposed to me. Their members owned blinking, swallowing, and breathing, and I would be depriving them of profits by nationalizing these assets. Their income from the Charity Gift Economy would also drop since my government-funded charity would reduce resource yield and my fine increases would raise Delivery's operating costs. It is, after all, precisely because they oppose such policies that the Syndicate funds Absolute Choice and opposes Moderate Choice. But the participation of Anisha, and by extension Fertilex, in the Gyges Circle, was an enigma. It was in Fertilex's interest to destroy the CG Economy altogether and decreasing its profitability only worked in the MegaGlom's favor, which is one of the main reasons it and the rest of the SpawnU Consortium support Moderate Choice. I just couldn't see what could have brought Anisha into the fold of this clandestine group. There should have been no common ground for cooperation."

"What about the Birla inheritance?" said Rick. "That must have something to do with Anisha getting together with them. I mean, she was the surprise heir and her parents died the day before the Gyges Circle took you out—on the same day we crashed Kitao! You must have considered that?"

"Of course. I had a discussion with my advisors about what bearing the surprise transfer of Fertilex's executive control to the younger sister might have had on her choice to join up with the Birlas' traditional rivals and on their decision to intimidate me, but none of us could draw any explicit connections. At the time I was too busy dealing with the threat to my person to investigate the Birla parents' accident through my own sources, so I have nothing to add that wasn't already on the news. My suspicion is that Anisha was involved with the Gyges Circle much earlier but that, once her parents died, she gained enough Freedom to start putting their plans into action. What those plans are aside from eliminating me, and I'm guessing you two as well given that you're here, I have no idea. But, as you point out, the connection with the inheritance seems clear."

What Barrow said made sense to Amon, as it fit with everything he had puzzled out about the conspiracy. If the copy of his own AT readout that Amon had received from the PhisherKing was accurate, the fines for the identity murder he'd committed against Barrow—and most likely for a variety of related crimes including Archivist record forgeries and Sekido's later attempt to ID assassinate Amon himself—had been paid for by a Fertilex subsidiary called Atupio. Presumably, then, Atupio was a front company that had been set up to disguise the activities of the Gyges Circle and that the inheritance had enabled Anisha to fund.

A thought occurred to Amon and he turned to Rick. "This reminds me of something Sekido mentioned to both of us." Rick nodded for him to continue. "That big project close to the Executive Council he kept hinting at. He told me several times that I might become an assistant to it. Anisha seemed to be involved too, in the guise of a GATA recruiter. Could that have been the Gyges Circle?"

"I would guess it was," said Barrow. "I mentioned earlier that someone in my cabinet leaked my breathing and swallowing nationalization plan. I suspected Sekido because he was my only minister, as far as I knew, that was involved with the radical faction, as I had appointed him as Liquidation Minister to appease them. Thinking back on the fake bankruptcy report that was issued to you, I realized that he must have authorized it and assigned you a fraudulent mission. This suggests to me that he learned of our plans from someone else in the cabinet. He may have even been the leader of the faction and my guess is that it was funded for whatever reason by the Gyges Circle."

"Bastard," muttered Rick.

Amon thought for a moment and said, "But if Sekido is the leader of the Moderate Choice faction that opposed you and your policies, and those policies are beneficial to Fertilex, why would Anisha work with him?"

"That is the center of the whole tangled knot and I never have managed to unravel it. Good chance of that here, in this information wasteland . . ." Barrow winced and dropped his gaze to the tatamifoam.

The men went silent, thinking over this convoluted chain of events, the white glare of a sunlight pin that caught the corner of Amon's right eye seeming to sear his mind blank.

"So, to conclude my story," said Barrow after a time, raising his head to catch their gazes, "once I had this inkling of what was happening, I fired all my guards and household servants, not knowing which one had placed the parasite. I then hired an entirely new crew, doubling the number that was around me at all times just in case. When twenty-four hours passed without me meeting any of their demands and nothing happened, I started to wonder if I was being paranoid and let down my defenses for just one hour to have my nightly bath. Then you appeared in my spa . . ."

Barrow's expression remained docile and attentive, but a tightness appeared in his throat, as though his breathing had stopped, and his husky-pale blue eyes widened ever so slightly as a sort of angry aura seemed to buzz over his face, surely remembering what Amon had done to him. Amon felt the dull, heavy coal of guilt in his chest smolder anew with each breath. Although he couldn't help feeling a touch of betrayal and wariness towards Barrow when he thought of him pulling the crossbow, Amon recognized even more clearly after everything Barrow had said that the man's deceit had been justified. Here was one of Amon's many victims, banished mercilessly from the Free World, though he hadn't even been bankrupt and probably deserved it the least of anyone. He wanted to apologize, but felt odd doing so in front of his partners, especially Ty.

"The truth is, I hadn't fired *all* my staff," continued Barrow. "I kept my museum curator, as he had been with me for decades and had my complete trust. I felt camaraderie with him as a fellow nostie who seemed to derive true joy from tending the various collections in my Tsukuda getaway. He had even helped me design the building itself. But I'm certain now that he was the one who betrayed me. To forge a real-time AT readout of the kind they used to trick you"—Barrow's gaze honed in exclusively on Amon—"into assassinating me would have required surveillance of what I was doing at that moment and the only person with access to the sensors in my residence was him. The parasite in my pajamas was no doubt his doing as well. My guess is that they must have offered him the anadeto I refused along with the anadeto I left behind for GATA to auction off with the rest of my assets."

Barrow closed his eyes for a moment and let out a slight sigh through his nostrils.

"However they got him to turn on me, I suppose they were originally planning to use the images from my sensors to promote the scandal that I was a nostie. When I refused to play along, they decided that such mild defamation wasn't enough. Instead of being portrayed as a mere nostie, false evidence of my molesting an adolescent girl was produced, and this harsher character assassination was complemented with identity assassination."

"What about Kitao then?" said Rick. "We crashed him the day you say you got the threat and the Birlas died. How do you think the Gyges Circle was involved with that?"

"Although Minister Kitao wasn't a member of the radical faction, they pressured me to appoint him on my cabinet in addition to Sekido, as a condition for propping up my administration, and it seems clear to me now that they did this knowing he would fall apart. He appeared qualified on the surface, but anyone who'd done a bit of digging knew his psychological state was fragile at best, and Moderate Choice only agreed to appoint him because the faction absolutely refused to budge."

"It was obvious he had issues," said Rick, and Amon remembered the minister sniffing the heads of passersby. "But what exactly was wrong with him?"

"In politics, it's often useful to know what's happening in the bedrooms of your opponents as much as your colleagues, if it's even sensible to draw lines between the two, and what I know of his problem comes from the reports I received from those who knew him best. He'd married at a young age and got his wife pregnant the natural way without any medical assistance, which shows he must have been remarkably virile back then at least. But since he hadn't yet received his hefty inheritance and was still on a starting Archivist's relatively low salary, he would have had to limit his actions to raise his baby and he worried that this would interfere with his ability to fraternize among the connected circles that were the key to career advancement, so he asked his wife to get an abortion. She agreed, and he rose up the Ministry of Records ranks, but the decision led eventually to their divorce. Although he would later remarry, he had apparently loved his first wife, and after she left him, he developed an obsession with pornography that was so severe he used to walk around with it playing wherever he went."

"But we never saw any exorbitant habits when we were reviewing his readout before the mission," said Rick. "At least not until about two years ago."

"That's because his habit was not beyond his means. The erotic overlay he painted over the world contained no smut or illegal content. He was satisfied, it seems, to build it from generic amateur uploads that were cheap to procure. However, the cost in itself wasn't the problem. It was what the images did to his nervous system. Once he had become an influential politician with a big salary, he was accepted into high society and soon sought to elevate his standing further by having another child the natural way. But after watching such copious amounts of porno, his new wife failed to excite him. A single willing sexual partner had long ago stopped exciting him, as he was used to having whole hordes of digital partners that could be refreshed at a whim to arouse him visually. He tried to augment his sexual advances on his wife by overlaying her body with them. When that failed, he hired multiple women to engage him at once, before going through the whole smorgasbord of erectile drugs, Manhood Dust, you name it. None of them could keep him interested for long. Overstimulation had formed deep grooves in the arousal areas of his brain, and this had made him neurologically impotent when faced with a lone body of flesh and blood. Ironically, he had given up his natural baby to achieve success, but now his further success was hindered by his lack of a natural baby."

"When we took out Kitao," said Rick, "he was obsessed with this one kind of flower. How did he get from porn to *that*?"

"The connection between his neurological deficiency and those blossoms was never entirely clear to me. As a hobby, he'd been keeping desert cactuses, also known as 'fair ladies under the moon,' in a greenhouse behind his house for years. We had psychiatrists analyze segs sold to us by his gardener, and according to their report he began to associate their smell and appearance with women somewhere along the way, either seeking a mental aphrodisiac or an escape from his frustration and sense of inadequacy. Eventually he came to derive pleasure from the association itself.

"Looking back, it was only a matter of time before his pathologies led him to bankruptcy, and that was why the radical faction and the Gyges Circle must have wanted him on my cabinet. They knew exactly which bureaucrats GATA protocol dictated would be in charge of the Ministry of Records in case the minister was unable to fulfill his duties and made sure to buy them out in advance. With this strategy, the Archives fell into their hands the moment you two crashed him, which allowed the Gyges Circle to falsify your records to make me look like a pervert and have you assassinate me. Kitao's disgraceful downfall and then mine in quick succession was guaranteed to doom Moderate Choice in the upcoming election. I have received no information about what has happened in the Free World since I came here, but I'm sure Absolute Choice must have won. The supply reduction is proof enough that their polices are already being implemented, though why it was important for Anisha and her Philanthropy Syndicate allies that make up the Gyges Circle to bring this about I simply do not know."

"What about Jubilee?" asked Amon. "Do you know anything about jubilee?"

"Jew-beh-lee?" repeated Barrow. "I think I've come across this word. Originally from the Hebrew *yovel*, isn't it? What about it?"

"Do you know how it might be connected to the Gyges Circle and everything that's happened?"

"I'm afraid I don't have the faintest idea. Why do you ask?"

"We ask questions, you answer. Don't mix it up," cut in Ty, who had just finished polishing his tricycle and now stood with it strapped to his back again. "Are you finished with him yet?" he asked, turning to Amon and Rick.

Amon and Rick looked to each other for confirmation and then nodded reluctantly.

"Hey friends!" Ty called out the doorway, and the two men that had led them there immediately materialized from the dim hallway. "Old man is going back to the Peaks so please point him in the right direction."

The men nodded and began to approach Barrow across the room, but Barrow stood up and put his right palm up. "Now hold on. I would like to ask just a few questions of my—"

"No!" barked Ty. "This community is under Xenocyst protection and you're gonna let your friends know what happens when someone challenges our authority.

"But—"

"Get out of here!"

"Wait, I—"

"Get!" Ty plucked a wheel from his back and held it ready to throw.

Barrow flinched and then looked up at Amon with a doleful, pleading expression. "Amon," he said. That one word, his own name, spoken in Barrow's resonant voice, thrummed the biting sharp strings of guilt in his chest. For it summoned his memory of introducing himself that night in Tsukuda, the only time Barrow could have heard it. With what hatred had he remembered that name all these months since his cash crash? And Amon deserved every drop of his venom, but here Barrow was, showing no signs of anger as he asked for his help with such delicacy. For this great, generous man, he had to make amends.

"Ty. Just give him a second."

"What? Forget it. We've wasted time here long enough. We need to get back to Xenocyst before dusk or—"

"Come on. You heard the story. He was assassinated for trying to help the bankdead, people like us. The least we can do is give him a moment to sp—"

"This *OpSci*?" Ty's loathing oozed from his voice. Amon imagined that he could hear the pain of what the cult had done to his parents in it and was reminded of when Ty had suspected him of being a believer after Vertical found a gang of them sampling him. What would have happened to him if she hadn't convinced Ty otherwise?

"They took him in against his will."

"That's how they all start out. And I'll bet my spokes he's lying."

"Ty," said Rick gently, who seemed to have been swayed by Amon's words, and put a hand softly on Ty's shoulder. "Just a few seconds. Then we'll be out of here."

Ty shrugged off the hand and stared with blazing eyes into Rick's, but after a few tight breaths finally lowered his wheel. "He gets to speak for one minute. But we can't have information going to the OpScis, not about your life in the Free World, not about anything! So no questions! If he's got something to say, let him say it, but he gets nothing from us. Issues?" He glared back and forth between Amon and Rick, who exchanged frowns and nodded.

"Thank you very much," said Barrow, looking up at the three Xenocysters in the way skilled speakers have so that he seemed to meet all three of their gazes at once, as the two local men slipped back into the hallway. "I fully understand your caution. After seeing the OpScis destroy valuable artifacts such as antique computers and engines because of their inane superstitions and their awful abuse of women, I would never trust them either. I now want nothing more than to bring them to heel. No doubt, it will be to the benefit of peace and order for all who live here. So allow me to show you the way to something that can help you turn the tide in this nascent war. I hesitate to tell you this, but through the anadeto dealers that helped me stock my collection, I came to hear of a legendary trove in the District of Dreams. Although it sounded like a specious rumor, the mere possibility was so exciting I purchased every bit of information I could get: from other collectors, from the

PhisherKing, and from anyone else who seemed to know anything. I uncovered nothing credible and eventually came to disregard the legend completely. Because why, I ask you, would great cultural heritage end up in a melting nightmare like this?

"But then I woke up in a LimboQuarium and I had a lot of time to think about the past. In the absence of my usual digital distractions, I found some of my memories strangely vivid and clear like never before. One of them was of a paper map a slum explorer had sold me which claimed to lead to this trove. It had seemed like indecipherable nonsense at the time, just a bunch of childish Xs and squiggles. But when I got out of Er, I learned how to navigate here, and this seemed to alter the way I had thought my entire life. Suddenly the map took on a completely new meaning, and I could read it in my mind's eye as easily as a picture book. The nostie collective I mentioned earlier used to guard this place until the OpScis drove them out. They were hostile when I first encountered them, but when they saw my passion for anadeto we began working together to preserve everything and they taught me some of their coded gestures so I could move around in their community. Then Kitao found me."

"You've seen him since you cash crashed?" Rick asked.

"Yes. He had been taken in by the OpScis, deep into their organization. I think he may already be some kind of priest there, a Lab Reverend if I'm not mistaken. From what he told me, his ex-wife paid the Philanthropy Syndicate to mark him as gifted for life even though his genome doesn't qualify for the standard of any of the plutogenic algorithms. This got him into a regular Er facility where he was able to recover quickly and also made him part of a brandclan that is highly respected by the OpScis. He recognized me and seemed to think I had something to do with his ending up here, because he had his men haul me off to Opportunity Peaks and . . . The only way I could earn a little respect from them was to show them the way to some anadeto—that is where the gang you just saw acquired their weapons—just a piddling, peripheral heap, mind you. I would never lead them to the real treasure.

"But for you, for Xenocyst, I am willing to share. Among decorative furniture and other impractical art pieces are perfectly good weapons and equipment that will give you a strong advantage over the Opportunity Scientists. All I ask is for a fair chance to take one of your membership screenings. Then if I'm accepted, we can all put our heads together and try to figure out what this whole supply depletion business is about. Maybe we can even do something to reverse it. So what do you think? Can you give me a chance?"

13
THE DIGITAL QUARANTINE, BEFORE TEA

In the council chamber, Hippo sat facing Amon in front of the wall stenciled with the girl in the bubble just as at his initial hearing. Except this time Amon sat cross-legged on the cold wooden floor instead of kneeling, Rick was there to his right, and most of the council had vacated the room. The last few stragglers were chatting by the doorway, and Amon watched them along with Rick and Hippo, waiting patiently for them to leave so that the three of them could talk.

He could still feel the cold sweat not fully dried beneath his armpits from the unrelenting eyes of the councilors skewering them all afternoon. They had finally been granted a screening after numerous delays, with the council bogged down by the supply crisis, and the debate that ensued the moment they sat in the circle still echoed faintly in Amon's recollection. Most—including the young councilor Yané—had been vociferously opposed to their inclusion. Compared to average crashborn residents, they were ill-adjusted, incompetent, psychologically unstable, cognitively stunted, distracted, poor speakers of Hinkongo, and socially awkward. They had also worked as Liquidators, a brutal profession that deserved their censure. With the supplies now reduced and a newly instated policy indefinitely cancelling all applicant hearings, even considering their membership was preposterous. Numerous incidents related to Little Book by their supervisors were used as evidence to establish these failings. In response, Hippo had raised examples of their strengths: their remarkably quick adjustment, their fluency in Japanese, their solid grasp of the

Free World. But what seemed to sway the council in the end was Book's summary of Ty's report of their valor in the Gifted Triangle and the way they had guided the encounter with Barrow to Xenocyst's advantage, the final vote being two to three, with five of the nine councilors abstaining and Hippo breaking the tie.

Just before the meeting adjourned, Hippo had requested the room to speak with Amon and Rick in private, but many councilors had lingered to talk about minor logistical matters. Only now, nearly an hour later, as the last man stepped out the doorway and closed the door behind him, did they finally have the space to themselves, and Amon looked to Hippo, eager for his initiative. Yet Hippo remained silent, embracing them with his troubled eyes, until Rick said, "So what is this about? Is something wrong?"

Although there was no impatience in his voice, they had both been there for hours and Amon knew Rick must want to return to their room as badly as he did. His feet were like icy lumps beneath his calves on the patch of floor his body had only partially warmed, his skin was goosebumped from the draft through his holey clothes, and he sniffled occasionally, perhaps about to catch a cold. The hunger panging in his gut with every breath ensured thoughts of food were never far away, while visions lurking half-perceived beneath his consciousness seemed to stoke his anxiety, the whole slum crumbling atop him as they all writhed in a naked heap. While the fact that they had just been accepted as Xenocyst members was a relief, it did little for his discomfort and restlessness and fear. He could only trust that Hippo had a good reason for keeping them.

"Yes. Many things are wrong here, as you know. You are both feeling the effects of the supply drop, I'm sure, and I can guess how worn out you must be after the screening. It's tiring enough for us whose lives are not hanging on the result. But please bear with me. Though I cannot tell you how delighted I am that you two were accepted—you both deserve it after what happened with Barrow, you really do—I also want to ask for your help."

Hippo frowned, furrowing his forehead with a crisscrossing web of worries. His face had grown haggard, with dark crescents beneath his eyes, all traces of joy drained away with the color from his skin.

"The whole council is stumped as to how to respond to the crisis. All of our customary ways of thinking and responding are turning out to be useless. I'm hoping that you two, with your backgrounds so different than most of us and your familiarity with the present world outside the camps, will be able to think of something that has so far eluded us."

The way he looked at them, Amon felt like a distant, glowing planet for a ship lost in the void. Could they possibly match up to such hope?

"We'll do what we can," said Amon in the most confident voice he could summon.

"Yeah," said Rick with a firm nod. "Just let us know how we can help."

"Well there's not much you can do until you understand our situation better, which is why I've set aside this time for us to talk. When Gura asked me about my past at the festival, the timing was wrong and we lacked the privacy of the Digital Quarantine."

The council had just named Amon Mogura, Japanese for an almost-blind subterranean mammal, on the basis of his story. Figuratively speaking, he had chosen to live in a dark place for many years but had eventually learned how to see with only a bit of light. Now, apparently, Hippo had decided to shorten it to Gura.

"But now that you two are full members," Hippo continued, "there's no reason to delay any longer. So allow me to tell you about who I am, and how Xenocyst came to be what it is today."

"In my banklife, before I founded Xenocyst, I originally trained to be a medical researcher. I graduated from medical school in my early twenties and, just like you and Rick when you graduated from the BioPen, I hoped to work for Fertilex. Also like you two, I failed the entrance application and was instead picked up by GATA Osaka. I spent a few years there as a technical assistant in the Ministry of Access before receiving a promotion to Identity Vitalator.

"Although I was reasonably good at my job, I had no passion for it. Not only was it outside my field, but I had a very specific idea that inspired me—and the only way I could see to bring it to fruition was by working at Fertilex. The topic of my dissertation had been the problem of so-called 'assisted natural impregnation.' As you know, the Fertilex monopoly over action-properties related to life gives them a corresponding monopoly over artificially generated human resources, whether cloned or otherwise, and the MegaGlom does good business charging introduction fees for access to the profiles of promising young workers. But they also cater to the top one percent of income earners who want to make babies through sexual intercourse, as heirs produced naturally in this way are very rare and are therefore considered a symbol of the highest success. While some of these couples choose to have their fertilized ovum implanted in a SubMom to avoid the fuss of nine months' pregnancy and simply purchase a fake certification of natural birth, most are concerned about the embarrassing possibility of being found out, especially since the Phishers who sell such forgeries are known to use their knowledge of the sale for extortion, and so there is a high demand for natural birth among the apex class.

"Now do you know what one of the main problems with impregnation through intercourse is?"

There was a pause as Amon and Rick exchanged glances to see who would speak first.

"Um . . . it's expensive?" said Rick.

"Well that too, yes, but I'm thinking of the fact that most Free Citizens have fertility difficulties. I had a hypothesis for a novel treatment that would improve their chances of success more safely and effectively than the other treatments on the market. This hypothesis remained in the back of my mind for years until, over the course of my ID Vitalator duties, I had a chance to speak with Shiv and Chandru Birla. I had been called in to oversee what my supervisor described as an 'important' Identity Birth. As is sometimes the case with such high-profile assignments, I was invited out to celebrate afterwards and was entertained at a restaurant. It was about an hour in when I discovered that the young man I had bestowed with an identity signature was a nephew of the Birla founders, and that the quiet, dignified Indian couple sitting beside me were them.

"I spent the remaining hour smiling cordially and pretending to enjoy the fine drinks and food, of a level of refinement I never experienced before or since. All the while I was thinking of my idea. If I was ever going to realize it, the Birlas might be my only chance. Finally, as the dessert plates were being cleared away, I mustered the courage and made my pitch. I was expecting them to sniff and perhaps make some noncommittal remark before excusing themselves politely. But to my amazement they both seemed intensely interested. By the following week, I had my own lab and several talented young researchers to help me put my idea into practice.

"To describe the method I developed in the simplest terms, I would take numerous semen samples from the father-to-be and use a device I invented to locate the most potent individual sperm. I then separated and recombined them with superior sperm from other samples. Sperm, of course, are polymorphic, meaning they have different shapes and characteristics. Some are bigger or smaller, faster or slower. Some are fatter or have multiple tails. These differences mean that compatibility between the individual sperm in a given ejaculation has an impact on the probability of one of them fertilizing an ovum. Therefore, I had to recombine not only the strongest individuals, but the ones that would work together best as a cohesive unit. Once I'd discovered a technique for calculating this ideal combination, I designed a method to alter the testicles of the patients so that it would be reproduced, more or less, in each ejaculation. Although the procedure was pointless if the ova were defective, it increased the odds by a higher margin with fewer side effects than the alternatives, which was good enough for our clients, who wanted a natural birth by any means necessary. While in principle my method had multiple applications and could have been used to raise the efficacy of test tube samples as well, it was cost-intensive and time-consuming because it needed to be personalized for each man's reproductive organs. So it was targeted at a very particular, read 'highly liquid' niche.

"Our lab's marketing team gave the treatment the ridiculous name All Star Natura. In spite or perhaps because of this, it was a big success. For moving so rapidly from concept to popular product, Fertilex gave me a huge promotion and provided me with a state-of-the-art laboratory, staffed by a team of the best and brightest in the field. Another team of 'all-stars,' if you will."

Hippo smiled to let them know that this was a joke, but Rick merely snorted and Amon could only force up one side of his lip in a mirthless smirk. Genuine humor eluded them in their predicament, it seemed, and Amon wished for days when they might laugh again.

"Now I had a seemingly limitless amount of funding—whatever equipment and personnel we requested they provided—and we were rumored

288 ★ ELI K. P. WILLIAM

to be developing these treatments for the Birla parents themselves. Decades later, I am now confident that this is indeed true, as the Birla sisters are said to have been produced naturally, perhaps with the help of All Star Natura itself.

"Almost overnight, I was wealthy and respected, both as an entrepreneur and a specialist. In the beginning, the Birlas had arranged for me to retain my position at GATA, since they were only hiring me on a trial basis and were kind enough to ensure I stayed employed if my idea failed. Now GATA named me 'Honorary Identity Vitalator' for 'notable contributions to the Freedom of the Market.' The title was as symbolic as it sounds: I was only expected to facilitate Identity Births on an occasional basis. Though in such a capacity, I did preside over the ID birth of Rashana and Anisha Birla. This is no accidental digression, as I'll soon explain.

"In our new lab in Tokyo, we continued to refine and improve the treatment. Soon several of our more creative assistants were developing unique ideas of their own. When I had finished training several of my staff to serve as independent supervisors and the research operation began to run itself, I turned my attention to a deeper problem, as I was not at all satisfied with the method upon which I had built my name. Undoubtedly, we had made it easier for a select group of men to impregnate their partners without artificial insemination. But we had employed the greatest of artifice in altering the bodies of these men in carefully planned and intentional ways. It hardly seemed that impregnation following from this would count as natural. On the contrary, it was hard to see how it was any different from all the so-called 'artificial' in vitro methods you can imagine. No, rather, for me to be satisfied that we had truly facilitated a natural process, we had to go beyond a mere symptomatic approach to resolve the root causes of infertility itself so that each impregnation would arise spontaneously from the amorous relations of two individuals without such designed interference. In this way, we would expand the sphere of freedom so that people could reproduce of their own volition without helping hands. You're probably thinking I was caught up in a purely academic, dare I say philosophical, problem. In actuality, I was still thinking within the constraints of my role as an inventor and developer of marketable products. Because, you see, if we could permanently and completely cure infertility for our patients then we would be able to assert, without any disclaimers or exceptions, that we had totally and absolutely endowed people with the capacity for natural impregnation. Against such a categorically superior product, I was convinced that competing Fertilex subsidiaries wouldn't stand a chance.

"Driven only by these enterprising motives, I began to investigate the root of the fertility problem. Quickly I discovered that very little research had been done on the subject—or that was how it seemed. It would be many years before I became convinced, as I am now, that the reports had merely been hidden from the gold-class academic databases I was given access to. At the time I naively thought the topic had been neglected and fancied myself a pioneer in a new sub-discipline. Following the chain of cause and effect, I would journey out into the dark unknown and locate its first link so as to forever eliminate the ills of humankind, or at least of the demographic that could afford and appreciate my services. What a fool I was."

Hippo shook his head ruefully and continued.

"Infertility can arise due to all sorts of factors, from deformities in the Fallopian tubes to dysfunction in the thyroid, but we had no evidence for any one of them or a worrisome combination of them being widespread across the populace. So our first step was to gather the necessary data. The easiest place to start, I thought, was with the bankdead. Only a minuscule percentage of bankliving reproduce and only a minuscule percentage of these do so in a human body. Since that wealthy segment is very tight-fisted about personal details, their cooperation in a study was out of the question. In the District of Dreams, however, was a large population that reproduces exclusively in this way. With the Birlas' backing, I even had the funding to break the international credilaws against enrolling individuals of low social standing into clinical trials and was able to use bankdead as subjects. I set up my own clinic and subject-recruiting center near Delivery. In retrospect, this was the very first beginnings of Xenocyst, though it hardly resembles anything like the community today. Although we did provide some basic medical care, this was only to attract subjects that met our selection criteria, and the overnight accommodations for our staff were only for temporary stays during test periods rather than permanent living.

"What we seemed to discover was that the fertility rate among bankdead was much higher than among bankliving. Particularly fascinating for me, likely due to my specialization, were the sperm samples we analyzed. They were like nothing I'd ever seen in all my years of research. If I were to boil our final statistical results down into the simplest laymen's terms, they were just buzzing with vigor and *genki*. By contrast, bankliving samples were lethargic, indecisive, distracted, and aimless, even the fine specimens selected for All Star Natura teams.

"But why? To answer this, I would have to isolate the factors that might explain the difference. Was it diet? This seemed unlikely as the bankdead subsist almost exclusively on nutritional inks. Although the adverconsensus is that these technically meet all the body's needs, I doubted the studies that supposedly demonstrated this as they were sponsored exclusively by subsidiaries under the same MegaGlom ownership as the manufacturers. Moreover, the quantities were slightly low, leaving many on the threshold of malnourishment. Therefore, for these and other reasons, I determined that the bankliving diet would be more conducive to fertility in general.

"So could it have been toxins then? No, because here again I found the bankliving to be in a better position. Bankdeath camps are usually built on unwanted lands and the District of Dreams is no exception, as the island is composed mostly of garbage and chemical waste. This foundational pollution is compounded by the Fleet flakes blowing around, which again are perfectly safe according to research done by the manufacturer. In fact, these nanoparticles are liable to slip inside cells and do not-insignificant damage over years of exposure—notice the low lifespan here and the fact that Fleet products are not approved for Free Citizen use. After ascertaining all this and performing a variety of other tests on our subjects, we concluded that the bankdead environment should be more detrimental to overall health than most environments in the Free World and that we would predict on this basis that bankliving ought to be more fertile than bankdead, though we were observing the opposite.

"The other possibility was that the difference was inherited, but investigating whether there were salient differences in the two gene pools turned out to be surprisingly difficult. Although plenty of data from related studies were already available online, these turned out to be useless as they didn't indicate which samples were taken from Free Citizens adopted from bankdead parents and so mixed up the two populations. To proceed, we needed to perform genetic and epigenetic analysis on our own samples, after ascertaining their descent, whether bankdead or bankliving. However, we were surprised to find no documentation available about the ratio of clones to natural births to order-grown babies to bankdead orphans. When we tried inquiring with the BioPens about the origins of their wards, we were told that this was private information and were refused, even by facilities owned by Fertilex. The putative justification was the prevention of discrimination. But if that were so, the BioPens should have at least had anonymized statistical breakdowns that could be loaned out for a fee, which they didn't. The other puzzling inconsistency was that BioPen kids don't themselves have access to this information, so clearly it was not about protecting *their* interests."

Amon thought back to when his SubMom had told him he was half Persian and half Japanese, and wondered if she'd had special access to the Green Ladybug database or had just made it up.

"The approach I finally had success with was to speak with the venture charities. With my clinic situated right beside Delivery, we had developed relationships with some of the managers and it only took a few modest bribes to get what we needed. What I discovered shocked and surprised me more than anything else. As it turned out, the vast majority of Free Citizens—approximately 90 percent—were in fact crashborn babies given up for adoption. But if that were true, then both bankdead and bankliving were, by and large, coming from the same population and there would be no genetic basis to explain the difference in fertility.

"At this point I was stumped. Against the advice of a colleague, I decided not to visit the PhisherKing because I was uncomfortable trading him the lucrative information his services usually require. In the meantime, my team had developed new marketable fertility treatments. These included novel drugs that equaled or surpassed All Star Natura, but such progress no longer interested me. I wanted to understand the fertility gap. It was an unyielding enigma that seemed to lie at the center of everything I did and now perplexed me unbearably. This was forcing me to think in unfamiliar ways. The first step, I decided, was to understand the bankdead—who they were and how they came to be this way—as they were the stock from which most living people were derived, and this led me to the idea of the Charity Gift Economy for the first time."

"I understand that the Books have been giving both of you lessons in here?"

"Yes," said Amon, and Rick nodded.

"And I suppose they've told you something of our origins?"

"The history of the bankdead was one of my first lessons. I think Rick is caught up now too." Rick nodded again. "There's still a lot that I'm confused about though."

"It never ends, does it? Well I'm sure you understand much better than I did back then. Information was extremely hard to come by in spite of all my resources and connections, and every one of my questions seemed to only spawn other questions. Once I began to get an inkling of how the whole Philanthropy Syndicate business functioned, I saw that there was a reason for my ignor—"

Hippo stopped short and his eyes turned to the entrance. Amon's gaze followed, catching the end of the door's swinging inwards. In stepped Book, with Little Book in tow cradling a stack of plastic sheets that rose to his chin.

"Speak of the rumored, and their shadow falls upon you," said Hippo.

"We have come to decode a number of highly sensitive letters from proxy enclaves for council intelligence," Book explained. "We were unaware that you would be occupying the digital quarantine for such a lengthy time period."

"We have many things to discuss today, I'm afraid."

"Understood," said Book with a slight bow. "Excuse us."

"Hold on," said Hippo, and the two Books stopped in the doorway to look back over their shoulders in the same posture.

"If our talking isn't going to disturb you, you're welcome to work in here."

"Such an opportunity would be much appreciated. I believe the disturbance will be minimal for us. A more significant concern is that our tapping will disturb you."

"Naw," "No problem," said Rick and then Amon, both shaking their heads. Although Hippo's talk was meant to be private, the Books appeared to be an exception, and Amon could see no reason why they shouldn't be.

"Go right ahead, Books," said Hippo. "But can I ask you a small favor?"

"Yes."

"Would you mind having someone brew us a pot of my special *gyokuro*? We are also celebrating the council's ruling."

"Certainly," said Book. "We will return shortly." Then, turning to Amon and Rick with his unevenly magnified eyes, "And congratulations. We look forward to working with you further." For the first time Amon could remember, Little Book's face showed emotion as he smiled at them, before he put down the stack of sheets against the wall and the two of them shuffled out into the hallway, closing the door behind them.

At the council, the Books had maintained their neutral demeanor as facilitators and conveyers of information, showing no signs whether they supported Amon and Rick's acceptance or not. So receiving their gestures of welcome now brought a quiver of warm gratitude to Amon's chest that almost made him want to cry.

Hippo was staring at the door frowning distantly, as though fretting over various thoughts stirred in the air by their departure.

"You were saying about the reason for your ignorance," said Rick.

"Right," said Hippo, relaxing his brow and embracing their gazes again. "I was going to talk about pitypromo. I realized then how it fueled a certain kind of consumption that the Syndicate satisfied, thereby funding the whole charity gift operation. In the process it generated a particular perception of the bankdeath camps that kept the Free World functioning. It was in this perception that my mind had been entrapped.

"The videos of the conditions in the camps fabricated by the MegaGloms that I and other Free Citizens often saw made them appear horrible enough to guilt us into donating, but just hopeful enough that we could feel as though our donations might make a difference. In particular, they were highly effective in encouraging impulsive donation even in those of limited means. Here the venture charities were selling the promise of satisfying the needs of the poor as a product, which simultaneously satisfies the customer's desire to alleviate their guilt in that moment. And the higher you move up the income scale, the larger impulsive donations become, with philanthropy motivated to a certain degree by the credicrime fine deductions offered by GATA to major donors. At the same time, the videos had the effect of making us afraid enough of bankruptcy to work hard to stay out of it, while also keeping up the façade that the AT market was a utopia that produces the best of all possible slums. Since independent research and investigative reporting went unfunded, unorthodox presentations of the camps were rare and could be labeled as anecdotal quackery. They would then be sorted into silver, gold, and platinum search engines. Unsearchability is the new censorship, after all. In this way, pitypromo kept up economic morale while bringing in enough capital from investitarians and philanthropaneurs to pay for bankdead supplies and thereby fund the rampant consumption of the poor that is an unavoidable part of the Charity Gift Economy. Decades later, my guess would be that the situation hasn't changed much. Am I right?"

"Yes," said Rick. "Everything you said fits."

Nodding in agreement, Amon recalled the satisfied looks on the faces of the slum tourists when they watched the bankdead eating the food they had given them. "Can I ask you a question?" he said.

"Of course. If you two are going to be able to help us in the way I'm hoping, I need you to have a solid grasp of what I tell you today. Is anything I said unclear?"

"Sort of. I mean, it's something that's been unclear to me for a while. So you say that pitypromo keeps the camps funded, but I don't see how donations could possibly be enough. Providing supplies for millions of bankdead, maintaining all those vending machines, and paying the salaries of career volunteers and freekeepers has to be incredibly expensive. It seems impossible to me that the MegaGloms of the Philanthropy Syndicate could recover their costs from donations, even if we add on the introduction fees for human resources twenty years down the road. Wouldn't it be much cheaper to simply buy resources off Fertilex from the start?"

"I thought so too when I began looking into this issue, but no. To bring expenses in line with donations and introduction fees, the Philanthropy Syndicate cuts costs in various ways. Action fees are kept low through automation across the entire supply chain, from distribution to security.

To reduce labor costs further, construction of the camps is left to the bankdead, and maintenance drones do the minimum required to keep infrastructure like suspension pillars and open sewers functioning. Meanwhile, risks and losses are offset through plutogenic hedging. For example, investments are made to establish brandclans that are not expected to produce marketable resources but that would be expected to do so if current expectations turned out to be false. Or a brandclan might be packaged as a derivative that will pay out in case a particular industry doesn't require as many employees as expected, so that investments in raising youth for those jobs are hedged.

"A variety of other derivatives help to generate additional profits, on top of the introduction fees, as part of the thriving industry of plutogenic speculation. Such assets are based on rights to assign brand membership to particular genomes, the expected value of a future profile, and so on. For example, investitarians often buy shares in "unmined genomes," with the value fluctuating depending on how close the genome or genetic sub-population approaches gifted status or, if gifted, how close it drops to the threshold with giftlessness. After all expenditures—PR, labor, supplies, security, and so on—are subtracted from income, the Charity Gift Economy remains slightly in the red for the Philanthropy Syndicate. But they are able to acquire human resources while preventing Fertilex's global hegemony, which is the whole point."

"If the Philanthropy Syndicate is doing so well acquiring their own human resources," said Rick, "then wouldn't they run Fertilex out of business?"

"Once again, my train of thought in those days was much like yours, but no, because Fertilex is still left with a number of incredibly profitable businesses. For one, the Syndicate MegaGloms must still purchase a portion of their human resources from Fertilex. This is partly due to population limits in the bankdeath camps. Only a certain percentage of bankdead are gifted in any particular sample group, and while it might be theoretically possible to increase the population in the camps to ensure that quantity meets demand, when density reaches beyond a certain threshold the population becomes too expensive to manage. Through adjustments of supply disbursement, the population of the camps is kept growing at the same rate as the Free World but no higher so as to keep resource supply steady. Yield of extractable marketable resources is also subject to random fluctuations, whereas the supply of engineered resources is stable, so Fertilex must be relied upon in times of scarcity.

"Note moreover that it controls several niche markets. In addition to the market for naturally born babies that my research contributed to, one such market is for top-quality resources. While gifted bankdead can produce highly marketable candidates, they're never as likely to be well suited for their future jobs as those that Fertilex specifically engineers and rears for them. By providing personalized laborers for even the rarest jobs, Fertilex can charge significantly higher fees than the cost of securing candidates through charity, since any company unwilling to pay will be stuck with whatever the camps offer. Fertilex also has its own venture charities that it uses to secure resources, and in many cases launder them. Baby laundering obscures their bankdead origin so their profiles can be sold at a higher price, and only Fertilex can pull it off because none of the other MegaGloms can claim to have acquired their resources anywhere else.

"You also need to understand that Fertilex is the exclusive supplier of the six SpawnU Consortium MegaGloms, who have banded together to keep the Syndicate in check. Fertilex provides them with rebated human resources and they in turn cut costs for Fertilex on a range of essential action properties. This is the bulk of Fertilex's sales, and all of these businesses', not to mention its enormous share in properties unrelated to life, maintain its position as the largest MegaGlom in the world in spite of the Philanthropy Syndicate challenge."

Hippo paused for a moment, his eyes shifting back and forth from Amon's gaze to Rick's. When neither followed up with further questions, he continued. "So after I learned about the Charity Gift Economy and the way pitypromo had so effectively roped us into supporting or acquiescing to it without knowing, I was utterly stunned and appalled. Due to the success of my research, I happened to be in a privileged position, with plenty of funding and access to the best information money could buy, but very few knew what I did about how the Free World functioned and I began to worry about my role within it for the first time. Up to that point, as I've told you, my inquiry had been driven by the desire to produce an unbeatable product. Now I was losing sight of why that was important. Every business and individual livelihood seemed to operate on the basis of an arrangement that was horrendously unjust, with the whole mess obscured and tucked carefully out of sight. The treatments I hoped to market suddenly seemed like a contribution to this state of affairs and I felt no attraction to pursuing their research further. Nonetheless, I was still engaged by the fertility problem, and for the first time in my life I felt something driving me that had nothing to do with profitability.

"At our fertility hospital in Free Tokyo, I got to know a number of our wealthy clientele over the course of their luxury treatments, hoping in my naive pragmatism to make influential friends and connections. In gratitude for a successful delivery, they would occasionally invite me into their private worlds, where I witnessed them spending time with their babies. At meditation gaming soirees and massageathon health food tastings, my hosts would keep their babies on hand in elaborately digimade cribs and carriages, often lidded with glass cases and placed under bright lights. They would always find a way to mention the baby's natural pedigree, slipping into the flow of the conversation the fact that he or she had not been test-tubed or artificially transferred, though as their doctor I could see this for the concealment of bragging it was. The unwavering cheerfulness of the babies was a sign of the infant mood enhancers in their nutritional formulas. They would smile and blink wide-eyed on display along with the furniture, rugs, and other elements of the domestic overlay the parents wanted to show off. If they did happen to cry, rearing staff hovering nearby would handle and feed them with the utmost delicacy while their parents simply watched and talked about them from a distance, or picked them up with feigned tenderness for a social media photo op. Their expressions and embrace were so stiff it was obvious that they never did this without an audience, except perhaps to practice for such moments.

"The bankdead parents who visited our fertility research clinic in the District of Dreams couldn't have behaved more differently towards their children. Most of our subjects who brought infants and children were giftless who had decided not to abandon their rejected babies in the Sanzu River as many do when they turn one and are no longer considered malleable enough for BioPen education."

Amon thought of the floating faces that had slapped the side of the boat as he crossed with Tamper and shuddered, wondering if that's what they could have been . . .

"The rest were those rare gifted who decided in spite of the bonuses to keep their offspring. In other words, they were all parents who genuinely wanted to raise their children. I remember vividly the very first subject that walked into our clinic. A woman cuddling a baby boy with a young girl clinging to her leg. I was immediately struck by how gently and tenderly she rocked her baby, and the way the girl looked so safe, as though all the dangers in the world could never touch her if only her mother were there. This was mutual caring and affection. This was intimacy and humanity. Perhaps there are people like this in the Free World, people like you, Shaké, who really want a family from the bottom of their heart."

The council had decided to name Rick Shaké, Japanese for "salmon," on the basis of the story from his hearing. He had had a family, lost it, and now wished to return to how he started out, like a salmon swimming upstream to its birthplace. Glancing over in concern as Hippo reminded Rick of his dream, Amon saw the brooding sadness in his eyes, and something else in his expression, a hint of melancholy in the lines of his brow that had never been there before. But he had no time to think what it might reveal as Hippo went on.

"But all the ones who could afford it were as I described, so I'd never seen anything like this. Though my bankliving patients had all the money, Freedom, and standing they could hope for, I caught glimpses of the emptiness lurking at their core that I knew from speaking with psychiatric colleagues was hidden only with the help of PharmaJoy cocktails. Meanwhile the love and hope my bankdead subjects shared for their offspring seemed to give them infinite determination and strength in spite of all the adversity and humiliation they suffered.

"It was while I was thinking about the correlation between this difference and the fertility gap one night in my lab that I was suddenly overcome with the strongest emotion I had ever felt. For the first time in my life, I was truly angry—no, not anger. Rage is a better word. I was enraged. I wanted to take it out on something, anything, and I saw a vision of my lab destroyed. Our diagnostic drones were battered wrecks along the walls and glass shards in puddles of gunk from shattered sample containers littered the floor. It took all of my self-control not to fly into a frenzy and make my imagination a reality at that moment.

"While people who deserved so much better were being stripped of their *dignity*," Hippo said, his voice trilling with an echo of that emotion, "all we did was pity them from a distance and allow others to profit off our pity while preventing change, not realizing that our own wealth and donations were only possible on the basis of that exploitative arrangement. I could not forgive us, them, myself, for continuing to live this way, and if I didn't channel my rage into more productive directions I knew it was only a matter of time before I gave into pointless destructive impulses and lashed out in ways that I would regret. Either that or I would go on as before while my newfound knowledge and rage catalyzed together and began to eat me from the inside out.

"I soon came to a profound and irreversible decision. My expertise was wasted on Free Citizens. I had been working all my adult life since graduating conglommercollege to serve them, and ever since the Birlas had set me up with a lab I had toiled away developing new solutions for those who wanted babies. In that endeavor, I had achieved as much success as anyone could hope for in their mid-thirties. But what was I doing?! Wielding nature to help the wealthy use living creatures as trinkets to impress their friends?! Shouldn't I have been dedicating myself to people who actually *cared* about their babies? Even the question of the fertility problem stopped interesting me. I began to feel convinced that it was not answerable through science at all and rapidly lost faith in my profession. Churning my mental juices over abstruse theoretical concerns seemed like so much wasted energy when people who deserved better were being disgraced. Let there be mysteries! Something had to be done.

"So I would use my know-how and reputation to set up a hospital in the camps—not a research center, but a place that would give aid and shelter to those who needed it most. I resigned from Fertilex, sold off my shares in All Star Natura, and began to seek support for my project, financial and otherwise. In my youthful idealism I expected everyone to wake up to the iniquities of it all. Unfortunately, the cost of accessing the sources that justified the need for my project despite the existence of countless venture charities, the contradictory view spread by pitypromo, and general skepticism and disinterest, served as obstacles as I tried to get the word out to colleagues, journalists, politicians, and other influential people. Though the reality propped up by vested interests was not to be toppled easily, I rallied all my resources and connections with persistence, and began to gradually increase my list of supporters. Soon I had wealthy philanthropaneurs willing to assist me, knowing they would receive no return on their investment and would relinquish all say in how the organization developed to the bankdead that composed it. I insisted on these conditions and was willing to reject many donors who disagreed because, as much as I needed funding, I had seen the way other venture charities had gone—even ones that started out with good intentions—when their backers began to meddle in their affairs. If you were dependent on corporations or individuals, it was only a matter of time before they began to pull the strings their money was attached to and the aims of the project were distorted until they lined up with profit margins. If I was going to realize the vision crystallizing in my mind—a union of bankdead run democratically by bankdead for bankdead that was completely independent and self-sufficient—I would need to ensure all decision-making power remained completely internal.

"I began to set up a foundation that would pay for everything we needed. Not just shipments of essential items like medicine, diagnostic tools, and bedding that we couldn't yet produce ourselves, but also the salary of a team of doctors, nurses, lab technicians, mercenaries, engineers, and other core personnel from the Free World who I needed to train bankdead staff to eventually replace them. We purchased a condominium full of nostie squatters and convinced most of them to join us or lured them away with attractive supply packages before modifying the building to our needs—this became the Cyst. Over time, we used the same combination of persuasion and bribery to take control of larger and larger areas. There our urban planners began to assemble structures similar to the disposable skyscrapers you see today, though of a more longer-lasting variety, which we hoped to later replace with permanent buildings. By the time the Opportunity Scientists learned of us and began to send in violent bands of Quantitative Missionaries, we had already set up defense systems including human guards and drones and were beginning to make pacts with surrounding communities to establish the buffer ring we have today. Once we'd reached a large enough size, we began to divide up our territory into administrative units, the residents of which began to elect representatives to the council. Everything was decided democratically, except that I stayed on as a special advisor to the council and still retain tie-breaking power in case of an even split. It was at this stage as the medical, social, infrastructural, diplomatic, military, political, and administrative facets began to take form that the project finally began to seem less like just an agglomeration of disparate humanitarian services and more like a city of its own.

"Our resources were limited, so we couldn't help everyone, and our main goal at the Cyst was to serve those the venture charities ignored. The gifted already received some limited services such as basic pre- and post-natal care insofar as these helped to increase yield. We would not simply provide services as the charities did, but provide the opportunity for those most in need of such services to provide them to each other.

"As you mentioned at the festival, Gura, Free Citizens are said to have all the freedom they can earn, or capital F Freedom, whereas the bankdead are said to have lower case f freedom because they're unable to earn anything but are otherwise free to do as they like. The venture charities deprive them of even this nominal freedom by making them dependent on the hand that feeds. They're driven to exhaustion by the constant need to get new supplies by, how did you put it, 'a tough slog'? At the same time, they're forced into idleness because they're prevented from finding livelihoods to support themselves in any other way or resisting the system that regulates them. Whether rushing about or lounging around, all bankdead are kept completely passive, unable to actively pursue any goal that they set.

"I wanted to help them help themselves, to lead them back to their own self-determination and autonomy. Because only in this way, by taking back some power to control their own lives through their wills, could they realize any kind of freedom worthy of the word. Unlike the venture charities, we would not decide what people needed and force-feed it to them. We would help them to discover their own needs and realize how to satisfy them themselves while opening up ways for them to spend their time meaningfully.

"Still, as much as I wanted to help *all* the bankdead in this way, I knew we couldn't go head-to-head with the venture charities. If we began depriving them of marketable resources, the Philanthropy Syndicate would surely invest in having us destroyed. On the other hand, if we refrained from interfering with their profits then they would have no reason to interfere with us. To achieve this neutral state, I decided that we would only accept the giftless as members. In particular, we would take in orphans, abandoned infants, pregnant woman, single mothers, the postmenopausal, the infertile, and others that are not of interest to the Philanthropy Syndicate because they are not or do not produce marketable resources. I had seen other alternative communities outstep their bounds to become too revolutionary and get squashed by the MegaGloms. If we were antagonistic in the same way, we would inevitably meet the same fate. Instead, neither capitulating to nor resisting the Charity Gift Economy, we would become a xenocyst."

"What exactly does that mean?" asked Amon. "I thought 'xenocyst' was just a name."

"Just a name? Names are important, Gura! Do you think we would make such a fuss about choosing names to fit each of our members but pick something meaningless for the whole membership? When our community had grown enough that we needed something to call it, it was a challenge to choose the right one for us. We started out with a number of ideas like 'Open Arms,' 'Roof Over Heads,' and 'Habitat For All,' but they all sounded too much like the names of venture charities that spun them as kind and compassionate while marketing human lives. That was when I remembered something I'd come across at conglommercollege. I think it was in a Canadian textbook or essay collection, although I'm not sure. A xenocyst is a foreign cell trapped within another organism. Although it does no harm to its host, it can neither be incorporated into nor rejected by the body that surrounds it, an indigestible outsider right in the belly of the beast.

"Our emblem, which I hired a well-known designer to produce, is the image behind me." Hippo gestured to the stencil of the girl in the bubble. "Back when we still produced much of what we use, it appeared on all our uniforms and equipment to set us apart from the brandclans and OpScis.

"By the time we decided on the name Xenocyst, the systems were in place to gradually increase our self-sufficiency and wean ourselves off the funds of my foundation as much as possible. I was beginning to spend more and more money on the project and was on the verge of going into debt when I realized I wasn't afraid of cash crashing anymore. Not only had I spent enough time with bankdead at this point that I was habituated to the idea of living as they do, but I began to think that there was no other way I could make this hospital work.

"One of my reasons for believing this was purely financial. I'd been delegating as much of the work as possible to bankdead members so as not to accidentally perform any of the exorbitant counter-cultural actions owned by one of the Philanthropy Syndicate's most active members, No Logo Inc. I'm thinking of properties such as *grassroots organizing, community building, awareness raising*, and so on. But as a result of this delegation, I had already been fined heavily for *exploiting* and *enslaving* in spite of having consulted lawyers every step of the way. This all had to be paid out of the foundation, and if I continued functioning as the central manager while remaining bankliving it would have eventually been depleted entirely.

"More importantly, I realized that the digital divide not only separates the two cultures of bankdead and bankliving, but also their cognition and consciousness itself, so that their worlds are almost mutually unintelligible to each other. If I didn't want to help the bankdead as a form of charity, removed from them, I had to become one of them. I had to abandon the apps and databases I'd always depended on to understand the issues they faced in the flesh and in full solidarity. That is, I had to sever myself from the ImmaNet and the AT market forever."

Again Amon thought of the slum tourists, and all the impassable barriers between their minds and the education the pamphlets promised.

"At the same time, I had no intention of undergoing the traditional humiliation of being liquidated. So while I started to prepare by undergoing a rehabilitation program similar to those offered in Er, I began searching for a way to cash crash without going bankrupt. First I made a special request to the Liquidation Ministry, but they had no protocol for such an exception and refused. When I tried to bring a petition to the Executive Council, they ignored it despite the assistance of my GATA contacts. Finally, an old colleague who'd been transferred from the Ministry of Access to the Ministry of Liquidation introduced me to a young Identity Executioner who was sympathetic with what I was trying to achieve. I arranged to have him meet me off duty and execute my identity. And guess what his name was? It's someone you both know."

Amon frowned and glanced at Rick to see if he had the answer, but found him crooking his neck quizzically. He thought about it for a moment and tendered a guess. "Lawrence Barrow?"

Hippo shook his head. "No. I never met Lawrence Barrow personally until a few days ago. I mean Yoshiyuki Sekido."

"Sekido?!" Rick shouted in exasperation as Amon flinched backwards in surprise.

"Yes. I was surprised to hear what you both said about him in your hearings. He was a different man back then, and not just an able Liquidator with a strong sense of duty. He was also a true contributor to various humanitarian causes in his spare time as a way to give back for what his career took away. His girlfriend was an activist involved in an Ogasawara community that served in part as my inspiration to create Xenocyst, and it was her that woke him up and showed him the true impact of his job."

Sekido had had a girlfriend? Amon couldn't even imagine it. And that wasn't the only puzzle. "How did you arrange this without getting Sekido into serious trouble?" he asked.

"I sought legal advice beforehand. To ensure Sekido-kun's action was classified as ID euthanasia rather than ID murder, I was told to not merely consent but to specifically request the execution. Apparently, I was the first person in history to have ID euthanasia, just as you were probably the first to commit ID suicide, and when the case went to the Fiscal Judiciary a new precedent was set. At the time, Judicial Brokers in the pocket of Moderate Choice outnumbered the pro-banklifers in the judiciary, and while ID euthanasia was designated a credicrime, the fine they decided upon was nothing compared to ID murder. In fact, it was small enough that I could leave Sekido with the last of my personal savings to cover it. However, my lawyers also predicted that the Liquidation Ministry would punish him severely for using the Death Codes contrary to their intended purpose. It seems that Sekido-kun was giving in to his activist tendencies at the time and was willing to take the risk. Perhaps he was hoping that his otherwise exemplary record would lessen the punishment. I cannot say for sure how GATA responded to his subversive behavior, as he's never visited Xenocyst and I haven't seen him since. But as for his apparently meteoric rise up the ranks in the years that followed, I find it simply baffling. Sekido-kun the Liquidation Minister!? Something must have happened in the interim to save his reputation, though I cannot even guess what.

"In any case, I had arranged to be transported immediately to the Cyst after the execution, and following a brief recovery period, I continued to assist with administration. I seemed to have been right that I needed to become bankdead to guide the community properly, as I found myself imbued with fresh inspiration and enthusiasm. Although we couldn't open the doors to everyone as I would have wished, since this would have increased the community to a size that would threaten the venture charities, we began to send out doctors and educators to our satellite communities and were planning to eventually expand our facilities so we could allow in the handicapped.

"Xenocyst was functioning so smoothly, in fact, that we started to get media attention, especially from the organization run by Rashana, about whom I will have more to say in a moment. This brought industry leaders, scientists, activists, and regular citizens who offered funds so we could provide more care to more people or set up a sister organization using ours as a template. I refused them all. We were Xenocyst and our objectives were modest. Aim too big and our host would see us as malignant and do everything it could to eliminate us. But I had miscalculated here, and it was just as our future stability seemed assured that everything started to go wrong."

14
THE DIGITAL QUARANTINE, AFTER TEA

The subtle earthy bouquet of the *gyokuro* lingered at the back of Amon's mouth as he placed his empty ceramic cup on the wood board to his left. He was grateful to Hippo for letting them sample the reserve leaf he rationed out for special occasions—which was delicate glowing ambrosia after months of sugary, fizzy vending drinks—and for having the Books procure some of the Cyst's scarce supply of hot water to steep it. The nearly twenty minutes in which Hippo had poured the tea from a small gray teapot into their brown cups and Amon and Rick had sat before him sipping away without saying a word had been a much needed respite from a day of nearly continuous discussion on an empty stomach. The Books, by contrast, had wasted no time in carrying their sheets to the back, from which the alternation of tapping and low-spoken words could be heard as they set to decoding the letters, their teacups long empty. Though the stimulation of Amon's pallet and warmth in his belly seemed only to stir up his hunger pangs, his awareness felt sharper now, and he met Hippo's gaze with his full attention as he began again.

"The problems started with our vertical nutritional ink factory. Some of our key equipment was malfunctioning. We were struggling to deal with this when a newly constructed building collapsed. It had contained the purifiers we were using to process the sewage and rainwater we collected. This was a major loss already, but the building also struck a neighboring building as it fell and did damage to the medical equipment factory housed inside. We were still trying to figure out whether the accident was caused by a negligent mistake during construction when the batteries for two separate solar and biochemical energy stations located in different places malfunctioned inexplicably within hours of each other. I had chosen these devices based on their reputation for durability. They were meant to self-power for centuries and had been installed by engineers with my complete trust. It seemed unlikely that all these problems would occur within the same week by chance, and we began to suspect sabotage. The council and I first started to investigate within Xenocyst—our screening procedures were strict though certainly not infallible—but when our supply centicopter didn't show up one day, we realized that the trouble undoubtedly originated externally.

"Whoever was trying to ruin us had waited until I was bankdead and our first-generation bankliving staff had moved on after passing on their skills, leaving us with few agents able to liaison with the Free World and gather information about the supply disruption. Nevertheless, by relaying messages to the managers of my foundation through career volunteer contacts, I discovered that all disbursements had been halted. Apparently, a group of businesses, that I later found out were all subsidiaries of Philanthropy Syndicate members, had sued my foundation. It had allegedly breached the Sustainability Promotion Act, which contrary to its name is primarily concerned with encouraging economic stimulus. Though no monetary exchanges were taking place between bankliving and bankdead at Xenocyst, Syndicate lawyers claimed that our foundation had nonetheless done harm to the economy and was therefore in violation of this legislation. Essentially, their case was that any enterprise using funds to generate any kind of value that is not subject to action fees but that reduces demand for them causes the market to shrink and is therefore illegal. This is similar to the laws that place a time limit on anything remaining in the public domain, which I'm sure you're familiar with. The more bankdead consumption is satisfied with products and services that are produced, marketed, and supplied by MegaGloms collecting licensing fees for this production, marketing, and supply, the more the economy will grow. The less bankdead consumption is satisfied in this way and the more they become independent, the more the economy will shrink. Every need not satisfied by the AT market is a chance for profit at the bottom of the pyramid lost and therefore a hindrance to growth. This is why sustainability law bans initiatives that attempt to satisfy bankdead needs by any other method. Since our foundation was funding bankdead activities that allowed them to produce and supply their own goods and provide their own services, it was supposedly preventing Free Citizens and MegaGloms from producing and supplying those goods and providing those services through actions that incur fees, which equates to a reduction in total transactions. In other words, it was siphoning large amounts of money from the AT market into a black market that fed nothing back into the market. Legality and illegality were irrelevant from the perspective of us in Xenocyst since we were outside credilaw jurisdiction, but my foundation was not and it was charged with 'supporting anti-economic industries and obstructing sustainable profitability.'

"The applicable legislations were extremely convoluted, and it was unclear to us whether the prosecution had a solid case. Unfortunately, the legal fees required to challenge this lawsuit had absorbed all my foundation's assets, and since debtors refused to lend when they saw our risky prospects, we had been unable to pay our suppliers. Although our suppliers were willing to continue shipments for a time in good faith, this sudden drop in revenue weakened them significantly and the Philanthropy Syndicate soon bought them out. The lawsuit succeeded to boot, and what remained of my foundation was bled dry by the prosecution. So, while I thought I had established a shipping network that would guarantee us with the essentials for decades to come, my foundation turned out to be on much weaker footing than I expected. As they say here in the camps, 'a building is only as stable as its weakest floor.'

"My research had told me we were the first independent community established right in the heart of a bankdeath camp, run exclusively by giftless for giftless. In retrospect, I should have noticed from the beginning how strange it was that the bankdead had such a low level of self-sufficiency. Why were there no other initiatives like mine? Surely there must have been at least a few others in this whole wide world who had wanted to empower them without asking for anything in return? But I had seen no similar examples in the District of Dreams, only the community in Ogasawara that I mentioned, and assumed in my pride that I'd hit on something original. In actuality—though even gold search engines are silent about this—it is standard procedure for the Philanthropy Syndicate to sue any such organization based in the Free World out of existence, while a special jointly funded task force from the Charity Brigade nips grassroots bankdead initiatives in the bud. Apparently, there is simply no room between the market and the black market for anything but the Charity Gift Economy."

"I remember seeing news coverage of incidents like what Xenocyst went through," said Rick. "They described them as random acts of vandalism in the camps."

"Yes. I'm not surprised. That's how the Philanthropy Syndicate works sabotage into their docucharitisements. And that wasn't the end of it either. Soon after, representatives of the 'world without slums' movement were smiling before reporters as 'reconstruction workers' sprayed demolition dust across whole blocks of our semi-permanent skyscrapers that had been labeled 'dilapidated' or 'unhygienic,' much like the academy where Book was raised. Of course, the upgraded housing promised before the public never materialized. In other targeted areas I've seen feeding stations 'rezoned' conveniently too far to reach practically on foot so that all residents must vacate."

"What's the point of all this?" asked Amon. "I mean, I understand that donations cover the costs of supplies as you explained, but surely not the large fines for the actions of the saboteurs? Wouldn't it be infinitely cheaper for the venture charities to help the bankdead become self-sufficient? Then they won't have to keep funding all the supplies and the donations become pure profit."

"Actually, the situation is the opposite of what you think. What you need to realize is that the cost of sabotage is actually low. Since bankdead cannot own property, destroying or taking their items is perfectly legal. In fact, keeping the bankdead from becoming independent is crucial to the human resources industry. If they aren't in constant need of disposable supplies, they won't be motivated to gift and yield will drop. Moreover, Free Citizens will have nothing to pity and fundraising through pitypromo will turn ineffective. Either way, the Charity Gift Economy collapses. The trick to running a successful humanitarian operation is to appear to be constantly alleviating poverty without solving any of its underlying causes and ensuring that no one else does either.

"As to your question about why the Philanthropy Syndicate doesn't simply keep the donations, the reason is that they are beholden to charity-accountability apps like TransparaKind that allow investitarians to check where their donations are going. If the various venture charities were to simply keep surpluses or divert them to hiring superfluous workers, their bureaucracy would appear bloated and donations would drop. In some cases, they might even pay fines to GATA for embezzlement. Therefore, since the Syndicate must make it appear as though donations are going to those in need, they have two choices: increase funding to services or to supplies. The challenge for them is to do so without improving the *quality* of services and supplies, since these must be set at the ideal level to increase bankdead propensity to gift while minimizing unrest. Improve conditions any further and yield will drop, since bankdead won't feel the urgency of relinquishing the burden of an extra mouth to feed and of giving their offspring up for a better life."

"I don't get it," said Amon. "How do you increase funding to services and supplies without raising quality? Where exactly does the money go? Into increased quantity?"

"Yes and no. The key here is Fleet. The best method the Philanthropy Syndicate has discovered for appearing to use donations efficiently without improving conditions is to provide disposable supplies made out of the substance. When donations increase, production of supplies is increased proportionately and the expiration date of each item is programmed to be shorter. Conversely, when donations drop production is decreased and the expiration date is programmed to be longer. In either case, the ephemerality of items supplied is set so that whether more units are produced or fewer, the total sum of the time all units exist remains constant—relative to bankdead population of course. More donations mean more items with higher ephemerality. Fewer donations mean fewer items with lower ephemerality. Ironically, the result is that increased donations not only fail to help the bankdead since they'll get the same usage out of the supplies either way, it actually inconveniences them since they'll have to make more trips to the supply stations to get replacements for the faster-dissolving items. The ephemerality of items is lower for the gifted, so they're inconvenienced proportionally less, but the net effect of increased pity and the pitypromo that wields it is an increase in suffering to a certain degree for everyone in the camps.

"Meanwhile, the income from sales of supplies all goes to the Philanthropy Syndicate, since the members have nearly equal share in the entire supply chain, including the patent on Fleet. The costs are negligible as each stage of production—from energy harnessing to synthesizing the materials to manufacturing to shipping—is entirely automated, involving almost no action-transactions. The difference between sales revenue and costs is diverted as donations to venture charities, which gives the MegaGloms a reputation for compassion while helping to pay for Delivery infrastructure and labor, including the salaries of career volunteers and freekeepers. By this time, the accountability apps have lost track of the original donations, as they've already cycled from the donors to venture charities to Fleet manufacturers to the MegaGloms that own them before trickling their way through various subsidiaries back to the charities. So to the investitarians it appears that their money is going to those in need—and it is. Except here is the central point: the quality of service and total existence time of supplies relative to population stays at the optimum level to ensure yield tracks Free World population growth irrespective of how much they give. And if any questions are raised about the short lifespan of the supplies, the MegaGloms simply claim it is to prevent waste accumulation and urban blight, earning them extra points for environmental and socially responsible initiatives."

Suddenly Amon was filled with the glow of clarity. For weeks he had built Fleet buildings, lived in Fleet rooms, and worn Fleet clothes, sensing a contradiction in the short-lived design of the ubiquitous material as everything within reach flaked and dissolved and crumbled around him. Now he saw the reason behind it all, and as convoluted and devious as the arrangement was, it made sense of all his daily experiences the moment he grasped it.

"Since bankdead need is indispensable for this system to function," Hippo continued, "it is well worth the small investment in occasional sabotage, even if fines sometimes apply. They must be deprived as much as possible of the greatest asset the poor have possessed since time immemorial—resourcefulness. Thus there is no soil to grow crops, or materials to build anything—even the sewage-ridden Tokyo Canal and

Sanzu River are too contaminated to fish. Xenocyst was intended to be a bubble of self-sufficiency that resisted these paralyzing policies and you're probably wondering why it still stands in spite of what happened, so before we discuss this topic any further, I'd better tell you about that."

"When Xenocyst was on the verge of collapse, a man came to strike a deal with me. Until I spoke to him, I'd been perplexed by the timing of the sabotage. The venture charities had known for a long time what we were doing, so why hadn't they launched the lawsuit earlier? Now I understood. They could have easily crushed us when we were weak. But they could make better use of us now that we were strong.

"The man introduced himself as an independent investitarian. I've never seen or heard from him since, so I cannot verify who he truly was. In retrospect he must have been a mouthpiece for the Philanthropy Syndicate. He offered to arrange for supply shipments to be centicoptered in on a regular basis. Although they wouldn't be exactly the same items as before, we would receive everything essential to our operations. He spoke as though he and his undisclosed partners genuinely believed I was providing real help to the bankdead and so on and so forth. Then he explained that his support had two conditions. First, I would stop providing our members with education of any kind about the Free World. Second, I would stop providing contraceptives.

"Why these two conditions? Well, the rationale wasn't hard to work out when I considered the pre-existing educational arrangements in the District of Dreams. Delivery offers no educational services whatsoever, partly to reduce costs—though that isn't all. For several generations, the crashborn have been without any kind of academic education or reliable information about what lies outside the camps. So by remaining silent on all of this, the venture charities encourage them to form their own understanding, or rather misunderstanding, of the Free World and the CG Economy. They know that the hole they insert their finger into reads their DNA and other hereditary structures and that their DNA determines whether the Market demands their offspring. However, as the majority have no background in even the most basic of scientific knowledge, most are unaware what 'DNA' even means, and few have ever used money so they are unable to grasp the word 'market' any better, let alone complex concepts like plutogenics. Since a person's status as gifted or giftless can shift without apparent reason, DNA and the Market have come to be understood as the arbiters of fate and this has opened the door for the spread of superstitious beliefs like those of Opportunity Science, which is perfectly compatible with the interests of the Philanthropy Syndicate."

"May I contribute to the discussion at this juncture?" asked Book from the back of the room as Little Book's tapping drew silent, and Amon realized for the first time that they had been listening. "This is related to my field of interest as you are aware."

Hippo nodded his assent.

Tap-ta-taptap . . . "The Xenocyst curriculum that the Philanthropy Syndicate representative requested us to abandon I specifically designed to combat Opportunity Science dogma and propagate a more empirically accurate understanding of our age. Hippo, in his wisdom, recognized that Free Citizens were a lost cause as their PR-opaganda inculcation filled them with a stock of truthy 'facts' to contradict anything we might teach them, whereas bankdead, lacking information technology, were tabula rasa as it were, and just as receptive to false religion as to our contrary lessons. Although our scope was limited due to resource restrictions, we held classes on basic literacy, mathematics, and other rudimentary subjects, for both children and adults, with more advanced seminars for precocious learners.

"On the basis of this primary education, we attempted to dissuade our students of prevalent misunderstandings about the Free World: that it is not a holy, otherworldly place or even all that exceptional a place; that the apparent health, cleanliness, beauty, and strange attire of the slum tourists, career volunteers, and other bankliving that visit the camps do not in any way prove they are blessed; that the drones, vending machines, and other technologies are in no way magical or ordained; that the preemptive foiling of resistance is not a manifestation of some supernatural moral order; etcetera, etcetera. Moreover, we made various positive assertions as well; that babies are considered so precious most bankliving are unable to afford them; that the bankdead are the ones who are the most truly alive and free.

"None of our instructors told anyone explicitly to refrain from gifting their babies—everyone in Xenocyst was encouraged to live as they deemed most appropriate. However, the slant of our pedagogy was manifestly obvious. Our objective was to help all bankdead—albeit women in particular—to realize that they had reproductive rights, including rights to their offspring, not to mention dignity, and that they ought to be honored at the idea of being a parent. Ideally, our graduates would learn to accept the adversity here and live the best lives they were capable of, rather than trade away the next generation for some *fallacious* ideal and *pathetic* bonus."

As Book described the curriculum he had created and overseen, Amon heard his deep, nasally voice rise at points with something that sounded like passion, and his closing words he spat out with unmistakable contempt. Usually he spoke with such dry erudition that Amon was caught off guard by his sudden display of emotion and felt his own chest resonating with it. While Ty's lifelong response to his struggles in the form of the tricycle was flashy and palpable, Book's was less dramatic but perhaps a much greater threat in the end. The knowledge he provided was subversive, offering a way to make sense of the District of Dreams without succumbing to Opportunity Science or any other oppressive misperception, and Amon appreciated for the first time how important the education he had been given was.

"So, if the council were to accept the investitarian's offer and cancel our academic program," said Hippo, "our citizens would uncritically swallow the plutogenic hierarchy as before and might convert to Opportunity Science, or at least believe it inwardly. When I thought about how this would work in combination with the ban on contraceptives, the purpose behind the man's offer became clear and I saw why the Syndicate had allowed Xenocyst to exist for so long.

"As you know, giftless parents occasionally give birth to marketable resources. Since Xenocyst had dramatically lowered the infant mortality rate and extended the average lifespan of fertile adults, we produced more total babies than a comparable area—and therefore more marketable babies. Some of our first-generation giftless had also produced gifted babies and we had not simply cast these out on genetic grounds, so over time our gifted population was increasing as well. This meant that we had unintentionally built up a store of human resources. Without education our members would be more likely to gift, and without contraceptives the growth rate would rise, increasing yield further. So by conceding to his conditions, we would produce a swelling population of giftless inclined towards gifting, some of whom would produce valuable people. Running services for the giftless like ours would have been too expensive for the MegaGloms because of all the labor costs involved. But if they could ensure already existing services fell in line with the Charity Gift Economy by investing a small amount in bringing us to our knees and then donating some cheap supplies to keep us in thrall, they could cultivate a more marketable gene pool.

"When first establishing Xenocyst, I had hired a team to do a cost-benefit analysis and they had determined it would be more expensive for the Philanthropy Syndicate to destroy us than to leave us be. Our attracting a segment of the giftless population would generate a marginal drop in yield, but this would be vastly outweighed by the costs of sabotage and other interventions. Although these calculations turned out to be correct, we hadn't considered that greater long-term profits might be had by co-opting us. Arrogantly we had only done our calculations under the assumption we were a threat. None of us had considered that we might instead be an opportunity. The lesson was clear—no pun intended. All attempts to help the world's poorest, and really help them by helping them help themselves, will either go up against the MegaGloms and become more profitable to destroy or appear lucrative and become profitable to take. There are no such things as xenocysts, no independent outsiders persisting in the belly of the beast. You are either part of the beast or in its maw.

"When the undeniable truth of this set in, I felt rage as powerful as that that night in my lab, and I had the man thrown out, though not before he calmly and smarmily told us where to find him in Delivery. As I stewed over what had brought us to this point, part of me began to regret using the funds I had amassed to build a passive xenocyst rather than organize the giftless into an armed insurgency against the Philan-thropy Syndicate." Hippo's eyes widened fearsomely and his jaw shook as though he were imagining such a battlefield. "This was an entirely emotional response of course. I never seriously entertained the idea on an intellectual level because I knew it would be crushed before it gained any momentum whatsoever."

"Is standing up to the charities really that hopeless?" asked Rick. "There must be some form of resistance out there."

"Well, there are occasional incidents, but these are kept manageable."

"How? There are so many people here, together they'd be unstoppable, wouldn't they? And what stops them from turning to terrorism?"

"Terrorism? In the Free Era? Go to the library if you want to read about other times when terrorist cells were allowed or even encouraged to operate in underprivileged communities. As Book will tell you, this was to cultivate fear against an amorphous enemy and maintain national cohesion while focusing attention away from deficiencies in the ruling order. Nowadays, such benefits are thought to be outweighed by the economic instability terrorism causes. Instead, discontent is diverted from corporations and the elite with pitypromo, among other distractions. Aside from inducing donations with pity for those who have fallen into the bankdeath camps, promoguiltumentaries and all the rest make Free Citizens afraid of falling in themselves, as I was saying earlier. This keeps them too busy scrambling to earn enough for basic actions like breathing and eating in an extremely volatile market to even think carefully about who profits from this arrangement.

"As for organized resistance, the Philanthropy Syndicate can easily discourage it before it occurs through the simple regulation of supplies. Near-total dependence on supplies prevents bankdead from procuring the necessary weaponry and other tools while fostering a feeling of gratitude and reciprocity that counteracts discord. Feeding station calories are set in accordance with supply ephemerality so that needs are fulfilled just enough to encourage complacency but not so much that bankdead have the energy to try and better their situation after the exhaustion of constant shelter resettlement and supply pilgrimages. In other words, the total 'quality of life' provided by the supplies and services—from clothes to shelter to medical treatment—has been calculated and refined through research to approach as close as possible to despair without slipping over the line into desperation.

"Supply *branding* also discourages resistance by creating division. Visible differences between items disbursed to unbranded giftless and branded gifted, and between the different gifted brandclans, help the MegaGloms cultivate marketable gene pools while setting bankdead apart from each other psychologically. The gifted treat the giftless as inferior, and many giftless accept this, though not without friction and fighting. At the same time, the different brandclans develop rivalries, which can range from sport-fan-like aggression to mortal combat, though CareBots are sent in to reduce resource losses when conflicts escalate. Whatever the particulars may be, branding keeps bankdead groups too busy squabbling to even conceive of an external enemy. Meanwhile, the ephemerality of disposcrapers and the unpredictability of the plutogenic algorithms prevent the formation of excessively strong group solidarity and intergroup alliances by keeping them constantly on the move and making them uncertain when their membership in a brandclan or status as gifted/giftless might suddenly shift.

"Let's not forget the threat of surveillance posed by the PanoptiRoaches either. This is a major obstacle to cooperation against the Syndicate as it leaves few with the courage to express their gripes and find others who share them. On those rare occasions when dissidents do take the risk of banding together, they are often tackled before they properly organize, which perpetuates fear of speaking out, as it suggests they might have been tipped off by monitoring equipment or spies."

"So there *are* cases where affordable discouragement strategies fail, as there must be," said Rick. "But I don't see how the Syndicate can afford to respond to actual uprisings. If there was a coordinated push-back, we could throw off their whole business model!"

"If only it were so easy! I like your rebellious spirit, Shaké. Too bad you're naive. The venture charities know just how to protect their business model—they've done so successfully for decades—by applying different compliance protocols in order of their cost. The least expensive of these is blacklisting. If the DNA of dissidents can be identified—and this is not difficult if SampleQuitos are deployed—they become hungry ghosts and are eliminated from consideration."

Amon had heard of SampleQuitos and hungry ghosts and was curious to know what they were, but didn't want to interrupt with such a minor question.

"If not but their general whereabouts are known, the skyscrapers in the entire region are demolished under the pretense of slum improvement. This is perfectly legal because bankdead are incapable of possessing property, and serves as an affordable way to encourage neighbors to snitch since no one wants havoc wreaked on their own heads. If in spite of all these preventatives, rebellious incidents occur, the last resort is CrowdCare."

"Which just means coercive force," said Rick.

"Yes. And?"

"Um, so, call me naive if you want, but isn't responding to resistance that way too expensive and unPRiendly to be part of a working business model?"

"Shaké, don't take what I said personally: all of us crashdead are naive in the beginning. Yes, interfering bodily with human beings is always a violation of credilaw. But unlike Free Citizens, since bankdead have no BodyBank, they cannot receive compensation for credicrimes committed against them, so only the 50 percent cut GATA takes has to be paid, which means half off all fines. Deployment of CareBots reduces this amount further as their partial autonomy deflects full culpability and cuts base action fees through the automation of violence. When human freekeepers are required in troublesome cases, labor costs are reduced with GATA-issued CrowdCare Licenses, which give the Charity Brigade rebates on credicrimes that supposedly 'protect bankdead from each other' and 'keep the freedom.' In all cases, non-lethal and semi-lethal weapons such as tear dust are preferred over deadly force that appears visibly harmful so as to avoid unflattering media exposure that might interfere with donations.

"The venture charity–run reporting outfits that provide most available coverage portray the bankdead as a savage mob mindlessly rioting against the freekeepers and drones who strive tirelessly to defend their Freedom. The more violent the bankdead resistance becomes, the easier it is to make them look bad and justify the use of force. The more peaceful it is, the less impact it has. So whether violent or peaceful, crowd and media care ensures that civil disobedience of all kinds is completely ineffectual without breaking the bank, as it were.

"I knew all this already when the man came to me with his offer. The right balance of generosity and ferocity encourages a don't-bite-the-hand-that-feeds mentality. All attempts by bankdead to support themselves without official supplies and deprive legitimate businesses of profit or change the state of affairs in some other way are squashed or sapped of strength. In our case, it never even got to violence. The only organization

I have ever heard of that has succeeded at holding out against these tactics is the one run by Rashana Birla, and I had no illusions that we wielded anything like the power that makes this success possible.

"So, after consulting with the council, I decided at last to meet him. It was a simple question of accept his offer or cease to exist. I had already tossed all my chips into this community, sacrificing every bit of money I'd had and even seeking ID euthanasia. If it fell to pieces I'd be ruined—bankdead like all the rest and unable to make any kind of difference. Not only that, but over a million people now depended on the services Xenocyst provided. We had become responsible for them too, and I couldn't let my personal feelings lead me to neglect that responsibility."

Again Hippo's eyes went wide and his jaw quivered briefly at the memory before he quickly regained his composure.

"The very day I agreed to the man's offer, the centicopter arrived. Ever since, we have slept in disposable skyscrapers, worn generic clothes, and lived in total dependence on donations. Though most of our sustenance comes from generic feeding stations, a few of these have been replaced with branded stations around the borders. This makes it difficult for the gifted born here to migrate out to the Gifted Triangle once they're old enough to take care of themselves and encourages growth of the branded enclaves I'm sure you've seen, which places the burden of managing and protecting their residents on us. Though our objective was never to help the gifted, the council mostly agrees that it would be wrong to kick out the ones who grew up here and could invite further reprisals. The result is that traces of plutogenic hierarchy have taken hold here. In not providing education or contraceptives, we're complicit with the Charity Gift Economy. It's not as though we actively fool anyone into gifting, but we don't correct them either and that leaves them susceptible to misunderstanding. I try to make the excuse that we're letting everyone make up their own minds. There are many texts in the library that explain what's actually going on, if anyone would bother to read them. But few are literate and so in practice we allow them to be deceived into gifting to keep this place running. This makes us hardly any different from the venture charities I sought to avoid becoming. In many ways I think the Opportunity Scientists are more deserving of respect than we are, since their principle of Universal Marketability makes them willing to embrace even the most inforaving maniac whereas we continue to discriminate and only let in a select few. The Philanthropy Syndicate certainly doesn't see us as any different. Do you understand what I'm saying?! As far as the MegaGloms are concerned, we're no better than a misogynistic, brutally authoritarian religion that breeds slaves, abducts babies, conducts bizarre pseudo-scientific rituals, and promotes self-mutilation so long as we produce the same yield at comparable cost. But there's little point in complaining about the situation; we only exist by the grace of the Syndicate, and there's nothing we can do to change it."

Hippo paused to gaze back and forth between them, and for the first time, Amon understood the pain in his eyes.

"So, Gura, you asked me at the festival why anyone bothers to get up in the morning, and I evaded your question. At one time, I would have told you that Xenocyst residents gain satisfaction from taking charge of their own lives to better themselves and the lives of others. Monetary payment is irrelevant to those who feel solidarity in constantly striving for something more. But that has all changed and I no longer know how to answer you.

"Now the supplies we depend on have been reduced and it's no longer just our dignity that's at stake; if this continues I fear the end of our community is inevitable. This time, no one is making us any conditional offers, and the council's requests to the venture charities for negotiation have been ignored without explanation. So ask more questions if you will—your understanding is key, as I've said—but please lend us your minds. You must have unique contributions to make and we're in no position to overlook even the slightest chance for a solution."

Amon had been so intent on listening to Hippo he only realized now, in vague recollection, that a guard had entered a few minutes earlier, gathered up the teapot and cups, and carried them away. His crossed legs were cold, half-numb slabs beneath him, and he switched them, hearing Little Book's tapping and the faint *rakhaw* of crows somewhere outside, as he struggled to assimilate everything Hippo had told them. At last, he could see how the different elements of the District of Dreams he'd been learning about came together: the Philanthrophy Syndicate, the SpawnU

Consortium, the Charity Gift Economy, Delivery, pitypromo, vending machines, plutogenic algorithms, Opportunity Science, CareBots, freekeepers, Fleet . . . The way it all worked wasn't really surprising to him, though the fact that he wasn't surprised was. Only weeks earlier, he would never have believed such a bizarre, iniquitous arrangement could have been possible in the Free Era. Now it fit perfectly with everything he'd experienced since Rick had failed to show up for work that summer day. Hippo's story told Amon as much about the District of Dreams, Hippo, and Xenocyst as it did about himself. Without realizing, he'd changed immeasurably, ready now to swallow even the most rancid facts. The worst of which, he had to admit, was that he'd played an integral role in supporting all this, delineating the world of banklife and bankdeath by banishing those who couldn't cope with the AT market.

It wasn't as though thoughts of being a Liquidator had never made him feel guilty before. He had always cringed at the sound of bankrupts screaming when they got nerve dusted, and began to have inklings of doubt about his job when Makesh (Rashana?) had suggested to him that banishing citizens to slums forever simply for making bad financial choices was wrong. This doubt had grown further when he'd crashed Barrow and seen that even the greatest men were susceptible to financial collapse, and when he'd nearly gone bankrupt soon after and seen that he himself was too. But his first-hand experience of the place he had sent so many had turned his doubt into a certainty—into a categorical denial of the justice of anything he had ever done. Now he was more guilty and ashamed than ever, and he began to wonder how long these two emotions would dominate his life—until a thought came to him for the first time. *What can I do to make up for my sins, to give back for what I have taken?* Answering Hippo's plea seemed like his best chance, though he had little hope of succeeding, as if a sad, fallen man such as he had the strength to atone for all the many wrongs that he had done . . .

"I have another question," said Amon, raising his head to break from his net of perplexity. Although he wasn't sure whether he'd have made the promise to the PhisherKing if he'd known what ordeals answering all his questions would entail, he felt somehow as though he was approaching the truth about jubilee and wasn't about to stop now.

Hippo nodded for him to continue.

"Well . . . ever since I met you, Hippo, you seem to have taken an interest in us. You argued in my favor at my initial hearing, you invited us to sit with everyone at the equinox festival, and now you're taking the time to talk with us when there are so many other people in this community who might benefit from your attention. So . . . I asked you a similar question at the festival, but why us? You know we were Liquidators, that we've done nothing but harm to people who didn't deserve it. We made all of this"—Amon waved his hand around as if to take in the whole slum—"possible, and yet you single us out and treat us with . . ." *kindness.* Amon's voice cracked and faded as he felt the urge to cry at the thought of it. No one other than Mayuko and Rick had ever given him anything without expectation of recompense.

"Please don't be offended about this, Shaké. I have immense respect for you and value your presence in this community immensely. But it's because of you, Gura. As I told you the day we met, I feel a special connection to you because of the strange symmetry to our stories. Don't you see it? I was an Identity Vitalator, you were an Identity Executioner. I gave citizens digital life and you took it away. I committed ID euthanasia and had someone take away my digital life. You committed ID suicide and took your own. Both of us chose to cash crash without going bankrupt, and here we are with our BodyBanks still installed. Do you realize the significance of this?"

Amon shook his head.

"I retain the codes for life, and you for death."

Once Hippo said this, Amon saw immediately that it was true. Identity Vitalators memorized the top-secret Birth Codes that allowed them to endow twenty-year-old youths with an identity signature, and Identity Executioners memorized the top-secret Death Codes that allowed them to erase it. GATA security protocol ensured that they were sent new codes to memorize at periodic intervals so that the old ones could be regularly reset, and their codes were annulled if one of them went bankrupt. Yet, since both Amon and Hippo were disconnected from the ImmaNet, the program that reset the codes would be unable to work on them, and since they'd cash crashed without being liquidated, no annulment would have been performed. In other words, protocol didn't cover the unique cases of ID euthanasia and suicide. Therefore, their codes would still be active. Amon had been too fixated on the fact that he'd retained his data to realize the value of his memory.

"Of course we cannot use our codes without access to the ImmaNet, as we have no way to interface with other BodyBanks," continued Hippo, "but in principle we still have the power to give and take digital life. To me this feels profoundly significant, though I cannot say how or why. Do you not feel the same?"

Amon thought about this and closed his eyes to visualize the code he still remembered, conjuring a string of jade digits on the black curtain there. *Vitalator. Executioner. Euthanasia. Suicide. Banklife. Bankdeath.* He saw something glint in the depths of the darkness, a diamond that winked into existence and then burst into ten thousand shards, the faintest aura left after its passing drifting towards him across the endless space behind his eyelids and filling him with wonder. *Something tells me your search is leading you to our rejuvenation . . .*

"Yes, it does feel important." As though they might somehow make use of this unique combination of knowledge if only they knew how.

"So perhaps you understand then why I feel a certain kinship with you and decided to persuade the council in your favor. When the Books, Vertical, and Ty reported to me that you were overcoming webloss quickly, adapting well to our less than luxurious lifestyle, and showing promise as a worker, I began to suspect that you might be of value to us. You see, there are few like us at Xenocyst who understand the Free World but can also cope with bankdeath. The giftless crashdead who get rejected from Er usually go mad and wither away or end up with the Opportunity Scientists, and we don't accept the gifted ones that get the treatment."

"So it was *you* who had me brought here, wasn't it!?" said Rick. Upon hearing these words, several facts snapped together in Amon's mind—Rick appearing suddenly on his supply crew, their assignment to be roommates, the special lessons with the Books—and he knew it was true even before Hippo nodded.

"Precisely, yes. Once I began to see potential in you, Gura, I remembered you talking during the hearing about your friend and partner Rick Ferro, and I doubted that he was dead as you seemed to believe. I thought he might complement your skills here, so I had some of our messengers run over to the Er facility run by Rashana to see if anyone by that name had been picked up. We have an agreement with them to take in some of their giftless graduates. Luckily my guess turned out right and I requested that he be brought here when his treatment period was complete. I didn't tell you in the beginning because I decided we should see what he was made of first. Otherwise, if he failed the trial period and we had to expel him from Xenocyst, I was concerned it would break your heart. Thankfully, he'd already recovered fairly well in Er and, when Book was done with him, I assigned you to join him on his first supply pickup. Ty's report about your behavior in the field was encouraging, but I made up my mind that we needed you two after I talked with Gura at the festival. All your concerns about freedom and the meaning of our lives here showed me your sensitivity and the depth of your conscience. That was why I had Ty take you out as guards and patrolmen. Not because I'm thinking these positions would suit you two, though they might be the obvious choice given your previous careers and your success on the last mission. Rather, I've decided to rotate you through a variety of tasks so you can see different facets of Xenocyst and better understand our many needs. No promises of course, but my hope is that you can one day serve as a supply coordinator and interpreter team. This involves communicating with the venture charities and expressing our needs in their bureaucratic language, among other tasks. For this we require personnel like you two who can bridge the linguistic, cognitive, economic, and cultural gap between bankdead and bankliving. You also have experience in administration, Gura, albeit in a totally different organization, and if all goes well I could even see you taking part in that here, perhaps by joining the council or serving as an advisor.

"I have faced much resistance to bringing you two in, in part because some resent my position as advisor, and I've heard rumors that they're secretly calling for my retirement. Most likely they view crashborn like you as a reinforcement of my outdated approach and I was only able to secure approval to summon Shaké and to offer you both lessons from the Books by forcing through a vote when certain councilors happened to be absent. This of course infuriated those who were excluded from the discussion and turned them even more adamantly against you. The number of councilors who abstained today reveals the controversy surrounding your membership, as many who would otherwise support it are afraid to take sides and possibly damage their relationship with other councilors over what they see as a minor issue. Their silence is a testament to the potential they see in you after your success on the Gifted Triangle mission, and I don't regret my decision to struggle in your favor, even if I've stirred up conflict, as I share their opinion."

"Thank you for your faith in us," said Rick.

"Yes," Amon concurred, feeling so flattered he was almost embarrassed. "We'll do our best to make useful contributions as long as we're here."

Amon remembered when he'd said similar things to Sekido, pledging his allegiance to GATA, but this time it felt different. Now he was offering his loyalty with clear eyes and a clear head. Assisting a community that genuinely gave succor to the poor was the least he could do.

"You know I would have laughed if anyone other than you suggested the possibility of leaving here," said Hippo, "but Rashana stakes such a strong interest in you I wonder if it might not be possible."

"So you heard from Rick about Delivery?"

"Yes. But not from Shaké. I heard it from Rashana herself."

"You spoke to her?" Amon's heart fluttered with a mix of excitement and alarm. "When?"

"She came here looking for you just last week."

"Rashana Birla came here? To Xenocyst? In person?" Amon was having trouble imagining the second-richest person on Earth setting foot in such a squalid labyrinth.

"Yes, and it wasn't her first time either. As I told you, my relationship with the Birlas goes back a long way. I never sought the funding of the Birla parents for Xenocyst, as I knew they would insist on having executive say, but I canvassed the sisters, and though Anisha was not interested, Rashana became one of our most generous patrons. Now that my foundation has been sued out of existence, she has shifted resources to her own organization, which as far as I can tell mainly focuses on dispatching independent journalists to raise awareness about the District of Dreams in addition to running Er for the giftless. If her parents had given her executive control of Fertilex, I'm sure she'd be doing much more, but sadly that's not what has come to pass, and perhaps for that very reason."

"So what did she say?"

"Well, last week during the council, I heard the electric whooping that Rashana's PhantoCopter makes when she's signaling that she wants to land on our helipad, and rushed to the roof to have our lookouts ring the landing bells. She requested a meeting, to which I promptly obliged and cut the council short. We sat in the center of the library, and after we'd caught each other up on the situation in our respective organizations, she asked if I had come across anyone by the name of Amon Kenzaki. I said I hadn't because I wasn't sure what her goal was in seeking you and whether you wanted to be found. She went on to describe you in astounding detail—probably using some criminal profiling app—and asked if I had come across anyone who looked like you. I explained that the Xenocyst council personally screens all new members and that I would have definitely remembered your face whether we had rejected you or not, especially if you were wearing a Liquidator uniform. She gave me a penetrating stare as though she suspected I was lying—you must be familiar with that terrifying thing the Birlas all do with their eyelashes—and she asked me if I was absolutely certain. She happened to know that Rick was here and as the saying goes, 'friends of a kind call each other.' When she saw Rick at Delivery and asked him about you, he claimed ignorance to your whereabouts but displayed nervous hesitation that made her doubt his veracity. Now I was evincing just the same hesitation. I assured her that she was misreading me—that I had not seen you—and told her that if there was nothing more to discuss we should call our meeting concluded. Still sending me those fierce, suspicious blinks, she requested that I have your description sent out to all our patrols and to contact her immediately if there was any sign of you. When I agreed and explained that your description had already been carefully noted by Little Book like everything else, she promptly boarded her PhantoCopter with her guards and left.

"Did I make the right choice here, Amon? I realized after you told us your story at the council that the Birla you were seeking was Rashana, and I could have offered to introduce her, but I wanted you to understand your position here before being confronted with that difficult choice. This time, I wanted to make sure to get your consent, given your complicated situation with respect to the two sisters. Now I wonder if I should have just told her and put you two together at once."

"Hmmm . . ." Amon thought about this, feeling the same uncertainty as when Rick had asked him a similar question. "I'm not sure. I did my best to hold back in line at Delivery so she wouldn't spot me because I wasn't sure if she was Rashana or Anisha, and just barely managed to stay out of sight. Then I heard from Rick that she'd introduced herself as Rashana, and since she seemed to have received the message I left before I cash crashed, I began to believe she was the activist. But then I remembered the way her guards surrounded her in a precise formation and it reminded me of the *tengu* around the emoticon man who hurt Mayuko. So I started to think that maybe I couldn't trust her after all. Now after hearing everything you said about how she funded Xenocyst and all the good work her organization does, that fits with what the activist Makesh said about wanting to help the bankdead, and the activist warned me I was in danger, so maybe . . . I don't know . . . I . . ."

Amon closed his eyes, took a deep breath, and exhaled the words, "I appreciate your trying to protect me. I just hope you haven't alienated Xenocyst from an ally on my behalf."

"Not to worry. Though I certainly wouldn't want to sour our relationship with Rashana, ever since the lawsuits she's become unable to support us in any material way, so we can get on well enough without her.

"As much as I'd hate to see you go now that you're finally members, I think you and Shaké would be best to seize the opportunity to speak with Rashana while it's still available and at least find out what she wants from you. It's not often that the Birlas pay so much attention to just one person—they're an incessantly busy family with connections to nearly everyone on Earth—so her interest in you may not last, and I don't think it's a chance to pass up lightly."

"What gives you such confidence I'd be safe to meet her?"

"Well, for one thing, I can tell you for certain that the woman searching for you is Rashana."

"How do you know that?"

"I've known the sisters since they were babies. You think I can't tell them apart? No twins are that similar. Maybe with digimake, but not in the naked world."

"Even if you're right, can I really trust her?"

"I understand your caution—getting involved with the powerful is as risky as it can be rewarding—but I think your worry about the guards is misplaced. They are all part of the Birla Guard, a carefully reared mercenary pool from which all members of the family draw. Since all recruits are trained in the same way, I imagine their deployment patterns are identical, whether it's one of the units serving Anisha or Rashana. So I don't think the similarity you witnessed is any reason to distrust her. But think it over. Ultimately it's your decision, and if you choose never to speak to a Birla again we are of course more than happy to have you here."

"Thank you. I'll consider it a bit more as you advise. But if I do decide I want to reach her, how would I go about it?"

"Just tell me when you want to reach her and I'll have someone ring the bells. We have arranged a signal that Xenocyst can use to request a visit. She'll be alerted as soon as the local sensors pick it up and should then fly over on her PhantoCopter at her leisure. Or you can go to Delivery and get in touch with one of the representatives of her charity yourself. It's up to you."

"What's her charity called?"

"Atupio."

"Atupio?!" Amon jolted back and frowned in surprise and fear. "Are you sure?"

"Of course. Many of Rashana's donations to my foundation were channeled through that corporation, and we've been partnered for decades. Why?"

"That's the name of the company that paid for Barrow's identity assassination and probably the attempt to identity assassinate me as well."

PART 6
EXPOSED?

15
XENOCYST, AMON'S ROOM

G*wong-ng-ng-ng-ng* went the sound of the bells, *gwong-ng-ng-ng-ng*, approaching incrementally as they went off in succession from the lookouts on the Xenocyst border inwards. Following close in their wake, warning calls leapt from mouth to mouth across the area.

"Typhoon. All residents to their shelters!"

"Typhoon. All residents to their shelters!"

"Typhoon. All residents to their shelters!"

"Typhoon. All residents to their shelters!"

"Typhoon. All residents to their shelters!"

Drenched in cool sweat after hours of lifting and carrying, Amon's skin stung as a fierce wind began to hiss and whistle through the narrow crannies of the District of Dreams, and he watched as Rick covered his face with his forearms and cringed at each gust. The tatters of his friend's jacket rippled against him as Amon felt the *thwap* of his own on his skin, the expired fabric releasing streams of flakes at the same moment as the buildings around them, all of it swirling up into a great confluence that shrouded the slumscape around them. With aching muscles, Amon plodded behind him along a ledge that wrapped the upper bulge of a massive disposcraper dome. Like Rick and everyone else in the line of people stretching around the bend ahead, he leaned on the curving wall as he went and shifted from foot to foot whenever the traffic stopped to rest his weary legs. They were doing their best to heed the warnings and return to their shelter as quickly as they could before the storm began, but so was everyone else and the paths were crammed with slow, grinding crowds as Amon's recollection turned with numb exhaustion to the harrowing events of the day.

For the previous few weeks, as the autumn air reached its chill tentacles into every alcove and corner of the slums, Amon and Rick had been helping with an ever-increasing variety of jobs, just as Hippo had told them they would. Instead of their construction, demolition, escort, and patrol duties, hospital managers had enlisted them for reproductive waste disposal. Wearing work shoes and overalls on loan, they would head to the birthrooms, where doctors and nurses huddled over pregnant women on cots squeezed into tight rows. From the base of some of the cots they took buckets of what looked like blood and hauled them outside to dump them into a steaming crevice. Wiped the floors with dissolving Fleet-cloth rags. Cleaned the postpartum latrines. Removed ragged bedding that had passed its expiration date. It was grueling, sometimes nauseating labor, but it quickly became part of their routine. And while Amon was absorbed in it, he could almost forget that he'd ever known another way to live.

Then, the previous morning, a whole twenty-five-story-tall, fifty-room-square swathe of Xenocyst buildings had suddenly caved in, and Amon and Rick were called in to assist with the rescue efforts. The cause had been premature lower floor decay due to room replacement delays, and the sudden influx of hundreds of injured patients into the hospital only made the supply shortages worse. Not only were the bed-ridden unable to pick up their own supplies, but the already scarce medical equipment became overstretched with the wards filled beyond capacity, until doctors and nurses could do little more than offer their kindness and attention as many perished. While OpSci skirmishes and malnutrition, as well as increasing numbers of suicides, were already taking their toll on the Xenocyst ranks, this new crisis created a backlog for the undertakers. And since all survivors had been liberated from the rubble the night before, Amon and Rick were asked to assist them at dawn.

Subsumed in damp chill beneath fragments of gray morning sky, they had found themselves with two other men holding the corners of a large, opaque plastic envelope that served as a hearse and hid its contents from the onlookers they passed. The two of them were worn out already from rescue efforts that had stretched well past midnight (groping and shoveling under the glow of the now precious firefLytes), and their arms and legs strained under the load as they climbed dark stair-strips. With each step the *rakhaw* of crows grew louder and a foul smell stronger, until a direct waft of air thick with putrescence struck Amon's nostrils and he gagged despite himself. Moments later, he learned the source of the stench as they reached a platform overlooking a large square rooftop about ten meters below, tucked out of sight by the backs of disposcrapers built encircling it. A man with a shaved head at the brink of the platform chanted over a body around which a family leaned, as four other men loaded another body onto a huge basket attached to a pulley and began to lower it over the side. Finally, Amon saw the crows he had so often heard, a glistening black mass perched on the edge of every rooftop around them, wheeling and swooping over the mound below that swarmed with their greedily pecking brethren.

Neither Amon nor Rick had ever attended a funeral before, as they had no family and few friends. And so the two harbingers of bankdeath finally became familiar with death of the body—the fact that a person could be wiped out with naught a trace but their bones, not merely economically and socially but straight from existence. To be sure, Amon had once thought Rick was murdered, but he had never confirmed it with his own eyes, and his friend had turned out to be alive all along. They had also occasionally glimpsed fallen bodies as they rushed through the slums on their different errands, and had dug up the rubble too late for some during the rescue the night before. Yet nothing had prepared either of them for the horror they now saw, all words that might have described it abandoning them to the raw presence of the scene.

They remained silent even after their duties were complete, walking along winding causeways and roofcourses beneath the ever-darkening sky-slivers, and it was then, before the signal bells were rung, that Amon decided he would seek out Rashana. Whatever happened, he was going to find her. By whatever means possible, whether the chances were slim or not, he and Rick were getting out.

Now, reaching a roomslope partway along the curving ledge, they slid down it onto a small raised landing that fed the pouring crowd into a packed elevated trenchway. As Amon slowly jostled his way ahead behind Rick, he could discover no chain of reasoning that had led him to this resolution in that moment—after the experiences of the day, his head was empty of definite thoughts altogether. But he felt a kind of certainty when he considered the decision and knew it had been motivated at least in part by a mysterious incident Vertical had related to him a few days earlier and a story she had told him soon after.

According to Vertical, a Xenocyst border sentinel had said that a woman had come looking for Amon. Escorted by a group of private mercenaries serving as her bodyguards, the woman had approached the sentinel's lookout block in the buffer canyon near the northwest tunnel. The sentinel had refused them entry as armed visitors were not permitted. Apparently the woman, who he had described as "young and beautiful," had asked if a man called Amon Kenzaki was there. The sentinel had told her he hadn't heard of anyone by that name and sent her away, but had later related the incident to his squad and the story soon spread to a man who served on Vertical's scouting crew. Vertical had overheard him mention Amon's name on their lunch break and, after prying for details, had sought out Amon at the first opportunity.

Though Amon's initial idea was that this woman might be Rashana, his confidence in this weakened the more he thought about it. Although she could be considered "beautiful" in a refined sort of way, and might plausibly be called "young," as she was likely still around forty, Amon doubted these were the first adjectives that would come to mind when describing this strong-willed, commanding corporate demigod of a woman, with her fearsome eyelashes. And it made no sense for her to be escorted by regular mercenaries rather than the Birla Guard, nor to be on foot outside the gate when she could fly right into the Cyst more safely on her specially designed stealth rotorcraft, the PhantoCopter. But if it wasn't her, then who could it be?

Amon's heart began to flutter when he allowed himself to entertain the only other likely possibility: that it had been Mayuko! This seemed too exciting to be true, and he wanted to speak to the sentinel to confirm that the guards had indeed been run-of-the-mill mercs and to ask him about this young, beautiful woman's hair, whether it had a certain sheen, like a comet laced with mercury.

He asked Vertical to bring him to the scout from whom she'd heard the rumor, but as the man had been shifted to reconstruction, it took several days to locate him. Then, when the scout finally took them to the northwestern lookout just three days ago, the sentinel could not be found. According to his fellows on shift, he had gone on a supply run a couple of days earlier and never returned, a mishap that was becoming more and more common as the OpScis turned increasingly aggressive. To make matters worse, the sentinel had apparently been at his post alone when the woman had approached, meaning there were no further leads.

Hearing this, disappointment fell heavy upon Amon like a great avalanche of sand, and he sat on a ledge overlooking the buffer canyon, too laden with thoughts and feelings to remain on his feet. From his perch, he watched the hordes of residents pour up and down the stairpaths on the outer wall of Xenocyst, cross the broken canyon floor in both directions, and stream in and out of the cracks in the petal-flurried, crumbling roomcrags on the far side, a splash of amber-cream released by the sunken sun glowing with incongruous beauty along the serrated tumbling skyline above. Yearning to see Mayuko more intensely than ever, Amon wondered whether the story had been true; whether she was indeed safe and, if so, why she might have come to find him.

To his surprise, his sad ruminations were interrupted by a warm hand on his shoulder. He traced from its fingertips up the arm with his gaze to find Vertical, who had sat beside him on the ledge without his realizing. She looked into his eyes with an expression of tender sympathy Amon wouldn't have thought possible on her usually grim face. For a moment he was uncomfortable at having her burst his bubble of solitude, but realized quickly that her touch was reassuring, that he was glad to have company.

"You okay?" she asked.

"I don't know," mumbled Amon. "I guess so."

"I heard your stories. She was important to you and Rick."

He hadn't said who he thought the visitor was. Somehow Vertical had put it together on her own.

"Yes . . ." he half-whispered as he blinked back the tears that came to his eyes, "she was—is . . ."

"I know how you feel. Something similar happened to me once."

"Oh yeah?" said Amon, looking at her somewhat hopefully as if she might have answers to his sorrows.

"Yes. You remember when I talked at the festival about my husband?"

Amon nodded, recalling how Ty had called her out for cutting her story short and not properly explaining her name. "I guess he came here at some point?"

Vertical sighed and looked off at the bloom of milky-dapples-on-peach wavering along the slumscape horizon. "If you think it'll help, I can tell you about it."

Amon turned to her, catching the glint of sadness in the corner of her sunset-filled eyes, and nodded, "please," curious to hear the rest of her tale as much as he was hoping for a distraction from his own.

"I had been living in the Gifted Triangle for five years when my husband found me. Searching for someone out here is no easy task. There are so many people in this tight labyrinth it's just too expensive and time consuming. But he was persistent and lucky. I was so shocked when I saw him. I'd already gone through all the grief, thinking we'd never meet again. But he'd held out hope the whole time and wanted me to come back with him to the Free World. He told me that he'd graduated law school and found a position at a decent firm. He could afford to let me stay in his home now, provide me with food, everything I needed. Though I was reluctant to leave the new life I had made here, I was happy to see him and amazed that he'd put all that effort into finding me on the time off from his new job. The decider for me was when he told me there was a track in the shared gym at his apartment. I was sick of sprinting back and forth on whatever short patches of rooftop I could find. The idea of really letting go on an open track seemed like a godsend.

"But it only took a few days to see that I had made a mistake. Without a BodyBank, I had to depend on him for everything—not just food and water. I couldn't turn on the tap in his apartment or the stove, or open the front door. As soon as he went out, it was like being in prison. And that's exactly what the Fiscal Judiciary called it. According to CrediLaw, keeping bankdead in your home is a form of kidnapping and unwillful imprisonment. They say we lack the ability to give digital consent. So he was paying enormous fines just to have me around. He said he could afford it, but I had no way of checking his readout. For all I knew, he was just saying that to reassure me.

"His apartment looked a bit worn out to me, but he saw no need to fix anything. It was immaculate in his eyes. There were furnishings I couldn't see, like the mirror and the wallpaper. And the window looked out on a wall only a few centimeters away for me, while to him it overlooked a wide, open square full of people and trees. It was so enclosed and dim in there. The nighttime was the worst; the whole city went pitch black and no one knew it. They were like slugs crawling through caves. He bought me a little flashlight and a lamp from some nosties, but there was something so depressing about being alone in this one dim circle of light. And when I went outside at night a whole city's worth of mosquitos and moths would swarm around my flashlight. It was awful. Then there was the problem with digimakes. He'd look so obviously exhausted but get irritated that I could see it. He'd set his apps to hide his expression and felt like I was cheating in being able to see through. I had no idea what I looked like to him. I know my living in the camps had weathered and aged me in those five years we were apart. So was he augmenting me? Had he applied youthening filters? I saw his naked face and I didn't want him to see anything other than mine.

"The worst part was that we couldn't communicate anymore. We'd be talking and suddenly he'd get the Elsewhere Gaze, or he'd smirk or giggle or grimace at something I couldn't see. Other times he'd start typing out a response to someone but try to keep our conversation going with his divided attention. Sometimes I'd ask him about what it was, but he didn't want to explain every little thing that popped up on his eyescreen. There was so much information flowing through that constantly narrating it would have been a full-time job and then some. If I'd had a BodyBank he'd have been able to share his screen easily. Now so much of his life was inaccessible to me. I had grown used to life in the naked world and, when we were together, I wanted him to be there with me all the time.

It was like living with a writer or an artist always thinking about their work, except far more lonely. I tried to explain this to him but the idea of focusing only on what was there was incomprehensible to him. How could he know what was there and what wasn't? He couldn't afford to access only the naked world as I could. There was no way for him to draw the borders. And even if he could, who was to say that what I was experiencing was really there any more than what he was? Maybe his experience was just richer than mine and I was acting like a child jealous of another child with more icing on her slice of cake.

"Then there was winding down after work, which meant watching docupromos and entertisements that I couldn't hear or see. He went to Jinbocho to get books and manga for me to entertain myself, but these were expensive and I wanted to get out more. Going out alone, I could only wander the streets. The doors wouldn't open for me so I couldn't get inside the stores, or if I followed someone in while a door was still open I could get trapped inside for hours. The default was to edit bankdead out of the ImmaNet feed, so usually I was invisible. If they could see me, I was fixed up to look like an office lady. I became something generic that fit into their view of how the city ought to be. They couldn't see who I was any better than he could. He'd take me out sometimes when he had a bit of time. This turned into a nightly after-work ritual. It wasn't really enough. I still had cabin fever. It was better than nothing, but I felt like a dog being walked. We weren't a husband and wife in a sharing relationship. I was a weak, dependent thing that he held in the palm of his hand and sheltered from the harsh winds of the world. He had all the power and, as much as he wanted to let me take part in decision making, he started to decide where we'd go on our walks. He chose what restaurants he'd take me to and what we'd eat. Unconsciously, he was taking control of everything, and I was growing too weak to resist him. For the first while, he'd take me down to the track every morning or to a park about once a week. But I was growing lax in my training. One day I decided to stay in and just lie on the couch for hours. I knew then that I had to leave.

"I couldn't tell him I wanted to return to the camps because I knew he'd never accept it. So I waited a few days and stockpiled food and drinks for the journey. Then one morning I followed him out of the apartment as he headed off to work. He was so immersed in whatever was in his eyes and ears, he didn't even notice. I broke into the District of Dreams by scaling the barrier on the Bridge of Compassion. At Delivery, I found that I'd been demoted to giftless and spent a few weeks in the Tumbles before applying at Xenocyst. At my hearing, the council asked me if I would ever go back again, implying that I might abandon the community. I told them no; I'd much rather be cramped physically and have to run vertically than be cramped mentally and have all the space in the world.

"Still he comes looking for me. The first time he came back I explained why I couldn't live with him—but he's stubborn. Ultimately, he isn't willing to go bankrupt to be here with me and I've learned that I can never return with him, as much as I might have loved him once."

When Vertical was finished, Amon sat there stunned, his thoughts whirling in the wake of her tragic tale. He was struck by what she'd said about the people of Tokyo being like slugs in the dark city and remembered that he'd been no different—his new name was Mogura after all. When he'd thought he was walking clearly lit streets, inhabiting clearly lit rooms, it had all been a graphical fabrication—the light not radiating from the world *to* his eyes but painted on the world *by* his eyes and the technological network woven through them. Except perhaps in those rare moments when he'd been under the light of the InfoSun, Amon had existed in shadow and murk his entire life.

Vertical had been absorbed in the skyline the whole time she spoke, occasionally casting her eyes down into the canyon as the peach-and-milk burned fiery purple and began to fade into the darker blue of evening. Now at last she turned to Amon and looked him up and down carefully, as though trying to read his feelings in the lines of his body.

"So what I want to say is maybe that was her. Maybe you'll see her again and maybe you won't. But there's no telling how it would turn out if you did. So don't hurt yourself by obsessing over something uncertain and distant. All we can do is focus on what's within our reach every day and hope."

Vertical put her hand on Amon's shoulder again and Amon looked into her quivering, sympathetic eyes. A wave of gratitude glowed in his chest for her caring attention and he felt as though he was finally beginning to understand her. Vertical had treated him with disdain from the beginning, always seeming cold and impatient, and though he could tell that she was hurt somehow, he could never guess why. Now he sensed the warm, sensitive pith beneath her prickly exterior and was happy to have earned her respect, wishing the circumstances were not so dire so that they might have more opportunities to communicate like this.

"Thank you," said Amon with a slight bow of his head and a wry smile. "I still don't know how I feel, but I'll think about what you said."

The trenchway continued until a meandering pegway arrived on their right. A misty drizzle on the wind now tickled their faces, and Amon began to toil up ahead of Rick this time, squeezing the slippery handholds hard, his wary eye on the many hundreds climbing above for fear one might lose their footing and come tumbling down.

To Amon, Vertical's advice had seemed sincere and he didn't doubt there was wisdom to it. But in the present situation, it seemed almost impossible to follow. For how could he focus on the day-to-day when all he experienced was misery? It was far too tempting, when he had a moment to breathe, to imagine somewhere else—a city where Mayuko was waiting, a simple comfortable apartment, the forest—especially since Mayuko had drawn close, whether as fact or figment.

After the continuation of Vertical's story, Amon had reflected back on the autumn festival when she had told the first part, which reminded him of Tamper, whose name story Hippo had told not long after. When he considered how both Vertical and Tamper had tried to reunite with family members in the Free World, it seemed to him that their stories were like the flipsides of one coin and he became more curious than ever about Tamper's letter. So, two days ago, he had visited the library to ask the Books about it and they had kindly agreed to make the time. Now, clinging to the pegs with the crowd halted above for some reason and the moisture whish-pattering on his head, Amon recalled the tapping of Little Book's decoding and the nasal thrum of Book's interpreting while the three of them sat in the center of the stacks, the scrambled characters on the plastic sheets in his hands like a spell summoning Tamper's soul.

Dear Xenocyst, Apologies for silence. Had little peace of mind to gather info.

Writing to amend for misbehavior. Xenocyst kindly fed and sheltered me after I skipped my hearing. An unfair exception to your good rules. So paying my story debt. Hope it's not too late.

In my twenties I married a doctor. An obstetrician. Mostly in-house midwifing for wealthy. Very successful in her niche. But she felt inadequate for having no baby. Studied hard her whole life to finish medical school ASAP. Never had time to think about starting a family. Because of her specialization patients would ask if she'd given birth. Had to say no. So they saw her as a girl not woman. Or that's how she saw it. Maybe she had their trust as doctor but she couldn't stand their superior looks. Whatever it took she wanted a baby of her own.

I was vending machine designer. Mostly repair work when maintenance drones couldn't fix a prob. My income was no joke but I wouldn't be paying for a kid—not at Fertilex rates. Other hand my wife had large salary and inheritance of derivatives from uncle. So budgeting we might scrape by.

I was surprised at my excitement. Few electronic engineers could dream the luxury of a child. Started imagining myself as father for first time.

With no fertility treatment we succeeded at impregnation, pregnancy, birth. A miracle. But our last good fortune.

When our son was two my wife got cervical cancer. Enrolled her in best oncology ward in Tokyo. Ordered most advanced treatments money could buy. Wanted to cure her fast. But she fought over a year. Medical costs drained her savings. Soon we wouldn't be able to support our son until ID Birth. She asked advice. I loved her. Recommended she continue treatment. The rest figure out later. But she was never type to trust chance. Spent years in school, worked her way up from internship to steady salary job and benefits. Stable prospects were everything to her. I tried to convince her. Invest in your own life! Thought I succeeded. Misunderstood the doubt in her eyes.

Night she died in hospital I discovered she'd canceled all treatments months ago. Continued renting out bed to appear looked after while skimping on every other cost. Including medicine. Chose not to waste our last days together arguing. Left me with just enough to care for son until twenty.

The stupid irony of life! Wife wanted a child to feel more secure in career. At end she chose child above career and everything else.

I fell apart. My wife blessed me with opportunity beyond my means to raise a son. In exchange I lost her. Didn't blame him for it. Loved my little boy as much as her. My grief took other forms.

My engineer co-workers were all grime nosties, the machine-loving kind. Told me about pachinko parlor in Nakano with vintage pinball machines. From before Free Era, around 1970s. Designed so you could actually play for profit and make living with enough skill. At least back when they came out. With inflation you maybe earn a bit of *sake* money. On first day I won ten times what I brought. Not just my luck and talent that drew me back again and again. Also the mystery of the machine. More mechanical than electronic. Parts and functions beyond my technical understanding. My friends were congratulating. Said I might make FlexiPedia pachinko hall of fame article one day. Gave me wild fantasies when wife became ill. I could pay off medical bills with winnings.

Had just enough sense to know this was delusional. Resisted impulse to play in wife's final months to stay by side. But after she passed I wanted to badly. Had put it off too long. Pachinko the only way I could forget the loss.

Finances held up till son turned three. Then vintage parlor went out of biz. Me and friends had to frequent newer parlors accessible from home. More expensive. Higher stakes. Rigged in favor of house no matter your skill. But habit wouldn't let go. My wife, so brilliant, had foreseen my direction. Somehow. Set up inheritance as trust fund. Just enough money disbursed each month for childcare.

When savings were gone, debt building, I feared myself. Would I withdraw even this for addiction? No! Clicked the fund away to foster parents who would raise my son. Carefully selected from database. Responsible. Infertile but full of affection for children. Profiles seemed ideal match for him. But this was worst gamble of all. On visit I discovered spacious condo. Used fund to buy while sending son to lower-grade school than promised. And they wouldn't give him his favorite drink Cloud9 Nectar. Only cheap knockoff brand. Swindled! I threatened fosters with legal action, bluff I couldn't afford. They preempted with lawsuit. Claimed gambling problem made me unsuitable for custody. Over my son! This trick finally woke me from grief. Quit pachinko entirely but too late. Already deep in the red and legal defense fees pushed me into bankruptcy. Cash crashed in the end. Just before my son's sixth birthday.

Lucky to find Xenocyst. Wanted to stay longer. Build more for community. But had to find my son. You taught me to seize control of my life even where choice is impossible.

Now I visit him daily. Bring him Cloud9. See him so close. Want to touch him. But his overlay would label me an obstacle and he would see whatever it made me. Not his father. Then fosters could review his LifeStream. Find me stalking. Keep him from his favorite drink or worse. And I'm ashamed to be seen. What kind of father can I be? A bankdead stealing to stay alive. Already my hack to fake inventory uncovered a few times. Fended off CareBots sent by vending machine owners. One day they will judge cost effective to sic freekeepers I cannot beat. Only a matter of time. I live in fear. Who could drag a child into such life? Better not knowing I'm here. Better to forget his father and mother. But can't leave him entirely. Want to provide him with best I can offer. His favorite drink and my thoughts of him.

This in between life is my penance. Hope this letter finds you. Let me pay my story debt at least. Tamper

By the time their disposcraper was in sight, a fitfully pounding bluster threatened to knock Amon's tired body off the edge of ladder footholds and pry his fingers from rungs, as the sky slivers above oozed with black clouds and the whole slumscape swayed with slow menacing force. Though it was hardly the time to focus on anything but trying to keep his grip as he scaled wet, ephemeral towers that refused to stay still, Amon couldn't help thinking that he would soon be alone with Rick in their room, where he might finally tell him about the incident with the woman. He knew that as Mayuko's ex-lover and old friend Rick deserved to know anything that might hold clues to what had happened to her. But initially he hadn't wanted to get his hopes up when it might turn out that the incident was a complete fiction, that the woman was someone else, or that she was Mayuko but they had missed their chance to meet her forever, so he'd planned to wait until he'd confirmed the details with the sentinel. Yet even today, after he had learned the sentinel was gone, Amon had said nothing, and in the occasional glimmers of self-honesty that reached his consciousness he saw the deeper reason for his hesitation: neither of them had mentioned Mayuko's name since the day they had reunited in Xenocyst. Now Amon was afraid that once the topic came up, Rick might question him more directly about the past and Amon would be forced to tell him the parts he had omitted from his story, or perhaps to explicitly lie, neither of which he was prepared to do.

Amon wasn't sure why he'd deceived Rick in the beginning. Without any premeditated thought or planning, he had simply found himself trying almost automatically to hide his final moments with Mayuko. At the start, Amon knew he'd been driven in part by his pride: he was ashamed to admit that he'd failed her in the moment of reckoning. Would Rick have understood the split-second calculations that led to Amon's decision to run alone? Would he accept the fact that the only way for both Amon and Mayuko to stay alive had been for Amon to leave her in grave danger? Now that he'd told the incomplete and thus dishonest version of events in which she had never been attacked, he didn't see the point in making Rick worry when there was nothing they could do to help her—or at least this was Amon's best excuse for continuing to seal his lips. There were also simpler, less noble reasons that he could sometimes admit to himself. Like the fact that the longer he remained silent, the more the elision became habitual and the harder it was to even broach the topic.

If they were going to discuss this sensitive issue that had profound bearing on their friendship after these several months had passed, they would need to find the right moment, when they could go slow and open up, not just exchange breathless words during their exhausting labors. Yet Rick usually excused himself right after work these days, and came back to their room after Amon was asleep or when it was too late for serious discussion, so such chances seemed ever less likely to present themselves. It was sad for Amon that Rick was spending less and less time with him, especially now that he was feeling the lack more and more and could have used an ear to speak his troubles. That was why, after the typhoon had been spotted and Rick agreed to hole up with Amon in their room to ride out the storm together rather than wander off alone, Amon felt a strange tinge of gladness to his foreboding, hoping that he would find the courage to speak at last and make everything clear between them as it had been once long ago.

Arriving in their room, Amon and Rick peeled off their sweat-drenched clothes and lay side by side beneath their Fleet blankets. They pressed the side of their bodies against the walls in an effort to plug up some of the expanding cracks in the expiring room and reduce the drafts for each other, hoping for the advent of dreams. (Would they ever come? Could they truly forsake Amon forevermore?) But when heavy droplets of rain began to pelt the upper reaches of the roof canopy and the floor began to rock, they sensed the growing force of the storm and, giving up on any pointless attempt to sleep, began to chat.

Apparently it was common in the fall for typhoons to enter the shallow mouth of Tokyo Bay and head straight for the District of Dreams, which served as a sort of storm barrier for the rest of the metropolis, perhaps intentionally positioned so by urban planners half a century ago. Though both of them had waited out typhoons many times before—inside the sealed, sturdy confines of the BioPen, their apartments, GATA Tower, or wherever they happened to be in Free Tokyo—never had they felt its raw power like this before, and Amon was unnerved by the absence of the cajoling ghoulish voices and heavypromometal always brought by InfoTyphoons.

In the utter darkness of the fracturing windowless chamber, deep in the belly of the ever-dissolving architectural beast, enveloped in the swelling tumult of elemental power, they tried to forget where they were and talked of many things—the quirks of their co-workers and neighbors, their work schedules, their plans for tomorrow—carefully orbiting but never confronting the indescribable horror they had seen in the hidden heights of Xenocyst that day. All the while, Amon's resolution poked out from a corner of his mind, his urge to tell Rick tickling at his attention as he kept up his end of the conversation, the right opening never seeming to present itself.

"Fucking shit I'm hungry," said Rick after a short lull in their chatter. It was his constant refrain of late.

"Oh, me too," said Amon. "But it feels good to do this, don't you think? Just talk like this."

"Yeah. It's been a long time, what with everything that's been happening here . . ."

"Who would have thought back in Free Tokyo that we would ever go even a single day without speaking our own dialect?"

"It's not the same, is it, Hinkongo?"

"No. I mean, I'm starting to feel comfortable with it, but even if I understand what they're saying and my point gets across, it always seems like . . . well, like something is missing, you know?"

"Like the words are never quite the right shape to fit what you want to say."

"Yeah, that's it. Something like that."

Now that Amon and Rick were frequently working in close cooperation with crashborn residents without the supervision of standard Japanese speakers like Vertical and Ty, their Hinkongo had been improving rapidly. Amon had always thought of the camp dialect as a crude, lowly pidgin, but despite its many foreign words it turned out to be easy to pick up without rigorous study once his ears had adjusted, as it had the same grammar as the standard dialect they were used to. Now that the linguistic door was open, they often made small talk with co-workers, though the best opportunity to practice had been the stargazing rooftops, where Xenocysters sat around telling stories, much as Hippo and his group had at the festival. If they were lucky, Amon and Rick would hear the fast, unsoftened Hinkongo of talented raconteurs, and found the crashborn residents just as eager to hear their stories, as chances to interact with crashdead were rare. No one had ever met an actual Liquidator, let alone an Identity Executioner, and they were eager to understand what these jobs signified, to imagine a world they had never known. With their limited vocabulary, it still took much pausing, backtracking, and gesturing to get across complicated messages, though the effort only raised their proficiency further. Yet now that the *suposhu* and embyrbrycks were scarce, and people were too hungry to climb any higher than they had to, these circles had mostly stopped gathering, and without Rick to accompany him Amon had stopped attending the ones that remained.

"But don't you think," Amon continued, "it's also kind of depressing?"

"What is?" asked Rick. "Not being able to communicate the way you'd like to?"

"No. The opposite. Being able to understand what everyone's saying now. You don't find that disturbing ever?"

"I don't know. Not really. How so?"

"Don't get me wrong, I'm happy to finally get a handle on the language. Work is so much easier now and we're finally starting to make a few friends. But . . . well . . . talking with everyone, we're learning about their lives, right? Not just elite members like Ty, Book, and the councilors, but regular people, and now they don't seem like just 'bankdead' anymore, the way we used to understand what that meant. Do you know what I mean?"

"I think so. Like how we never used to really respect them."

"Respect them? They used to be faceless to us! Faceless! Just a category we could stick labels on. All of them. If we were feeling mean, they were 'lazy,' 'lecherous,' 'discreditable.' Or if we were feeling generous they were 'underprivileged' and 'left behind.' We didn't even see them as individual people. And now that I understand how the Charity Gift Economy works, I can't stop thinking back on our previous life. We used to believe we were making the world a better place, just by working and living. But that was all bullshit! Trickle-down charity from our actions!? The best of all possible slums!? Maximal freedom for all!? Through liquidation!?"

Amon remembered his talk with Makesh in Sushi Migration, and all the things he had said with such certainty about the justice of the AT system. *What a fool I was*, he thought, and felt the harsh, clenching tingle of shame climbing his back as he sympathized with the Birla sister's impatience with him.

"I know," said Rick. "It's painful to think what we used to do. I always—"

Broosh-krah. Rick's words were erased by a juggernaut blast of wind, the force of which Amon felt slamming the wall to his right and heard bending the surrounding buildings too far for comfort—*kricka-kra-kra-kra-kra*—the floor now tipping to the side so that he had to grip it with the flat of his palm to stop from sliding.

No other blasts followed, and the floor soon righted itself, the wind settling to a sharp, whistling hiss. Still, Amon couldn't help imagining their building collapsing and, in his mind's eye, he was back wading through the rubble during the rescue efforts yesterday, calling out and digging for survivors. What if they were the ones buried next time? Would they have the luck to be found?

He was reminded of one crisp, sunny afternoon when a skyscraper avalanche forced them to change their supply route on the way back from Delivery and they saw Welcome Chasm for the first time. With shelters being replaced less frequently, the carefully constructed buildings in Xenocyst were somewhat unstable, as the cave-in would soon demonstrate, but in the haphazard architectural mess elsewhere, collapses were happening on an almost hourly basis. Finding a heap of shattered walls, squarish hunks of room, and a powder of crushed Fleet blocking their way, they were diverted to a rooftop that ran along the jagged edge of a thin chasm. With a glance of concern at Rick and Amon, Ty ordered everyone in the crew not to look in under any circumstances. But, sensing from Ty's expression when he'd met their gaze that the chasm concerned the two of them somehow, Amon couldn't resist his curiosity. And when Ty was busy arguing with a gang of locals who insisted on receiving supply tolls for the right to pass an alley ahead, Amon lay down on his belly to peer in, with Rick following close behind.

Past the layers of sharply jutting ridges formed of room corners that composed the sides of the chasm and the layers of dark petals fluttering between them, they saw a truck driving along a two-lane road at the bottom. It was unmarked, without any brand name or logo, though they both guessed soon afterwards that it was operated by venture charities who received giftless crashnewbs from the GATA Displacement Crews— what Amon had always thought of as the last social program. They watched as the truck stopped, a stretcher was rolled out, and a person lying inert atop it in bankliving clothes was carried off and laid down on the concrete. There, before their eyes, was the fate of the majority of those whose identities they had executed—the ones who had genomes unlikely to produce marketable resources and who were therefore denied admittance to Er (with the exception of Atupio facilities that only took in a select few).

Unlike Amon, the nerves of their visual and auditory systems would have been surgically repaired during BodyBank removal, so these crashdead were not blind and deaf, though they still had to cope with cogwither, crowdcrave, and all the other symptoms of webloss. He could hear the raving shrieks and cries of those who had crawled away upon awakening echoing up to his ears, and wondered how many would survive the week. Some would be assimilated by the Opportunity Scientists, who offered religious practices and beliefs to help them deal with their psychological deficits and madness. Others, like those who'd crashed because they couldn't pay their medical bills, would already be on the verge of death upon arrival. Most would be unable to cope and become so-called fragparrots: men and women whose identities were so fragmented they spoke in promotation scripts and whistled edutainment jingles until they were too weak to stand.

Ty was too busy haggling with the gang to notice what Amon and Rick were doing. Nevertheless, after he'd negotiated the crew's passage he tuned in to the gape-mouthed, harrowed expressions they wore the whole way back, and swore at them with wheel clenched in fist for abandoning their guard posts during a potentially dangerous confrontation. For days Amon and Rick hardly spoke, having only the will to barely fulfill their duties. Amon lost his appetite and had to force himself to eat, suffering a relapse of the dissonance he'd felt after first seeing the supply crews returning to the Xenocyst border. If not for Rick budging him out the door each morning and forcing him to down his rations, he might have shriveled up on the floor and starved.

"I guess the one consolation," said Amon, "is that we managed to bring Barrow to Xenocyst."

"Sure. He did earn us a place here."

"No. I mean consolation for everything that we've done."

"Oh. For you maybe. I never knew him personally so it doesn't really matter to me either way. Though he does seem to be fitting in pretty well."

"I'm amazed at his energy. After everything that's happened to him and all that he's lost, he just seems to accept his place here and get on with it."

"You always were a fan of Minister Larry."

"What do you mean? You voted for him too!"

"Only after you twisted my arm with all that bullshit about the equality and fairness of nationalized bodily functions. If it wasn't for you I would have abstained."

"You mean would have 'been a politically apathetic asshole.' And don't try to pin the responsibility for your decisions on me, even if it was a good decision. They do call it the *Free* World for a reason."

"Sure. But is it a good reason?"

"Let's not get sidetracked. You know what I mean."

The moment after Barrow had offered to guide them to the stockpile of analog detritus and asked for permission to take the Xenocyst screening, Ty flew into such a rage—cursing and kicking Barrow repeatedly as the disgraced politician curled up in the fetal position in the corner—that Amon and Rick had to restrain him. Anyone who had ever followed Opportunity Science, Ty snarled, was forbidden from ever joining Xenocyst, and that was that. Besides, the council had ruled that they had no resources for new members and how did they know he wouldn't be leading them into an ambush?

Once Amon and Rick got Ty to calm down, Amon spoke up in Barrow's defense, feeling obligated to protect him in return for bringing him to this pathetic fate. First, while the rules might forbid OpScis from joining Xenocyst and urge rejection of new applications, admission was ultimately up to the council to decide, not mere patrolmen, and if they brought Barrow in for a hearing the council would likely extract further information that would aid them in their conflict, whether or not he was allowed in. Second, if you knew anything about Barrow's career, then it was impossible to take seriously the idea that he might be a sincere believer. If Barrow worshipped anything, it was anadeto—a nostie through and through. Finally, the chance to acquire a stockpile of equipment and weaponry that wouldn't dissolve, if it could be found, was too good to pass up in these volatile times, and didn't the presence of the rare machine pistol in the hands of the field priest prove that it likely existed?

Frowning with stone-faced indecision, Ty had nothing to say in response and Barrow had filled the silence with a plea for his own case. Infusing each syllable with his enchanting timbre, he insisted on the sincerity of his desire to join. Since cash crashing and losing his position as CEM, his plans to help the bankdead had been cut short, but Xenocyst offered a chance to continue his work, if in a much-reduced capacity. Only months earlier he'd been the most powerful politician in Japan, and he promised that if he was accepted he would harness his unique set of skills and know-how for the good of the community.

Between Amon and Barrow, with Rick interjecting occasionally as mediator, the two of them managed to convince Ty to reluctantly let Barrow take them to the trove. But only under the condition that he stay two meters in front of him at all times and with the understanding that Ty would wheel-rim his skull open at the slightest hint of disobedience.

When Barrow agreed and the argument was settled, Ty asked the local residents to send word to the Cyst that they would be delayed a few days and the four of them embarked on a long journey, much further than Rick and Amon had ever traveled from Xenocyst. They started off south—crossing the outer room-hills of Opportunity Peaks that rolled outwards from its base in progressively smaller corner-jutting undula-tions—cut west when they reached a sharp cliff of disposcrapers to scale its stairpaths to the roofways above, and gradually descended winding ledges and tunnels until they reached the dark confines of ground-level tarmac. There they had lunch at a feeding station and began to spiral upwards again in a westerly direction, eventually reaching the top of several faux-bronze towers leaning out over the Tokyo Canal. By this time night had fallen, and they marched south on a course that zigzagged to and from the edge of the bank, following the canal's straight form that glimmered gray below them under the flicker of crumbling cookies hung sporadically along its length, dark blots of unmanned boats and cruise ships bobbing up- and downstream, an ocean breeze on their skin. A cloud-hazed crescent floated above the serrated mound of architectural pitch that loomed against the sky on the far side and, when the fireflLytes ended, they trudged on carefully under the dim moonlight it cast. But when fissures opened in their path, Ty judged it too dangerous to proceed, and they took shelter in a cobblestone nook.

Waking with the silver-gray light before dawn, they continued along the shore to a highway that angled north-east across the island from the Miura Peninsula towards downtown Tokyo. Amon heard but didn't see cars roaring high above, the massive road propped up on sheer concrete cylinders around which CareBots whirled. Rick reminded Amon of one mission motorbiking along this highway years before, and Amon recalled the blue infosea stretching to the horizon on both sides, an ImmaNet veneer nothing like the transient labyrinth they now traversed.

This highway marked the border of the Tumbles. As the region was inhabited exclusively by giftless and was more than a day's journey from Delivery, the buildings were always more worn out than elsewhere, leaving a tumbled and often tumbling sprawl of stunted disposcrapers poking from shattered rubble. After passing between the highway's pillars and crossing the cold bar of shadow it cast, they turned east from the canal into an enclave that appeared to be made of cracking clear plastic. It was abandoned, the reek of decay drafting from dark crevices and tunnels, and Ty supposed that it was too distant from Delivery to be nutritionally sustainable since the supply drops. Hiking the broken roofsteps of this ghost town, they watched swirls of flakes from brittle translucent shafts glow persimmon-lavender under the sunrise trickling through cracks above, staying well clear of the edges from which huge sections kept breaking off and crashing far below into splinters like calving ice from arctic glaciers.

To prevent Barrow from leading them into a trap, Ty often broke his own rule of having him stay in front and instead had their captive guide tell them which direction they were going but chose the route himself. This added time onto what was already a marathon expedition, and they were forced to camp out in unknown alleys for several nights. Deep in the Tumbles, far from Xenocyst, not even Ty—a crashborn with more wanderlust than most considered healthy—had any idea where they were, and their one landmark was the distant outline of Opportunity Peaks to the north-west, visible only during lulls in flakefall. Over the desert of Fleet petal dunes and low shelter clusters that rolled in endless tracts around them, great hordes of residents kept streaming north and south like migrating herds, looking even more thin and weary than elsewhere. The ribs of adults showed through the slits in their loose disintegrating shirts, the bellies of children were bloated, and many slumping or laying flopped out on ledges appeared to lack the energy to move altogether. Though they seemed too dissipated to be threatening, Amon and the others tried to avert their gazes, not knowing their affiliation, and Amon feared this was a sign of things to come in enclaves to the north. To ward off brigands as they traveled during the day, Ty made a show of hurling and retracting the wheel of his tricycle when the slumscape opened up while Amon rested his hand on the exposed holster at his side and Rick held out his newly acquired double-barrel machine pistol. At night, Ty, Rick, and Amon took turns keeping watch while the one member they distrusted, Barrow, slept soundly. But perhaps due to their display of force, not one person stepped into view from dusk to morning twilight.

Not long after setting out with the dawn on the fourth day, Barrow told them that they had reached the trove. He led them through a maze of downward-sloping corridors, along narrow causeways and catwalks over raw sewage, facedown bodies, and worse, up dim tunnels that often branched in dozens of directions using the mental map he had somehow decoded in his memory. All the while Ty ordered Amon and Rick to take turns gripping the scruff of Barrow's neck to make sure he couldn't abandon them, for they would be mortally lost without him. At last, they reached an underground chamber delved into the island itself that was piled to the domed ceiling with what appeared to be broken junk. The flattened frames of cars, ripped panty-hose, empty lip balm tubes, used batteries, snapped brooms, tangled netting, holey plastic bags, bent bicycle seats. Yet when Barrow instructed them to dig beneath the surface, they discovered that the garbage had actually been propped up and counter-balanced carefully to create pockets that sheltered items of greater value beneath. In one such pocket, they found salvageable electronic components, transistor radios, tablets, smartphones. In another, materials like screws, nails, plywood, poles, metal sheets, planks, cables. In another various tools like wrenches, knives, abacuses, flashlights, slide rules, binoculars, hourglasses. Elsewhere there were toys, figurines, antique furniture, oil paintings. And finally, as promised, in a great alcove beneath a reinforced gray tarp, an array of weapons and armor: flak vests, shotguns, rubber bullets, longbows, whips, swords.

Barrow explained that such stashes were unheard of these days because they had all been seized by anadeto dealers, who could affordably take what they wanted from the legally unpropertied bankdead and auction them off to dandy nostie collectors. The fact that this one had escaped their notice, obscure and unguarded, was a miracle, he said, and noted that they had the nostie collective that took him in to thank for it, now eliminated like the ghost town earlier. This, to the other men's surprise, brought tears streaming down Ty's cheeks, and he knelt atop an area of the heap full of bicycle-related items, picking up bunches of various parts and tools and then letting them fall from his hands. When he'd regained his composure, he explained that this might very well have been bequeathed by the community that raised him, or his parents themselves. For Ty, the trove wasn't just useful to get them out of the pinch: it was a part of his heritage.

From then on, Ty stopped being suspicious of Barrow and, when they departed for Xenocyst the next morning, no longer told Amon and Rick to keep watch on him. They made much faster progress this day, as they were close to southern proxy territories that Ty was familiar with, and reached a Xenocyst checkpoint by early evening. After dropping Barrow off in the library to describe his map for Little Book to draw, Ty promptly gathered a recovery team with Amon and Rick and left for the Tumbles that very night to haul back whatever useful wares they could find. By the time they returned the following night, the council had finished its ruling on Barrow. He had been granted a trial period in Xenocyst. Asking the Books about it later, Amon and Rick learned that, after the council had subjected Barrow to an intense round of questioning and extracted a lengthy narrative confession, there had been little opposition to allowing him in in spite of his OpSci history and the ban on new memberships, with Hippo himself being his most vocal supporter. Though the Books had been too busy for them to glean further details, Amon had no doubt that Barrow's humanitarian political aspirations, expressed with heart-resonating eloquence, had played an essential role in winning them over.

Now Barrow was surely busy with whatever menial job they had assigned him, as Amon only saw him occasionally at night, huddling with a group of crashborn around some scrounged-up embyrbrycks on a low rooftop near the Cyst. It was the only story circle still going that Amon knew of, and he could have used company now that Rick was around less, but he never approached, feeling awkward to intrude on Barrow's personal sphere given their history. Though when he saw the exuberant sparkle in Barrow's eye over the lurid glow as he told some tale with great animation and held his listeners rapt, Amon almost felt for a moment that he could forgive himself, one day, for his gullible sins.

"Sometimes being here feels like a penance for what we've done," said Rick, and Amon remembered how Tamper had used the same word in his letter. "The hunger just nibbles away inside me and the chill comes through the holes in my clothes, and I'm always afraid something is going to collapse on my head especially in this typhoon, and I feel like we're getting just what we deserve. But then I remember the other crashdead who don't deserve it—at least not as much as we do—and they're suffering in the same way because of us. Under the circumstances, I might feel better about who we are and what we've done, you know, if there was a little bit more to go around. But there's no way I can even begin to forgive myself when I see what everyone's going through. How long is this supply problem going to continue?"

"No one seems to know," said Amon. "And if it keeps going on like this, I wonder how long it's all going to hold together. I mean, with so many essential things missing, is the community going to keep functioning? And if everything breaks apart, what happens to us?"

"Yeah. I can't stop worrying about the same thing. Have you noticed all the hungry ghosts around lately?"

"So sad," said Amon, remembering the first time he'd seen one just a few weeks earlier. On lunch break from construction duties, while he was standing on the edge of a feeding zone eating with Rick and some of their crew, one of their members had approached, unwrapping his rice ball. When he went to take his first bite, it crumbled and slipped between his fingers like sand. Wearing an expression of astonished horror, the man dropped into a squat and hung his head between his knees. One of the others went to pat him on the back consolingly, and their crew leader kindly dismissed him early.

Now Amon saw emaciated wraiths in all the feeding zones, lurking around the edges as they eyed the feeders covetously. According to the Books, their genomes had been blacklisted so that vending machines ejected different food. Though their meals looked normal, they were printed with a highly ephemeral molecular structure, lasting just long enough to reach the target's lips. Hungry ghost labeling was supposedly punishment for dissent—trying to rob vending machines, insisting on more supplies to career volunteers, talking revolution—though it wasn't always clear what the alleged perpetrator had done, if anything. Those who complained to Delivery consultation officers were told they had already received their supplies, which was true in a way, and inventory would always back such claims, so that no one, not even the officers, could believe otherwise.

"If only we had Tamper's vendor hack," said Amon. "Then we could give them all the food they wanted."

"Sure. A feast until the CareBots come."

"But a feast all the same."

"Okay. I know I started it, but can we stop it with that word? It's too painful to even think about. Not even the gifted have enough these days. Have you seen how they've stopped tossing their wrappers?"

"Yeah . . ."

"Before, I took it as a sign of solidarity, the way the privileged ones would kind of share out what they got, even if it wasn't much and the gift-less had to scrounge for it. They don't even do that anymore. Everyone's keeping every scrap, looking out for themselves instead of the group."

"I know," said Amon. "But what worries me more is the kids."

"What about them?"

"The other evening I saw this group of boys around ten on a rampage. They were kicking holes in the walls of a disposcraper slated for demolition and hurling chunks of Fleet at other kids that passed by. They were bashing in the heads of the action figures and dolls that were about to disintegrate, probably stolen ones. I just hope their behavior isn't a barometer for how the situation is progressing. Kids do have a tendency to, you know, give away what everyone is thinking when no one wants to say it and . . ."

A few moments after Amon trailed off, another blast of wind shook the building, tilting the floor so that Amon had to grip it again. But instead of righting itself like before, their shaft began to sway steadily in circles like an egg-beater, buffeted by gusts from all directions. This continued for several tense minutes until the floor seemed to bob up and down as though the patch of artificial island their building stood upon was trying to break off and float away. Soon a mist of rain began to slip in through the cracks of their decayed room, spattering onto the side of Amon's face and dampening his thin blanket. Gradually, a cold seasickness-like nausea set in, and they tried making a bit more chit-chat to distract themselves from the fear. But having trouble hearing each other's voices over the architectural grind, liquid hammer-tap, and whistle-roar of the winds, they soon gave up on asking each other to repeat what the other was saying. Instead, they lay there hanging on queasily in the churning, bumping darkness for perhaps half an hour until the rain shrank to an intermittent patter and the gale waned to mere brushing along the exterior. Then, at last, their voices could carry again and Rick said something that Amon could hear clearly.

"Fucking shit I'm hungry." Something in the tone of his refrain sounded different to Amon this time, the desperation he sensed in it reminding him of his resolution earlier that day. The time had come for them to get out.

"Rick?" he said perhaps a minute later.

"Yeah."

"I finally decided today."

"Okay. Decided what?"

"About Rashana."

"You're going to see her?"

"Yeah. I've got to."

"When?"

"As soon as you want. Tomorrow?"

"As soon as *I* want? You want me to go with you?"

"Of course."

"Mmmm . . ." Rick hummed pessimistically.

" . . ."

" . . ."

"What? You don't want to go?"

" . . ."

"Why don't you want to go?"

" . . ."

" . . ."

" . . ."

"Rick?"

"I—I don't know . . ."

" . . ."

"I . . ."

"What?"

"Talking to Rashana is kind of dangerous, don't you think?"

"Well, we can't be entirely sure about her," said Amon, "but you heard what Hippo said about the Birla Guard?"

"What about the files that link Atupio with the Gyges Circle?"

Towards the end of their talk in the digital quarantine, Amon had reminded Hippo and Rick about files from the PhisherKing that he'd mentioned when telling his story. They were marked as authentic and showed that Atupio had paid the fines for Amon's ID assassination of Barrow along with the cover-up at the Ministry of Records that hid these crimes from his AT readout. He had also discussed how Sekido's crime of infecting Amon with a parasite had been covered up in a similar way, suggesting that this had been funded by Atupio as well. Since, according to Barrow, the Gyges Circle was behind his assassination, Amon had concluded that Atupio was funding this secret organization.

"I think Hippo argued pretty convincingly," said Amon, "that Atupio was most likely manipulated by Anisha to frame Rashana."

Hearing Amon's conjecture, Hippo had suggested that Anisha might have temporarily seized control of Atupio to divert its funds to the Gyges Circle's coup d'état while framing her sister for it in the process. After taking the reins of Fertilex, it wouldn't be difficult for her to tamper with one of its subsidiaries, and—given the sisters' hatred for each other since long before the inheritance issue came to light—that was just the sort of rivalrous machination he expected from her. While Anisha, in Hippo's experience, was downright devious, Rashana had his whole-hearted trust, having supported Xenocyst and other genuine humanitarian initiatives for years. After Amon hemmed and hawed skeptically for a while, their conversation had ended with him saying he would think Hippo's advice over. Today, at last, he had arrived at his conclusion.

"Hippo was just making an educated guess," said Rick. "I don't think you should risk your life on a character recommendation."

"But if there's any chance for us to get out of this, Rashana is it. We both know that there's no way for bankdead to live outside. Someone with her type of resources is our only hope."

Contrary to what their infoadvercation had implicitly emphasized, the bankdead did not congregate in the camps simply because proximity to donation points was convenient, free to come and go as they might. Even if they could cross the toxic, freighter-clogged currents of the Sanzu River or Tokyo Canal without any materials for rafts or boats but non-buoyant Fleet, or somehow bypass the security barrier on the Bridge of Compassion, a feat only an athlete like Vertical might achieve, all they were free to do was wander the streets and starve or dehydrate as Amon almost had on his way out. Lacking expertise like Tamper's, their best hope to secure sustenance was begging, though getting attention would be hard while rendered as a generic salaryperson and the few Free Citizens who cared would be reluctant to indulge in the exorbitant action of almsgiving. It was for these reasons that Amon had never seen bankdead walking around Free Tokyo, and Tamper's and Vertical's stories seemed to teach the folly of leaving even when it was possible. But all this only made Amon certain that he had to try. For he was an exception. He knew someone with more than enough Freedom to support him if she chose.

"What, you think she's just going to wave her magic money wand and give you back your identity signature and then you'll turn on your BodyBank and everything will be okay?"

"I don't know what she's capable of. But don't forget, you are standing here right now thanks to the Er center that she funded."

"I'm grateful to Rashana. I really am. But that doesn't mean I have to trust her completely."

"Of course not. All I'm saying is, there's a possibility she can help us and she's the only possibility we've got, so it's worth a try. Otherwise, we'll be stuck here forever. Or as long as we last anyways."

"But if that's Anisha, or if Rashana has some secret motives, we just don't know what she'll do to us. We could die right there. Or worse. So yeah, maybe Hippo makes the odds sound a bit better, but it doesn't change the basic fact that you'll be gambling with your life."

Amon frowned at this uncharacteristically conservative response from his usually gung-ho friend and looked at him in disbelief, wishing he could see the expression on his face in the darkness, his words alone mere broken bridges to the thoughts and emotions they attempted to give him passage to.

"You know I'm no gambler, Rick, but we're always gambling with our lives, every choice we make. Whatever decision we come to, we always stand to gain or lose something, whether in the short term or the long run. The only difference between one decision and another is how likely it is to go either way. It's just like we've been talking about. The situation here is getting worse and worse, right? So doing nothing is the biggest gamble of all. We could lose everything, and even in the best-case scenario, we'll just go back to the same pointless routine. Sure, going to see Rashana is a risk too, but we don't have all that much to lose to begin with and if we guess right we have so much to gain. She could help us get the answers we need and find justice, maybe help Xenocyst somehow—there's obviously no way to make a difference here, you can see that. She might even set us up with normal lives when this is all over. So don't you think we should just take the plunge and go see her as soon as we can? I mean, I just don't see what you're stalling for."

Rick exhaled audibly, seemingly on purpose.

Amon waited for him to speak.

" . . . "

"Rick?"

"You act like everything would be so much better if we went back to the Free World! And yes, I want to eat! I'm hungry and I don't like what's going on here one bit. But will it make any difference if we cross back there? We're still going to be in this shitty world, contributing to this shitty system, so what would it matter?"

Amon looked in the direction of his friend's voice but the darkness of the room revealed no more of his friend's mind than it had before, as rain began to patter and hiss somewhere several layers of building away. He was shocked to hear Rick speak like this. While he had always harbored a brooding sadness in his eyes that sometimes seeped into his character, and he seemed to be struggling with the constant lack more than Amon since he had not cultivated his frugal willpower, Rick had always approached life's many challenges, in both the Free World and the District of Dreams, with bold, sometimes wanton, optimism. Clearly something here had changed him, and Amon wasn't sure what that was, but decided, for his own reasons, that he could relate.

"I understand how you feel, Rick," said Amon, reaching out from under his blanket and putting a hand on his friend's warm, damp shoulder. "There was a period of time when I first arrived at Xenocyst that I was almost ready to . . . well, kill myself. And I don't think I'm totally over it even now. I used to be worried that one of our targets might recognize me and try to get me back for liquidating them. They would have only seen my digimade face for at most a split second, hardly long enough to remember, but what if my face was burned in the memory of some of them because of their trauma in that moment or something? What would happen if I ran into one of them? It was a scary thought then because I was still feeling the webloss and didn't know my way around, and I would have been pretty helpless if one of them tried something.

"Then we met Barrow and he actually did recognize me. His cash crash was unique because I hesitated and actually talked to him for a while. Unlike all the others, he had time to commit me to memory. I'm guessing it was my voice as much as my appearance that called it all back for him, because I hardly resemble my former self at all without digimake. But even if that was a total fluke, the fact that one target recognized me proves in principle that others could too. My paranoia was justified! So you'd think I'd be even more afraid than before. But that's not how I feel at all. Just the opposite . . .

"I've stopped worrying they might recognize me. Maybe you'll think this is crazy, but now I'm so guilty I sometimes hope that they do. So whenever I see a face that carries that familiar feeling and their eyes meet mine, it always seems like their gaze lingers over my face too long. And in the moments when I really just hate myself completely, I see our targets lurking everywhere, hiding in shadows and little nooks, just waiting for the right moment to ambush me . . . and I want them to do it so bad, to strangle me or bash my skull in, blow my head off, and soon I'm imagining all these different ways they might repay me . . .

"I know this is morbid. What I'm trying to say is that I understand how you feel about wanting to give up. But isn't the fact that this place makes us feel this way all the more reason to get out as soon as we can? We can't just let the weight of being here crush our spirits. We've got to go, Rick. Let's go!"

"Amon," said Rick, shaking Amon's hand off his shoulder. "You're misunderstanding me, so let me be clear. I'm not saying that life is pointless in general, though maybe it is. What I'm saying is, I don't want to go back anymore. You have your promise to the PhisherKing and your questions about jubilee and your desire for justice and all that. And I don't want to discourage you, but I just don't share your curiosity or your faith . . . Maybe life in the Free World will be more comfortable, for you . . . for both of us I guess . . . but what's left for me there? Now that I see how it all works, there's just nowhere for me to go, and nothing for me to work towards. At least here we have friends and our relationships with them don't cost even a single hundredth of a yen. These people took us in and taught us and gave us everything we need. I have no illusions that we can save their souls in the way Hippo expects of us—I know you agree that his hopes for us are beyond unrealistic. Still, if there's any way for us to make up for what we've done, it's by supporting those around us in any way we can, in little ways if that's all were capable of, not by running away when the going gets tough and chasing after vague dreams and ideals."

Suddenly Amon remembered Vertical's story and what she had said about focusing on the day-to-day. Could Amon accept it? Could Rick and Vertical be right?

"So where's the really good reason that balances out the risk of meeting Rashana?" Rick demanded. "Why should I take the gamble? It's not worth it."

Because Mayuko is going to be waiting there for us, safe and sound, Amon wanted to shout, but bit his lip. For he knew that even if the unconfirmed third-hand story meant what he wanted to believe it meant, Mayuko wasn't going to be there for Rick in the way that *he* wanted. Definitely as a friend, but not as the lover and mother of the child he desired. She had expressed her feelings for Amon, and telling Rick would only add new cracks to his already fractured sense of purpose, perhaps shatter it completely. Not only would it mean the death of his only aspiration—to start a family with Mayuko—but it had the potential to drive Amon and Rick further apart when they needed each other more than ever.

Then suddenly a flicker of clarity came to Amon like a firefly springing to life in the darkness, and he realized how selfish he was being, keeping his mendacious silence to ensure that Rick stayed by his side. Wasn't it this very deception that was driving them apart anyways? Wasn't every second he delayed just prying the rift between them wider? Now was the time to speak, the time for truth.

Amon opened his mouth to say something when a *shooshing* crack and rumble of earth, air, and water all at once announced the typhoon's resurgence. The rains began to whip and the slum was pried first one way then the next under the gale, each shaft creaking as it wrenched to the limit, each room quaking violently as they all bashed rattling into their neighbors. Spray fizzed in through all the cracks with a great hissing roar as though the sky itself were smashing down on them. No longer safe to recline on the floor, they got to their feet and clung to each other with their blankets wrapped around them, cold water pooling at their feet as they combined their warmth to fend off the wet chill that subsumed them.

For the next few hours, they spent most of their energy trying to stay on their feet as sudden blasts hurled them about, careful not to collide with each other bone to bone and sustain injuries. Shivering through the night with their skin touching, Amon had never been so physically close to his friend and felt their hearts drawn together like never before, warding off the misery of that night with their shared flesh and love. They might not have been able to agree in words, but their bodies were in agreement that they were still friends.

At the same time, Amon could sense something in his mind that stubbornly resisted their full communion, and knew it was his secrets— an invisible but unbreakable dividing power like the membrane that sometimes separated his two selves in his dream. *I'm sorry Rick*, Amon whispered to himself too faintly to be heard above the din as he embraced the fragile quivering being that was his friend in the night. *I'm sorry.*

16
THE COUNCIL CHAMBER

Bedding 10%, incubators 13%, antibiotics 12%, catheters 8% . . ." Sitting to the left of Hippo at one end of the council circle, Book read off a list of supplies and how much they had been reduced since the previous month, prompted by the tapping of Little Book on Hippo's right. "Bandages 9%, disinfectant 11%, intravenous fluid 9% . . ."

Amon sat with Rick outside the circle near the back right corner of the room, listening to Book's dry enunciation as the last few councilors came in through the door and took their spots on the floor. An inspector stood just inside the threshold and waved a small wand over the body of each person entering. It occasionally let off pulses of bluish light, disabling any electronic devices they might be carrying—even dormant ones that could not be seen by the naked eye—so they would not be purposefully or accidentally carried in. In combination with the nanodevices that warded off PanoptiRoaches, this completed the digital quarantine and Amon felt grateful for Tamper's work, as privacy had never been more important than it was that day, given the dire topic they would soon broach.

"Thank you for your report," said Hippo when Book had finished, sweeping his gaze slowly around the room to acknowledge the presence of everyone in attendance. Ty and Vertical sat facing each other inside the circle. With no applicants to oversee, the usual guards were not with them. The inspector bowed to the circle once the final councilor had been checked and departed, leaving about fifteen people in total in the room, including Amon. The wood floor was cold on his buttocks and heels as he sat with his knees propped up, feeling a chill creep up his spine. Yet he didn't let this uncomfortable sensation trouble him, not any more than his hunger or exhaustion. Mostly, he was just glad to be there, and to be included, even if only at the periphery, in the momentous choices they confronted.

"Now that we're all assembled," Hippo continued, "let us move on to the main issue at hand. I have called this emergency council today to discuss the future of Xenocyst. As the Books' data illustrates, the quantity of our supplies has been dropping steadily since the first day of fall. We have dealt with supply fluctuations in the past and this has sometimes forced us to re-negotiate our terms with the venture charities to secure what we needed. But this time their representatives deny that any such drop is occurring and obstinately refuse our requests for negotiation. Moreover, the reduction is much greater than we have ever experienced before, to the degree that our capacity to provide medical assistance and basic administration is being severely challenged.

"While our internal conditions deteriorate in this way, escalating conflict with the Opportunity Scientists is further straining our resources. Under pressure from the OpScis, several of our proxy enclaves have already defected, including most notably the TriTinkers. Other southwestern collectives such as the CrestBloods have been toppled and occupied. With the situation so precarious, it is difficult to know who to trust. The number of reported kidnappings coming from those territories that still call us their ally increase by the day. Although we have stuck to the policy of forbidding our residents from wearing branded clothes outside the walls of Xenocyst to discourage this from happening to our own, the Opportunity Scientists seem willing to take anybody now, on the off chance they might be gifted and have supply privileges that can be milked. None of our sources can confirm what is motivating the Quantitative Priesthood to pursue such aggression, but the desperation with which they seek supplies makes it clear that they are suffering from shortages as well. In fact, the reductions seem to apply to the entire District of Dreams. True, they have been less extreme for the gifted, but this only deepens plutogenic lines. Unfortunately, we suspect that, due to increasing tension between our gifted and giftless residents, a gifted exodus to the Triangle has already begun. This is the most worrisome development of all. While the exodus may have freed up more space in our compound, it has left us with even less hands to assist with our already patchy defense and illustrates that morale is dropping within our ranks. Already rumors have reached my ears of secret cells discontent with our ruling order. I do not know how imminent or likely it is that they will act. Nevertheless, their movement is not something we can ignore. If we cannot maintain solidarity here and these trends continue, the fate of Xenocyst is obvious."

Hippo paused to sweep his urgent gaze slowly across the assembly before continuing.

"Although no one has been able to determine exactly why the supplies are dropping, clearly the Philanthropy Syndicate is cutting back on its investment here for whatever reason. From what we've gathered from our sources, including a crashnewb recently interviewed by the Books, this is related to the political situation in Free Tokyo. Would you mind filling us in, Books?"

"We have been aware for a considerable length of time," said Book, *tap-tatap-tap* . . . "that GATA has been affected by a coup d'état. Former Chief Executive Minister Lawrence Barrow, who is present in the chamber tonight"—Book's uneven eyes flicked to the left corner of the room at the back across from Amon and Rick, drawing the gaze of several councilors along with it. Amon too looked over and saw Barrow sitting on his shins with his hands folded in his lap—"was recently ID assassinated in the preliminary phase prior to an election. Moreover, one of the members of his cabinet, former Minister of Records Shota Kitao, who is currently rumored to be a Lab Reverend, was subject to cash crash only the previous day. Subsequently, both men were portrayed as perverts in media reports as one component of a campaign to undermine the credibility of the Moderate Choice party to which they belonged. The preceding is all news we have reported previously. More recently, we have learned via interviews with an incoming crashnewb that an extreme right faction of the Moderate Choice party led by the Minister of Liquidation, Yoshiyuki Sekido, has splintered off to form its own party, Full Choice, in response to the scandals, thereby dividing the Moderate Choice party immediately prior to the election. As the leader of the the remnants of the Moderate Choice Party, Yoshino Sawanoi, has proven himself extremely inarticulate, Absolute Choice was thereafter able to increase its share of votes significantly in the election. However, it nonetheless failed to secure the majority of seats and was consequently forced to partner with Full Choice in forming a new coalition government.

"Due to our new crashnewb source's high level of affluence until shortly prior to her liquidation, she enjoyed access to gold search engines and was able to tell us with a high degree of certainty that this new coalition government has been enacting policies that are connected to the supply quantity shift. Rather than legislate Absolute Choice's campaign promises, including privatization of urination, defecation, and heartbeating, the ruling party instead moved firstly to reduce a particular set of credicrime fines. This policy is not particularly surprising in and of itself, as it is consistent with both Absolute Choice's and Full Choice's avowed fiscal conservatism. Their lobbydealogy perceives any decrease in disincentives on performing criminal actions as an increase in total freedom. However, the fact that the fine reduction was not universal *is* surprising. According to the crashnewb's account, the party only reduced fines for crimes within an exceedingly narrow category, namely crowdcare and the like, including *semi-lethal assault*, *corralling*, *CareBot operation*, and *mass intimidation*. This is the extent of the information we have at this juncture."

Little Book's tapping stopped, Book gave a slight bow where he sat, and Hippo took over. "Last night we assembled a committee to discuss these findings, so allow me to tell you our conclusion about the relation between these political developments and the Philanthropy Syndicate slash on investment in supplies. The Syndicate seems to maintain peace and stability in the camps by keeping a balance between generosity and ferocity. The venture charities provide enough supplies to make us bankdead relatively contented, which works as an incentive towards complacent good behavior. The Charity Brigade implements violent responses severe enough to make us afraid to lose the contentment we have, which works as a disincentive towards dissent; the fewer supplies we get, the less we have to lose and the more worthwhile it will seem to resist. The Syndicate is aware that with less being given out, the bankdead are more likely to riot and that the Charity Brigade will need to utilize more crowdcare in response. Such violence would incur credicrime fines greater than the revenue saved from reducing supplies and lead in turn to a loss of profit, if not for the reduction in crowdcare-related credicrimes. Therefore, it is clear that the rise of Absolute Choice and their reduction of these fines is what is making the supply reduction possible, and that the change in government was orchestrated by the Syndicate in advance to realize this. To be more specific, the change seems to have been orchestrated by Syndicate executives working together with Anisha Birla.

"This partnership between the heads of the Syndicate MegaGloms and the head of Fertilex has been called the Gyges Circle. The GATA coup d'état they funded must have been astronomically expensive, so they no doubt have a well-plotted agenda that justifies such expenditures, although we know nothing more about them at the moment and have yet to guess at their motives. However, I have not called this meeting to inquire into the whys of it all. We are here to discuss the how. How can we respond to our current predicament and keep Xenocyst, this great community we have all built together, from falling apart? I wish I had a brilliant proposal to make, but I'm afraid this quandary goes far beyond my wits. Xenocyst has done much for the bankdead here and continues to do so in spite of what the Philanthropy Syndicate did to us. Mothers, infants, orphans, and others who have been neglected are safer, healthier, and more autonomous in spite of the education and contraceptive restrictions placed on us. Hundreds of thousands depend on us and it would be irresponsible of us to let them down. So let's open this up to the floor. All ideas are welcome. What do you all think we should do?"

The past few weeks leading up to this meeting had been tough for everyone, no less so for Rick and Amon. The air was getting colder, the daylight hours were shrinking, and the sky had been covered in clouds for so long that Amon almost wished another typhoon would come just to have the one clear, sunny day that always followed. Amidst chill and gloom, the vendors had gone from dispensing five meals every two days to two per day, and Amon felt consistently weak and hungry, his eyes taking on wills of their own to jitter anxiously across every vista that confronted him in search of food; even crumbs would have been welcome. With more and more buildings collapsing and further medical equipment shortages, Amon and Rick's reproductive waste disposal and undertaker responsibilities began to blur into each other, with many pregnant women, as well as babies and children, no longer able to hold on.

In the hospital, he noticed that they were serving mothers a mash of their own placentas for a bit of extra nutrition in their depleted state. At the same time, as there was no longer enough water flow for thorough cleaning, the floor in the hallways were covered in a layer of scuff-marked grit, the walls mucked with handprints. With less PeelKlean coming in, even patients were starting to look visibly dirty and the stench of body odor filled the wards as much as the jam-packed byways outside. On his various errands, Amon often spotted kids with distended bellies, and even those that looked better nourished seemed little interested in flying kites or playing games anymore, though he continued to see gangs on sprees of bullying and senseless destruction.

The storytelling circles were nowhere to be seen, and the sounds of lovemaking around Amon's room no longer woke him at night—though the swelling racket of crows sometimes did. These scavengers, who had always remained hidden in the heights, now seemed to crowd every perch. They stayed well out of reach but close enough to watch the crowds, as if expectant of an opportunity to swoop in. Frail figures could be seen huddling together in almost every available nook and shelf, fending off the cold in the open now that embyrbryck stocks and room replacements were dwindling. Although city planning in Xenocyst made traffic smoother, certain stretches of the lower passages were so crowded it was nearly impossible to move along them, while the external enclaves Amon crossed on patrol and supply runs were crushes of grimacing heads and flailing limbs, each body squirming and clawing just to shuffle one step down an alley. Even the Road to Delivery and its many branches, usually tended by the Charity Brigade and CareBots, were becoming so perilously clogged as to be nearly useless. This delayed people from acquiring new roombuds, which forced more onto the ground floor and led to more crowding, creating a vicious cycle.

The sign that conditions were approaching their nadir was that even crashborn denizens like Ty and Book, who always hid their emotions behind a grim deadpan, were beginning to look fearful and distraught. Vertical's multi-directional sprints were noticeably slower, and Hippo, who usually remained in the Council Chamber, could be seen pacing the hallways of the Cyst, his shoulders slouched in defeat, his eyes wide with indignant disbelief, his jaw set, tight breaths squeezed from his nostrils as he frowned with such intensity his thoughts seemed to radiate from his brow like a vague flame of jumbled words. Even when Amon walked right past him, Hippo didn't notice he was there, and when Amon had said hello one evening, he had only given him the faintest mumbled sound in response, as though he lacked the will even for simple greetings.

With no mirrors except the one in the council chamber reserved for screenings, Amon began to take Rick as his reflection, since they had both crashed at nearly the same time, and he watched as their appearance deteriorated in tandem. While on the day of their reunion Rick had been a bit skinnier than in their Free World days, now he was properly gaunt, his skin grayish pale and drawn tight to his cheek bones, his eyes bulging somewhat from his taut face, his once intentionally mussed hair now shaggy and knotted; his bulky, muscled arms and legs stringy and lean, bulging veins running from his hands to his shoulders. Amon could sense that the same changes had come over himself when he patted his own body in the privacy of their room, his once neatly shaved head a cauliflower top of frizz, his torso now grooved with divots beside his ribs that he could fit his pinky into. Meal replacement ink was advertised to provide all essential nutrients, but clearly they weren't hitting the minimum quantity, and lying in hungry torpor on his floor at night Amon sometimes imagined his meager flesh sliding right off his bones, leaving a bare skeleton that soon dried and crumbled into white dust, blowing off in the wind with the rest of the city.

When Vertical brought word that Hippo was inviting him and Rick to the next council, Amon was happier than he could remember feeling in a long time, as it would give his voice a chance to be heard. Not that Amon had any grand solutions in mind, but if he could contribute something, anything, to the discussion, it might lighten the leaden ball of helplessness in the pit of his stomach that seemed to grow heavier with each passing hour.

After Hippo had set up the conundrum for everyone, there was a minute of fraught silence where the councilors looked back and forth at each other to see who might be the first to speak.

"I've got a proposal," said Yané, his gray-streaked beard puffed up to an unruly bramble. "We get more women to gift their babies. That way we reduce hungry mouths and boost individual supplies just like that. Plus it'd send a message to the charities that Xenocyst is a rich mine for resources. Then our negotiations—"

"Are you suggesting we force mothers to sell their babies?" said Jiku, the woman with the clam-shell face Amon had met at the equinox festival. "Who are we to order them around on such a sacred choice? And how on earth would we decide who makes the sacrifice?"

"On the assumption that this is a proposal the council deems worthy of serious consideration," said Book, "perhaps we could make the selection by lot. Practically speaking, this would require producing a roll call of all the women who do not wish to gift voluntarily and marking those who are requested to procure one baby so that they will be exempt from procuring the next."

"All of them could be made to gift," said Yané. "Parents with marketable babies only raise them here 'cause of our standard of living, but that's dropping fast. Unless we cut back on hungry mouths. So giving them away is what's best for all of us—the parents, the babies *and* the community."

"Taking that choice from parents is monstrous!" Jiku exclaimed. "We'd be no better than OpScis. And there's no guarantee that the charities will increase our supplies. We might violate Xenocyst's core principles and still end up no better off than we are now."

The two councilors sat staring at each other with intensity. Yané's cheek twitched a few times as though he was going to speak, but he never opened his lips.

"Fine. So we have two proposals now," said Hippo. "Force some mothers to gift by lot or force all of them. I think we've heard a few arguments for and against. Does anyone have anything to add to this particular discussion?" There was no response from the circle. "Then let's put this aside and see if we have any other suggestions."

Again heads and eyes rotated. When no one spoke, they settled facing straight ahead, some staring at the floor. Throat-clearing, swallowing, and the rustle of dissolving clothes reigned until Ty said, "How about we try the opposite?" A circle of necks craned towards him. "How about we refuse to give up any resources at all? And not just in Xenocyst. We'll partner up with our allies and as many other enclaves as we can get. Then the charities get nothing until we get steady shipments."

"A human resource embargo?" Vertical scowled in disbelief. "Good luck maintaining cooperation with that! All the charities have to do is toss us a few scraps of useful materials and we'll be snarling at each other like hungry wolves."

"With the new weapons we've got, it doesn't have to be a request," said Ty, reaching around to grip a wheel for effect. "We can make it an order."

"And push more of our allies onto the OpSci side? All that does is leave us isolated from other enclaves. Then we'll be facing the Brigade alone with even less supplies than we have now."

"I agree with Vertical," said a man with a grating voice at the rear of the circle. Amon could see a horseshoe-shaped bald spot on the back of his head. "If Ty's plan goes wrong, those slum-free-world people could show up at the gates of Xenocyst tomorrow. We'll be demolished! Crunched into nothing! Then what will we have achieved?

Ty just hung his head, wearing an unconvinced smirk, and said nothing.

After a few scattered coughs, Hippo said, "Alright. Do we have any more ideas?"

"Tip-a-tap. Yes taptataptap," said/tapped the Books. "I do not believe this qualifies as a solution, per se. However, in the short term, I propose that we permanently dismantle the library."

The entire room stopped breathing, the muffled *rakhaws* of crows outside filling the silence like an underworld choir, while Book and Little Book just sat there impassively taking in the crowd with their tired, studious eyes.

"What's that?" said Ty, raising his weathered forehead to give them a hard stare.

"I can surmise precisely how surprised you all must be to hear me of all people putting forth this recommendation, as I have long defended the utility of the library," said Book *ta-taptap*. "However, as you are all aware, we are sorely deficient in space. Without some means to alleviate lower floor population congestion, some of our buildings will need to be demolished to make room for foot traffic, and our existing structures will have to be built higher. However, the former will only exacerbate the problem and the latter will be a significant strain on those living on the upper floors, as calories are already critically under-provided. Whatever urban planning strategy we employ, we are approaching an overcrowding crisis. I am proposing that we begin with the library, as it is the most precious area to me personally. My hope is that others will follow my example by making changes they find undesirable to accommodate everyone else. In the future, we might perhaps consider downsizing the hospital and diverting the running water we have specially piped in for medical purposes into a storage tank in case the feeding station beverages are depleted any further. Our books might also be traded for supplies to nosties, some of whom may value such items more than a meal. If there is no demand, then we will have plenty of fuel to keep ourselves warm during the upcoming winter."

The *rakhaw*-filled silence returned as most of the councilors stared with looks of perplexed astonishment at Book, and Amon remembered the passion in his voice when he had spoken of education after tea, no better able than anyone else to process such words coming from his mouth. But three heads were nodding in agreement and Amon wanted to call out *Come on! You can't actually support this!* Yet his feeling of indignation was so strong he couldn't gather his thoughts to produce convincing counterarguments and would have been too shy to speak out as a first-time guest if he could have. So he remained simmering in the corner, thinking how perverse it was that the idea of trading babies had become so normal that he'd hardly blinked at the previous proposal while wanting so intensely now to save something that only a few months earlier he had thought was entirely worthless.

Amon had recently been spending most of his evenings in the library. With Rick rarely around, calories too few for climbing to stargazing platforms, and the compound too dark at night for wandering now that the remaining stock of firefLytes had been distributed around the border to assist the night watch, Amon's options for passing the time after work were limited, and this was the best one remaining.

He continued to pick up *Woman in the Dunes*. For the first week or so, the text still looked like incomprehensible runes. Nevertheless, he found the process of turning the pages and scanning their rows of alien scrawls inexplicably addictive. And strangely, when he recalled the act of reading afterwards, images would arise behind his eyelids, as though some subliminal dimension of his mind were absorbing the meaning even though he wasn't conscious of it in the moment.

In this way, he "read" *Woman in the Dunes* several times. He would stand still in the aisle between the shelves, holding the book open in both hands until his feet ached and the faces of the readers browsing around him had all been replaced. Soon he could imagine the entire story from beginning to end and somehow knew that Kobo Abe had written it, though he still couldn't see this name on the cover. He was even able to recall specific phrases word for word. One in particular kept resurfacing in his recollection:

> *The man's eyes began to sting. Neither tears nor blinks could fend off all the relentlessly falling sand.*

The novel was about a man imprisoned with a woman at the bottom of a pit in a sand dune, forced to shovel the sand that is constantly encroaching. Only by performing this endless, utterly unproductive task can he prevent the sand from burying them alive and earn food and water from the locals while struggling against the seductions of the woman, with whom he might produce a baby that would tie him to that place. To Amon, this scenario seemed like a perfect metaphor for life in the bankdeath camps generally, and this quote in particular felt personally significant. He often ruminated over it at length while lying on the floor of his room before sleep while Rick was away, feeling sad and helpless but oddly consoled, as it reassured him that others, at the very least the protagonist, shared suffering like his.

Then one evening he entered the library and found he could read the spines and covers of all the books. Though the pages of the dozen or so he picked up and consulted remained an inscrutable wash of lines and squiggles, it was not long before they too began to resolve into the ideograms and phonetic characters he was used to. A few visits after he reached this stage, these began to coalesce into words, then words into whole phrases, and eventually phrases into paragraphs, as though day after day he were adjusting to a voice in a crowd. Soon he discovered a certain way of looking at the page that would make the script take on a discernible shape and order, like 3D pictures.

Though he had little patience to read more than half a chapter at first, slowly he began to sample sections of various documents. The selection may have been limited, but Amon's progress was gradual and so to him it seemed inexhaustible. He took stabs at various novels, short stories, poems, and plays from Japan, both ancient and pre-Free Era, as well as translations from here and there. He briefly experimented with non-fiction and a few textbooks, but found it frustrating that they had not been updated in some cases for decades, rather than in real-time as they should have been.

It was confusing to him that the content in the library was organized by type of medium and author's name rather than by price, as it had been with the gold, silver, and bronze search engines. Such arbitrary ordering seemed as good as a senseless jumble, for without any indication of each unit of information's market value there appeared to be no way of guessing at its quality, as determined by the endorsement of specialists, intelligent demand, and other objective factors. But soon he realized that the equality and accessibility of information was presenting a challenge to him. While alphabetization was admittedly arbitrary, it was also egalitarian. Available to all who might reach out their hands for them, the books were asking him to decide for himself what their value was, to sort and stratify them in his own mind, to accept the responsibility born by all autonomous agents of endowing signals from others with an interpretation and evaluation that only their unique consciousness can provide.

Before bankdeath, he had considered himself literate—fairly uncommon in the Free World, where many got by purely on video and audio. But he was used to short, pithy articles, clickbaity listicles, fragmented blogs, and jumpy webchat that read themselves to him if he grew tired and were equipped with explanatory hyperlinks or songs, sound effects, and animations that played when he scrolled to a particular passage. The thick volumes of the library filled margin to margin with inert script felt dead to him. Though he could skim them rapidly, he struggled with careful reading, which many of the books, because of the careful way they were written, demanded. To draw out the meaning of each line and the interlinking nuance buried between them, he had to learn how to ponder, an intellectual effort that taxed his focus all the more now that he was hungry, and he never managed to finish another book.

Nonetheless, Amon derived such fulfillment from the bits and pieces he could parse that he began to wonder why he'd never discovered this pleasure before, and it wasn't long before he realized the answer. It was the scarcity of information that made it precious—not as a rare mineral goes up in price as supply decreases, but the way gold only shows its authentic glinting majesty to the eye in darkness. Plenty, it seemed, had flooded his mind with a great torrent that drowned out the significance of each drop, the constant effort to find signal amidst all the noise numbing him to the importance of deeper content while reducing media consumption to an unconscious and automatic cost-benefit metric, a frantic scramble for that which provided the most concentrated jolt of truthiness and entertainment in the shortest span of time. Everything else had to be dismissed as banal, irrelevant, cognitively toxic. A mind so attuned, he now understood, could never grasp the pleasure of literature, with its gradual accumulation of polysemic complexity and ambiguity that took hours, days, and sometimes weeks to culminate. Although he was still learning to immerse himself in this way, he found the effort rewarding and sometimes enthralling, until his brain chugged gradually to a halt and all he could do was stagger home to sleep.

The library was his refuge from the boredom, absurdity, and misery of his life. It seemed to open the way towards answering his many questions and fulfilling his promise to the PhisherKing. It was the sole bastion against the ignorance that had made so many unwitting pawns of the powers that be. And while Amon might have agreed it should be trashed back when he had little respect for nosties, the mere suggestion now seemed like a personal attack, and so he felt fully vindicated when Hippo leapt in to its defense.

"Well," said a middle-aged man on the left side of the circle with big round cheeks that were freckled so thickly he looked spotted with tiny gum wads. "I for one second—"

"I couldn't disagree more," cut in Hippo, his eyes wide and challenging. "I know there are those of you who have long petitioned to get rid of the library and I'm sure you agree with Book, but I will do everything in my power as special advisor to stop this. The closing of the library is to me synonymous with the death of Xenocyst. Since the Philanthropy Syndicate has coerced us into shutting our schools, we need a place to learn and educate ourselves. Yes, we have other arts here—our skyscraper comics and reliefs, our embyrsculptures and cinderworks, our music—and these are of supreme value for giving our residents just that much more reason to exist. But here, behind the Digital Divide, books offer us the only way to have sustained dialog with minds and epochs and cultures beyond what is familiar to us. Without such dialog, we are doomed to lose the knowledge and know-how that sets us apart from our peers and rivals in the District of Dreams. If we're going to let that slip away, we might as well just give up now."

"But we must prepare for the worst," said Yané. "If the crowding get any thicker, what do we do? Tell residents without rooms to test their luck outside? No one reads anyways!"

Three heads nodded.

"Abandoning the library only postpones the problem," said Hippo. "If the decrease in roombuds continues at this rate, overcrowding will reach critical levels. But once the library is gone we'll have no more spaces to sacrifice."

"How about this chamber? The helipad? The storage floors?" demanded the freckled man. "Nothing can be sacred anymore. We must do everything we can to hold together!"

"It may be that delaying the inevitable is the best we are capable of in the present situation," said Book, bringing all breaths to a standstill once more.

Only the *rakhaw* of crows could be heard until a sonorous voice said, "May I contribute something to the discussion?" Amon looked along the back wall to the opposite side where Barrow knelt, his back straight and his broad shoulders raised just as in his former days as the great leader Amon had admired. The entire council had turned towards him as one, those on the left side of the circle twisting their torsos and craning their necks, called to attention by the music of his words.

Over the past few weeks, Amon had observed Barrow ingratiating himself rapidly into the community. A lover of anadeto, he could be seen in the library chatting with Book about the collection and perusing the shelves. From what Vertical had told him, Barrow had already rotated through several jobs, earning high praise from his supervisors and co-workers, and Amon spotted him soon after talking with Hippo in the Cyst hallway, a sign of just how high his respect was rising. He had even witnessed Ty allow Barrow to touch the gears of his tricycle while they were chatting on a rooftop at night, Ty's hatred for anyone with connections to the OpScis forgotten in their mutual appreciation for old mechanisms.

While all other storytelling gatherings had degenerated into glum, irritable, muttering affairs and eventually dispersed, the one Barrow attended was still going strong and actually seemed to be growing. On the way to his room after work, Amon continued to spot him at the center of the group, listening and laughing and sometimes patting one of the other men or women on the back with a smile.

Amon guessed that part of the reason for his instant acceptance was general gratitude for the equipment he'd provided, as it was generally recognized that Xenocyst would have already been overrun by the OpScis without it. No doubt his innate charisma and work ethic had played a major role as well.

Initially, Amon kept his distance from Barrow, assuming that he would never forget what Amon had done to him despite his help liberating him from the Opportunity Scientists, and feeling ashamed to be in his presence. But one night, when Amon was passing by such a gathering, Barrow called him over and invited him to join. Unable to refuse this offer of reconciliation, Amon took a spot across from Barrow and watched him guide the conversation with his firm but personable aura. Under his influence, everyone was eager to contribute and the speakers seemed to summon the faith and cheer they had possessed in brighter days.

When others told tales, even intriguing ones, there would always be a few people whispering here and there. When Barrow spoke, everyone was hypnotized—his husky-blue eyes sparkling with exuberance as they seemed to look at everyone in the audience at once, and yet made Amon feel they were somehow directed specifically at him. Barrow clearly had a talent for languages, as he was already fluent in Hinkongo after only studying the basics in banklife (to make rooting out anadeto in the camps easier) and speaking it for the past few months since his bankdeath. During a lull, Barrow had asked Amon to share the story of his cash crash and Amon had accepted despite his great tiredness that night. Though Amon's words didn't seem to enthrall the group like Barrow's did, everyone still gave him their full attention from start to finish, and Barrow's gaze never wavered, as though he were eager to understand and grow closer to Amon.

"You do know what the unique character of your cash crash means, don't you?" said Barrow after Amon was finished and the audience was sitting quietly, digesting his tale.

Amon thought for a moment. "Hippo once pointed out that, because I was never liquidated, I still have the bankdeath codes. Is that what you mean?"

"Not exactly. What I'm thinking of is the fact that your genome was never deregistered even though you still retain your BodyBank."

"I guess that's true. But I'm not seeing how it's important."

"Well, first of all, I'm confident that you can trust Rashana. Through Atupio, she strived to raise bankdead self-sufficiency by supporting organizations like Xenocyst, so it's impossible for me to believe that she would try to eliminate me, as my redistribution policies were perfectly in line with that objective. In other words, I don't believe for a second that Rashana funded the Gyges Circle, and now that I know you committed ID suicide I would urge you to meet with her."

"Why? Do you think she can help me get out of here?"

"The chances are very slim, but in your case not impossible. As you know, the only viable way to live in the Free World is as a Free Citizen, and usually the sole gateway to becoming one is for marketable babies."

During Liquidator training, Amon had learned that only babies under the age of one could have their genome registered with the Ministry of Access, only those so registered could use a training bank and acquire a BodyBank when they reached twenty, and only those with a BodyBank could receive an identity signature from an Identity Vitalator. These requirements were strictly maintained, as any attempt to register the DNA of someone of the wrong age, surgically install a BodyBank in someone under twenty years old, or give an ID signature to someone unregistered all warranted the bankdeath penalty.

"The GATA system also rejects any DNA that has been deregistered, so crashdead don't have the slightest chance of getting back their Body-Bank—I'm speaking, of course, of identity rebirth. Only if someone gave up their banklife for someone else could this be possible, and good luck convincing someone to agree to that.

"But you and Hippo are in a slightly different category than other crashdead. Since you cash crashed without being liquidated, your genomes were never deregistered, so you are both in the unique position of being registered BodyBank wearers over twenty that happen to have no ID signature. Theoretically, this means that you might use a training bank if someone leashed you and paid for all your actions, and since you kept your BodyBanks you could acquire a new ID signature if someone convinced an ID Vitalator to give you one. All the bribes, fines, and bureaucratic string-pulling would be enormously expensive, so Hippo would have no chance. But for you? Perhaps Rashana might be willing to pay. She certainly does take a special interest in you that is rare for the Birlas."

Amon was reminded that Barrow had started out his career as a Liquidator and then Identity Exectioner like Amon, but clearly his expertise in the liquidation system had been sharpened by his years of administrative experience at the higher levels of GATA as Amon had been unable to put together the implications of his situation in this way. While Amon had thought of leaving the District of Dreams in a vague, hopeful sort of way, this was the first time it seemed truly possible, and immediately he felt his breath quicken with excitement, seeing that Barrow's assessment was correct.

"Thank you," said Amon with a slight bow. "What you've told me gives me new hope."

"It's the least I can do."

Amon frowned quizzically at Barrow. "Why? You don't owe me anything."

Barrow locked his eyes with Amon's. "You must understand," he said, "that part of me still bears a grudge against you for what you did to me."

"Yes, of course."

"But I'm doing my best to forgive you in light of what you did for me. If it hadn't been you who assassinated me, it would have been some other chump, no offense intended. Here, you gave me another chance, and no one else could have done that. Why else do you think I would have called you over tonight?"

"I appreciate that."

"No. There's no need for gratitude. We have more important issues than grudges. There's the Opportunity Scientists and the supply shortages. Friction between our members will only wear us down when what we need more than anything is our strength.

"So I can't promise I'll ever fully forgive you. What you stole from me was far too precious. But won't you join with me in letting bygones be bygones?" Barrow said, extending his hand. "We can work together for our own sakes, for the sake of Xenocyst, and for the sake of all bankdead."

Recently, Amon had heard Hippo refer to Lawrence Barrow affectionately as Larry-kun, and now he had invited him to the council even though he was still on a trial period. Amon wasn't surprised that Barrow was getting along well with Hippo. Both were adept leaders in their own way and seemed to share similar concerns for the welfare of bankdead. It relieved him to see that he had come so far so quickly, for he deserved to have success, to have exactly what Amon had taken from him . . .

"By all means, please tell us what you have to say," said Hippo. "All opinions are welcome here."

"Thank you kindly. Let me begin by saying how much I appreciate your allowing me to be here at this council and to speak before you on this most dire occasion. As most of you know, I was an OpSci slave for several months and it was only by your good graces that I escaped my bondage and was accepted into this great community. I am forever in debt to your kindness and cannot express how grateful I am for the chance to attend today."

Barrow held the circle with his husky-blue eyes and bowed his head to the floor. He remained prostrate for a few beats, sat up straight, waited another moment to gather their gazes again, and continued. "Now then, my proposal concerns the OpScis. Having spent time living in close quarters with them, I know first-hand just what they're like. The superstitions they use to justify their plutogenic castes; the slavery and the deception of those blind followers they milk for supplies; the farming of women and the rape incorporated into their rituals; the human sacrifice they perform in the name of salvation in the Free World; and although I have not witnessed it myself, there are rumors of cannibalism that I don't doubt for a second. I'm sure we all agree how despicable it is that the venture charities cooperate with this sick cult. The Opportunity Scientists should never have been allowed to exist for as long as they have, and certainly not to flourish as they do now in spite of the shortages."

Barrow paused for just long enough that Amon felt almost unbearably eager to hear what he had to say next.

"But now we have a chance to right this injustice. We have the weapons, we have the personnel, we have the strategic knowledge, and we can be certain of the support of our residents in this grim crisis. The time has come to declare an all-out war on the OpScis and destroy Opportunity Peaks once and for all. Then we can form a coalition with all the enclaves that remain to strengthen our bargaining position as Ty has proposed, and if the Philanthropy Syndicate wants resources, they'll have to come to us."

A few heads nodded slightly in agreement, but everyone else was frozen, stunned by this powerful new idea spoken in a powerful voice.

"This proposal is just reckless," said Vertical, addressing the council. "Fine, so maybe we have new weapons, but we can't underestimate the OpScis. They outnumber us, and if push comes to shove, we'll be overwhelmed. Then it would be Xenocyst that gets destroyed once and for all."

"But we're almost warring already," said Ty. "The border fights are getting rougher and, with the way things are going, they won't just be isolated incidents anymore. Soon I could see them flaring up into something big."

"Don't you see that this is exactly what the venture charities want," said Jiku, "to make us bankdead fight among ourselves? Then they can distract us from who's creating the conditions that gave rise to the conflict in the first place. As you yourself know, Ty, the reason for our soft-handed approach to the OpScis has been to resist such top-down manipulation. We haven't worked out the Syndicate's grand plan, but allowing them to divide us now would—"

"Divide?" scoffed Ty. "Since when were we ever close enough with those OpSci pieces of shit to be divided?!"

"Listen to his rage!" cried Vertical, pointing at Ty and flicking her gaze around the circle. "Ty and Barrow are trying to sway us with their personal vendettas, but we can't lose sight of what's good for everyone. A war right now could destroy us all. Win or lose, the supplies we use up in the military efforts will leave us with a full-blown famine. Then what if the supplies drop further? We might start the war thinking that more supplies will come eventually, but our negotiations could fail for all sorts of reasons. I can't imagine a worse ending to what we've created here. A suicidal war? It's just too risky."

The intensity of the dispute between Ty and Vertical disturbed Amon deeply, the rift between the two of them seeming to reveal the rift between all of them.

Ty sneered at Vertical, and looked ready to deliver a tongue-lashing when Hippo intervened. "All risks aside, there is a far more important reason why this plan is folly. I appreciate your contributions, Larry-kun, Ty. In my time here, I have considered fighting back in the way you're describing, not just against the OpScis, but a guerilla war against the venture charities as well. In all honesty, part of me wants that right now . . . but the temptation must be resisted! Xenocyst was not established to take lives. It was established to save them, and our best protection of all is our status as a neutral haven. Yes, defense of our borders is important for our continued existence. We cannot simply provide medical help and pray no one interferes with us. But we must avoid bloodshed at all costs and a direct assault on the Opportunity Scientists will be a bloody affair indeed. Thousands of innocent lives will be lost in battle and many thousands more in the aftermath. If we initiate the war, all of that suffering will be on our hands. Then what will we be? Not healers or teachers or leaders by example, but murderers. No. If we are drawn into a war against our will, then so be it. But so long as we have the space to choose, we must seek another way."

"Of course war is not a good in itself," said Barrow. "It is a last resort. But making a futile effort to avoid violence now that we have been pushed into this corner is only going to perpetuate the systemic violence that reigns over innocent lives. Instead, we must take the initiative while we are in a position of strength and make this bold sacrifice—to improve the security and welfare of all people in the District of Dreams as Xenocyst has always sought. Once the OpScis have been brought down, we can free the men, women, and children straining under their yoke. We can unite the various collectives in harmonious cooperation. We can send out medics to far-flung communities that have been unfairly cut off from services. So I say, for the sake of true compassion, order, and a deeper commitment to pacifism, we have no choice but to seize the day and face the demon we have tried too long to ignore!"

Glowering at Barrow with that same expression of indignant disbelief Amon had seen in the hallway, Hippo took a deep breath, just as other councilors sat up straight, obviously raring to express their support for either side. Amon could sense the tension saturating the room as they debated a question about which there were no clear answers. All paths seemed to beckon evils, and Amon could imagine no way to determine which were greater and which were lesser in the crucible of deprivation they all found themselves. Judging by the mixed expressions of despair and determination on all the faces Amon could see, the disagreement looked ready to split the council, to rend asunder Xenocyst's leaders, and perhaps Xenocyst with them. But before anyone could get a word in edgewise, someone seized the brief pause and spoke into the eye of the storm. "Can I suggest another plan here?"

That someone was Amon. Surprising himself as much as anyone else, he had given voice to the nascent idea in his head and everyone now turned to hear what this other newcomer had to say. Rick's surprised, searching gaze right beside him touched Amon with more tender intensity than all the rest put together, and he paused for a moment as the memories and feelings of the past few weeks bubbled to the surface of his mind.

Much of what had led Amon to speak up in that moment, he had discovered in the sky, where he continued to seek respite when all else failed to settle his restlessness. During the day, whether at work or after, he sent his gaze upwards in search of roof canopy gaps at every opportunity, and in the evenings when he had no patience for reading he sometimes rallied his energy for the climb to the viewing platforms.

Now that he had no access to weather reports, the unpredictability of the sky still made him anxious. Yet when he could find the focus and time to contemplate it more carefully, to breathe deeply and observe with all the equanimity he could summon, he began to feel intrigued by its impassiveness, by its indifference to him. The way clouds formed, rolled, and vanished in unending patterns. The way hues were always transitional and so subtly distinct that there were no words to differentiate them. The way a unique mood or half-hinted emotion seemed to seep into him depending on changes in the light at each moment and time of day.

The naked sky was unlike anything he had beheld in Free Tokyo, where everything from the streets to the InfoFlux had arisen from human willing, formed within the constraints of anthro-consciousness and cognition and capital. It wasn't completely devoid of artificial taints, even with the InfoSky peeled back. Sunsets were sometimes blue and green, perhaps from the faint nano-mist left by the decaying flakes, perhaps some other fume; azure days were littered with the blurring rotors of centicopters, the sparkling translucence of CareBots, the white streak of carbonjets; and the stars were cluttered with slow-scrolling satellites and space stations. The sky was altered by our excretions and pollutions and motions, no doubt, yet only in subtle ways we could never guess in advance. It resisted our control and unfolded according to its own principles, independent and unfazed by whatever we might paint and piss atop its transient ethereal canvass.

Gazing skyward in this frame of mind, Amon felt as though his thoughts were escaping from the narrow tunnel that had always entrapped them, no longer echoed back to him by walls built by the collectivity of other minds. Then he could forget his exhaustion and his hunger and his body and his thoughts and lose himself in some spaceless outer strata between strata, where he began to see something else unsmeared with artifice and embellishment, another sky behind the sky. In such fleeting moments, he understood his desire to meet the forest in the flesh, to forego the chicanery of graphical simulation and finance and actually visit the place where it was found, as though he had sensed somehow in that phantasmagoric cavern of his former life the ever-present profundity that it obscured.

Amon still wasn't sure if color was "color" or if he had opened the right eyes, but veridical or oneiric, he was here now, wherever and whenever that might be, and the sky's tireless play seemed to contain a lesson. The beauty of its protean transformation in the slivers between roofs seemed to reveal the beauty in the transformation of all things: the sublimity of the grooves in his dissolving ceiling, the music in the mumbles and groans of a sick ward, truth even in a river of shit. How many of these opportunities had the audio-visual jibber-jabber stolen from him?

At the same time, while the sky seemed to promise wisdom, it reminded him often of his great ignorance, in the form of the sun that still eluded his perception for some reason. While his eyes seemed to have recovered in every other way, he sometimes spotted that strange visual lacuna—an absence that was neither black nor white nor any color, but simply not there to be seen—floating in a crack in the slumscape from which the light and heat shining around him radiated. In this bright, warm celestial nothing that stubbornly resisted the unveiling power of his naked gaze, all Amon observed was his own lack of knowledge, and sensed somehow that the sky had more to teach, though he could not fathom what that might be.

Then, on the perfectly clear day after the typhoon, Amon was walking back to his room after sundown when a breeze snaked its way down through the clutter of towers to brush his skin. Carrying with it a distinctively autumnal scent, it reminded him of a similar breeze that had beckoned him up to the stargazer's rooftop that first time. Instead of just carrying a hint of fall, this breeze was thick with it, just saturated with its chill, melancholy essence. Again he followed it, zigzagging and spiraling upwards along a busy stairpath until he reached a wide ledge, bordered on the left by the summit of a disposcraper mound rising up and on the right by a steep ridge that dropped sharply away. Not the same viewing platform as the first time, for the whole slumscape had shifted and been replaced, but one with similar dimensions and location. It was just as crowded as before except, instead of gazing upwards, everyone crouched and sat in huddles with their heads drooping, muttering quietly to each other or simply resting.

When the breeze blew again, Amon looked up to find a diamond-shaped patch of sky filled with stars. Immediately the nostalgic feeling returned, a precious memory just out of reach, when finally he grasped it and found himself transported to that moment with Mayuko on the rooftop of the BioPen that he had forgotten until he met Tamper. *Fall. It must have been fall when that happened*, he realized. They had seen the first star of the evening appear in azure, and wanted to stay there together to watch more of them twinkle into existence until the night came and the sky looked just like it did now. Amon savored this earliest of recollections with bittersweet longing, imagining Mayuko looking up at that same sky from a rooftop in Free Tokyo, remembering that same moment, their gazes set at just the right angle that their attention was reflected off the distant galaxies into each other's eyes, jointly partaking through this subtle exchange of awareness in both past and present in spite of all the distances that might divide them.

Sorrow quickly overtook him, for he realized that he was indulging in fantasy and that they were not really together—nor could they be. Even if Mayuko managed to find them, if she was indeed searching, there was nothing she could do to help Amon and Rick escape. Maybe Rashana could liberate them with her great amount of freedom, but unlikely exceptions aside, the free and unfree worlds were all but impossible to bridge. Vertical, Tamper, Ty, Book, Little Book, Barrow, Kitao, Hippo, and so many others were trapped here and forced to suffer in countless ways because of the system Amon had supported. The crowding, the volatile architecture, the pointless effort of constant resupplying, the hunger and fighting and boredom and stigmatization, the ignorance, the self-loathing and guilt, the apathy and despair, the charity-sponsored religion that took advantage of all these feelings . . . He wanted these horrors to end. Not just for his own sake, not just so he could escape from it, not just to placate his guilt, but so the others, the ones he had put here personally as much as everyone else, could have a chance for a respectable life. Only then could he make amends for the harm he had done, and hold Mayuko's hand beneath the trees of his forest, gazing together at the stars between the leaves with his soul at peace.

All this had been roiling just beneath the surface of Amon's awareness as he listened to the discussion and considered the various proposals made. Then disparate elements in his memory had collided suddenly—Tamper's vending hack<<>>the supply mixup at Delivery<<>>Rashana's interest in him<<>>Atupio's media campaigns<<>>the Philanthropy Syndicate<<>>the SpawnU Consortium<<>>Opportunity Science—and a vague flicker sparked to life in the back of his eyes, impelling him with its faint light to speak. Now he had to take a moment to form its glow into words, to blow a sentence out of molten thought.

"Yes Amon," said Hippo, when his pause had stretched out to an awkward length. "You were going to make a contribution?"

Amon nodded and took a deep breath to muster his courage before opening his mouth.

"All the proposals so far have had their strengths and weaknesses and might aid us to varying degrees if we could make them work. But what if we could cut deeper to the core of the problem . . . the issue . . . The political issue is that the Philanthropy Syndicate is forcing the Absolute Choice and Full Choice coalition to reduce credicrime fees so that they can reduce supplies. This is only possible because the public, and probably some of the lobbies, aren't aware of this policy and its impact. So what if we could show Free Citizens that the charity and gifts are two sides of an economic exchange based on genomic discrimination? Then pressure could be put on Absolute Choice and the Syndicate to treat us better or at least return the supply levels to normal."

When Amon stopped, the councilors who had been ready to challenge Hippo as the debate about war was heating up now directed mocking snorts and sour expressions of derision his way that seemed to say *as if!* But Amon hardly cared, because he could see the sheen of hope on Rick's brooding eyes beside him. And Hippo regarded Amon with solemn seriousness, as though reevaluating the very fabric of his being, when he said, "How do you propose we go about that?"

17
THE BRIDGE TO DELIVERY

The glass forms of multifarious drones swirled above and around the bridges. Butterflies, moths, dragonflies, hummingbirds circling and orbiting each other in fixed patterns—an elaborate, aerial parade of glittering graceful force masquerading as fragility beneath the fall-blue firmament. Afternoon sunbeams shone over the mirror-plated rim of Delivery, refracting through the drones into a whirling constellation of light flecks that dazzled Amon and warmed the exposed skin of his face after the dark, congested chill of the labyrinth.

Only a few paces from the entrance to the looming distended cube, he looked around one last time. There was Rick beside him and the other members of their crew just behind, all wearing the generic autumn uniform of Opportunity Scientist research assistants: sneakers, tight pants, and a tight hoodie all stitched of various fabric patches. Into the crisp air, flakes drifted about like slow-falling multicolored snow. Puffs of white breath wafted from the mouths of those pressing close around them in line and those on all the other bridges reaching over the moat, a lavender-turquoise mist rising from the flake-heaped bottom. The supply pilgrim crowds appeared different from before. Each time the quantities were reduced, they seemed to get skinnier and dirtier, their skin more haggard, their clothes more ragged, their eyes draining of vitality.

Glancing over at Rick, he saw a look of tense, fearful determination and knew it reflected his own feelings, his friend a mirror not just for Amon's body but his soul as well. Amon gave a firm nod. *Let's do this,* the gesture said, and in Rick's nod back he knew that he had understood perfectly as they took the final step to the end of the bridge.

"Okay . . . Well . . . first try to imagine the supply line at Delivery," Amon had said at the council. "Reporters and sousveillers like the ones working for Atupio sometimes go in there to record what they see. But their videos alone reveal almost nothing to Free Citizen viewers about what's going on there. Everyone lines up and puts their finger in a hole. Those with a baby put their baby's finger in the hole. Sometimes a tray comes out to accept a baby into the receptacle, sometimes not. Since the dispensing of supplies in Delivery is automated, it's impossible to tell which bankdead are getting what and why. Watching the vending machines carefully, you might notice that some get more and some less, but it isn't clear that the difference is connected to the result of sticking their finger in the hole or whether their baby was accepted, and it's not immediately clear that some get better quality goods. Very few Free Citizens have an opportunity to view this process from start to finish because only a tiny minority can afford to search for it on a platinum engine, and only a tiny portion of these would even bother to look it up. But even for the ones that do, there's no way they'd be led to the conclusion that some bankdead are getting more than others depending on the structure of their genomes, or that this is decided by MegaGlom designed algorithms, or that these algorithms are designed to maximize yield of human resources. They might think that people getting less now got more on a different day or maybe that the supplies are divvied out for each in accordance with his needs, with some getting more or less calories than others, for example, depending on their body size and metabolism.

"The fact that an exchange is occurring is no clearer from watching the bankdead called over to the manual supply tables. A few people put their finger or the finger of their baby into a genome reader. Some babies are given a quick health check and accepted into a crib before being stacked out of sight in containers. The lined-up bankdead are then given a pre-prepared bag of supplies, but it's unclear what they contain.

Once again, the connection with the genome readers is impossible to determine just by watching a video.

"And this is assuming that they're naked recordings. Most footage released comes from Philanthropy Syndicate reporters and gets carefully edited so it can be incorporated into pitypromo, with the containers being rendered as smiling volunteers, the health check cribs as nurses, and so on. Few other reporters are allowed in the vicinity, and if they're able to get in as Atupio staff do, they're quickly escorted out the moment they cause trouble.

"But the day the supply reductions started after the equinox, when I was on a supply run and saw a bunch of dispensers refuse to give out their contents, the situation was a bit clearer. The brandclan who were denied created a disturbance, so to keep the crowd flowing, the freekeepers redirected them to the tables. This forced the career volunteers to prepare new bags of supplies on the fly. If there had been any sousveillers there, it would have been obvious on video that some bags contain more and better supplies. Even so, it was only a small group that was denied, and the incident was short-lived so I doubt there would have been enough footage to show that this depends on their giving up babies.

"So what if we could have Tamper engineer a total breakdown of all the receptacles and vending machines in an entire lane when Atupio reporters were there? Then, if we could release the recording online, Free Citizens would see hundreds of people come through, some getting more than others, and witness the direct handover of supplies for babies. To anyone watching, it will be obvious that some babies are accepted while others are rejected depending on their genes and the health check. They'll also see that parents who gift their babies are given more supplies than those who don't, and more than those who are rejected despite the fact that they have an extra mouth to feed. Though viewers still might not immediately connect it to the human resource trade, if a reporter were asking tough questions and providing commentary the scene would be easy to understand and persuasive. The usually heart-warming spectacle of mothers voluntarily offering up their babies for a new life of Opportunity will become the horror show of babies sorted by their genes and packed into boxes.

"Once the public sees this, it won't be difficult to connect with the BioPens and convince everyone that donations are being used to secure human resources. Then the entire Charity Gift Economy and the pluto-genic principles it's based on will spill out into the open. Everyone will see that the charity and the gifting are not two separate activities, but the two sides of an exchange supporting a whole massive industry that makes the existence of the Free World possible.

"Of course this isn't going to magically rouse the masses or anything, but once this revelation is out, it will discredit the MegaGloms that form the Philanthropy Syndicate. The viewers will see many sick, skinny, dirty bankdead in the video, and this can be linked to the Syndicate supply reduction and from there to the slash on crowdcare fines that enables it. Then it will be clear that the giftless are living near starvation levels because of policies concocted by MegaGloms. What the result of citizens' realizing this will be is difficult to say. At the very least, I bet it would lead to a drop in funds from angry donors and a corresponding rise in Syndicate pitypromo investment, which will force them to decrease the ephemerality of supplies in order to balance donations with production, and so we'll end up with more durable supplies. In the best-case scenario, the Full Choice Party may turn on Absolute Choice, collapsing the coalition, and maybe the policy will even be canceled. Then the situation here might just return to how it was before the reduction began."

Once Amon had made his proposal, a debate broke out. Most spoke out vehemently against it, but the fact that the discussion continued at great length without any new plans being proposed told him just how seriously even its detractors were taking it.

The first objection was raised by Yané. He was skeptical that the Charity Brigade would respond as Amon was predicting. Rather than conduct the entire charity-gift exchange manually, they might simply send the bankdead on their way.

Ty jumped in to defend Amon's description of Delivery procedures, saying that he had seen such a manual handover when machines had broken down on multiple occasions. Yané responded that just because this was how they dealt with a single malfunction, it didn't guarantee that they would deal with a large-scale breakdown in the same way, especially if sabotage was suspected. But the freckled councilor raised doubts in support of Ty about whether any other response was feasible. The Brigade couldn't shut down the lane or try to send the famished bankdead away empty-handed, as that would cause a crowdcare disaster with everyone pushing their way in along the Road to Delivery. Moreover, quick reprisals were unlikely, as the freekeepers wouldn't expect the desperate bankdead to disrupt their own lifeline. Eventually Yané conceded that they might pull the sabotage off temporarily, but reviewing their sensors later, the Charity Brigade would surely discover it and realize that Xenocyst was to blame. Well then, they'd just have to acquire Opportunity Scientist outfits and disguise themselves, Ty proposed. Then they could bring Charity Brigade retaliation on an enemy and boost their relative position, whether or not Amon's PR plan succeeded.

But Jiku objected that it wasn't worth it just to frame the OpScis, and the Philanthropy Syndicate would use their ownership of Delivery image rights to keep the naked video relegated to gold search engines. There it would go largely unwatched except by the wealthiest, who were likely to have a stake in the Charity Gift Economy and the status quo it supported. Only the edited version would appear on bronze search engines where most people might view it, ensuring their perception of the incident would be distorted. As was well known, this was precisely what happened to the blog exposés of slum tourists and activists who traipsed a bit deeper into the camps than their guides recommended, so there was no reason to think this time would be any different. Hippo disagreed, saying that Rashana had the funding and media influence to pay the fines for having a naked seg with an authenticity stamp disseminated on bronze engines and mainstream sites. She might even collaborate with the SpawnU Consortium, who would be eager to cause problems for the Syndicate and the coalition government it colluded with. But usually, Yané countered, information on bronze engines is drowned out in a flood of noise, making it unlikely anyone would take note of it, let alone be swayed to change anything. Vertical, unexpectedly taking Ty's side, suggested that if they could orchestrate a short, easy-to-understand scene, and the SpawnU Consortium was buoying it on social media, there was a good chance it could go viral.

While the circle was discussing this issue, a senior councilor who Amon had never heard speak queried whether Rashana would actually fulfill her role. They would have to rely on her to record the incident, compile the naked video into a punchy seg, and seek the assistance of the Consortium to propagate it. If she refused to cooperate or failed in any of these tasks, they would be taking a huge risk for nothing. Hippo then pointed out that Rashana and her organization, Atupio, were already committed to spreading information that counteracted the Philanthropy Syndicate's pitypromo, and now that executives from the Syndicate were partnered with her sister Anisha to make conditions even worse for the bankdead, she would surely leap at this opportunity. Disagreements lingered, but the discussion was speculative and ended when someone suggested that the only way to resolve it was to consult directly with Rashana and confirm her intentions.

The final doubt was raised by Book. Even if the sabotage went smoothly, the venture charities responded as expected, Rashana collected good footage, and the seg went viral, there was no way to be sure it would have the impact they wanted. As everyone knew, elections were merely public dramatizations of backroom deals and competing interests. The electorate was largely irrelevant, and even if the public eye was brought to bear on the Charity Gift Economy, it might have no effect on the allotted supplies.

"Furthermore," Book argued, "if we consider the manner in which the entire system of the CG Economy is programmed into the objective workings of the machines, it appears improbable that there will be any recourse against the MegaGloms. If, let us suppose, the existence of the CG Economy was exposed and someone accused the Philanthropy Syndicate of, for example, operating an illegal black market or embezzling donations, individual engineers might be held culpable. However, each engineer is employed by a different MegaGlom sub-subsidiary designing the software and hardware for particular sets of machines according to specific instructions from research teams, and no one set of machines produces the CG Economy alone, just as no individual polluter caused global climate change but only the sum of all polluters. As it is the coordinated total effect of the set of all the vending machines of all MegaGloms that realizes this economy, the Syndicate could simply shift responsibility for each set onto the various technicians immediately in charge and deny they are in any way involved in coordinating their projects. An inquiry could theoretically succeed in holding responsible the technology managers in charge of creating and constantly updating the plutogenic algorithms. However, the command chain is too diffuse and convoluted for liability to ever reach any higher. Thus, as much as I support the theoretical possibility of educating the world about the iniquity of contemporary reality, I do not believe the Philanthropy Syndicate or Absolute Choice Party would ever be implicated."

This highly technical argument had the room befuddled for a time, and soon some of the councilors who had been nodding their heads during Barrow's speech used this opening to begin insisting upon the superior advantages of going to war after all. But to everyone's surprise, Barrow himself spoke up against Book. "Actually, from my understanding of the political situation, I believe that there is a good chance Amon's viral exposé will have a major impact. You see, Full Choice is originally a Moderate Choice faction. This means that they have traditionally received funding from the SpawnU Consortium. Since the death of the Birla founders, Fertilex has been breaking away from SpawnU under the influence of Anisha and she has been funding Full Choice to advance her own ends. However, the fact that the Full Choice party maintains its identity as an organization distinct from the Absolute Choice party, even nominally, tells us that it is not fully in the hands of Anisha and must continue to receive part of its funding from SpawnU. The Full Choice party, therefore, is still a swing variable in the current political arrangement, and SpawnU will be trying urgently to cut deals with it to bring down the coalition government. For this reason, I believe that the coalition is highly fragile and that the SpawnU Consortium will seize the chance to take advantage of this exposé.

"A massive scandal implicating the coalition could very likely spur Full Choice to blame Absolute Choice for everything. Whether this would be in an effort to return to Moderate Choice or to strengthen itself as an independent third party depends on what the SpawnU lobby behind them wishes to achieve. Either way, I believe that if such a recording went viral, it could bring the government crashing down, and this would open up the possibility for the crowdcare fine reductions to be reversed. Then supplies might be increased to their former levels as Amon suggested. At the very least, it will direct public attention towards the conditions here, and the economic power of pity and guilt can only improve them, Book's objections notwithstanding. Because, while he is entirely right that an inquiry would struggle to nail the Philanthropy Syndicate with any *legal* responsibility, that wouldn't prevent the media from making them appear *politically* responsible if the seg was compellingly spun, a task I'm certain the SpawnU Consortium and Rashana will pursue eagerly."

Stunned by Barrow's eloquent defense of Amon's plan, despite having energetically proposed his own only minutes earlier, the room went silent for a while. When discussion started up again, it shifted to the logistics of how to realize it in practice. And soon, without a definitive vote being held, Amon watched as all the councilors began working together to make it happen, reluctantly or enthusiastically.

While the details were being finalized, a task force was assembled and the digital quarantine became their center of operations. Select residents were delegated specific roles, weapons and equipment were gathered, and a gang of Opportunity Scientists was robbed for their uniforms so Xenocyst could have a template to sew more of their own.

Everyone came to Hippo frequently for advice, as he seemed to take to his role as central coordinator with renewed relish. The look of smoldering rage and defeat he'd worn for weeks had vanished, to be replaced by a sort of lucid determination, his eyes now receptive again to those who needed him. Amon even heard him laugh a few times, noting how he became particularly absorbed in planning the defensive strategies of Ty's armed backup crew. To Amon, he seemed relieved to finally have an excuse to resist—to do something, anything, for those who suffered—without compromising his long-cherished resolution to be a xenocyst, and Amon was happy that his plan had offered this kind man, this friend who had saved him from death and despair, a new source of hope.

Vertical led a scouting crew charged with recruiting Tamper. With binoculars and telescopes salvaged from Barrow's trove, her scouts took posts on the disposcraper rooftops along the bank of the Sanzu River, and she instructed them to ring a signal bell to get Tamper's attention if they spotted him. Over the course of several days, he was sighted numerous times, wandering in and out of view along streets that ended at the far shore, and after a dozen rings he finally stopped and took notice. Seeming to spy the watch stationed high across the river, he walked over to the railing along the bank, commandeered a boat, and parked it beneath the building where the bell had sounded. Vertical dashed over and had only briefly described the situation when Tamper disembarked through a crack in a shelter, climbed to their post, and began to head south without a word, taking for granted that Vertical would follow along and guide him directly to Barrow's trove for the electronic components he would need. When Tamper arrived at the Cyst the following day, he had merely greeted Hippo, his old friend and benefactor, with a nod, and went straight for the elevator Amon had once slept in. There he holed himself up for weeks, designing the new devices they would need. When they were complete, he went off to Delivery to test them and—leaving a coded message with Book that they had worked satisfactorily on both a receptacle and a dispenser—vanished, presumably back to haunt his son on the edge of Free Tokyo, leaving the devices neatly arranged on the floor of the elevator.

At the same time as the search for Tamper began, efforts were underway to enlist Rashana. The signal bells on the roof of the Cyst were rung in the pre-decided pattern and that very evening her PhantoCopter landed there. In the privacy of the digital quarantine, compromised only by the presence of Rashana's BodyBank, Hippo told Rashana everything and requested her support. To everyone's relief, Rashana seemed excited. She confirmed their read on the political situation, with only a few minor revisions and additions, explaining that from all the sources she had consulted it seemed likely their plan would have a huge effect if successful, and promised to do her part. Her first step would be to call a strategic brainstorm on the ideal media presentation, and Hippo suggested inviting the Books to contribute their psychological expertise.

During the meeting, Hippo had also delivered a message directly from Amon: he was living in Xenocyst with Rick and they would appreciate if she could meet them on the roof of the Cyst at midnight the day of the sabotage. This had required Hippo to admit that he'd lied to Rashana about Amon's being there, but when he'd tried to explain that it was only to protect Amon, etcetera, etcetera, Rashana had interrupted, saying, "There's no need to explain. I know. Just tell him that I'm glad to hear he's finally ready to speak with me and that I'll be here at the time he requests."

Amon had considered meeting her with Hippo, as he and the council surely would have let him do so if he'd wanted to. But after much wavering he'd decided to approach her indirectly in this way. If they talked now, Amon was afraid that she might insist he come with her right away, and he wasn't ready to leave just yet. First of all, he hoped that, once the exposé operation was complete, Rick might change his mind about avoiding her, for if Rashana did her part, Rick would see for himself that she could be trusted. (Though Rick might not be able to acquire a training bank as Amon might, since he had been liquidated and lacked a BodyBank, Rashana had to be able to do *something* for him.) But a change had also come over Amon. Yes, the ever-increasing lack was excruciating and their precarious relations with the OpScis were terrifying. After Mayuko, or whoever it was, came to find him, he felt the need to leave more urgently than ever. And understanding jubilee, vindicating himself, finding the forest, were all still of profound importance to him. Nevertheless, he couldn't forget what Rick and Vertical had said about focusing on what was close at hand. Through helping Barrow, Amon had begun to earn his forgiveness, and he wanted to do so much more for others so that he might one day forgive himself. Here was his chance to show Free Citizens what iniquities made their lives possible and give something back for what he had done to make it this way. The people he'd met here too—Hippo, Ty, Vertical, Book, Little Book, Tamper, and all the rest—though he'd only known them a short time, were closer to his heart than anyone he'd met in the metropolis, except for Rick and Mayuko. He wanted to make sure that they were okay, that they survived the greatest challenge Xenocyst had ever faced, and since it was his idea, he felt obligated to see it through. So instead of rushing off before the imminent cataclysm, he volunteered to be one of the frontline saboteurs, willing to risk it all if anything went wrong.

★

And so it was, once everything was set, that he trudged up the Road to Delivery with a crew of Xenocysters dressed like OpScis and crossed the bridge to the entrance, his head swimming with thoughts of what might happen when he met Rashana at midnight, his chest tight with fear of what lay ahead as he put his foot over the threshold.

18
INSIDE DELIVERY

The moment Amon stepped into Delivery and began to line up in the lane of receptacles, he made eye contact with someone familiar and felt an eerie chill mist up his spine. *Was that really Minister Kitao?* It was difficult to tell at first because the man's lower back had given out, his whole torso hunched forward to the right from his waist, and it was unclear if he would reach the minister's two meters when stretched out to full height. What should have been neatly gelled short hair on his head was a frizzy mop, and he was even skinnier than the gangly man Amon remembered, his broad face drawn ghoulishly tight, his long arms nearly dangling to the floor. Even so, it was difficult to deny the resemblance with the minister's former digimade features. He was also wearing the brand name patchwork robes of an OpSci priest, which matched Barrow's story, though Barrow had said nothing about back problems, so could Kitao have been injured somehow?

Judging by his place in line, the man must have been walking just a few paces ahead of them along the bridge outside, and Amon was surprised he hadn't noticed someone with such distinctive posture and dress until he'd looked back at them. Crooking his neck around, his face about level with his solar plexus, the man's gaze had traveled up Amon's body from his toes to his eyes and remained locked there ever since. The man—Kitao, yes, the delirious glaze over his eyes was unmistakable, it had to be Kitao—wore a perplexed expression as though he thought he remembered Amon's face but wasn't sure. Had yet another of his targets recognized him, now, at this most precarious of moments? It seemed impossible that Kitao would remember Amon's face when he had mostly seen him rendered as an aphid and had only spoken to him when he was digimade as himself for less than a minute. Perhaps the intense stress of the experience had burned Amon's face into his recollection, as Amon had often feared. Then again, perhaps Amon's patchwork pants and jacket had caught his attention. Were their disguises flawed somehow? Could OpScis see through them? Amon felt harrowed under the stare of this hunched apparition from his past, his guilt scraped out to the surface of his mind, and he imagined Kitao headbutting his way back through the crowd like some enraged, hobbling dinosaur to choke him with his long-fingered hands.

But without saying or doing anything, Kitao turned his tired grimace away and continued to shamble ahead in line. Amon peeled his gaze from the man's back and turned it towards Rick to inquire with his eyes whether his friend had noticed him too. Apparently oblivious, Rick was already stepping towards the receptacle on the left row that the council taskforce had assigned him, and Amon realized that he had almost missed his receptacle, third from the door on the right, and stepped up to it quickly before the inexorable crowd behind could push him past it.

He reached his right hand into his pocket to put a small electronic device like a closely fitted thimble onto the tip of his pinky finger and inserted it into the machine. Tamper had designed the device to block the genome reader from taking a sample of him, while impersonating the genome of a recently deceased resident of Xenocyst, thereby reducing the chances of the Charity Brigade learning his identity and potentially blacklisting him as a hungry ghost. At the same time, it transmitted malicious inputs. When Amon retracted his finger and slipped the device off into his pocket again, the virus was already doing its work. Other members of their crew, including Rick, had inserted their fingers into five other receptacles in the same way. They had lacked the materials for Tamper to make devices for all the machines, though they could have made more than six if they'd wanted to. But the taskforce had decided on this number, in consultation with Tamper, because it would create a serious enough disturbance for their purposes without immediately appearing intentional.

Amon and the other five men in the line behind him all moved ahead, past the intersecting hallway where the supply tables stood to the vending lane, and inserted their thimbled fingers into the machines there. No supplies came out as the vendors instantly stopped working, and at around the same time the receptacles began to break down one by one. The virus for the receptacles had been programmed to delay the malfunction to coincide with that of the vendors. This way the Brigade would have trouble seeing the connection between certain people inserting their fingers into machines and certain machines going haywire. They might analyze data from the sensors monitoring the room and discover people with little devices on the tips of their fingers. But the sabotage crew was expected to be long gone by the time such conclusions were reached, and since they were dressed like OpScis and hadn't provided their own DNA it would be their rivals that took the blame. The vending virus, on the other hand, had been designed to work immediately, as this was crucial to the next stage of their operation: the riot.

"What's this!" Rick called out to the freekeepers and career volunteers around the pitypromo table. "Nothing's coming out!"

"Yeaaah!" Amon shouted, pointing to his hole-filled sneakers with a what-the-fuck scowl. "Where my shoes!?"

The other four men in their crew began to growl at the Delivery staff with similar pretend anger. Soon the weight of the line had pushed them ahead. Amon and the rest tried to put their fingers in the next set of machines, but when these broke down and failed to eject their supplies in the same way, they began to shoulder their way back to the first machines that had supposedly betrayed them. Those next in line also found that supplies wouldn't come out of several of the machines, almost half by this point, and began to join in the clamor. "I'm not goin' anywhere till I get my fuckin' shoes!" Amon bellowed as he shoved against the tense, squabbling tangle that had formed in the lane, the functional machines now the locus towards which the weight of the crowd surged. There was no resisting the immense force of all the bodies, and Amon found himself pushed backwards step by step, but refused to give in and saw dozens nearby digging in their heels. Soon he was squashed against the back wall that overlooked the Bridge of Compassion, his cheek flattened on the cold glass. Turning around, he leaned in to resist turning left into the exit line and a barricade of other bodies assisting his, including Rick and their partners, soon formed. Amon could almost see the pressure of the rapidly swelling crowd clog on the vending machine walls as the jostling back and forth grew more violent, and he feared they might soon rip out of their mooring in the ceiling and topple onto innocent heads, when a freekeeper poked her torso into the space between receptacles and vendors that opened into the intersecting hallway, the assault duster in her hands bespeaking her authority. "Due to technical difficulties, we will now be providing supplies at the tables," she shouted. "Those at the end of the vending lane, continue immediately into the exit lane. Everyone else form a line right here." She swung the barrel of her duster forward to indicate the start of the line at the mouth of the hallway.

With Rick right in front of him, Amon allowed the crowd to shuffle him into the exit lane and started to push his way towards the intersecting hallway and the exit to the bridge beyond it. HandyPedes peeked out from holes in the ceiling and crawled down in their strange jittery, tottering way on dozens of tiny prongs and tools of different sizes poking from their long, slender torsos. When they reached the backs of the vendors, they began prying open small panels and inspecting inside with flexible lights and lenses. From beyond them, past the hallway, Amon heard baby wails contributing to the racket and saw two career volunteers unloading the compartments from the backs of the receptacles. With the devices shut down, the air-conditioning inside was no longer working and the babies needed to be ejected immediately to maintain their commercial viability. The occupied compartments—teary-eyed grimacing babies visible through the walls of the glass cubes—were being stacked on the back of an electric cart, presumably for shipment elsewhere.

When the line had moved forward a few paces and Amon was passing the HandyPedes, they were fiddling with something behind a detached panel just above him and he could see right, down the intersecting hallway, to the table where supplies were being frantically handed out. The female freekeeper who'd spoken earlier directed the incoming bankdead line towards the tables and the outgoing line to the exits while two other freekeepers flanked the supply stacks behind the table. They tried to keep the crowd orderly, but the bankdead pressure from behind and their eagerness to get their share were too great, so that the lines just kept widening and spilling into an even greater area of the hallway. Once someone got to the front of the line, a career volunteer would have them insert their pinky, or the pinky of their infant or child, into the hole in the genome reader cube. Those with potentially marketable babies were waved over to another career volunteer, who took the babies and lowered them into a diagnostic crib, where scriggling robotic limbs attached to the bars began their health check. The babies were then removed from the crib and either returned to the mothers or inserted through a plastic flap into nursery crates stacked behind the table. Each bankdead then received different supply packages from two other volunteers depending on their plutogenic category. Already the volunteers were running out of pre-packed bags and were beginning to gather supplies from crates behind them to stuff into empty ones. Two of them who had pushed their way to the back of the vendors to retrieve supplies from the shorted-out dispensers were struggling to get back to the tables, resorting instead to tossing them over the heads of the crowd to the table. Amon watched the famished bankdead eyeing these near-flying items with palpable covetousness.

Deeper in the hallway past the tables, Amon could see about a dozen of the Birla Guard standing in a square. It was the same formation they used when protecting the Birla sisters, but no one was visible at the center this time and Amon guessed that Rashana was there as a digital figment. By appearing to be there for anyone with ImmaNet access, she could observe the scene and direct her mercenaries without being present bodily at this volatile and politically charged event. Six of her reporters accompanied by sousveillers were already accosting the Delivery staff.

"This black cube you see here is the same type of genome reader many of us are familiar with from our local hospitals," a male reporter before the supply table said, gesturing to the reader on top. "The venture charities claim that these are used to check for congenital diseases in infants and thereby offer personalized care—but some of the babies are not accepted after inserting their finger. Others are not accepted after the health check. Something else is obviously going on here. But what? The answer is . . ."

"Could you comment on the reason behind the difference in supplies?" a female reporter was asking a volunteer handing out bags.

"Where will these boxed infants be sent?" another man asked a volunteer unloading one of the receptacles. "Can you confirm or deny the reports that they are sorted by genome for specialized BioPens?"

The staff ignored the reporters as they scrambled to gather their exposed human resources and distribute the supplies fast enough to clear out the backed-up line. Aside from the three freekeepers occupied with directing the crowd, two more stood near the square of Birla Guards, watching impassively. They seemed strangely uninterested in restraining the reporters, and Amon guessed that they had been paid off by Rashana. The crowd squeezed his body and released it as it pulsed and swayed around him, impatient blather, shouts, and baby cries roaring in his ears. As chaos reigned, it was now time to move on to the next stage: the drama.

Right on cue, a woman shrieked up ahead—it was Vertical—and Amon watched as she hopped over the supply table and reached through the flap in one of the nursery crates. A career volunteer grabbed her arm to restrain her, but she shook him off and succeeded in wresting the baby from its enclosure. Then, sheltering it in her arms, she crawled back over the table and pushed back those at the front of the line to make space for her to stand. Although her scream had drawn the gaze of the freekeepers flanking the table and the one guiding the crowd in the midst of the fray, none of them made a move to stop her as Rashana's reporters soaked it all up intently.

"Give that boy back immediately!" demanded the career volunteer.

"Noooo!" keened Vertical, cradling the crying baby close to her chest. "This is my baaaby."

"Listen ma'am. You've already offered him up for adoption. You can't just—"

"I never agreed to anything. I thought you were just giving him a health test."

"Well, he's already passed that test and now he's . . ." The man faltered, and Amon guessed he was thinking "is property of MegaGlom X" somewhere deep in his mind, though it had probably been twisted into some other thought more compatible with Charity Gift Economy principles. What he said was, ". . . he's been entered into the system."

"Cancel it then!" she shrieked. "And give me my supplies! I want a home to go to with my baby boy!"

"We can't do that, m'am . . . you have to . . ." The man was tongue-tied.

"You can't give me my supplies you say?" Vertical shrieked again, cringing as though on the verge of tears. "Unless I give you my *baby*?"

The reporters and sousveillers crowded in, eagerly soaking up the scene while the Birla Guard stood back, observing with strident eyes.

This performance had been proposed by Barrow once he'd become a supporter of Amon's idea, and Vertical had volunteered, followed immediately by Rick, though the council had decided on Vertical because they thought a mother would be more compelling than a father. Vertical had been given a finger device much like the one Amon's crew had used, except rather than cause a breakdown it impersonated the genome of the baby's dead mother. This subterfuge allowed Vertical to gift the baby, since Delivery only processed gifts from their genetic parents (a measure that prevented marketable resources from being damaged in kidnappings and from being stolen by giftless who lacked the supplies to raise them safely, though also encouraging Opportunity Scientist chattel herding). Vertical had inserted her thimbled pinky and the baby's pinky into the reader. They had met the plutogenic standards of some MegaGlom's brand and she had handed the baby over. A career volunteer had then put the baby into the diagnostic crib and, when he'd passed the health check, inserted him into one of the nursery crates. But Vertical, just as she'd rehearsed, pretended to be shocked that her baby was being taken and went to retrieve him.

Her demand for supplies now created a bureaucratic problem for the venture charities. The table was meant to be a manual realization of the automated receptacle and vending lines, but the receptacles drew any baby that passed the health check inside, meaning that passing the health check and receipt of the baby were equivalent and inseparable within the system. If a baby was tagged as marketable and healthy without being detected in the inventory, then an error would occur and the parent's assignment to a supply category—gifted, giftless, or gifter—would be pending until it was resolved. This meant Vertical, in her genetic guise, currently had no category and was not technically entitled to any supplies. The career volunteer was rendered indecisive, therefore, because he knew he was in charge of ensuring there were no discrepancies between human resource receipts and supply disbursement, yet couldn't admit before the media that there was any connection between them.

"Hurry up!" barked a man behind Vertical as the crowd continued to pile in behind this disturbance.

"Just give him the damn baby already!" cried a woman, and several others shouted in agreement. "Yeeeah!" "Come on!" "Move bitch!" To the bankdead, it was clearly Vertical at fault for not following the rules of the game and holding everything up. The two lines—Amon's line coming from the glass wall and the other line coming from between the receptacles and vendors—were converging, causing vicious arguments and tussling to get ahead to the open tables, the freekeepers utterly failing to keep the crowd in any semblance of order as it seemed to grow denser and more irritable by the second. Feigning fear of the mob behind her with a tense shudder, Vertical handed over her baby to the man demanding it and went over to another career volunteer for her supply bag.

Giving back the baby had been part of the plan, though it was only decided after a heated debate. The council had sent a dozen orphaned babies from gifted parents to an Atupio laboratory to test whether they were marketable according to any MegaGlom algorithms, which Rashana had seized access to through her information channels, and this boy, whose name was Koki, had been the only one that passed. His father had been crushed in the big disposcraper collapse and his mother had died of an infection, leaving him under the care of the community. Their responsibility for him didn't mean they could simply endanger his safety to garner media attention, so it was agreed that he should be handed over once Vertical had raised a fuss. Some had argued that it was wrong to gift him, but Xenocyst was now heavily burdened with orphaned infants, many of whom were not likely to see their first birthday given the shortages, and Koki would have a far better chance of survival where he was going. During the present crisis, there was little justification for keeping babies any longer.

Once Vertical received her bag, she slung it over her shoulder and made for the exit, getting shoved and buffeted back and forth by the agitated crowd as she passed. Her leaving was the sign that they had captured the footage they needed and should now head back to Xenocyst. All Amon, Rick, and the sabotage crew had to do now was move casually through the supply line so as not to arouse suspicion and their job was done.

Then, up ahead, in the open area beyond the tables, just in front of where the Birla Guard stood in a box around Rashana's figment, Amon spotted Kitao again. He was whispering with his mouth tilted to the side towards the ear of a freekeeper, who was leaning over to listen to the hunched priest. Suddenly another ominous chill misted up Amon's spine and he looked towards Rick, squeezed in place just in front of him. "Hey, Rick."

"Yeah," said Rick turning to meet Amon's gaze over the tossing head-scape.

"You see that man over there, past the lineup? The one who's bent over?"

Rick looked the way Amon indicated. "Yeah. What about him?"

"I think that's Minister Kitao."

"You sure? He looks short for—shit! Maybe you're right."

"A second ago he was talking to a freekeeper."

"And?"

"He spotted me when I came in, gave me this weird look, so I . . ."

Amon trailed off as the eyes of the whole crowd shifted, drawing his along with them to the door in the wall just beyond the table, which had slid open, letting out a dozen freekeepers. They trotted into the hallway and the man in the lead immediately began to shout at the two freekeepers who were standing around doing nothing. Jumping to attention, they gave quick, surprised bows and began to clear away the reporters and sousveillers. Three of the Birla Guard moved in to interfere, but three of the newly arrived freekeepers stepped into their path and met them face to face while the others began to shunt the rest of the guards towards the door in the hall, addressing someone in the center of the square who to Amon's naked eyes wasn't there. The half-dozen mercenaries marched in formation as though Rashana had agreed to leave, while those that remained refused to yield to the freekeepers blocking them. A scuffle soon broke out between them, two of them gripping each other by their polymer armor as though ready to brawl, the rest raising their assault dusters in position to fire. Screams of fright mingled with yelling as the crowd began to mill about in pressurized panic, and some of the maintenance workers curled up on the floor at the base of the machines, perhaps obeying warnings from the freekeepers. Amon felt himself tossed and twisted about helplessly while Rick gripped the right sleeve of his hoodie so they wouldn't be pried apart.

How did they find us out so quickly? flashed through Amon's awareness. After Vertical's rabble rousing, they were expecting the Charity Brigade to realize that the malfunction had been staged, allowing Rashana to bring them cracking down on the Opportunity Scientists when she claimed to have made a pact with the religion to create the viral video. But they weren't expecting them to react immediately, and the presence of the sousveillers was supposed to ward off a heavy-handed response. Now freekeepers kept filing in until Amon couldn't count them all in the tumult, though he was sure he had never seen so many in one area, and the remainder of the Birla Guard were forced to begin their retreat. For security reasons, the freekeepers stationed near other supply tables in the hallway were not allowed to leave, and reserves like these new arrivals were usually stationed in the upper levels of Delivery. It should have taken several minutes for them to arrive even after a decision was made to deploy them, which was supposed to take even longer since it required human executive clearance. But several squads of them had appeared so quickly it was as though they'd been dispatched before Vertical had even snatched the baby . . .

His eyes darting about in panic, Amon spotted Vertical a few paces from the exit, still trying to squeeze her way out. Then, just as the last of the reporters and Birla Guard were shunted through the hallway door, one of the freekeepers stepped in front of the exit portal, aiming his assault duster forwards to block those trying to leave.

Vertical dropped her supplies, ducked low, and dove out the door between the legs of the freekeeper faster than he could close them or lower his aim. Amon felt someone grab him around the shoulders and tackle him chest-first to the floor. Winded, he tried to struggle free from his assailant, who hissed "Stay down!" with a familiar voice, and he realized it was Rick. Lying on his belly, surrounded by tight layers of legs, Amon couldn't see what happened next, but heard a sound he knew well: the *chrinkle* of dust fired through the air, then screams and water began to patter on the floor. Tear dust, the eyes of the crowd around him erupting like storm clouds. A great roar of panicked voices as Rick yanked Amon to his knees and began to headbutt and thrash open a path through the seams in the pandemonium of waists. Amon followed in his wake, punching and elbowing all who closed in on them. Bodies toppled on his back but he bucked them off and kept going. Then a shoe pressed someone's weight onto the back of his calf, painfully pinning him in place. He had to stand up straight or the crowd would crush him, but if he did the Brigade might dust him.

His body now reacting of its own accord, Amon found himself half-charging, half-falling towards the door, dozens of hands tugging him back so their owners could get out ahead of him. *I'm going to be sucked under!* he thought as his feet tangled up with other feet, an arm hooking under his left armpit and a chin smashing into his right shoulder as he teetered off-balance. *I'm going to be stomped into nothing!* But just as his forward momentum died and he felt himself spinning towards the floor, a force pushed him from behind, a current of bodies moving in the same direction, carrying him ahead as though on the crest of a tidal wave, and he batted and flailed in violent contortions he was hardly aware of, spit flying from his mouth. Then Rick was there beside him and together they stepped over the fallen freekeeper in their way, sprawling on top of more writhing limbs and torsos onto the bridge outside.

19
THE BRIDGE FROM DELIVERY

The moment Amon and Rick spilled out onto the bridge, Amon felt an intense, burning sensation flare up on the skin across his body and time suddenly seemed to slow down. The feeling of heat enveloping him from head to toe brought with it a knee-jerk compulsion to escape and return the way he had come, but the crowd thundering behind kept him going straight ahead. Sudden exhalations and yowls told him they were being seared in the same way, and he found himself part of a stampede plowing helplessly ahead into the empty space left when the lineup had frozen several minutes earlier.

Turning his head right towards the source of the heat, Amon saw several DragonFrys hovering above him off the side of the bridge. They looked just like glass dragonflies, but with large mouths stretched wide open, concentrating the invisible rays of a hot miliwave towards Amon and those around him. They had first taken aim at the door, but as the crowd leapt ahead to avoid the ovenbeam the DragonFrys pivoted and directed the angle further along the bridge to corral everyone in Amon's exit line and the approaching entrance line away from Delivery.

Just as Amon was out of range of the beam and gasped in the sudden rush of crisp fall air, he saw other translucent forms approaching in his peripheral. Peeling off from the churning cloud of CareBots that encompassed their bridge, DusterFlies swooped in on them, fluttering over the rapidly bobbing heads before him and flicking their wings downwards. Though Amon couldn't see the minuscule nanobots as they fell, he could tell from how the crowd reacted that these vitreous butterfly drones were sprinkling various kinds of dust on them. One woman stuck out her tongue in mid stride and scraped wildly at it with her fingers as if to remove an unbearable taste. A man shuddered violently and batted at his body as though clearing away insects that coated him. A teenage boy began swinging about stupidly with his fists. A few lost their balance and toppled to the floor like drunks. Some looked utterly relaxed despite the uproar. Those unaffected just charged onwards, knocking aside and trampling those in their path, and Amon felt someone's hand crunching underfoot.

Though the different kinds of DusterFlies were unmarked, he recognized the dust each one sprinkled: bitter dust, crawly dust, tantrum dust, vertigo dust, putre dust, mellow dust. Strangely, despite the cornucopia of precisely targeted discomfort and disabling euphoria visited upon the crowd, all those hit were completely silent. He heard yelling, wails of terror, trampling, flapping, gun shots, the *chrinkle-chrinkle-chrinkle* of dust, but vocalizations of pain were oddly absent. Then TazerWasps began to dive in, and the man directly in front of Amon who had been violently bumping and digging through those ahead of him in the mayhem took a stinger in his right temple, whereupon he began to twitch and gurgle while crumpling beneath the charge.

As Amon was about to pass under a cluster of DusterFlies, he pulled one of the batons Tamper had designed for them from his left pocket and tossed it up towards them, watching as it arced downwards and the DusterFlies dive-bombed after it towards the moat. An approaching pile-on of wriggling bodies blocked the middle of the bridge, so he stepped onto the ledge between the in-and-out ramps to run along it. He had made it past the worst of the clog when the unbearable heat of another ovenbeam swallowed him, indicating he was out of bounds, and he leapt back onto the bridge to find himself crowdsurfing towards the opposite edge. Sensing the drop to the moat approaching, he bucked his legs downwards to squeeze himself into the crowd just in time.

Jammed immobile into an off-balance, panicking crush, everyone lurching forward for their lives, Amon saw a half-dozen SampleQuitos swarming in and smacked one away, knowing that they were strong enough to survive swatting and would blacklist his genome if he let them close. Several TazerWasps rocketed towards him from his right side to disable this violent offender, and he hurled another baton into their midst, sending them on a sudden vertical U-turn, plunging out of sight. Amon climbed over another small heap, totally oblivious in his half-conscious rush to what body parts he was stepping on—a head there, a thigh here, a buttock there—and got his feet back on the ground. He saw the end of the bridge approaching, the slumscape rearing beyond it, when suddenly a screech filled his ears. Or not ears per se. Rather, the noise seemed to originate in his head, though somehow he instinctively knew which direction it came from and involuntarily looked that way, diagonally up to his left where he found a BansheeBird about five meters away. Its glass hummingbird body hovered elegantly, its see-through pin-beak aimed right at his forehead, the beat of its fast-blurring translucent wings adding a sharp thrum to the sound wave that seemed to scrape along the pleats of his brain as though ten thousand tiny chainsaws were grinding on rusted lumps of metal in his skull. *There's no point going on*, called a voice from his depths in metallic-shriek syllables that were just barely intelligible. *End it!* A razor-whirling headache seemed to scream down his body as he fumbled for another baton in the right pocket of his jacket. He got the cylinder in his hand but the pain was so bad he wasn't sure if he should throw the baton or just leap over the side of the bridge to stop all sensation forever. *Not death. Dream Mayuko! Forest jubilee!* Summoning every fragment of his splintered will with this incoherent mental battle cry, Amon quelled the suicidal impulse and withdrew the baton . . . but when he looked towards the BansheeBird to take aim, something just to the right of it pulled in his gaze. A fireworks display of multicolored lights pulsed at varied frequencies on the clear wings of a DazzleMoth fanned out towards him and his headache crescendoed, his visual field melting into a searing blaze of white as the bone of his cranium felt ready to implode. Convulsing and dry retching with rib-cracking strength, Amon put his hand on the ledge, followed by his right foot, and prepared to jump off towards the drone.

Gatah. Gatah-kroonch. The chainsaw squeal suddenly stopped, and Amon collapsed backwards in shock onto a warm, lumpy, twitching bed. *Gatah-gatah-blamkreesssshhh.* With fluorescent afterglow spots still blinking in his vision and elbows in his back, Amon saw Rick standing over him holding the gun he'd taken from the OpScis, its smoking twin barrels pointed out to where the two drones had been, a sparkling glass cloud expanding in the air from that direction. Lowering the barrel, Rick reached out to grip Amon's right bicep, hauled him to his feet, and smacked him hard in the face. A sharp buzz in his right cheek, Amon allowed Rick to pull him along, punching, kicking, and pistol-whipping at anything in their way. Something tiny alighted on Amon's forehead and he went to brush it off with the back of his hand, but his reflexes were too slow in his lingering daze and it took off before he reached it. Only as the red blur of blood-filled wings receded into the sky did Amon realize it was a SampleQuito off to label him a hungry ghost or worse. Then he looked down and found the spiral off-ramp right in front of them. After seconds that felt like hours, they had reached the end of the bridge at last!

But before they could get to the barrier at the end, reinforcements arrived—a swarm of fluttering, humming, glittering things headed straight for them, far too many for Rick's one machinepistol to handle. *Fuck.*

THWAP. Three balls flew down from the looming disposcrapers ahead and exploded near the drones into nets that wrapped around them. With their multifarious wings all tangled together, they began to plummet into the moat or onto the heads of the crowd on other bridges below. Retracing the parabolic course of the net to the ledge where it seemed to have originated, Amon could see no one there, but he knew Hippo had positioned Ty and his crew on the rooftops just across the gap at the end of the bridge to cover the sabotage crew in case CareBots were roused—and were they ever roused. Amon could hear machine gun fire and saw a few butterflies burst like smashed candy before the rotating barrel of a Gatling gun poking from the doorway of a room several stories up.

Still disoriented and nauseous, Amon let Rick pull him to the end of the bridge and watched him fire at a bunch of DusterFlies glide-creeping up below a protruding room. His shots missed but drew the attention of Ty, who leaned out into view from behind the room and swung his three wheels out one after the other in three great arcs—*whoosh, whoosh, whoosh*—so that each skipped from head to head of drones at three different altitudes, sending their short-circuited forms plummeting onto the end of the Road to Delivery. Yet the bots Ty missed amassed with further reinforcements into another murmuration above him, whirling and looping in a complex formation that looked like a crystal-river gift-ribbon, and Ty shouted an alarm call before his crew leapt from their cover and scattered into the shadows of the slumscape, tailed by vitreous insectile blurs.

Looking down, Amon saw that the spiral ramp was packed, with many hang-dropping off the side onto the heaving headscape below. Rick glanced over his shoulder and whipped out his gun-arm—*gatah-kro-onch, gatah-kreesch, gatahkreeshahh*—shooting down a BansheeBird, DazzleMoth, and DusterFly trio that approached from behind as the people around them dropped to the floor to take cover. Seizing this opening, Rick dashed ahead, stepped onto the barrier at the end, and leapt forward—all in fluid succession. He launched out across the gap, wedged his upper body into a cranny left by two poorly aligned shelters, and pulled himself in before waving Amon over and sliding forward into a dark cavity out of sight. Terrified he might lose his friend, Amon gave his head a swift shake and followed after Rick with a dash, a step, a leap, and a *thwachk*, crawling into the slumscape.

20
THE GIFTED TRIANGLE, AN ELEVATOR

At the end of the cranny was a hole that dropped into darkness, the bottom out of sight. Amon hesitated at the edge for a split second, but it was either take the leap or return to the madness, so he twisted around between the tight walls to get his legs in front of him, dangled them into the hole, and dropped in. His soles took the ground hard and he fell, rolling to absorb the impact until his left hip slammed into a wall and he came to a stop.

When he got up, he found himself in a narrow cleft between walls of bamboo-board shelters that leaned over top in gappy rows like a closed mouth with missing teeth viewed from the inside. Beside him, Rick was lying on his side in a low alcove.

"'ts go!" barked Amon, and started to run down the alley, but noticed Rick wasn't following and stopped, turning to find him cringing and gripping his right ankle. "What's happened?"

"I fucked my ankle on that drop."

"You okay to go on?"

"Not much choice, is there? We've got to get away from those drones."

Rick rose slowly to his feet and took a few tentative steps. He managed to limp along several meters, but winced every time he put down his right foot. After about twenty steps, he stopped to stand on one foot, keeping his right heel up and toes floating above the ground, clenching his jaw in pain.

"Here," said Amon, stepping beside Rick and wrapping his left arm around his waist. "Put your weight on my shoulder." And they began to proceed, with Rick hopping along using Amon like a crutch.

Together, they moved with as much stealth as they could, peeking around corners before turning into new alleys, creeping up stairs to scope the path ahead and climbing down again if the route looked too open, aiming their guns forward when crawling through tunnels and squeezeways, gradually losing themselves in the maze of this unfamiliar territory in the hopes of losing their pursuers, of putting as much distance between themselves and the battle as they could. It was difficult for Rick to climb and they would be easier to spot on the more open upper levels, so they stayed as close to ground level as they could. Everywhere they went, the paths were almost deserted, with only the occasional furtive figure appearing and then vanishing into the interstices of the slum, the local gifted surely taking cover from the violence in their disposcrapers. But eventually Amon and Rick heard the blather of many voices ahead, which told them they were approaching one of the branches of the Road to Delivery, and they steered their course away from it, knowing that the air above would be filled with CareBots. By now the drones might have been taught what they looked like using images culled from the Delivery sensors—or just to search for suspicious armed men dressed like OpScis. All the men and women on the sabotage crew, including Vertical, had volunteered to do their parts knowing that there was a strong chance they could be labeled as hungry ghosts or dangerous targets. Plastic surgery could be provided to throw off facial detection, as a few bankdead doctors recruited at the founding of Xenocyst had passed on this archaic art (which had been rendered obsolete by the ubiquity of digimake). And Rashana had offered, without anyone requesting it, to do everything in her power to remove anyone whose DNA got sampled from blacklists, either by bargaining, bribery, hacking, or, if that failed, by giving them amnesty in her Er facility until anonymous relocation could be arranged. Yet for the time being, the crewmembers had to hide and Amon and Rick did their best to stay clear of more heavily populated areas. Despite their distance from the main foot traffic arteries, they occasionally spied a DusterFly or TazerWasp ripping past in some crack overhead and had to cower at the base of the nearest wall or inside the nearest nook until they were sure the threat had passed. The translucent bodies of the CareBots were as difficult to spot in the gloom as flitting shadows, and Amon now understood why they were constructed of such a vitreous material. The only other motion was the flakes drifting about them, colorless and gray, as they crept further into the cold depths of the labyrinth where sunlight never touched.

After some time, the bamboo-board transitioned into copper and then to limestone before the shelters turned motley, and the air began to fill with the reek of sewage and rot, telling them they had left the Gifted Triangle and reached a giftless area.

"We need to get off the streets and find shelter before the drones secure the Triangle and move in to lock down the surrounding enclaves," said Amon as they walked along a narrow strip of tarmac between precarious crumbling towers of misaligned blocks.

Rick nodded. "If only we could ditch these uniforms. With no one else outside, we're the easiest targets on Earth."

Though the original plan had been to give the saboteurs a change of clothes so they could remove their disguises after the mission, the OpSci uniforms had turned out to be too tight to wear over the more baggy standard supplies and they would have looked strange carrying bags *to* Delivery. Instead, the council had decided to have Xenocysters waiting on their return route to hand them changes, but Amon and Rick had missed the rendezvous, leaving them stuck with what they were wearing. OpScis had been passing ever more frequently through the Gifted Triangle of late, so while it wouldn't be obvious that they were the saboteurs, they didn't blend in either as the residents were all gifted.

Amon looked around at the disposcrapers. "Should we try to commandeer one of the rooms?"

"How about there?" said Rick, pointing to a stub of alley that ended at a narrow dead end wall. It was made of concrete—not shelters of Fleet concrete but a solid slab—with an empty doorframe cut into it on the ground floor. "That looks like the entrance to a condo, doesn't it? If we hole up in an elevator the drone sensors won't have a chance."

Amon nodded. Then both men drew their guns and Amon helped Rick to the end of the alley. Through the doorframe, Amon could see shadowed figures huddled everywhere—on the floor, along the walls—the milky half-circles of their low-hung eyes tracking them from the darkness.

"I hate to disturb these people in their homes," whispered Amon.

"I know, me too," Rick replied. "But can I leave this one to you? With my leg like this, you'll be more persuasive."

Without replying, Amon held out his gun and stepped confidently through the frame. The figures all melted away from him as though his duster were a torch dispelling shadows, clearing a path for them across the dim, dilapidated lobby. The ceiling over their bowed heads bent down in the middle as though some heavy weight were on the floor above, the walls dark in blotchy patches with what appeared to be holes, the de-tiled floor bumpy and warped, as Rick clung to Amon's arm and hobbled along just behind him.

"There," said Rick, pointing to the battered metal door of an elevator open just a crack, a faint vertical line of light slashing out. The opening was too narrow for them to fit, so they both stuck their hands between the doors and, with a surge of muscle, managed to pry them a notch wider. Beneath the glow of a fresh firefLyte, a group of six scrawny, pugnacious-looking boys sat against the walls surrounded by an assortment of anadeto and bits of plastic that cluttered the chamber. Startled, they leapt to their feet and snatched up mismatched weapons: a chipped scalpel, a razor on a string, spiky pieces of metal and plastic.

"Tell them to leave," Rick muttered to Amon.

"Out!" Amon shouted, standing outside the doorway with his barrel trained on the inside of the chamber. "You'll get it back tomorrow when we leave."

The boys froze, holding their weapons ready to fight, but five of them flicked their eyes to the eldest boy as if wanting his instruction. Not more than thirteen, their young leader was unusually pudgy for bankdead in these days of scarcity, clearly having secured more than his share. He nodded to the others and they all began to gather up tools, knick-knacks, and scrap from the mess on the floor, bundling them in their own pieces of tarp. A boy who looked about nine sent a venomous glare at another boy of about the same age when he picked up a hole-puncher. He looked ready to call him out for stealing until he glanced at Amon furtively and seemed to think better of it.

In the order that they finished bundling their meager treasures, the boys crept timidly for the doors and Amon stepped back to let them out through the slit. Their pudgy leader was the last to leave and went to take the firefLyte on his way out, but when Rick gave him a piercing glare and a firm shake of his head, he abandoned it, slipping past them into the lobby in the wake of his friends and stepping around the huddled shadows out into the alley. When Amon looked back through the crack, the floor of the elevator was completely bare, as though no one had ever lived there.

Amon didn't feel good about kicking people out of their shelter, even this gang of young thugs that was probably terrorizing the local denizens—otherwise there was no explaining their possession of this prize elevator and their many weapons—but in the circumstances he and Rick had little choice. In the frenzied struggle to escape Delivery with their lives they had already fought and stepped on however many innocents, and there was no restraining their beastly wills to survive now, though Amon, and surely Rick as well, hoped to mitigate the harm they might do as best he could.

Rick turned his body sideways and Amon stuffed him through the slit from behind before squeezing into the elevator himself. Amon sat against the wall left of the door below where the firefLyte hung from a hole in the ceiling and Rick took the wall opposite him. They then laid their guns on the floor and Rick breathed a sigh, drawing Amon to let out one of his own. He almost felt a hint of relief.

But it was then, beneath the glow of the lantern, that Amon noticed Rick was crying.

"What's wrong?" Amon asked, staring at his friend as tears dribbled slowly and steadily from his eyes.

"What?"

"You're crying!"

"Yeah, and you'd think it's because of my ankle and everything else that went wrong today," said Rick almost casually as he continued to cry, his voice not audibly perturbed by sadness or any other strong emotion, his expression almost flat if displaying signs of tiredness. "It started when we were about halfway across the bridge. I'm guessing it was one of the DusterFlies."

"Tear dust?!" said Amon in alarm.

"I think they got me when I fired warning shots for Ty and them."

"We'd better go find you something to drink."

They had received extra food and beverages that morning, provided by the council to fortify them for the mission, and Amon had felt more contented than he had in weeks. Now, after the extreme exertion of the sabotage, he was parched, and saw that Rick was losing water even faster.

"Oh yeah. I'd love something to wet my lips. But I don't think I can walk." Rick pulled off his right shoe and rolled up his pant leg to reveal his ankle, bright red and swollen to the size of a Fuji apple. "I guess I twisted it worse than I thought. It just keeps throbbing harder and harder and now that I'm sitting down it feels all stiff, like it's locking up."

"Shit. What are we going to do? We need to rehydrate you fast."

"Don't worry. The trickle has been so small since they got me on the bridge you didn't even notice. Right now must be the peak."

"I hope so . . . but I'd better go find you something anyway. You never know," said Amon, getting to his feet. "Just wait here."

Picking up his duster, Amon slipped between the doors. Strangely, he found the lobby completely empty, the huddled figures gone, and realized why when he saw a faintly glinting blur hovering outside the open doorway. Several DusterFlies fluttered in the alley, wantonly flicking about the dust on their wings, and a BansheeBird *thwapped* the air as it blurred by an intersecting path above. Without turning around, Amon slunk back into the elevator, resisting the panic thumping in his chest to retreat as quietly as he could.

"What is it?" Rick whispered urgently, clearly startled by the suddenness of Amon's return, and picked up his gun.

"The CareBots are here! They're in the alley and all around! What should we do?"

"Shit," said Rick, taking aim at the slit in the door. "I guess we'll just hunker down here for now. We can go search for a feeding station once they clear out. My leg should be better by then."

Looking at Rick's still-exposed swollen ankle, Amon frowned with concern, doubting that he would recover as quickly as he seemed to believe. He sat against the wall across from Rick again, wondering how they might get him something to drink. In spite of Rick's hopefulness, the flow of tears seemed to be picking up now, a droplet making its way down each cheek nearly every second, the cold metal shell of the elevator so unnervingly quiet that Amon could hear each one spatter onto the floor. The firefLyte above began to dissolve, little flecks of light drifting down into the space between them and extinguishing into nothing before they hit the ground.

When a few minutes had passed and no drones appeared, Rick lowered his gun to the floor beside him but kept his hand on the grip, poised to whip it up in a hurry if need arose.

"Oh, I hope we can get out of here in time," said Amon. "If we don't make it to Xenocyst by midnight, we might not get another chance."

Rashana had a special agreement with the venture charities that allowed her to pick up giftless crashdead for her Er facilities and gave her media access to Delivery only under the condition that she refrain from overly subversive activism. As the exposé was clearly a violation of this agreement, she would soon be forced to withdraw all Atupio agents from the District of Dreams, and there would be no way to reach her if they failed to meet.

"Are you still sure that's a good idea?"

Amon had been hoping that Rick would see that Rashana was trustworthy and reliable after she assisted them with the mission, but her position wasn't that clear anymore. Nothing was clear anymore . . . "Let's not jump to hasty conclusions."

"Then what the fuck do you think happened back there?"

"Shit, I don't know. Those freekeepers came on fast!"

"Too fast. Weren't they supposed to be stationed ten floors up? They were gathering around the supply table before Vertical even got out the door. It was like they knew exactly what she was going to do and were just waiting for her to do it. Then without even blinking, they started firing on us. Don't they need authorization from the top to invest in violence here? How could they have been so prepared?"

"Maybe they picked up our plans through surveillance."

"In the council chamber? That Tamper guy's devices worked beautifully at Delivery. Why doubt his digital quarantine?"

"True. The hacks he used in Free Tokyo work so well he's been living off the machines for years, still haven't caught him . . . So maybe a spy then? Hippo says he trusts everyone on the council, but there's so much less to lose these days by ratting us out."

"But what's there to gain? Maybe they could make a deal with the venture charities for a supply bonus to ride out this crisis, but in the long run they'd never get anything better than what we already have at Xenocyst: security, community, culture, respect. The charities can't offer anything like that, which is exactly why we all stick together. Xenocyst really is the best deal any sane bankdead could hope for. Surely our councilors would agree with that?"

"Okay. Maybe. So what about Kitao then?"

"Fuck . . . That was really weird. What the hell was that guy doing there?"

"Remember I told you I saw him talking to one of the freekeepers? That was right before the backup busted into the hallway. So maybe he was warning them about us."

"But how would Kitao know what we were doing? I mean, even if there was something obviously wrong with the uniforms we made, all that would tell him is that we were frauds, and he could complain to the freekeepers all he wants about our little masquerade, but why would they care? Plus their response was way too quick if he'd only just told them."

"Hmmm." Amon thought for a moment as Rick frowned in his direction, his tears and the fireflies falling out of synch as though visually representing different beats. "So what if . . . Well, it seems way too coincidental that he'd be there, an OpSci priest that we know, that we cash crashed, suddenly appearing on the day we dress like OpScis to frame them for sabotage. Don't you think? So maybe . . . Could Barrow have been working for them all along? Then he might have told his old political buddy about our plans to curry favor with the Quantitative Priesthood."

"Whoah. Just what you'd expect from a politician I guess . . . I'm surprised to hear you talking shit about him when you're usually all over his knob."

"Hey! I respect him for what he did as a leader, but I'm not some brown-nosing idiot!"

"Okay. Fine. Calm down. So let's assume he's linked up with the OpScis. Then why'd he make that speech about going to war with them?"

"Maybe he meant to destroy Xenocyst by luring us into a fight we couldn't hope to win."

"Devious. I wouldn't put it past him. But I never took Barrow for a believer. So maybe it was all a big act, but that speech he gave was just full of hate. You couldn't hear it in his voice because he's got that perfect control; it was something about the way he emphasized certain words, you know, you could just tell. I really think he despises them. For how they treated him. Maybe the way they treat anadeto too."

"I guess I got the same impression from him. If I think about it, there are other reasons to believe he was genuinely behind our plan. Like his history with the Philanthropy Syndicate. They were the ones who partnered with Anisha to have him ID assassinated, so he probably hates them even more than the OpScis, and I can imagine that having the chance to disrupt their plans in the way we tried must have been exciting for him."

Rick nodded and then hung his head, apparently thinking. "So what about Rashana then?"

"I doubt it," said Amon. "Just look at her interests. They seem perfectly aligned with ours. We get that viral seg out there, the coalition maybe goes down, the Philanthropy Syndicate loses some funds and influence, and she gets to mess with her sister by screwing with the Gyges Circle."

"But that's exactly why I think it might have been her," said Rick, raising his head. "Forcing the Charity Brigade to unleash their full brutality on video would make for an even more persuasive seg. What could suit her interests more?"

"I'm not sure if it's fair to be that cynical about her. I mean, if Hippo and Barrow can be believed, then she would never let all those bank-dead get hurt for her own purposes. Plus those weapons are designed specifically not to look brutal on video." Amon remembered the lack of screams on the bridge and supposed that each dose of dust of whatever kind had been laced with mute dust. This would minimize the appearance of suffering to any Free Citizens that might by chance be observing the scene or watching naked segs of it. In general, since the non-lethal crowdcare weaponry employed by freekeepers and drones left no visible wounds or bruises, their effects looked merely uncomfortable rather than damaging—especially if footage was edited—and could be promoted as a necessary means to protect anarchic rioters from themselves. "Her reporters got cleared away before the attack got started anyways, so if that was her plan it failed miserably."

"Okay," said Rick. "So what about Anisha then?"

"What about her?"

"I don't know. Maybe word got out to her about what her sister was planning and she arranged to have the Brigade ready to interfere."

"Could be. But now we're just speculating. We have no idea what's going on between the sisters. We don't even know one hundred percent that Rashana *is* Rashana."

Nothing was certain, nothing ever had been, and Amon began to doubt his resolution to see Rashana on the roof of the Cyst that night. There was no way to get in touch with her to cancel the meeting, so his decision whether to honor it or not would likely be final, for he would have to blow it off or trust her fully, as all of Xenocyst had trusted her in bringing her in on the sabotage. But had that been the right choice? Could the whole plan have been doomed from the start?

"Aw," Amon sighed, his spine quivering with toxic pulses of guilt. "What a disaster I created." Or was it the sky, the seeming profundity he'd discovered, that had led them astray? Somehow he couldn't believe that. There must have been something he misunderstood.

"You shouldn't blame yourself," said Rick. "It's not your fault we were betrayed. And overall, I'd say the mission was a success."

"A *success*?! How?"

"I'm pretty sure Rashana's reporters got a clean shot of Vertical's drama and everything before that, which was what we set out to do, right?" Rick's voice sounded hopeful as he said this, but then he wiped his tears away and Amon saw his hand shake for just a moment. Seeming to notice Amon's searching gaze of concern, Rick averted his eyes to the corner of the elevator, as though that might help him dissemble his emotions from a friend he knew could read them like no other. Amon could sense Rick's fear anyways, in his tense posture and the tightness of his breathing, and suddenly realized the mortal danger he was in. For the flow of tears was not dwindling as one would expect with a normal dose of tear dust. No, the flow was increasing steadily, the size of each succeeding droplet seeming to grow.

Like other crowdcare weaponry, tear dust could be set to different levels of non-lethality. At level one, it overstimulated the tear gland. At level two, it additionally paralyzed the gland that coated tears with oil, increasing overflow onto the cheeks. At level three, it induced swelling of the tear ducts to cut off drainage from the eye. Additional exposures simply increased tear gland stimulation, raising the intensity and duration of the effects cumulatively. The symptom outbreak speed was also adjustable, ranging from "instant outpour," which had been applied to the lineup inside Delivery, to "gradual flood," which Rick seemed to be suffering.

Although the crying only lasted for a few hours at the lowest setting, when applied repeatedly it could continue anywhere from days to weeks to months. In such cases, dehydration and malnutrition became a serious risk, especially in summer, as water and electrolytes drained from the body more rapidly. If enough beverages could be secured, some people were said to live for an entire season with this condition, though buildup of residue could often cause pain, tear duct infections, vision impairment, and even blindness. Rick too might be kept going for a long time, even if he'd been exposed to multiple doses as his intensifying symptoms suggested, but he had already lost plenty of fluids in the intense exertion of the sabotage, ensuing battle, and their flight here, so if they couldn't get to a vending machine soon—

"I'm going to check and see if the drones are still there," said Amon, getting to his feet. Leaning towards the elevator doors to stick his head through the gap, he scanned the lobby. It was still vacant, but so too now was the alley, no hovering glints anywhere. Pulling back into the room, he met Rick's eyes. "Looks like we're all clear for now," he said. "Let me just peek outside and be back in a minute."

Rick nodded, flicking tears off the twin rivulets draped down his cheeks. "Here, take this," he said, picking up his machine pistol from the floor and proffering it to Amon. "Your duster's no good on drones."

"Thanks," said Amon, taking it by the handle, "you take mine," and pulled his duster from his holster to hand it to Rick. "In case someone shows up while I'm gone."

"Okay. But Amon?" said Rick, his voice lilting with urgency. Amon stopped at the door and looked back. "There's no need for you to come back here."

Amon was speechless as Rick glared at him with defiant terror.

"I was trying to be positive about my ankle, but I won't be walking to Delivery tonight. You have your appointment with Rashana and, all the things we talked about aside, I think you should honor it. I'll look after myself."

Stunned, Amon stood there frowning, his mouth agape, lips twitching wordlessly until, "What?"

"Amon. I'll be fine. By morning—"

"Fine? Just look at yourself! All the water is leaking out of your body and you can't even stand. What if you fall asleep, alone, in the middle of—"

"Amon! Can you just do what I ask? It's not a good idea for you to stay here."

"Don't be crazy. Why?"

"If you don't go now, it'll be too dark and you'll never make it. Like you said, this is your last chance."

"But what about—"

"GO!" Rick bellowed suddenly, the elevator booming with his voice, spit and tears flying, his body shaking, his eyes wide with distress. "Just fucking GO! You hear me, GO!"

"What's the matter with you?" Amon whisper-hissed, trying to imply Rick should quiet down. "You want—"

"No more arguments. Go already, *please*." Rick's voice cracked with emotion. "I'm begging you. It's what's best for you. For both of us. You've got to get out of this place."

What's happening? Amon wondered. It harrowed him to watch his friend, who had struggled so bravely that day—saving his life and the lives of Ty and his crew—break down so incomprehensibly like this.

"Look. I'm stepping out now. But I'm just going to get you a drink and then I'm coming back."

"NO! That's just what I mean. Don't. Come. Back."

"I'm not arguing anymore," said Amon, prying his gaze away with a shake of his head, and stepped out the door, Rick's muffled howl of *GO, Amon. Please just GO!* making him cringe and tense his back as he crept across the still-empty lobby.

★

Amon crouched at the doorway to the lobby and stared up at the over-hanging jumble of shelters, watching out for flying glitters. Spotting nothing but steady flakefall, he slipped furtively into the alley and began to search around the condo perimeter for vending machines. He peered down the connecting squeezeways and zigzagged around to what he thought was the back of the building, but found nothing. He decided he would need a better vantage to scope out the routes and climbed a stairpath about ten half-stories when he spotted a DusterFly flittering by and rolled softly into a shallow alcove. Between the edges of the rooms that enclosed him, all Amon could see was a section of wall a meter away and couldn't tell if more CareBots were passing by—though he thought he heard a faint echo of gentle flapping and the patter of raining flakes. The fact that his ears caught these subtle noises told him just how quiet the surround was. The sounds of battle had long since faded and they were well away from the Road to Delivery. No footsteps on the streets. No chatter through the thin Fleet walls. Amon could imagine the locals tucked away in their rooms, holding their breath, perhaps snuggling with each other in mutually protective embrace, and envied them. That was just what he wanted to be doing: cowering in a tight, out-of-the-way hole, like that elevator, or, better yet, their room in Xenocyst, as he had done with Rick during the typhoon. But such fantasies were not to be indulged. Not at least until he found Rick something to drink.

So Amon waited until he heard no passing drones for several minutes before slowly peeking his head out from the nook. Although he was relieved to find no threats lurking about—just a roofway snaking upwards to the left and discontinuous jutting platforms separated by gaps to the right—his sudden dive into the nook seemed to have joggled his sense of direction and he was no longer sure which way he had come. Even after he crawled out and looked around more carefully from the ledge, he saw only a rabbit warren matrix of strange alleys and stairpaths. Careful not to drift too far, he wandered tentatively along each of them. Stooping, crawling, climbing, he wound back and forth through this unknown chunk of ephemeral city, terrified that he might never find his way back to the elevator where Rick needed him, even if he said otherwise. Thick layers of shadow petals swirled round, obscuring the lay of the slumscape, some of it skimming Amon's face and hands on its way down, as the dredges of sunlight that had seeped into the area faded rapidly. On the rooftop ground, Amon saw piles of shards like faintly glowing broken ice here and there, and guessed that DusterFlies must have shatter dusted the firefLytes to enforce a lights-out policy. Soon it would be too dark to see at all and he would have to wait until morning to find the condo entrance. Either that or he could climb to higher ground where the sun still glowed, and use the remaining light to do as Rick had demanded: return to Xenocyst for his meeting with Rashana. Only the residue of a vanishing day remained, and he would have to begin climbing immediately if he were to have any chance. His choice was now or never: keep searching or ascend.

Yet Amon only considered these two possibilities for a fleeting second, as leaving Rick alone in his present condition—without at least finding him something to drink—seemed like no choice at all. Though he felt the heavy weight of despair settle in his stomach as his dreams winked out in the black emptiness of his consciousness—jubilee, Mayuko, the forest extinguished forever—escaping from the District of Dreams would mean nothing to him, no matter what he achieved afterwards, if it had been earned by abandoning his best friend. And to his relief, after a few minutes of wandering, he spotted the familiar stub of an alley below.

After hang-dropping down the side of the wall to land before the condo entrance, Amon ran his fingers restlessly over his face and through his puff of hair with distress and confusion—*What will happen to Rick? How can I help him?*—dithering outside, unsure whether to continue on or return to the chamber empty-handed. But it only took a few seconds for him to accept how pointless and dangerous it would be to traipse blindly through the shifting labyrinth in the drone-infested dark, almost certainly to be separated from his ailing friend forever, and he reluctantly stepped through the doorless doorway.

A few residents had gathered in the lobby again, the silhouette tableau of their huddle along the walls barely visible in the glow from the elevator. Had the glow grown fainter? Amon held out Rick's gun to ward off anyone that might approach, and crossed back to the thin beam of light between doors, slotting his body in.

Inside, the lantern hung on a wire from a small hole in the ceiling dissolving furiously, sparkles showering the room, the gray-walled chamber flickering from dim to semi-bright like a noncommittal strobe. Rick was lying flat on the floor of the elevator with the top of his head touching the wall opposite the door. A circular puddle of liquid now ringed his head like a glistening halo that slowly expanded as the tears fed it one after the other. If Amon wasn't mistaken, they seemed to be growing a bit darker and—was it a trick of the light? No!

"Rick! Your eyes!" cried Amon. "They're *bleeding*!"

Although the droplets slipping down his cheeks were not as dark as blood, there was a reddish tinge to them whose source seemed obvious.

"What are you doing here?" said Rick. His tone was firm, but his voice was overly subdued as though he had been sapped of strength, while heavy quivering exhalations betrayed his fear. Despite his unwelcoming words, Amon thought he looked relieved to see him.

"Come on Rick. I don't understand you. You know I can't leave. Definitely not now. What's happening to you?"

"Those drones must have dusted me more than once. I never really believed it until now, but I heard rumors that you can cry blood with an overdose."

Amon clicked his tongue and ran his fingers through his hair, baring his teeth.

"I wish you'd done as I asked."

"It's too late. The sun is down."

Rick paused for a moment as though thinking. "Did you find anything to drink?"

"No. Damn, Rick. I'm sorry. I looked around for a bit until some drones came. Then I had to hide for a while. They destroyed all the lanterns and the sunlight started to fade so I kind of got lost and just barely found my way back. I thought it would be too dark to go searching anymore, but maybe I should head back out there."

"What about going to Xenocyst?"

"I told you, the sun is down. There's no way I'd make it there before morning. We don't even know where we are."

Rick let out a long, quivering sigh. "Then forget about it. Getting yourself lost out there in the night with all the drones on patrol would be suicidal. We're just going to have to stick it out till morning."

Amon looked down at his best friend, at his dull, enervated gaze, at the puddle of pale, bloody tears soaking the back of his head, at his slack open mouth, and he decided that he had to try his luck out there once more. Day or night, unknown or familiar, dangerous or safe, it didn't matter. He would find a drink for Rick, even if it meant losing his life in the process.

"Don't worry," said Amon. "I'm going to give it another shot, but I'll be careful. There are other directions I haven't tried yet."

"No. Forget it, Amon. What if you can't find your way back this time?"

"Just give me a few minutes to find something. You must be thirsty as hell."

"I am. Thirsty. Really, really thirsty. But . . ." Rick trailed off and closed his eyes.

"Okay. So I'll be right back."

" . . ."

Amon stood up, his intense worry for his friend impelling him to the door. He had only taken two steps when Rick said, "Wait" quietly, but with such charged inflection that Amon's legs froze and he looked back at him again.

"I really don't think you should go this time," said Rick, his bleeding eyes staring pleadingly at Amon. "Not just because of the darkness and the drones. I don't think you've thought this situation through."

"First you say go, and now you say stay? What is this, Rick?"

"Listen, okay? Do you realize we're in a war zone? Sure, they call it crowdcare and make it look all fatherly for the vids, but violence is violence, whether it's non-lethal or semi-lethal or whatever the fuck they say. Every bankdead in their right mind is hiding in their room or whatever, so you're going to stand out like nothing else on those empty streets. If you do manage to find a feeding station, it'll be swarming with drones and you'll be lucky to get past them to a machine. That's assuming one of the SampleQuitos didn't suck on you because, if they did, those vending machines will be no better than deathtraps. So don't even think about going out there. If there's no way for you to get to Xenocyst and make your appointment with Rashana, the only thing we can do now is wait."

Rick's words reminded Amon of the SampleQuito on the bridge. Although he'd totally forgotten in the flurry of their escape, one had indeed stung him. This meant that some member of the Philanthropy Syndicate had his genome in their database and if they could link it to the recording of him taken by the sensors in the supply lanes, they might discover he was one of the saboteurs and put him on a blacklist. Then he'd *definitely* be a hungry ghost or, if the charities were really pissed off, the vending machine security systems would take him out on the spot and summon CareBots as backup. So while getting Rick some fluids was of the utmost importance, trying to access a vendor before they spoke with Rashana might get Amon killed or captured, and then his friend would be left crippled and helpless as he . . .

Amon stood there by the slit, staring at Rick, the spectacle of his friend shaking in his visual field as Amon's eyes twitched with concern. The tears had thickened further, oozing down his face to feed the darkening halo that warped as it expanded, the shadows on the floor growing with the gradual dissolution of the lantern as though they were sucking down the light from above.

"Wait?" Amon replied. "Wait for what? You're not going to last much longer like this."

"What other options do we have?"

"I'll be back soon," said Amon, stepping forward and putting his shoulder into the space between the doors. "Just—"

"Please!" Rick cried, his voice suddenly quavering, "Can't you see what's happening to me? My eyes ache. They *ache*! Everything's clouding over in red, and the whole room is so blurry I can hardly make out the walls. And I feel weak. Weaker and weaker each second, like my arms are dumbbells almost too heavy to lift and—and . . . When you went outside, I wanted you to leave, but I can't tell you how scary it was to think you weren't coming back and that I might—I don't want to be alone like this . . ."

Looking into Rick's desperate bleeding eyes, Amon finally understood their predicament. A bit of sports drink wasn't going to cure what ailed him. A sheen of blood kept forming over his eyes and then overflowing the bottom of his sockets, creating wine-red rivers that gleamed in the deepening dim with each sparkle from the crumbling sphere of light and dribbled down the sides of his cheeks to send ripples over the surface of the pool. If they were in the Cyst hospital, they might have amputated the tear gland and stemmed the outflow, but that was several kilometers of maze away, not to mention darkness, and drones, and gods and buddhas knew what else. Amon wished he had a scalpel or some kind of blade so he could do it himself, and darted his gaze around the elevator, but of course there was nothing and he realized it was mad to think his untrained, clumsy hands would do anything but kill his friend if there was.

Amon had seen other victims of tear dust—sprawled together in puddle-filled alleys, licking each others cheeks in rhythmic alternation to trade lost fluids—but never symptoms this severe, and his fear for his friend was suddenly tinged with the hot blush of anger when he realized that what had been done to him would undoubtedly go unpunished. Tear dusters were technically "non-lethal" or "semi-lethal," even if they might result in death or serious injury from lack of hydration, as the actual cause was limited water rations, which it was not the responsibility of anyone to supply, only an act of compassion from the charities. No single round could kill someone directly and it was difficult to assign responsibility for delayed, long-term, or cumulative reactions, since bankdead had no BodyBank sensors to collect verifiable evidence of the state of their health after initial dusting. The Fiscal Judiciary therefore only treated tear dust as causing temporary gland stimulation and fined the individual freekeepers who used it for the relatively cheap credicrimes of "assault," "inducing discomfort," and so on.

Freekeepers were nonetheless discouraged from firing their assault dusters except when it was a last resort—as it had been during the riot—because it was even cheaper to have CareBots employ crowdcare weaponry. While overdosing Rick might have been an intentional choice made by remote human operators, Amon guessed it was a "decision" made by the drones, which were programmed to look for "abnormal" or "disorderly" activities like the stampede on the bridge. The deterrence algorithms of several drones had probably labeled him a serious threat requiring dust with a high level of lethality, reaching the same conclusion independently rather than as part of a coordinated assault, so that responsibility for the overall result of his being hit multiple times would fail to stick to any one of them. Even if it did, the behavior of these machines was not considered an action any more than that of the bankdead—as they were non-citizens—and could not therefore incur fees, let alone meet the Fiscal Judiciary's definition of a credicrime. At the same time, the fact that they were nominally autonomous entities limited culpability for those who designed, maintained, and deployed them to cases of negligence such as "faulty programming" or "improper use," as blame for particular violations could be placed on the drones. This ambivalence surrounding the legal status of drone moral agency made it a cinch for Philanthropy Syndicate lawyers to prevent liability from climbing the chain of command; the end result being nullification, diversion, and reduction of any financial penalties.

Combined with the half-price rebate on crimes against bankdead always in effect, and the recent Absolute Choice reduction on fines for brutality, CareBots were an affordable mode of crowdcare indeed. In Rick's case, however much he suffered in the end, the most that might happen was some organization peripherally involved paying a negligible fee, and Amon squeezed his fist so hard with indignation just thinking about it that his whole arm shook. While he was beginning to accept that Rick was right about the futility of going to search for something to drink, accepting the implications of staying here was impossible. Could Amon really just do nothing? How could this awful situation be allowed to unfold?

Amon slipped out the slit and cried, "Hey! Anyone have any water? Please! My friend needs water, okay? He's dying. Anyone? Please?"

It could have been the darkness, but the shadowy figures showed no signs they had even heard him. Not a flinch or a turn of the head. They simply remained slouching along the walls and sprawled on the floor, silent, whether sleeping or awake Amon could not tell.

Their apparent indifference infuriated him and he squeezed Rick's gun with ruthless resolve, taking one stomp towards them, determined to find out if they had water and take it from them if he had to.

"Amon!" called Rick, his voice trilling with concern, and Amon suddenly realized what he was doing, his anger fizzling out as fast as it had struck him. Here he was in the middle of a famine, asking strangers for something to drink after busting into their home with guns and seizing the best room in the house. With the current supply levels, there probably wasn't a drop of water in the whole condo, and if there was, depriving these people any further could mean taking their lives, killing for the sake of his friend.

Filled with revulsion for what he had almost done, Amon retreated back into the elevator, letting Rick's gun fall from his hand with a *clonk*.

"I'm sorry, Amon," said Rick. "I know it's my fault you lost the chance to get out of here, but if that's the way it's got to be then please stay here and talk to me. Just . . . talk to me."

Amon turned towards his voice and saw Rick holding out his hand from the floor, looking up at Amon with a forlorn and terrified expression, the wine continuing to spill down his twitching cheeks, his jaw quivering. Amon looked from Rick's outstretched hand to his half-blind, red-clouded brown eyes, and grappled for a few moments with the words that had just launched from his lips. But their meaning outmatched him, and soon Amon resigned himself to taking his friend's hand, feeling the core of warmth beneath the cool surface of his sweaty skin, and slumped down to his right against the cold, hard wall.

"I don't know why you keep saying it's your fault," said Amon, shaking his hanging head. "So many people hurt and dead, our friends too maybe. And look what they did to you, all because of my stupid plan."

"Like I told you, don't even think about that now," said Rick, his voice surprisingly confident as he squeezed Amon's hand tightly. "Your plan was the only chance we had. It was a good one. We took a chance. Something we couldn't foresee happened and we got attacked. But it wasn't a total failure. We got the footage and now there's a good chance that everything will be better here."

Maybe, but will you be there to see it? thought Amon, keeping his despair to himself rather than polluting his friend's adamant hope. He knew he would never have spoken such optimistic sentiments in Rick's place, and admired his resilience. The idea that such an incredible person might soon be gone was just too sad and enraging to consider, and Amon squeezed back, quelling the shaking that seemed to arise from the pit of his belly as he held in his own tears.

"So please stop blaming yourself," Rick continued. "If anyone screwed up, it was me."

"What are you talking about? How?" But Rick merely sighed and continued to lie there in his blood and tears, his chest trembling slightly as it rose and fell with each breath, while Amon slouched beside him, not wanting to press him in his dire condition.

For a few minutes, they remained silent. The pool was spreading towards Amon, and eventually he had to raise his buttocks off the floor, his shoes becoming two islands. He thought he could feel his friend's pulse in his hand—or was it his own? Its steady pounding seemed to slowly dwindle, like the ebbing and flowing tide of the ocean being sucked down a drain. Before the world turned to desert, before everything was just sand blowing about, fluid and ephemeral like the city they cowered beneath, was there anything that had to be said, any last words to exhale in the roaring face of the inevitable? Yes, there was. But was it right to expose the truth when the lie could be so much more comforting; to slice open the soft veil of moss and reveal the sharp rocks beneath?

"Rick," Amon said, his tongue seizing the initiative and answering his own question for him. "There's something I need to tell you."

Rick's blood-veiled eyes turned to Amon expectantly. "Yes, my friend."

"The day we met up here for the first time, when I told you the story about what happened to me after you cash crashed . . . there was something I sort of left out."

"Yeah. I know."

"Y-you know?"

"Well, not everything. Just say what you were going to say. I'm listening."

Amon told Rick about how Mayuko had saved him in the Open Source Zone and then took him to a weekly mansion to hide from his pursuers. While this part was easy enough, the rest of the story was difficult to admit, especially when Amon went on to explain how he'd fled the next day after the emoticon man arrived, leaving Mayuko in danger. The final part was the hardest of all, and he hesitated, afraid to hurt his fast-waning friend, until he sensed somehow that maintaining the deception one second longer would only hurt him in some more fundamental way, hurt them both, hurt them all, and heeded the words of sincerity as they cried out to escape into the world at last.

"The last moment I saw her before we had to disconnect she told me

. . . I don't know if I should be telling you this now, but you understand? I need everything between us to be clear and true."

". . . Yes, Amon," said Rick, his voice wispy and frail. "Whatever it is . . ."

"Well, it was . . . I still want to understand jubilee. And I haven't forgotten the dream. But now . . . She told me she still had feelings for me, you know, and that's one of the things that's kept me going, the idea that I might get back together with her someday."

Amon paused and looked at Rick to see how he was taking it. His eyes were half closed, as though he lacked the strength to keep them open any longer, and Amon couldn't catch his gaze to read it. Watching the blood gather around the edges of his eyelids, Amon wondered whether any of those tears were shed by sadness. Was every other tear a sad tear? Or was each tear divided into a different proportion? Forty percent sad, 60 percent . . .

"I'm sorry, Rick . . . We—"

"You don't need to apologize. I'm . . . I'm actually relieved."

"Relieved? How . . . You told me you wanted to start a family with her, so I thought . . . I thought that . . ."

"How can I explain?" Rick opened his eyes wide and looked at Amon, his gaze bearing in with intensity from behind the red veil. "I was part of a family once . . . You know I was adopted. I remember those days as happy times. Then suddenly they abandoned me, and I was in the BioPen where the kids were cruel. They didn't like newcomers, but you and Mayuko were kind to me from the beginning. Like this one day—it came back to me so clearly in Er when the overlay was gone and I had lots of time to think—this one day when all the other kids were shunning me and just pummeling me in dodgefireball and our SubMom didn't seem to care, or maybe she hated me, and then I was crying. You and Mayuko took me out to see that star in the afternoon. Do you remember? There was this one steady twinkle in the InfoSky, untouched by all the images, like an oasis of the naked world."

Now that Rick mentioned it, Amon did remember and nodded. He had seen the daytime star with Mayuko when they'd first met, and wanted to share this beautiful mystery with Rick when he saw how upset he was, so they'd snuck up to the rooftop again, this time trapped in their training banks.

"You and Mayuko took care of me. I'll always be grateful. You two were closer to me than anyone I'd ever known. So don't fool yourself that I couldn't tell you were hiding something in that story. While I was listening, I thought to myself, *Where's Mayuko in all this?* The Mayuko I knew would be calling you about me non-stop after I disappeared. I could only think that you cut her out of the story because you two had sex or something. I was jealous. I should have asked you the moment I had the chance. Maybe I was afraid to hear you tell me what I've always known. Because being back together with you here in the camps, I learned something. I used to think I was in love with Mayuko, that she was the only one I could be happy with. But then you became a big part of my life again, not just as a distant partner, as a close friend, and I realized . . . I did love Mayuko . . . I loved her as a friend . . . but not in that way. I only thought our connection was something more because . . . because you weren't around anymore. We were just sort of filling in the gap that you left when you were busy chasing your dream . . . Getting involved with Vertical was the only way I could chase mine . . ."

"You and Vertical? What does she—" Amon stopped himself, remembering the look of joy on Rick's face when they danced together at the festival. In a flash of insight, he understood why Rick wasn't around in the evenings, why he'd been reluctant to leave the camps, why he'd volunteered to be the agent provocateur on the mission.

"She was the one who picked me up from Er. She listened to my story at the council, and she trained me . . . I got to know her a bit . . . a bit too well maybe. After Tamper's story at the festival, I saw her sitting alone on the edge of the roof . . . She looked down . . . and I wanted some company . . . why not go cheer her up . . . And we discovered we have a lot in common. Then they made us dance in the circle with all the booze and before you know it . . ."

Rick gave the faintest, momentary smile.

"After that, we started seeing each other . . . these few weeks . . . I was disgusted with myself . . . disgusted to be interested in other women. Especially when it got serious . . ." As Rick spoke, he began to pause now and then, as though summoning strength for his voice. "We were careful not to have sex at the wrong times . . . charted her cycle. Neither of us wants a baby in this place . . . but it made me feel like I was moving towards being a father, even if I knew it wasn't going to happen ... Do you have any idea how painful it was? Doing cleanup work in the Cyst with babies around all the time. Me and you ... we were never even in the same room with babies in Free Tokyo ... They were always something strange ... far away ... raised by SubMoms in distant BioPens for future industries we couldn't even imagine ... or pets for the super-rich. Then we were surrounded by all kinds ... babies, toddlers, children ... those fetuses we had to throw away ... I heard their cries and gurgles, I said 'hi' to the mothers cradling them in the hallways, I watched them lying under blankets while we swept around the incubators ... and all I could think was how much I wanted one of my own ...

"I wanted to teach my kid ... son or daughter, it didn't matter, but I imagined him a son ... teach him everything ... the truth about the Free World and this place ... I wanted to raise someone beautiful and wise and good ... and happy ... not a happy lie ... but aware and accepting ... I wanted my son to see the stars, not with ads on them, but pure, and to really see them ... Maybe someone like that could make a difference in the future ... be part of a generation that gets us out of this awfulness ... It was a dream destined for tragedy ... just like my family and Vertical's family and all families in this fucked up world ... but Vertical showed me how to believe in the impossible and keep going in the here and now ... just like her with her running ... and with Vertical I found out that it didn't have to be with Mayuko ... So ... I was ashamed to tell you ... I didn't know what you'd think after everything I said before ... I was worried you'd hate me after I was with ... your ex-girlfriend ... after I talked like I was really crazy about her and ... just moved on to someone else. I'm glad to hear I wasn't betraying her and you like I thought ..." Rick paused to shake a glob of blood that had collected in the hollow of his right socket. "I guess it's too late for me to be a father ... If I'm lucky maybe one of my seeds will come to fruit. But I don't regret being in these worlds ... the Free and now the naked ... because I got a chance to meet great friends like you and Mayuko ... Vertical too ... I admire her strength and decisiveness ... not just quick on her feet but quick-thinking ... And let me tell you, when Vertical is horizontal, she's just fantastic ..." Rick tried to laugh but it came out as a series of weak pants. Amon didn't react. It might have been funny at another time, but not here, not now. Was the flow from Rick's eyes beginning to slow, or was time distorting in Amon's mind?

"That was why . . . I'm sorry, Amon." His words came out as faint mumbles. Amon almost couldn't hear him over the quavering rasp of his own disturbed breathing. "I told you I wanted to stay to take care of our friends and everyone else . . . and that was true. But I knew you wouldn't leave . . . not if I refused to go. Whatever happened, I wanted . . . I wanted to keep you and Vertical by my side. Now you're stuck here . . . If it wasn't for me, you'd be safe already . . . and you'll never . . . I'm sorry . . . I'm so sorry."

Amon shook his head, cringing with sadness, but Rick didn't see as he closed his eyes and his body went limp. Then suddenly he opened them, squeezed Amon's hand so hard it shook, and looking at Amon said, "Now there are no more lies or secrets between us, right? Just two friends completely open with each other . . ."

Amon nodded, as a tremor of sadness shook him from his core and he gritted his teeth, clenching all his muscles to contain it before it could seize his body. While the light flickered and sprinkled the chamber with increasingly dim fireflies, Rick squeezed Amon's hand and Amon squeezed back, their tears streaming down, linking their bodies and souls in liquid sorrow.

"I-if only I could have . . ." Amon said, his voice faint, somewhere between a whisper and a whimper, the dripping of the tears almost loud enough to obliterate it. "I should have been there for you and Mayuko all those years. I should have made time and really told you what I thought when you asked for advice. But I let my selfish dream get in the way . . . I-I mean, I wish . . ."

"Forget what happened then . . . Just be here . . . now."

21
XENOCYST WEST CHECKPOINT, THE LIBRARY

Password!" demanded one of the two guards that faced Amon in the middle of Xenocyst's west tunnel checkpoint. Both held dissolving nightsticks recoiled, ready to strike, one right-handed and the other left, so that they mirrored each other in the same stance, crouching with their weight on their back foot and the opposite foot forward. It was the right-handed man who had spoken. He was broad shouldered with bristly hair protruding from his sunburned cheeks and huge knuckles gripping his stick. The left-handed man beside him was wiry and short, with worm-like blue veins bulging from the sides of his forehead, the bald spot in his shaggy mop aimed just above Amon's head. Both looked to be in their early thirties and stared at Amon with bloodshot, circle-ringed eyes, hungry eyes, eyes that seemed ready to stop at nothing.

Amon stood there with his fists upraised boxer style, his heart pulsing in his ears. After he'd climbed up the outer wall these two sentries had shouted out for him to halt his approach, apparently reacting to his Opportunity Scientist outfit.

"Nighthawk Star," Amon replied. Although the two men remained in the same offensive posture, he could see their shoulders relax. They were at ease enough now to pry their gaze from him and exchange a glance. Lefty gave a nod to Righty, who said, "Okay. We can let you in. But our orders are to escort you straight to the Cyst."

"Escort me? For *what*?!" Amon snapped, annoyed with this unfamiliar procedure. "I know the way."

"Thez in't about guiding you," said Lefty, who had a strong Tumbles accent. "Anywen with the michin passwod still has t' get approval frem from the councel before thiz allowed t' go unsupahvised."

"*What's this?*" Amon growled, his eyes going wide with indignation. "We risked our lives for all of you!"

"Our riginal ordahz were t' welcome membahz of your party," said Lefty. "But aftah th' attack on Xenocyst last night, th'z breaches all ovah our fortifications. No one knows who t' trust anymore."

"So that's . . . I saw the wrecked buildings on my way in . . ." Amon said, "and the bodies. Who did this?"

"We don't know," said Righty. "Some rumors say the OpScis, some say the Brigade. All I know is you're not going anywhere without an escort. Not till you report to the council!"

Amon gave the men a murderous stare, as though injecting the concocted poison of his exhaustion, guilt, rage, and sorrow into their eyes across the space between them. A group of incoming residents slunk past the three battle-poised men and down the tunnel, where other guards stood ready, watching intently.

"So you coming with us or are we throwing you out?" asked Righty.

The two men tightened their mirrored stances, declaring through posture their readiness to back up their words with force. Amon had no energy for their suspicions. In fact, he was so tired it took all his will just to hold his fists up, keep his eyes fully open, and stay upright on his feet. He thought of the duster in the holster attached to his waist behind his back. He'd left it hidden because he didn't want these men to sound the alarm, but was ready to dust or pistol-whip them unconscious if he had to. No one was stopping him getting in, certainly not a couple of grunts. Yet he could tell they weren't bluffing, and picking a fight by rejecting their escort was only going to delay and tire him further. Considering the destruction he'd seen just outside the tunnel, it was understandable that they'd be on high alert, and somewhere in his turbid mind he began to suspect he might be overreacting. So he decided to swallow his pride and impatience, for he had to see Hippo right away, to tell the council what happened, to rest, to grieve . . .

"'ts go," Amon said with a curt nod and then winced, the image of Rick that flashed behind his eyelids like a jagged hunk of slag bursting into the depths of his soul.

It wasn't long after Amon and Rick had opened up to each other and finally come to an understanding about Mayuko that Rick stopped talking or responding. For a short while, he let out the occasional enervated groan, but these too soon stopped. All Amon could do was crouch in the dark puddle beside him, his back against the wall, and hold his friend's hand as he became visibly weaker and weaker. Hours passed, though to Amon they felt like years dragged over the rough rocks of time. And as the uneven thumbnail-sized chunk of what remained of the lantern began to shed the last of its fireflies, the light faded to the faintest blue-white glow above them, leaving the chamber dim and colorless. Amon watched his friend's face carefully, as he continued to cry without crying, his life seeping away, drop by drop. With the night withering away, the nauseating tide of exhaustion pushed at the back of Amon's eyes, and it seemed as though his memory of Mayuko crying on the floor of the weekly mansion were doubling up with Rick, each one of Rick's red-black tears bearing his dream, an obsidian bead necklace of forests reeling from his best friend's eyes.

At first, he dismissed the expanding interval between each droplet going down Rick's cheeks as distortions in his own sense of time, but soon the change became so consistent and steady as to be undeniable. It was the most pitiful, revolting, heart-rending sight Amon had ever witnessed and, to his shame, part of him desperately wanted it to be over already almost as much as he wanted his friend to be healed and revived, his beautiful friend. As if to satisfy Amon's dark wish, Rick gave out one last spasm of body quakes, opened his eyes, and turned his gaze to Amon's. The look of brooding sadness that had often been in Rick's eyes was gone. All that remained behind the red, cloudy veil was raw pain and confusion that seemed to demand answers of the world and Amon as its nearest representative. Eventually the flow stopped, the oneiric excretions running dry, and when Rick's last tear fell, Amon knew that his dream was dead, once and for all.

Eventually, Rick's hand began to go cold and Amon gently put it down in the black liquid below. He sat there for a while longer, his head between his knees, his buttocks floating above the dark pool, the small ripples his own tears sent against his shoes visible only as hazy arcs of motion beneath the faintest hint of a lantern that remained. Before long, Amon began to think about leaving and stood up, sloshing over to the doors to peek out of the elevator. Into the lobby the palest glow of morning dusk was just beginning to ooze, outlining the shadowy figures of men, women, and children sprawled on the floor and along the wall. He had to get back to the Cyst as soon as possible to seek safety, check that the others were okay, and figure out what to do next, not to mention get some food and drink. Then he thought of Rick's body. Though he wanted him to have a proper sky burial, there was just no way he could haul him all the way to Xenocyst. While Amon would be in danger unencumbered as it was, the exertion of carrying him could literally kill him in his weakened state. But when Amon finally stepped out of the elevator, intent on returning to Xenocyst, he stopped in the lobby, ignoring the residents staring at him fearfully, and turned back around. The idea of just leaving his friend there to rot in his own fluids wrenched him open from the inside, and he began to clench his fists, gnash his teeth, quaking from head to toe, his every buzzing breath seeming to stoke the sickly flame of misery in his core like a bellows.

GRAAAHHHHHH!

Before Amon knew it, he was shrieking at the top of his lungs and delivering a swift kick of rage to the elevator doors. But rage at whom? The drones obeying their programming? The freekeepers that deployed them according to protocol? The engineers that designed them on spec? The managers following instructions from their managers? The executives working to satisfy investors and corporate principles and market dynamics? The MegaGlom subsidiaries of which they were all a part? The Philanthropy Syndicate? GATA? The systems that bound them all together like the Charity Gift Economy or the Action Transaction Market? Who or what exactly was responsible for this? In the end, he felt the flame of his rage turn inwards and scatter within him, finding nothing left to burn except Amon himself, the fool behind the plan that failed.

The door of the elevator had bent inwards like wet clay, surely built of a more malleable material than the metal it appeared to be. Amon wanted to kick it again ten thousand times, pulverize it, cave the chamber in on itself, and seal his friend in his own private coffin forever. But he stopped himself as he remembered the boys who made it their home. Space was precious in the camps and destroying this shelter would only displace them, pushing their gang to displace someone else. While it wasn't exactly nice to throw them out for the night or to leave a bloody mess in there, he couldn't do anything about that now and it was better than battering it to uselessness. He doubted his hole-filled, flaking shoes would have held up anyway. Seizing this moment of control over his anger, Amon peeked one last time through the crack in the elevator, at what remained of the person he had known for almost as long as he had memories, lying on a stagnant bed of glistening black gradually turning red in the heightening glow of dawn. He then whipped around to dash past the residents out of the lobby and into the alley, forcing himself to run away from the condo and never look back.

As Amon had wound his way up a long, continuous stairpath, wrapping his way around shaft after shaft and hiking over roomslopes, a petal blizzard fell on the camps, shrouding the nascent morning light. Chill autumn winds blustered his skin from narrow cracks and squeezeways, and raised a great flurry of flakes that slapped his skin as they swirled in all directions. Every structure in sight seemed to be decaying—holes eating their way through walls, rooms crumbling, shafts leaning at ever more precarious angles as their foundations crunched down floor by floor—as though undergoing entropy in ultra-fast-forward. Shocked, exhausted, sleep-deprived, and thirsty, Amon trudged and clambered along in a daze. He hardly knew where he was or what he was doing, but some part of him still sought Xenocyst and hoped, though he saw no familiar landmarks and had lost all sense of direction, that he was meandering the right way. Although it was too late to meet Rashana on top of the Cyst, he didn't know if she could be trusted anymore and wasn't sure if he cared. For whatever she might give him, wherever she might take him, Rick would not be there to share in his fortune.

Nevertheless, he climbed along furtively, ever on the lookout for drones as best he could with his dull, tired eyes, dancing frantically away from stairs that broke off underfoot and jumping gaps between the narrowest of footholds as the path came apart beneath him. Coughs sounded constantly from all directions as the emaciated droves shambling through every alley and ledge inhaled the flake-thick air. Amon tried to breathe through his nose, though he could only stand the smell of death that permeated the whole district for so long and occasionally had to use his mouth, choking like all the rest when he did so.

Eventually he reached a fan-shaped plateau of roofs, with a ridge of shelters curling over him on the left and the hundred-meter drop of a crevice on his right. Although the view beyond the crevice was shrouded by the petal-blizzard at first, the air soon cleared during a brief intermission of the winds and the shimmering cube of Delivery appeared above the slumscape in the distance, a murmuration of glass forms sketching glittering patterns before it. The upper five levels of the bridges were visible and Amon could see that they had all been retracted, now reaching only halfway across the moat. Though the disposcraper sprawl blocked the Road to Delivery from view, he could imagine the supply pilgrims jammed in like never before, the crowds at the front backing up so as not to be pushed over the edge like lemmings. Clearly Delivery was not designed to maximize disbursement efficiency but to protect against revolt, was not a welfare mall *for* bankdead as it seemed but a fortress *against* them.

Soon the plateau ended at a ledge, beyond which was a disposcraper valley, its gradually inclining slope disturbed by jutting corners and occasional pits. Amon scrambled down against the many climbing up, sidestepping the protrusions and crouch-hopping carefully down drops until he reached the valley floor. This was a winding, elevated alley lined with buildings all constructed of defective rooms—doors on the ceilings, the steps of stairs separate and scattered across different sides, convex or concave walls that resisted attachment to each other, the usually cubic shelters squashed into parallelograms with holes in them—the bodies of babies shriveled up like sundried fish littering the deformed ledges he passed.

Through a serrated rip in a wall, Amon spotted a packed feeding station several stories below. In one corner, children with bloated bellies were eating handfuls of Fleet powder from a heap, hungry ghosts hovered around them them with famished eyes, and plump crows filling the surrounding ledges jostled each other eagerly. Seeing no drones patrolling, he was tempted to approach and try his luck with the two vending machines poking up above the slow-shifting headscape . . . until the red wings of the SampleQuito receding into the sky flashed before his mind's eye. He was so hungry and thirsty, he imagined himself sneaking around to the back of the machine and somehow busting open one of the pipes so that he could drink the raw sports drink components and meal replacement ink it pumped in. But as all crashborn kids learned from their mothers, he would be no better than a lost sailor drinking sea water, for the ink would be in a chemically indigestible state until the machine processed it. All he would achieve was to disrupt a food source for his fellow bankdead during this famine and bring the wrath of the CareBots even more surely than his finger inserted into the machine. Wiser to find Xenocyst as soon as possible and ask for rations when he got there.

So he continued upwards, climbing a series of pegs in an uneven cliff, his limbs feeling weaker and weaker as he hoisted his weight up the leaning walls, his head light in the putrid petal-dense air. Soon he reached a series of warped roof islands and bounded from one to the next, careful his feet didn't slip into the numerous holes on top, seeing the dark forms of shattered bodies in the shadows far below. The blather of many voices and coughs became progressively louder as he proceeded until he reached another ledge, where he found himself looking down upon one of the Road to Delivery's main arteries. To his surprise, the crowd was thinner than usual, leaving numerous patches of empty space between them, and he guessed that word was spreading about Delivery being closed. Not far above them but a dozen meters below his vantage, a DazzleMoth and two DusterFlies fluttered, and Amon made sure to stay hidden behind a horizontal shaft that spanned the road as he crawled across on his belly, gripping stairs to steady himself against the rightward slant of its wall.

On the other side, Amon looked back during another flakefall lull, and through a crack between two stacks of shelters to the west, he spotted Opportunity Peaks in the distance, halting in surprise when he saw a scrap of sky through its once-monolithic form. An asterisk of blue filled a hole in the middle of the mountain, just below where the slopes diverged towards the two summits, as though it had been smashed by the blow of a great battering ram, and the uprooted left peak was leaning on the right one. It looked ready to collapse at any moment, and Amon could see the lower ridges darkened with squirming dots, hordes of survivors surely, perhaps enacting a ritual of lament. *Did Kitao's snitching do nothing to save them?* Amon wondered, befuddled about what might have happened and unable to rejoice at the apparent success of their plan when he thought of the innocent souls that been cloistered inside.

Then, triangulating the location of the mountain with where he remembered Delivery to have been, he was able to determine the direction of Xenocyst with some confidence and charted an easterly course straight for it. Once he had his bearings, it was less than half an hour before he reached familiar territory, and although this part of his journey was the hardest slog of all—tripping, stumbling, and lurching his way along step by grueling step—he felt a faint twinkling of hope amidst his utter misery, fatigue, and despair, that he might survive and see his other friends, even if Rick never would . . .

But when Amon had crossed one of the allied enclaves and at last clambered up to the wall overlooking the buffer canyon, he saw that the border of Xenocyst had been devastated too, and stood there stunned as even the suggestion of hope fled. Caverns of cross-sectioned buildings gaped in various places along the curving length of the outer wall where massive hunks from five to twenty stories had been torn right out and lay shattered on the floor of the canyon. Many of the broken shelters lying in the heaps of debris had not even begun to flake, which told him that this was not the result of regular dissolution but of some other cause. As he descended the stairpaths through the still-raging petal-blizzard, he saw bodies in the rubble, sprawled atop or buried with parts sticking out. Some looked as though they had been crushed by the buildings, some shot with bullets, patches of their blood and vomit staining the ground. These appeared to be the signs of a battle, and one that had ended very recently, as some locals were still picking through the waste for bits of cloth, food, and other valuables; more crows lined up patiently on the surrounding ledges.

Amon made his way across the canyon floor, avoiding the piles where he could and climbing over them when necessary, wondering who could have done this. He could only think of the tales he'd heard of demolition dust. But he had always thought that the Charity Brigade used it to crumple rows of disposcrapers in an orderly fashion, whereas here the damage was random and many shafts still stood only partially destroyed, with some of the residents curled up in their exposed rooms. In other words, it didn't look like Charity Brigade work at all. It was more like what Amon would have expected from the Opportunity Scientists, though they should have been reeling from the attack on their holy mountain, presumably at the hands of the Brigade, and weren't supposed to have such an arsenal, which was perplexing. For it seemed possible that one of them might have heard the details of Xenocyst's rabble rousing and come to exact their wrath, but surely not both of them, and surely not together . . . ?

As the guards took Amon through the Xenocyst compound towards the Cyst, he realized he was actually glad to have them there. Though he had made a big ruckus at the checkpoint, he now found the interior of the enclave confusing, as the havoc wreaked on the border extended inside as well and the slumscape had been radically transformed from the previous day. The buildings that had lined his familiar routes were blasted beyond recognition or lay in fragments, while roombuds blossomed rapidly along his path into new buildings according to some hastily devised city pattern. Even when he did spot some alley or roofway that he remembered, he lacked the focus to connect it to where other paths should have been and reconstruct the map in his memory as he staggered along, his vision blurry, barely awake, fallen into a daze of famished exhaustion and shock, his awareness blipping into oblivion for a second now and then so that he kept having to remind himself where he was upon awakening. With the two guards periodically glancing over their shoulders at him and muttering about him in concern, Amon hiked over mountains of debris, leaped the jagged maw of busted gaps in roofways, sometimes crawling through keyhole apertures in tottering shafts leaning into each other, nearly falling over when someone in the crowd bumped him even slightly, mumbling delirious nonsense to dissipate the pulses of regret that surged through him. If not for his escorts urging him along, he might have simply thrown himself down in a shattered rubbish-filled alcove and never gotten up, letting the flakes bury him like soft snow. The devastation here was his fault, everything was his fault . . .

They passed several of what had once been some of Xenocyst's many checkpoints. These were tunnels and lanes built intentionally tight so that a small number of guards could hold off a large horde of intruders in a crisis, and shelters could be thrown up to blockade them if necessary, turning the compound into a maze of well-defended dead ends. The fighting seemed to have been particularly intense around these bottlenecks as they had all been blown wide open, the neighboring buildings utterly decimated.

Yet soon, the signs of destruction began to dwindle and sections of the old slumscape that were intact appeared increasingly, so that Amon could finally tell where he was: not far from the Cyst. Still, the atmosphere felt unlike what he'd grown accustomed to. Passersby kept their heads down and slunk by nervously without meeting his gaze, while other men and women stood stationed on ledges with assault dusters, the fraught air like a bent pane of glass ready to snap. It amazed Amon how much change a place could undergo in a single night—especially one that had been tended carefully to remain stable for so long in spite of slight shifts that were constantly occurring.

Soon they reached a small alley-side entrance to the Cyst flanked by two guards holding assault dusters. Amon's escorts gave a password he'd never heard before and took him in, up the condo's dark staircases that he had walked countless times during his duties. The regular bustle of incoming supplies, outgoing waste, and staff coming and going was more sparse and sporadic than usual, though sentries with dusters were everywhere.

When they got to the eleventh floor and his guides kept ascending, Amon stopped on the landing. "We're not going to the Council Chamber?" he asked.

"Th' councilahz are out en their districtz ovahseeing th' reconstruction," said Lefty. "Thez supposed t' be convening latah th'z evening. We've been told t' take you t' th' library entil then t' eat and recupret."

"Great," said Amon, the idea of getting some food and rest immediately vanquishing all his other worries, though the next instant they were back. "But isn't there some way I can take my meal to wherever Hippo is? I want to know what happened to everyone else and I need to give him my report."

"We haven't received ordahz bout reporting t' Hippo," said Lefty. "Our job 'z 't take you t' th' library."

"Someone else'll be along," said Righty. "They'll explain the situation."

His awareness too foggy for him to argue, Amon nodded and followed them, going up more stairs and hallways lined with sentries. Presently the door to the library was there on his left and Amon crossed the threshold. He sighed with relief when he saw the stacks still standing there, his sanctuary intact, the familiar caramel-dust smell of old paper soothing him like nothing else. Then his eyes went to the tray of food and drinks on a low coffee table, his tongue suddenly swimming in saliva despite his great thirst, the ache of hunger in his belly so intense he thought it might sprout teeth and devour him from the inside.

"Is any of that for me?" Amon asked.

On the wooden tray was a glass of water, a bowl of multi-grain rice, a bowl of miso soup, and a small oblong plate carrying a piece of grilled salmon. There were also several tiny dishes holding a raw egg, a dollop of natto mixed with strips of nori, a few slices of pickled daikon, and a yokan for dessert. Wholesome comfort food, of the kind he'd rarely enjoyed even before he cash crashed.

"Help yourself," said Righty, and Amon hardly heard him say, "We'll be back shortly," so ensnared was his mind by the sight of the food. Almost tripping over his own legs to clear the several paces to the coffee table, Amon flopped butt-first onto a spot on the leather couch before it and poured the water down his throat. Then he picked up chopsticks of black glossy wood inlaid with mother-of-pearl and began to dig into the rice. He hardly tasted a bite of it, having just enough peace of mind to note that scarfing this fine meal too quickly was a waste but not enough to slow down. Just as he was chewing the last few morsels, a man wearing a brown-and-black silk kimono came to take the tray away and replace it with another carrying more of the same dishes.

"These are for me too?" Amon asked, looking up at the man, who nodded with a solemn expression before bowing and leaving the library. Amon set into this second meal with gratitude and relish. By the time he had finished off about half of it, though he could easily have eaten two or three times more, he felt his urgency to feed temporarily sated and lowered his pace to savor the taste a bit more. He was sipping at the last of his second miso soup when an exquisite voice called, "Amon!"

Barrow had just come through the doorway and was approaching Amon, holding a colorfully lacquered teapot and two teacups.

"Barrow!" said Amon, happy to find another familiar face after so much had changed.

"Wonderful to see you safe and sound!"

"You too. Have you heard from Vertical and Ty? Are they alright?"

"Thankfully, yes. Both of them arrived safely yesterday evening."

Amon breathed a long sigh of relief. "Where are they now?"

"Resting."

"And the rest of the crew?"

"One of your saboteurs has gone missing, and a woman from Ty's crew is in the hospital here, being treated for tear dust."

At these final two words, gut-wrenching sorrow filled him.

"What about Rick?" asked Barrow, as though he sensed the source of Amon's pain. "Is he with you?"

Amon shook his head ruefully, squeezing his eyes shut with his jaw clenched to hold back tears.

"Has something happened to him?"

"Drones. They overdosed him on tear dust . . . I was with him this morning when he passed away."

Barrow cringed with a look of profound regret, furrowing his broad forehead. "I'm truly sorry to hear that. I know he was your close friend and, during our short acquaintance, I saw what a strong-willed and talented young man he was, much like you. Why don't we have a cup of tea and talk about this further?"

"Yes . . ." Amon couldn't think of anything more inviting than a cup of tea to banish the autumn chill that lingered in his bones, and just the mention of it made him sink deeper into the couch, only a thin line of restraint keeping the weight of his exhaustion from dragging him down to sleep now that his belly was full. Barrow sat on the couch across from him, setting the teapot on an aquamarine-fish-against-indigo textiled coaster and two handcrafted ceramic cups straight onto the table. It was then that Amon noticed Little Book standing by the shelves staring at him, and gave him a nod. He wanted to ask where Book was, but knew

Little Book had no way to answer without Book there to interpret and, as a jumble of horrible scenes from the mission began to flicker in Amon's recollection, a different question leapt to his lips. "Does anyone know what happened out there?"

"Unfortunately not. We all have our theories, but no one knows for certain."

"And here? What happened to Xenocyst? Who attacked us?"

"That is another mystery no one on the council has managed to solve. Maybe the Charity Brigade, maybe those OpSci monsters, maybe both as an alliance. I'm sure your experience of the catastrophe can help us to understand this. So what happened to *you*, Amon? What happened to Rick?"

Feeling a powerful need to relate the terrible tribulations he had undergone to someone, Amon lost himself in rambling out the events of the past day. He began with everything that had happened since the moment he and Rick had arrived at Delivery, and, by the time he'd reached the part where Vertical started shrieking, two more men wearing kimonos entered. One of them cleared away Amon's tray while the other brought over a lidded ceramic jar and poured what must have been hot water into the teapot.

The whole time Amon spoke, Little Book stood to the side between the couches and the shelves, scrawling away on his tablet in the loud way he did when he had something to say, which Amon thought strange because no one there could decipher his code. This led Amon to wonder again where Book was and, faltering in his story, his attention turned to Little Book's tapping.

Tappatappa-tap-tatap-tappa . . . *Tappatappa-tap-tatap-tappa* . . . *Tappatappa-tap-tatap-tappa* . . .

Though Amon couldn't decode the meaning, he realized that Little Book was repeating the same pattern of taps over and over again with a space in between.

"Would you mind taking that somewhere else?" said Barrow. "We're trying to have a serious conversation."

But Little Book was undeterred, and with his eyes cast to the floor he kept on writing noisily away. *Tappatappa-tap-tatap-tappa . . . Tappatappa-tap-tatap-tappa . . .*

"What are you trying to say LB?" Amon asked, turning to look at the boy. Little Book paused his writing for a second when Amon spoke. Then he looked up at him from the tablet screen and the moment their eyes met he began to tap out the same pattern again. *Tappatappa-tap-tatap-tappa . . .* Though the boy's face was as unexpressive as always, Amon sensed his desire to communicate some message, as though a hand were reaching into his soul, either to leave or to take something. "Sorry buddy, but we just don't understand that tapping without Book. Can't you say it in another way?"

Little Book stayed his hand as though in thought, staring intently at the screen, completely motionless, not even seeming to breathe. Then, he lifted up his digital pen, looking straight at Amon, and traced a shape in the air that Amon immediately recognized.

"Looks like a crucifix," said Barrow. "Are you implying that someone needs to be sacrificed, boy?"

"No. I think it's the Roman letter T," said Amon. "Right LB?" But Little Book was tapping out the same pattern again, his gaze back on the tablet.

"T?" said Barrow. "Are you sure it wasn't the number ten?" Ten was ✛ in kanji.

"I don't think so. The horizontal line looked shorter than the vertical line, like in a lowercase t." And given Little Book's fixation with clean orthography, Amon doubted this was an accident.

"Well what does 't' have to do with anything?" The letter T must have connected to the drink "tea" in Barrow's mind at the same moment as Amon's because he turned to Little Book and said, "What? You want a cup of tea too, do you?"

Tea? Thinking about this word, Amon took another sip and savored the taste in his mouth. The bouquet was different than that of the *gyokuro* Hippo had once served, though no less refined as far as he could tell. Curious, he brought his gaze down to the ceramic cup in his hand. It had a beautiful pattern of vermillion flowers on obsidian blue. Fragrant steam rose from the golden water and the warm smooth thing in his hand suddenly struck Amon as eerily out of place. What were these nice cups and that teapot doing in the library? Hippo's ceramics had been plain and chipped. And where did they get the new tea leaves? Or the hot water? Or the couch he was sitting on? From his low seat, Amon's eye expanded to take in the library lobby in front of the stacks for the first time, as he'd been too dazed and delirious on his way in to pay attention to where he was. Various impressionist and abstract paintings now adorned the wall, and a stand had been set up displaying small chests of drawers painted with *maki-e*. A Persian carpet stretched along the floor and three antique lamps had been placed at equidistant intervals. The plush couch he sat on smelled of real leather and the coffee table glass was glazed in the Qing-style pattern of rolling hills and lake valleys. Here was a cosmopolitan smorgasbord of art and antiques, but none of it felt incongruous, as though each piece had been selected for meaning, color, and design to fit with every other.

Then he saw it. T. T for tricycle? There was a tricycle polished to a bright silver gleam leaning on the bookshelf along the wall furthest from the door. "Tricycle" immediately made Amon think of *toraishikuru*, which had been shortened to Tora, which meant Tiger and was shortened again to Ty. T for Ty?

A jolt of alarm went from the base of Amon's spine to the top of his head and out to the tips of his fingers. But he quelled the urge to leap to his feet as he'd done when he'd become suspicious of Sekido in Shuffle Boom—that had just brought Freg and Tororo to dispense with him and there were guards over by the door who might do the same. Instead, he directed his gaze to the golden liquid in his teacup as calmly as he could. Then he remembered the many sentries with dusters he'd seen on his way here from the border. Amon realized now that his feeling of security upon returning to Xenocyst had lowered his defenses. With paralyzed wits, disoriented and distracted further by the destruction that had rendered the closest place he had to home almost unrecognizable, he'd hardly noticed the dusters, but they could only have been acquired from the Charity Brigade. In a flash Amon saw the crowds gathered to hear Barrow speak around the embyrbrycks, his passionate speech in support of war at the council, his sudden flip-flop to agree with Amon's more peaceful plan. What had Barrow done? Had he seen Amon's surprise when he noticed Ty's tricycle, practically a part of his body, all its chipped yellow paint scraped off and unattended by Ty?

"Where did Xenocyst get this wonderful tea from by the way?" Amon asked. In Hinkongo, the English loan word "tea" referred to all different kinds of tea, including the *sencha* they were drinking, and Amon used the word in this way even though they were speaking standard Japanese, as he tried to dissemble his fear and remain seamlessly on the "T" topic. He took his first sip of the fresh pot but tasted only bitterness. "I haven't had anything like this for ages."

"A philanthropaneur stopped by recently, one of Hippo's old supporters, and donated a large supply of leaves from Uji. Not half bad, is it?"

More like you made a deal with the philanthropaneurs in Delivery and this was part of the payment, along with the dusters, thought Amon. *But what kind of deal, and why?*

"And what about all these antiques and things?"

"Oh, this junk? Now that we have all sorts of artifacts from the trove I provided, the council has taken my advice to make a kind of live-in educational space where people can learn about other eras by actually inhabiting them. This is meant to supplement the text-based educational materials on the shelves."

Amon nodded as though this made sense to him, but he was thinking what a consummate liar Barrow was, a born politician if ever there was one. So sly-tongued, it seemed, that he had deceived Book when telling his fabricated story in the mirror at his first visit to the council. If anyone could pull it off, it was Barrow.

"And how about the hot water? How did you heat it up?" The moment he said this, Amon knew it was a foolish question, for it would only alert Barrow to his suspicions. But his thoughts were in such turmoil he couldn't think how else to fill the space.

"I'd be happy, of course, to explain all the changes that have been taking place here, Amon, but shall we get back to your story first? I'm curious to know what happened, because it may help us decide what to do next."

"Right," said Amon, but in Barrow's devious husky-blue eyes, he thought he could see some glimmer that he knew Amon was clueing in. The doorway was to Amon's back and he didn't want to turn his head to check how many guards there were, but he had seen a couple of servers come in so there had to be at least two. He couldn't tell if they'd been armed but, judging by the equipment of the guards on the way in, someone with an assault duster couldn't be far off. Even if Amon managed to nerve dust Barrow and however many guards were present, their screams would surely draw reinforcements and Amon would have no hope of escaping alive. He needed to find another way out. "But can I use the toilet first?"

It was true that he had to pee, and Amon stood up.

"The toilet?" said Barrow, looking at Amon with narrowed eyes. There was a pause after that, and Amon knew with certainty that Barrow could read his doubts. Amon was just reaching for his duster when Barrow winked his left eye and Amon felt hands on him from behind. He jerked away but was already fast in the grip of two men who must have been lurking behind him, one gripping his shoulders to pin him in place, the other grabbing his right arm and twisting it up behind his back. Barrow nodded and a third man reached down to Amon's holster. Amon tried to knee his hand, but the second man wrenched his arm up hard and the pain drained all his remaining strength. When Amon had been disarmed, Barrow nodded again and the men released him.

"My apologies, Amon. I was trying not to upset you so that we could get through this conversation without having to resort to that. But I seem to have failed."

"Where's Hippo?"

"I'm afraid I don't know."

"You were lying about Ty and Vertical, weren't you? They're not resting at all."

"I'm sorry about that. I was trying to familiarize you with the situation gradually. If I revealed all our tragedies too quickly in your present state, I was afraid I might shock you and we would be unable to finish our conversation."

"The OpScis and the Charity Brigade never attacked us. It was you and your followers!"

"Now that is not true. I was being honest with you before when I said we don't know who attacked us."

"And who exactly are 'we'?"

"You must understand. This was the only way that the community could survive. We could no longer go on being a xenocyst. Our cell had to metastasize. We had to take on an antagonistic role and fight for our place in this world. Hippo couldn't see that. He didn't realize that the political situation has shifted and that old strategies no longer apply.

"Xenocyst is nominally a democracy, but Hippo still wielded immense power as an advisor. Nothing was going to improve under his influence. For the good of the community a change had to take place, and we were planning to pursue peaceful, democratic means. Then Xenocyst was assaulted in the middle of the night. We were overrun by a strange mix of intruders. Some were dressed as OpScis, some as freekeepers, and some as standard residents. In the confusion it was impossible to tell who was fighting on what side, and before anyone knew it, Hippo and the council were gone. Someone had to take charge in this crisis. That is the only reason we moved in here, to serve as the last line of defense against sheer chaos, and I see to warming Hippo's seat not with joy but out of necessity."

Spoken in the commanding, crystal lilt of Barrow's voice, Amon almost felt persuaded—but not quite. For if the coup hadn't been planned, how come they were already so well armed? The story was just too convenient to be believed.

"So what *did* happen to Ty and Vertical? Are you going to tell me they disappeared with the council?"

"Very likely, yes."

"Then what's Ty's tricycle doing here?"

"He must have rushed off without it." Barrow stared at Amon with husky-blue eyes that seemed to project the utmost sincerity, knowing that what he was saying was bullshit and that Amon knew he knew it was bullshit. Ty would rather die than leave his tricycle behind. Anyone who knew him personally knew that. So why would Barrow say something so obviously false? Amon thought of the guards behind him and realized that he was not the audience for the lie. Clearly something terrible had happened to Ty, but Barrow didn't want his followers to hear. Though discontent with Hippo's quietist leadership style had surged since the supply reductions, Ty was a widely respected member of the community, thought to be highly capable, dedicated, and formidable in combat. If Barrow admitted to harming him in any way—could he have held a grudge for the way Ty treated him the first time they met?—his reputation would suffer. The fact that he was so concerned about how the guards perceived him suggested to Amon that his hold on power was tenuous.

He had played a central role in organizing the coup, but perhaps there were those who questioned his authority, or others with equal claim to it. This fear of rivals also explained why he would fabricate the nonsense about how control of Xenocyst merely fell into his hands by chance after the battle, for some might support his views about reform while opposing the idea of a violent overthrow. But what was Barrow after? The moment this question occurred to him, Amon realized the answer.

"You charmed these men," he said, looking over his left shoulder behind him and waving his arm over the backrest at the guards, of whom he could see that there were four, "and betrayed our sabotage to the Philanthropy Syndicate to acquire their help in seizing power for yourself. Then you purged the council and had Ty killed to take his tricycle, all so you could turn the Cyst into a museum."

For a split second, a look of fearsome anger appeared on Barrow's face, muscles clenching the skin into deep wrinkles that radiated out from his nose, warning Amon to keep his mouth shut or else. Barrow had held perfect mastery over his emotions as he lied, only revealing them when it suited his purposes, as it just had. But in that moment, for the first time, he seemed to lose control, for Amon noticed a slight quiver to his pupils as his eyes took on a lost, disconsolate look that suggested fear. *Maybe Barrow doesn't just have rivals,* thought Amon. *Could someone else have him in their grasp?* Then Barrow relaxed his face again, the wrinkles smoothed out, the fear vanished, and he was wearing a kind, somewhat condescending smile.

"You know that's nonsense," he said. "My whole career as the CEM was dedicated to helping bankdead, and I have used all my energy since coming to Xenocyst to continue that work. Even those on the council who oppose me would admit that."

Amon thought of Barrow's story about turning down bribes to protect the bankdead with radical policies, which had earned him good repute at Xenocyst, as he glanced around at all the antiques in the room again. More likely Barrow had been diverting GATA funds to his personal venture charity that would indeed hand out supplies without requiring human resources, just as Barrow had claimed, but instead anadeto, for his personal collection of course. Perhaps he had even hoped to tap into the legendary trove that nosties often spoke of.

Then the moment he found himself in the District of Dreams, he had sought out this trove and lost it when the OpScis enslaved him. After he had willingly offered it to Xenocyst in exchange for a chance to meet the council, Amon had thought him over his obsession. But apparently this had merely been a temporary gamble for the sake of a much longer, slower strategy. Barrow's intentions could not be found in his words, only his actions. Collecting and preserving things of the past, it seemed, was all he had cared about from the beginning. Every gesture and mannerism and turn of phrase was just an expression of that desire. Yet if that were so, what was he bothering with Amon for?

"Why are we even talking right now?"

"Hippo saw your potential to serve as a messenger and interpreter for negotiations with the Philanthropy Syndicate, and we'd like to continue making use of your skills."

"You're offering me a job?"

"You must understand how short we are on qualified administrative staff after last night."

"This is ridiculous," said Amon. "You know I was a supporter of Hippo. You think I believe you that you're just going to forgive me and let me work here?"

"If we wanted to hurt you, we would have already done it, but my overriding policy is mercy. Take Little Book. Although we know where his loyalties lie, we have decided to keep him here for his cryptographic expertise. Otherwise, we would lack the right cyphers to encode our letters and reassure our allied communities that we are the sender. This could lose us their trust, and corresponding in plaintext would obviously allow enemy groups to intercept our messages. So our resident scholar is currently working on learning his tap language. You will serve similarly important functions.

"Of course your movements outside the compound will be restricted until we can trust you, but I'll make sure that life under our command is better, much better, than anything you could hope for elsewhere. Just think for a moment about what your options are. You're bankdead, so you have to live in the District of Dreams. But as you told me a moment ago, a SampleQuito took your blood, so you are now, in all likelihood, a hungry ghost. Here we'll provide you with everything you need, perhaps a few comforts in recognition of your achievements.

"So why not accept my offer of asylum? I've seen what you can do. You're a fine worker and a brilliant strategist. We're going to build a new community better suited to present reality and we need your help."

Amon saw that Barrow was right. Staying at Xenocyst might be the only way he could survive. So maybe he could play along with his offer while he tried to discover some way to escape, though he suspected Barrow would have tricks to maintain his obedience. This was assuming that anything he said was—

Whoozt whoozt whoozt whoozt. Just then, Amon noticed a repetitive sound, somewhere between the *thwap* of a propeller and the *zap* of electricity, and realized it had been going on faintly in the background for several minutes. Though it made him think of a rotorcraft and seemed to emanate from the roof, it was entirely unlike the whirring hum of the supply centicopters. Then he remembered something Hippo had told him. Rashana signaled her approach to the Cyst's helipad by setting the rotors of her usually silent PhantoCopter to make a loud "electric whoop." Had Rashana returned for some reason? Could she be here to meet with Amon? He imagined her arriving for their appointment at midnight in the midst of the battle and having to turn back when no one signaled for her to land. She would see that Amon's failure to show up was due to no lapse on his part and might still be willing to meet him. And now that it was clear who had betrayed them, it seemed certain that she could be trusted after all. But how could he get to the roof?

Tilting his ear upwards at the same sound, Barrow said to his guards, "One of you go up there and ring the landing bell. Tell her that I'll meet her for tea if she wishes."

As one of the guards left the library, Amon saw his last chance for escape, from Barrow and perhaps from the camps, rapidly receding. There were only three guards left in the room, two standing by the door and one behind his couch. Was there truly nothing he could do?

"If I accept your offer," said Amon, trying to keep the conversation going while he scrambled his thoughts for a way out, "maybe you'll give me asylum like you say. But once you find a replacement for me and I'm no longer useful, there'll be nothing left to protect me. Not after what I did to you."

"Don't forget. As I already told you around the embyrbrycks that night, I'm grateful for the chance you gave me in bringing me here and am perfectly willing to let bygones be bygones. But since then I have managed to go even further, and am now ready to forgive you completely. Shall I tell you why?"

Amon nodded.

"I hadn't yet realized this at the time, but your story brought me new relief, and within a few days of hearing it I was able to conquer any lingering ill will I bore towards you." Barrow took a sip of tea. "I remembered the part about the forest, how you said you'd once aspired to go there. Until then, I was struggling with a dark, vengeful part of myself that wanted to get even with you for taking away the life and career I worked so hard to create. But I realized that there was no need for me to obsess over it. Our score was already settled."

Barrow paused for an uncomfortably long time, staring at Amon with his husky-blue eyes, beaming his fatherly smile, until Amon couldn't resist asking, "How so?"

"There was a special forest that existed just as you described. I saw naked segs of it many years ago. My intention here isn't to gloat, Amon. In fact, I'm very sorry to have to tell you this. I just want you to understand how our relationship stands now. But you'll never make it there.

Amon was getting sick of Barrow's leading statements and didn't ask for clarification this time, but Barrow continued anyway.

"All that wood my residence in Tsukuda was made of. Didn't you wonder where that came from? Most people who saw it and learned that the wood wasn't part of the overlay did. It was Hahajima, in Ogasawara, the community that inspired Hippo to create Xenocyst in the first place. I had the whole island felled. Not a shrub remains. It's just a dusty rock covered in stumps. So by a rare stroke of fortune or a sad twist of fate—call it what you will—I killed your dream already, decades ago. Which means I don't have to do anything at all. My heart can be at peace with you because we're already even. A dream for a dream."

"A dream for a dream and the whole world is despair."

"Not if someone somewhere can find a new dream, and I have mine right here: to remake Xenocyst into a beacon of compassion. But I need your help in making that a reality. Perhaps I can help you rediscover your own dream in the process."

After all his consummate lying, Amon wasn't so foolish as to trust what Barrow was saying. And how could Barrow be so certain that the forest Amon saw was the one he had destroyed? It wasn't as if he could burrow inside Amon's dreams to check. Still, if Barrow didn't believe what he said was true, Amon could see no reason he would let him off so easily. Surely he would want to extract more satisfying revenge, however much of a pragmatist he was, than to simply keep Amon in thrall as a servant. So had the forest been destroyed? Amon didn't know if he was supposed to feel angry or disappointed, but the news hardly disturbed him at all, for all his emotions and mental gibbering were drowned out by a single thought: *It's because of Barrow's betrayal that my best friend is dead.*

Amon and Rick had dismissed their doubts about Barrow's loyalty because they believed he truly hated the Opportunity Scientists and the Philanthropy Syndicate, and wanted to use the sabotage to do damage to both. Now Amon saw that they had probably been right about his hatred—but not about his loyalty. For though he had indeed helped Xenocyst to weaken the Full Choice/Absolute Choice coalition, the Philanthropy Syndicate, and the Gyges Circle by cooperating and assisting with the exposé mission, Amon supposed that he had also informed on Xenocyst about said mission just as it was being completed. Once the Syndicate heard this, they had armed the discontented Xenocyst cell Barrow had been cultivating to topple the old leadership, as having them attack the sabotage perpetrators would be far cheaper than employing the Charity Brigade or even drones, since illegal arms trading was more affordable than direct crowdcare. Then with Barrow installed as decision-maker, or at least as puppet figurehead, they could be guaranteed a steady supply of human resources, and perhaps an increase in yield since Barrow would not be hindered by Hippo and the council's scruples. The damage to Opportunity Peaks showed that the Opportunity Scientists had also been implicated in the sabotage, and Barrow would be well positioned to fulfill his vendetta against them in the future with his new arsenal and power. Having his defectors dress as OpScis so that the Xenocysters were unaware they were being attacked from within would also help him towards this goal, since it would instill hatred in them and thereby make it easier for him to justify whatever antagonistic policies he chose—perhaps one day even war. In this way, Barrow had brilliantly played all sides against each other to his advantage as only a political prodigy like him could. Now, as an added bonus, his ID assassin had been delivered helpless to his stronghold.

But Amon didn't care what Barrow might do to him. All he could think about was Rick and his friends, and this called forth the rage he'd felt outside the elevator that morning. Still, there was nothing he could do about it. His duster had been taken from him and armed men stood not meters away. He had discerned his predicament too late, making Little Book's cryptic message all for naught. Unless—T? Tea!

Spish! Kachink! Amon flung his tea in Barrow's face and cracked the lip of his teacup against the metal bar running along the edge of the coffee table, splitting the cup in half. In the next instant, before Barrow could get to his feet, Amon lifted the coffee table with his foot to hurl it at at him. While Barrow brought his arms up to block the table, Amon jumped to his feet and leapt over the couch in front of him. Then, spinning around quickly as Barrow's hands whipped down reflexively to catch his precious antique before it fell, he wrapped his left arm around Barrow's chest and put the sharp edge of the broken cup to his throat, causing Barrow to release the now-cracked coffee table, which hit the ground with a clunk and a rattle.

"Raise an alarm and that voice of yours is done!" hissed Amon, keeping the point of the shard close against the top of Barrow's neck. The three guards now had assault dusters trained on Amon, but Barrow's body shielded him. Little Book, Amon realized, was nowhere to be seen, his tapping having stopped some minutes ago. "Tell them to put the dusters on the floor in the middle of the room!"

"P-put them on the floor as he says," said Barrow, trembling with fear.

"Tell them to stand against the wall away from the door."

"S-stand against the wall away from the door."

The three guards did as instructed, and backed up against the wall to the right of the door, just left of where the stacks began.

"If anyone enters, tell them to stand with the others and do the same, got it?!"

Barrow's neck twitched slightly as he began to nod and then felt the sharp ceramic on his throat and immediately stopped. "Y-yes," he stuttered instead.

Sure enough, two men drawn by the commotion burst into the room and wheeled the barrels of their assault dusters towards Amon and Barrow.

"K-k-keep quiet and put your weapons on the floor with the others," said Barrow.

The men had already taken aim, and stood there unmoving, looking confused.

"Put them on the f-floor with the others," Barrow repeated. "And stand with the other men. No noises."

The two men hesitated for a moment, exchanged glances with each other and the other men, and then reluctantly placed their weapons on the floor, sliding them over to the pile before lining up against the wall. There were now six dusters in the middle of the room—five assault dusters and Amon's pistol-sized nerve duster—plus five men standing near the exit, tense and unsure what to do.

"What kind of dusters are those?" Amon called out to the men.

They froze nonplussed.

"I asked a fucking *question*!" snarled Amon.

"He asked you a question," echoed Barrow.

"Fight'R'flight," said a man with a crooked jaw and deep-set eyes. "And typhoid."

"Okay. You. The one who just spoke," said Amon. "Go over to the weapons . . . Now! But no quick moves!"

Crooked Jaw hesitated. Then, under Barrow's urging stare, edged slowly over to the weapons.

"Slide the nerve duster over to me with your foot," Amon said.

"Do as he says."

Crooked Jaw put his foot on top of the nerve duster and slid it down the aisle beside the shelves and couch ends. It was a good, straight slide, and the duster stopped perfectly alongside Barrow and Amon.

"Kneel down," Amon told Barrow.

Barrow knelt and Amon went down with him, switching the shard to his left hand to keep it against his neck. He then snatched up the duster with his right hand, put it in his holster, and said, "Stand up."

Barrow stood up and Amon went up with him.

"Tell the man who spoke to pick up one of the dusters," Amon whispered.

"Pick up a duster," said Barrow, looking at the man indicated.

Crooked Jaw paused for a moment to consider the pile of dusters and picked one up.

"Tell him to shoot his four friends."

"Shoot your four friends."

"What?!" said the man, and the line of four men began to shift restlessly on their feet as though readying themselves to act.

"Do you want him to die?" Amon put a slight bit of pressure into the shard.

"Glah," Barrow choked as his trembling intensified.

"Do you want to be blamed for the death of your new leader when so little has been settled here? Do you want the crowds of his supporters who gave up everything to tear you limb from fucking limb?"

"Shoot!" said Barrow, his voice pinched but lilting beautifully.

The tallest of the four men said, "Don't be crazy. You're not shooting *us*."

"Yeah fuck that!" said another. "We'll kick the shit out of you if you even try."

"Shoot them or I'll make sure you end up just like the councilors!" Barrow growled.

What had Barrow done to the councilors? To Hippo? To everyone else? Amon felt his hand pressing the shard harder into Barrow's throat.

"Agggh!" Barrow cried in pain, and a drop of blood trickled down his throat.

"Yaaaaah!" One of the four men who'd remained silent let out a battle cry as he began to charge the one with the gun.

"Shoot!" barked Barrow. "Shoot now!"

Crooked Jaw fired—*chrinkle*—and the charging man suddenly stopped, turned around, and dashed out the door, the fight'R'flight dust having switched on his instinct to flee.

Another man began to make for the door in the wake of the first, and Crooked Jaw aimed at him reflexively.

"Shoot!" shouted Amon, knowing the dusted man was too absorbed in mindlessly running away to sound the alarm—but worried the second might.

"Shoot!" echoed Barrow.

Chrinkle. Crooked Jaw fired again. The fleeing man turned around, his fight instinct overstimulated, and lunged for the nearest of his comrades with over-expanded, bloodthirsty pupils but an incongruously calm expression, grabbing him by the shoulder and punching him in the face.

As the two men began to brawl, Amon whispered, "The other two men."

"Shoot the other two!" Barrow yelled.

When Crooked Jaw hesitated, the remaining two men, seeing what was coming, both dove in two different directions in the same instant, one to take cover in the lane behind the stacks and the other for the pile of dusters. *Chrinkle.* In that split second, Crooked Jaw chose to fire at the one going behind the stacks, by which time the other man already had a duster in his hand and was whipping the barrel up just as Crooked Jaw shifted his aim. *Chrinkle.* The diving man fired first and hit Crooked Jaw, who had a 50/50 chance of either fighting or fleeing since he was doing neither at that moment and dropped his duster before pouncing on the man who'd shot him, and the man behind the stacks came barreling out towards them with arms outstretched.

Amon began to push Barrow towards the doorway, but the other two men were still brawling there, the dusted man kneeing the other in the kidney as the non-dusted man pummeled his chest. Amon switched the shard to his left hand again and drew his duster, pointing it at them as he edged towards the doorway with Barrow in front of him. While he didn't want to shoot them in case their screams might draw reinforcements (if the fight hadn't already), he wanted to keep them in his sights for fear the fight-dusted man would go berserk on Amon or Barrow if they stepped into his field of vision or that the undusted man would attack Amon. In the corner of his eye, Amon saw the other three men all in a tangle slam into a bookshelf as he came within a few paces of the doorway. If he could just slip past them—

The two brawlers suddenly lurched, bumping Amon on the side and sending his shard a few centimeters away from Barrow's neck for a split second, whereupon Barrow ducked under Amon's arm, went to the floor, and scrambled away. Amon whipped his duster around to target Barrow but he was already out the door. Shouldering aside the two brawling men, Amon leapt out into the medical equipment–cluttered hallway to see Barrow running to the left, calling, "Intruder! Intruder! All guards! Intruderrrrr!" his clear, resonant voice seeming to ring the walls.

Gwong-ng-ng-ng-ng went the sound of the landing signal and *whoozt whoozt whoozt whoozt* the chopping helicopter as it approached. Suddenly time seemed to freeze as Amon was presented with a choice.

Barrow was headed for the stairwell at the end of the hall that led down to the ground floor and up only as high as the fifteenth floor, well short of the roof where the PhantoCopter was landing. To Amon's right was another stairwell that ran all the way up, the sound *whoozt whoozt whoozt whoozt* of the copter's spinning blades beckoning Amon to the only safety he could hope for. All he had to do was dust Barrow and fight his way to the roof, and he might get out of this hellish trap. But when he saw Barrow stumble and bash into a crash cart, sending a tray of used medical equipment flying before tumbling to the floor of the hallway, Amon remembered what Barrow had just said about the councilors and thought of Hippo and Vertical and Ty and Book, and saw Rick crying himself to death in the elevator just that morning, the wet sound of his cold hand dropping to the floor when he finally released it, and rage filled him anew—rage like he'd never known before—an inferno of rage that consumed his mind with a crackling roar. What did it matter if it was Amon who had plunged him into the camps? The time for guilt and compassion was long past. It was for these weak, pointless feelings that he had given Barrow the chance to betray them and stayed to concoct his plan that had gone so horribly wrong, his efforts to help others and make up for his sins turning to harm and punishment, as all such efforts must in this sick world. The only question that remained was who deserved it, and the thought that this deceitful demagogue would remain here, in charge of this community with his special luxuries from the venture charities, and his power, and his analog treasures, was unbearable, agonizing, and Amon charged straight for him while holstering his duster in mid-stride, caught him just as he was getting to his feet, grabbed him by the back of his right shoulder with his left hand and yanked to spin him around. *Thrunch, thrunch, thrunch, thrunch.* Amon's vision went white, only the sensation of his fist connecting with something soft and crunchy remaining in his awareness.

The sound of footsteps behind brought him back to his senses and he released his grip, stilling his pummeling arm.

"Glrawr," gurgled Barrow as he flopped to the floor, the muscles of his warped, bloody mash of a face convulsing, his hands scrabbling for his throat, where Amon realized he had been directing his storm of punches.

What have I done? thought Amon, spinning around to head for the stairwell leading to the roof as he drew his duster, hoping to flee from the maimed man at his feet, from his lapse in control. Immediately the footsteps grew louder, as four guards stepped down into the landing of the stairwell and one of the undusted men in the library popped out from the doorway in front of them, covered in bloody scratches and bite marks, all of them wielding assault dusters.

Chrinkle. Chrinkle. Chrinkle. Amon fired his duster first at the man near the library and then the four near the landing. The first went down with a scream but the others leapt for cover, two down the stairs and two up. There was no way Amon could make it to the other end of the hallway with four armed guards stationed where they were, and surely more men would follow soon. In the time it had taken him to wreak vengeance on Barrow, he had lost his chance to go to the roof and meet with Rashana. Suddenly filled with regret, but with no time to dwell on his decision, Amon did another about face and reached behind him with his duster to fire round after round to keep the men from returning to the landing as he dashed his way to the stairwell leading down.

"Intruder!" croaked Barrow behind him. His voice—carrying a raspy high-pitched hum like a half-clogged vacuum cleaner—was ruined.

Whoozt whoozt whoozt whoozt. The sound of the rotorcraft faded as Amon descended, with nowhere left to go in the naked world.

ACKNOWLEDGEMENTS

I began my second novel feeling confident that it would be easier to write than the first one because I already knew how to write a novel. I failed to realize that the unique approach it demanded would make much of what I thought I had learned writing my debut useless. Such authorial hubris may be as old as storytelling itself.

To overcome the parade of unexpected challenges I faced, I relied on the support of many people.

Thanks again to Ashley Davies, Chris Molloy, Logan Fulcher, Daniel E. K. Priest, and Eleanor Cruise for putting up with the (no doubt grueling) earlier drafts of yet another of my novels. (If they persevere through the final book in the trilogy, I will count myself blessed.)

Thanks to Alex Klotz for his ideas and expert assessment of the science.

To Perry Ge for his stimulating analysis and discussion about the first half.

To Robert Priest for his appropriately brutal comments on a later draft.

To David Boyd for reassuring me that the large scale overhaul was worthwhile.

To Marsha Kirzner for the finishing touch of her fine-toothed comb.

To my agent, Monica Pacheco, for her concise but incisive comments and continuing support.

A special thanks to everyone who emailed me or gave me a shout out on social media to say how much they enjoyed *Cash Crash Jubilee*. The bleak, oppressive mood of *The Naked World* often seeped into my spirits as I was writing it, and while I never dreamed of giving up, there were periods, especially in the winter of 2015/2016, when I slipped into a dark, introverted muddle. The kind words of complete strangers helped me in part to overcome that. I've written articles in the past that people presumably read, but this is the first time I've had interactions with those people and learned what it feels like to have "readers." There's nothing more encouraging than knowing there are people who resonate with my work and I am profoundly grateful that there are a few of them out there.